I

It was three minutes to ten on the morning of Monday 18 August.

William Wisting was shown into the vast office, different from how he had imagined it would be. He had pictured imposing furnishings of leather and mahogany, but the room was decorated in a simple, practical style. A desk, stacked high with documents, dominated the space. The armrests on the chair behind it were worn and family photographs of varying sizes surrounded the computer monitor.

The woman who had greeted him in the outer office followed him in and set out cups, glasses and a water jug and coffee pot on a table beside a small seating area.

Wisting gazed out of the window as he waited for her to finish. The sun was already high in the sky and Karl Johans gate, Oslo's main street, was filling up rapidly.

The secretary clutched the empty tray to her chest as she nodded, smiled and left the room.

Less than two hours had passed since he had received the request to come here. He had never met the Director General of Public Prosecution before. Although he had once heard him give a presentation on quality in investigation work at a seminar, he had never spoken to him or been introduced.

Johan Olav Lyngh, a big man with grey hair and a square jaw, stood waiting. His wrinkles and ice-blue eyes gave the impression of obduracy.

'Let's sit down,' he said, gesturing with his hand.

Wisting took a seat on the settee next to the table.

'Coffee?'

'Yes, please.'

The Director General poured out two cups. His hand trembled a little, not a sign of apprehension or disquiet, but a consequence of his advanced age. Johan Olav Lyngh was ten years older than Wisting and had held the office of highest-ranking prosecutor for twenty-one years. At a time when all the familiar structures in the police force were in a state of flux, it felt as if Lyngh represented something safe and enduring – someone who did not change course despite advice from consultants keen to run public sector operations in accordance with business sector principles.

'Thanks for making yourself available,' he said, 'at such short notice.'

Wisting nodded as he lifted his coffee cup. He knew nothing about why he was here but understood that the impending conversation would contain extremely sensitive information.

The Director General filled a glass with water and took a gulp, as if he needed to clear his throat.

'As you probably know, Bernhard Clausen died at the weekend,' he began.

Wisting felt a knot of anxiety and foreboding in the pit of his stomach. Bernhard Clausen was a retired politician, a former Member of Parliament for the Labour Party who had held ministerial posts in a number of governments. On Friday he had been taken unwell at a restaurant in Stavern. He had been transported to hospital by ambulance but the next day the Party office had announced his death at the age of sixty-eight.

'It was reported that he'd had a heart attack,' Wisting commented. 'Is there reason to believe otherwise?'

The Director General moved his head from side to side.

'He suffered another heart attack at the hospital,' he explained. 'There will be a post-mortem later today, but there's nothing to suggest anything other than death from natural causes.'

Wisting remained seated with the coffee cup in his hand while he waited for Lyngh to continue.

'The Party Secretary contacted me last night,' the Director General went on. 'He was at the hospital when Clausen died.'

Lyngh was referring to Walter Krom, head of Party organization.

'After the death of Clausen's son in an accident, there was no close family left. Krom was listed as next of kin. He took charge of the belongings Clausen had with him when he was taken to hospital, including the key to his summer cabin in Stavern.'

Wisting knew where the cabin was situated. When Clausen was Foreign Minister, security measures for it had been included in police planning commitments. It was located at the edge of the cluster of cabins near Hummerbakken, and strictly speaking was closer to Helgeroa than Stavern.

'He took a trip down to the cabin yesterday, mainly to check that the windows were closed and the doors locked, but also with the idea that some sensitive Party documents might be lying around in there. Even though he was retired, Clausen was a member of an advisory group involved with the Party leadership.'

Wisting edged further forward in his seat.

'What did he find?' he asked.

'It's a large, fairly old cabin,' the Director General added, as if he needed time to come to the point. 'His father-in-law built it in the fifties, and when Clausen joined the family, he helped to construct an extension. Did you know he originally worked as a structural carpenter and iron fitter before he went into politics full-time?'

Wisting nodded. Bernhard Clausen belonged to the old guard of the Party and was one of the few central figures in the Labour Party with a background as an industrial worker. Trade union activity was what had sparked his interest in politics.

'The cabin was extended with a view to accommodating a large family, children and grandchildren. Six bedrooms in total.'

The Director General smoothed out a crease on his grey suit trousers.

'One of the rooms was locked,' he continued. 'Krom let himself in. It was one of the smallest rooms, with only bunk beds. Cardboard boxes were stacked up on the beds – I don't know how many. Walter Krom examined some of them and found that they were filled with money. Banknotes.'

Wisting sat bolt upright. Throughout this conversation his thoughts had strayed in many directions, but he had not expected this.

'Cardboard boxes full of cash?' he repeated. 'What are we talking about here? How much?'

'Foreign currency,' the Director General explained. 'Euros and dollars. Approximately 5 million of each.'

Wisting's mouth dropped open, but he had to search for words.

'Ten million kroner?'

The Director General shook his head.

4

'If all the boxes contain similar amounts of cash, there might be as much as 5 million euros and 5 million dollars,' he corrected him.

Wisting struggled to calculate the total sum. It had to be in the region of around 80 million kroner.

'Where did it come from?' he asked.

The Director General spread his arms and took on an expression suggesting this was a mystery.

'That's why I asked you to meet me,' he answered. 'I want you to find out.'

The room fell silent. Wisting let his eyes wander to the window and settle on Oslo Cathedral in the distance.

'You know the area well,' the Director General added. 'The cabin lies within your police district, and what's more, you're more than cut out for it. This has to be a confidential investigation. Bernhard Clausen served four years as Norway's Foreign Minister and has been a major player in our Defence Committee. National interests may well be in jeopardy.'

Wisting considered what this meant. Decisions on Norway's relationship with foreign powers had been in Clausen's hands.

'I've asked your Chief of Police to release you from all other duties, without telling him what you are to work on,' the Director General said as he got to his feet. 'You will have full access to our resources and the laboratories at the National Criminal Investigation Service, Kripos, in Oslo will give your inquiries top priority.'

He crossed to the desk and picked up a large envelope.

'Where's the money now?' Wisting asked.

'Still in the cabin,' the Director General replied, handing him the envelope.

Wisting could feel that the contents included a bunch of keys.

'I want you to form a small team of well-qualified personnel to deal with this,' the Director General, still on his feet, told him. 'Krom has informed Georg Himle, the Prime Minister when Clausen was in government. Apart from that, no one knows about this. That's how it has to stay.'

Wisting stood up, realizing that the meeting was coming to an end.

'The cabin is equipped with an alarm. A new code has been generated, both for the cabin and his house. You have it there,' the Director General explained, pointing at the envelope. 'I suggest the first thing you do is take care of the money.'

2

Outside the colossal building the late-summer heat hit him full force. Wisting took a deep breath, crossed Karl Johans gate and headed straight for the multistorey car park where he had left his car. Before he drove off, he poured the contents of the envelope on to the passenger seat beside him. In addition to the bunch of keys, the envelope contained a black leather wallet, a gold watch, a mobile phone, a few loose coins and a piece of paper with the new code for the alarm – 1705.

The phone was an older model, solid and functional, and there was still some power left in it. The display showed two missed calls but did not say from whom.

He laid it aside and glanced at the wallet, which was scratched and worn and bent slightly out of shape. Opening it, he found four different credit cards as well as a driving licence, insurance certificate, a Labour Party membership card and loyalty cards from various hotel chains. In the notes section there were seven hundred kroner, several receipts and a business card from an *Aftenposten* journalist. There were also a number of photos of his deceased wife and son.

Lisa Clausen had died when her husband was Minister of Health around fifteen years ago and Wisting remembered the media storm it had provoked. She had worked at LO, the Norwegian Confederation of Trade Unions, and had been diagnosed with a rare type of cancer aged forty-six. An expensive experimental treatment was available around the world but was not recognized by the Norwegian health authorities. As Health Minister, Bernhard Clausen was indirectly the highest-ranking person responsible for the fact that his wife did not receive life-extending medication.

She was several years his junior and their son must have been in his mid-twenties at the time. He was killed a year later in a road traffic accident. Two tragedies had struck Bernhard Clausen within a short period of time. He had withdrawn from politics and public life for a while before returning as Foreign Minister a couple of years later.

Wisting replaced the phone, keys and wallet in the envelope and examined the gold watch. The face was emblazoned with the red logo of the Labour Party. He let the second hand rotate all the way round as he gathered his thoughts. Then he returned the watch to the envelope with the other items and started the car.

The first person he needed to get on board was Espen Mortensen, an energetic and versatile crime scene technician who could be relied on not to talk to others. Wisting had bumped into him that morning in the police station corridor and knew he was back from three weeks' holiday.

As he followed the signs for the E18 motorway from the city centre, he dialled his number.

Mortensen sounded busy when he answered.

'Have you managed to catch up with everything after your holiday?' Wisting asked him.

'Not entirely,' Mortensen replied. 'There's still a lot to do.'

'It'll have to wait,' Wisting said. 'I need you for a special project.'

'Oh, what would that be?'

'I'll be back in Larvik in an hour and a half,' Wisting said, casting a glance at the dashboard clock. 'Bring your crime scene equipment and meet me at the car park beside Stavern Sports Hall, and we can drive together from there.'

'What's going on?' Mortensen asked.

'I'll explain later,' Wisting said. 'But don't mention this to anyone.'

'What about Hammer?'

Nils Hammer was second-in-command in the criminal investigation department and deputized for Wisting in his absence.

'I'll have a word with Hammer,' Wisting told him.

He wrapped up the conversation and found Hammer's number.

'I've been given an assignment that will mean being away for a while,' he explained. 'You'll be in charge of the department in the meantime.'

'What kind of assignment?' Hammer asked.

'It's a high-level project.'

Hammer knew better than to ask any further questions. 'How long will it take?'

'I've no idea,' Wisting answered. 'I'm taking Mortensen with me for the preliminary stages, so he won't be available for the next week or so.'

He knew this would place Hammer in a difficult position. Resources were already scarce.

'OK,' Hammer replied. 'Anything else I should know?'

'I don't know too much myself,' he admitted.

'OK,' Hammer repeated. 'I'm here if you need anything else.'

The car radio reconnected when he ended the phone conversation and Wisting switched it off. All that could be heard now was the engine noise and the regular rhythm of the wheels on the asphalt. Thoughts about the origins of the cash were already forming in his mind.

Bernhard Clausen was a Party veteran with a long political career and countless power struggles behind him. He had always been sympathetic towards the USA and had been a supporter of the war in Iraq. This had led to disagreements in government, and he had suffered a setback when it was decided that Norway would not participate in any aggression. Later, as the chair of the Parliamentary Defence Committee, he had brokered an agreement to purchase American-produced fighter planes for the Norwegian Armed Forces. The contract was worth more than 40 billion kroner.

Wisting's hands curled around the steering wheel. Money was usually the root of everything that smelled of greed, corruption and abuse of power. This promised to be an investigation on a totally different level from what he was used to, but he had the optimum starting point. He had the money. Money always left traces behind and it would simply be a matter of following them back to the source.

3

The anonymous white delivery van that Mortensen used to hold all his equipment was parked in the shade outside the nearby sports complex, with Mortensen seated at the wheel eating an apple.

Having parked his car, Wisting stepped out and approached the van's open window. A group of boys were kicking a ball about on the artificial grass pitch.

'We're heading out to Bernhard Clausen's summer cabin,' he said.

Mortensen swore as he tossed the apple core into the passenger footwell.

'We're not dealing with another death,' Wisting hurried to add. 'This is something quite different.' He went on to explain his meeting with the Director General earlier that day and the discovery of cash made by the Labour Party Secretary. 'I know the way,' he said. 'Follow me.'

On returning to his own car, he adjusted the mirror to check Mortensen was following close behind before he swung out on to the road to drive the short distance towards Helgeroa.

The houses grew increasingly few and far between and soon abundant cornfields surrounded him on all sides. After several more kilometres, he turned off, out towards the coast and the cluster of cabins. The old asphalt was cracked and pitted, and here and there stones bulged up from the surface. At an intersection, he had to consult the map on his phone before turning on to a narrower gravel track that ended in front of an ochre-coloured cabin with a grey slate roof and a glass verandah facing the sea.

An older-model Toyota, probably Clausen's own car, was parked in front of the cabin. Wisting left his car slightly further off, leaving room for Mortensen to park his van near the door.

He fished out the keys from the envelope and strode towards the cabin, where a pennant fluttered sluggishly at the top of a flagpole. He could hear the sounds of a motorboat down on the water below.

The cabin was in a sheltered position, not directly overlooked by any of the neighbouring residences. Old, twisted pine trees cast shadows and a grassy field extended more than fifty metres down to the smooth coastal rocks and a shallow inlet. Two children lay on a jetty down there with fishing lines dangling in the water. Above them, a bank of clouds hung motionless in the sky.

Approaching the front door, Wisting searched through the keys to find the right one.

The alarm control panel flashed and beeped intermittently. When Wisting keyed in the code, a green diode lit up.

Two jackets hung from a row of hooks beside the control panel, with a pair of Wellington boots and a pair of sandals lined up on the floor.

Inside, the kitchen was combined with the living room and a swarm of flies buzzed around a pot on the stove. A plate of leftovers lay on the kitchen worktop. In one corner of the living room there was an imposing open fireplace and a door led out to the glass verandah. From there, a wide flight of steps descended to the outdoor area. A large picture of Clausen was prominently displayed on one wall.

In it he wore a singlet and stood beside an axe on a chopping block, wiping sweat from his brow with a checked handkerchief. The photograph had become an iconic image and was how people would remember him, as an ordinary working man who represented the Party's roots. He appealed to both employees and the higher echelons of society, and the forthcoming election campaign would not be the same without him.

The other pictures on the wall were smaller but showed Clausen with famous people he had met, mainly from his time as Foreign Minister. Nelson Mandela, Vladimir Putin, Dick Cheney, Gerhard Schröder, a number of Norwegian prime ministers and Jimmy Carter with his Nobel Peace Prize. Clausen's shock of grey hair was slightly fuller in these photographs than in recent years, but the steely blue gaze remained the same.

From the living room, a corridor lined with doors opened on to bedrooms on either side. Closest of these was the room Bernhard Clausen had used. The bed was made, a book lay on the bedside table and a few garments were folded on a chair, with a black travel bag on the floor. Directly across the corridor was a small bathroom.

At the far end of the corridor they found the room they were looking for. It had a different smell from the rest of the cabin – dry and dusty, warm and stuffy. The walls were covered in varnished pine panelling and it was furnished with bunk beds, a bedside table and a built-in cupboard that divided this room from the adjacent bedroom. Posters decorated the walls, various idols of the nineties side by side with posters peppered with political slogans. Nirvana, U2 and Metallica alongside *A Steady Course*, *Security in Everyday Life* and *If Welfare Is Paramount*. A rag rug covered the floor and the window had thin, flowery curtains. The window itself was closed off with an external shutter and two air vents had been inserted high on the wall.

They counted nine cardboard boxes altogether, four on the lower bunk and five above. On the lower bunk there was also a petrol tank for a boat, with a fuel hose, pump and coupling for an outboard motor.

The boxes all differed in shape and size. Some were the kind you can pick up in grocery shops.

Mortensen prepared his photographic equipment and Wisting drew back to the wall to give him space. In doing so, his shoulder accidentally brushed against one of the old election posters and it ripped from the drawing pin to fold down along the middle, exposing a round hole in the wall. Wisting put his eye to it and discovered another hole.

'What have you found there?' Mortensen asked. 'Peepholes?'

'I don't know,' Wisting replied, as he completely removed the poster.

Another two holes had been concealed. Producing a ballpoint pen from his shirt pocket, he pushed it in and came up against some thin paper.

As Mortensen aimed the camera lens at the wall, Wisting moved out to the corridor and into the neighbouring bedroom. Here, too, old election material was displayed on the walls. *Social Democracy Because We Need One Another. Renewed Growth for Norway. Health and the Elderly Come First.*

He tore down a poster exhorting people to *Vote YES to the EU.* Behind it he found four holes, each revealing different parts of the room on the other side.

Mortensen came to join him. 'Unusual,' he commented as he raised his camera to take another picture.

'Let's get a move on,' Wisting said, heading back to the room where the cash was stored.

Producing a pair of latex gloves, Mortensen pulled them on before lifting one of the boxes and placing it on the floor. It was heavy, heavier than a box of copy paper.

The flaps had been taped down with brown parcel tape. Wisting was unsure whether the Party Secretary had cut them open or if this was something Clausen had done himself.

Wisting opened the flaps to find the box full of American hundred-dollar notes. Some of the banknotes were in wads secured with grey tape. However, they were not packed neatly at all: it looked as if the box had been filled in haste.

Picking up a bundle, Wisting reckoned it contained one hundred notes. Ten thousand dollars. There were perhaps two hundred of these bundles in the box. Two million dollars overall.

After replacing the cash, he lifted down a cardboard box from the upper bunk and opened it. This time, there were piles of euro banknotes of different denominations: twenty, fifty and one hundred.

Mortensen took a step back.

'These must have been here for years,' he said. 'Just gathering dust. It doesn't look as if he's spent any of it.'

Wisting agreed. Nothing about Bernhard Clausen suggested he possessed great wealth. In fact, it seemed as if he had led a simple life.

Mortensen stepped forward again and picked up a wad of notes. 'Could it be some kind of secret emergency fund which was under his control as Foreign Minister?' he suggested. 'Cash to be used to pay terrorist organizations for

Norwegian soldiers held hostage, or something along those lines?'

Wisting shrugged. That was certainly one possibility. Cash would be required for crises of that kind, but it would be highly unlikely for it to be stored in cardboard boxes in a retired politician's summer cabin.

He crossed the room and opened the cupboard to find it filled with stacks of old newspapers and magazines. One shelf was crammed with various spray cans, everything from insecticide to hair lacquer. At the bottom of the cupboard there were propane-gas canisters. Wisting crouched down and looked under the bed, where he saw another two cans of petrol and another cardboard box. A cloud of dust swirled up when he pulled it out.

The box contained old comics. When he picked up some of the ones on top, he discovered a couple of porn magazines with German text on the front covers. Leaving these, he slid the box back in again, got to his feet and brushed off his hands.

'Let's get going,' he said, with a nod in the direction of the bunk beds. 'We'll record and document it all before taking it with us.'

'Where will we take it?' Mortensen asked.

'Home with me,' Wisting answered.

'Home with you?' Mortensen repeated. 'Do you intend to store it there?'

'Temporarily,' Wisting replied. 'Until we find out what this is all about.'

'Then I hope you've got a good burglar alarm,' Mortensen commented.

Wisting took out his phone and left the room so Mortensen could seal and mark the boxes.

He pulled off his rubber gloves, stepped outside and skirted around to the sea-facing side of the cabin. Beside a rocky outcrop, an attractive seating area had been built, with a fireplace, barbecue, refectory table and patio heaters. Wisting stood with his back to the cabin, going through the contact list on his mobile phone. After a while he found the one he was looking for and pressed call.

He and Olve Henriksen went back a long time. They had applied for police college together, but Olve had not fulfilled the entrance requirements for perfect vision. Today he owned one of the country's largest security firms, offering everything from doorkeeper services to transportation of valuables, and probably earned three times as much as Wisting.

'I need a burglar alarm,' he said.

Olve Henriksen suggested having a site inspection first.

'I need one today,' Wisting broke in before Olve had finished speaking.

'I see,' Henriksen replied.

A pause ensued. Wisting waited, watching as tiny black ants scuttled to form a line across the slate slabs at his feet and disappeared down a crack in the wall.

'I can send someone to your house at four o'clock,' Olve finally offered.

Wisting thanked him and provided his address. 'One more thing,' he said, before they rang off.

'Yes?'

Wisting held back, afraid that Olve Henriksen would put two and two together, but trusted him to be discreet regardless.

'Do you have a machine to count banknotes?' he asked.

'We do, at our main office,' Olve told him.

'Is it possible to move it elsewhere?' Wisting queried.

'We have three, in fact,' Olve answered. 'Two of them are portable. The other one is kept as a spare.'

'Could I borrow one?'

'Or you could bring the money here?' Olve suggested.

'Preferably not,' Wisting said. 'I can come and collect the machine.'

'Fine.'

They arranged a specific time and place before Wisting headed back to the cabin.

Mortensen was now seated on a chair in the living room, leafing through the guest book, still wearing his gloves. 'Hans Christian Mukland was here last week,' he said, showing Wisting a signature on one of the final pages. 'He was Justice Minister when I was at police college.'

Wisting took charge of the book.

'There are four more books on the shelf,' Mortensen explained, pointing. 'Everyone who's visited here since the fifties has written a message.'

Wisting riffled back and forth through the book. Famous politicians had given the date of their visit and written short messages. Sometimes photos of get-togethers, taken outdoors beside the cabin walls or around a dining table, were pasted in.

'We'll take them with us,' he said.

The sound of a car outside made them look at each other in surprise. Wisting moved to the door, pulled aside the curtain at the small window beside it and peered outside. A large black SUV was about to turn on the parking space.

'Is someone coming?' Mortensen asked.

Wisting shook his head as the car sped off. His eyesight was not good enough to make out the registration number.

'It's leaving,' he said, lingering to watch the car drive into the distance. 'Probably just a random motorist who's lost his way. After all, the cabin is at the end of the track.'

'Or some nosy parker who's heard that Clausen is dead,' Mortensen suggested. 'Shall we carry out the boxes?'

Nodding, Wisting slipped on a pair of gloves.

Mortensen had drawn a plastic bag over every box. They each picked one up and carried it through the living room and out to their vehicles.

'I need his fingerprints,' Mortensen said as he set down the first box. 'To see if anyone else has handled the money.'

'He's at Ullevål Hospital,' Wisting said. 'We'll arrange that tomorrow.'

'We'll need a biological sample, too, for a DNA profile,' Mortensen pointed out.

Wisting nodded. 'We'll do that at the same time.' He stayed outside to keep an eye on the cars as Mortensen carried out the rest of the boxes.

A gentle sea breeze rustled through the undergrowth, where wild raspberries grew. On the path down to the water's edge, a man with a fishing rod was walking, holding a boy in a red life jacket by the hand. A woman with a dog tugged on the lead as they passed. Further along the path she met a man wearing dark trousers, a short-sleeved shirt and sunglasses.

Mortensen emerged with the last box. 'We'll have to come back for a more thorough search,' he said, tossing his head in the direction of the cabin. 'He's got a massive desk in there with drawers full of handwritten notes. Could well be something of interest that might put us on the right track.'

Agreeing, Wisting cast a glance inside the cabin. 'Wait,' he said.

He headed inside again, making straight for the pot on the stove, and waved away a few flies. It looked like some kind of mixed stew. He found a plastic bag and scraped the contents into it, then placed the pot in the sink and filled it with water. Opening the fridge, he collected the various food items and poured away the leftover milk. He took the food scraps with him and activated the alarm before he shut the door behind him.

4

Wisting drove to his house in Herman Wildenveys gate and reversed as close to the front door as possible, with Mortensen following suit. He had decided that they would store the boxes in the basement, as he never used it anyway. The walls were made of brick and there were only two high, narrow windows.

With each box he carried inside, he looked down towards the house his daughter occupied at the bottom of the street. He would not be able to come up with a reasonable answer if she suddenly appeared and began to ask questions.

The man who arrived to fit the alarm was punctual, and Wisting chose a simple intruder alarm. It would be too laborious and time-consuming to combine this with a fire alarm. He instructed the fitter on how he wanted the basement to be secured with magnetic switches on the door and windows, and for the space itself to be equipped with motion-detector cameras. The control panel was to be fixed to the wall immediately inside the front door. He declined to have an alarm sign displayed outside. The alarm signal should go straight to his mobile phone as well as Mortensen's, in addition to an internal siren.

Mortensen stayed as the alarm was being installed while Wisting left to collect the machine they intended to use to count the money.

When he arrived at the alarm company's headquarters,

he was given a quick lesson on the operation of the machine. The specific currency had to be selected, but the machine had sensors to identify the denomination of notes. In addition, it used infrared rays and UV lights for automatic recognition of fraudulent banknotes. The capacity was 1,200 notes per minute, and the results of the count were printed out on a separate printer that had to be connected up.

On the return journey Wisting called into an office-equipment store and bought ten large cardboard boxes and a roll of parcel tape, as Mortensen had requested. When he arrived home, the alarm had been fitted and Wisting glanced up at the two motion detectors at either end of the basement.

'I had to choose a code,' Mortensen said, tapping in four numbers on the control panel to demonstrate. 'I chose 1808, today's date: 18 August.'

The alarm flashed red and emitted faint beeping sounds. When Mortensen keyed in the code again, the alarm was silenced and a green light came on.

They pushed a table against the wall and Wisting placed the counting machine on one side of it while Mortensen assembled the cardboard boxes.

'We'll count the notes and move them across into the empty boxes so that we get a complete overview,' Mortensen said. 'I can then examine the old boxes for fingerprints here – the cash, too – but we should also take a selection of them to the lab at Kripos for the experts to look at.'

Before they could make a start, the doorbell rang.

Moving out into the hallway, Wisting peered through the glass beside the door to see Line and Amalie standing outside.

'Have you locked the door?' his daughter asked.

Wisting opened the door and made a fuss of his grand-daughter, who threw her arms around his neck. He did not normally lock the door and Line and Amalie usually walked straight in whenever they paid a visit.

'Mortensen and I are busy working on something,' he answered, swinging Amalie up into the air. She gasped and laughed with delight.

'We've made some iced tea,' Line said, holding up a jug.

The ice cubes rattled as he used his free hand to take the jug. 'Lovely,' he said, still hovering in the doorway.

There was a moment's silence.

'She's a little thief, you know,' Line said, nodding towards her daughter.

Wisting put down the jug and looked his granddaughter in the eye. 'What's this Mum's telling me?' he asked in a stern voice.

Amalie usually chattered nineteen to the dozen, but now she kept quiet and looked away.

'She was sitting in the pushchair while we were in the shop,' Line told him. 'When we came out, she had helped herself to a packet of sweets.'

'What did you do?'

'We had to go back in again and hand it back. They were on display right beside the checkout.'

'Silly shop,' Wisting said, rubbing his nose on Amalie's cheek to make her laugh.

'Don't say that,' Line said, reaching out for her daughter. 'She won't understand that she's done something wrong.'

Wisting grew serious and again made eye contact with his granddaughter. 'Grandpa won't be happy if you do that sort of thing,' he said, handing her over. 'But it's not so easy for a two-year-old to understand the business of paying,' he added to Line.

'She knows the difference between right and wrong,' Line said.

Wisting smiled, glad to see that Line was such a good mother.

'Puss,' Amalie said.

'Puss?' Wisting asked.

'We've got a cat in our garden,' Line explained.

'Ah, I see,' Wisting replied with a smile.

'If you're busy, maybe we should come back later this evening,' Line went on.

'Good idea – I'll see you later, then. Thanks for the iced tea.'

He waited in the doorway until they were back on the street before closing and locking the door.

When Wisting was back in the cellar he and Mortensen pulled on latex gloves before he removed the protective packaging and opened the first cardboard box. Mortensen plucked out a few notes from the top layer with the intention of examining them for fingerprints.

'They don't seem to have been used much,' Wisting remarked as he fed the first wad of dollar notes into the counting machine and watched as they rattled through the apparatus.

Mortensen looked through the counted bundle. 'They're all from 2001 and 2003,' he commented, stowing them in the empty box. 'Notes usually circulate for ten years or so before they get too worn and have to be scrapped.'

Wisting put on his reading glasses and looked through the next bundle, also more or less unused notes. 'These are all from 2003,' he said.

'Well, that gives us an indication of how far back in time we have to go to unearth any answers,' Mortensen said.

Wisting was thumbing through another wad of banknotes. 'From 2001 and 2003,' he said. 'There doesn't appear to be any system in the serial numbers either. They're not in numerical order and don't come from a single consignment.'

Wisting fed the counting machine with another bundle of notes as Mortensen sat down with his phone to research American hundred-dollar notes.

'Their system is a bit different from ours,' he said. 'Two thousand and three is the year the note was designed. The 2003 series was printed through to 2006, when they changed the design,' he said.

'So even though it says 2003 on the banknote, it could well be from 2006?' Wisting asked.

'Not exactly,' Mortensen replied. 'In May 2005, a new boss was appointed in the US Finance Department. They began to print notes with her signature on them, and continued with a 2003A series until the hundred-dollar bill was redesigned in 2006.'

'Do we have any 2003A banknotes?' Wisting queried.

Mortensen shuffled a wad of notes through his fingers like a pack of cards. 'Not yet,' he answered.

The manual checks meant the counting took longer than Wisting had anticipated, and three quarters of an hour had elapsed by the time they reached the bottom of the first box. The printout told them it had contained $2,480,000, divided into one-hundred-dollar and fifty-dollar notes.

'The exchange rate is just over eight,' Mortensen said, checking again on his phone. 'Eight point one seven to be precise,' he added, doing a mental calculation to convert it to Norwegian currency: 'Sixteen point seven million kroner.'

Wisting taped up the first box. 'No A-notes,' he summarized. 'This means we will have to go back as far as May 2005, then.'

Mortensen agreed. 'Let's find a box of euros,' he said, removing the protective cover from one of the other boxes.

This one had not been opened previously and Wisting had to fetch a knife to slit open the tape. 'These are pounds,' he said. 'British fifty-pound notes.'

'Is there a year on them?' Mortensen asked, grabbing a wad to examine them for himself.

'Nineteen ninety-four,' Wisting read out.

He delved further into the box to check another bundle and discovered something protruding between two layers of banknotes. A black cable.

He used two fingers to fish it out. It was a severed length of cable with smaller red and blue wires protruding from the broken end and a tiny metal plug at the other.

'A mini-jack,' Mortensen commented. 'For transferring sound files.'

He produced an evidence bag while Wisting examined the small electrical component before dropping it inside.

'Very widely used,' Mortensen went on as he marked the bag. 'On almost all headphones, radio transmitters and walkie-talkies . . .'

Wisting nodded. It was too early to draw any conclusions or read anything into the case, but experience had taught him that it must have something to do with a secret operation where everything had happened quickly but something had gone wrong.

He picked up another wad of notes and checked through

them. 'Nineteen ninety-four here, too,' he said. 'On all of them, as far as I can see.'

He changed the currency setting on the counting machine and fed in the first bundle. Mortensen read up on British pounds on the Bank of England website.

'Looks, again, like the date follows the design,' he said. 'A new fifty-pound note was introduced in 2011. All the notes printed between 1994 and 2011 are marked 1994.'

After another three quarters of an hour, they had counted £186,000. 'Just over 1.9 million Norwegian kroner,' Mortensen calculated.

The paper dust in the air had given Wisting a dry throat. He had put the jug Line had brought on a shelf by the front door and the ice cubes had melted. Heading for the kitchen, he collected two glasses and poured the iced tea.

'We need something to eat,' he said. 'I'll phone for a pizza.'

They embarked on the next box while they waited for the food to arrive. This one contained euro banknotes of various denominations.

'When was the euro actually introduced?' Wisting asked, changing the currency setting on the machine once again.

Mortensen checked on his mobile. 'The notes first went into circulation in January 2002,' he answered.

'That narrows things down a little,' Wisting said. 'So far the money comes from a period of time between January 2002 and May 2005.'

'But that doesn't tell us anything about when they came into Clausen's possession,' Mortensen objected. 'The earliest it could have been was in 2003, when the dollar notes were printed.'

They went on working in silence. After half an hour they heard a vehicle stop outside. 'Grub,' Wisting said.

At that moment the counting machine gave a signal he had not heard before and stopped in the middle of a bundle.

'What's up?' Mortensen asked.

Wisting investigated. 'A scrap of paper,' he said, removing the offending article from the machine. 'It must have been between the banknotes.'

The piece of paper was the size of a matchbox and had two straight and two torn sides, as if it had been ripped from the corner of a larger sheet of paper. On one side, something was written in blue ballpoint pen.

The doorbell rang. Wisting handed the note to Mortensen, pulled off his rubber gloves and went upstairs to fetch the pizza.

'Looks like a phone number,' Mortensen told him on his return.

'Norwegian?' Wisting asked.

'Eight digits, without a country code,' Mortensen answered, and immediately looked it up. 'Registered to Gine Jonasen in Oslo.'

'Let's eat outside,' Wisting suggested.

Mortensen put the scrap of paper into a plastic bag and sealed it. They then activated the alarm, locked the room and stepped out on to the terrace on the other side of the house.

They ate straight from the box and drank cans of cola. Faint noises from the town below drifted up to them from time to time and Wisting fixed his gaze on a yacht making its way into Stavernsodden.

'Any inkling of what this is all about?' he asked.

'A secret hoard of money comprising international currency,' Mortensen replied. 'As I said before, this could be cash that the authorities have kept aside to buy their way out of tricky situations.'

The same thought had already struck Wisting. 'Clausen was Foreign Minister in the Himle government,' he said. 'Georg Himle must have known if there was a huge stash of money somewhere. If that were the case, surely the Party would have swept it under the carpet rather than approach the Director General.'

Mortensen reached out for another slice of pizza. 'I don't know much about politics,' he said. 'Nor about money either.'

'I'm not so sure the answer lies in politics,' Wisting said. 'If we're to find the answer, we'll have to talk to people who knew him.'

'It'll be difficult to combine that with a covert investigation,' Mortensen pointed out. 'Besides, it would be too much for just the two of us.'

'I've got free rein to take on whatever personnel we feel we need,' Wisting said.

'Do you have anyone in particular in mind?'

Wisting nodded, without disclosing anything further.

A grasshopper began to sing somewhere in the garden and the two men finished their meal in silence.

Wisting stood up. 'Shall we continue, then?' he asked.

Mortensen, keen to resume, followed him back down to the basement.

Wisting continued with the money count while Mortensen concentrated on the fingerprints. He folded out the old boxes so that they were flat and sprayed every surface with a chemical, leaving it for a few minutes to dry. Then he placed a special cloth on top and used a steam iron to recover latent fingerprints.

Each fingerprint was photographed, registered and prepared for inclusion in a search through the records.

'There are both old and new prints,' he commented. 'The most recent ones are probably from the Party Secretary, who found the boxes. Some of the faintest prints are most likely from Clausen himself. They appear to be years old.'

They continued working without making conversation, and at just before 10 p.m. they were almost finished. Wisting was nearly at the bottom of the last box when he discovered something sticking out between the banknotes.

'A key,' he said, holding it up. It looked like the key to an external door and the metal was corroded in several places.

Mortensen took it from him. 'It's not a regular key,' he said. 'There's not even a maker's mark.'

'A copy that's been filed down?' Wisting suggested.

Mortensen nodded. 'There's no way it can be traced.'

He produced another evidence bag, dropped in the key and sealed the bag, before placing it on the table beside the scribbled telephone number and the metal plug.

Wisting counted up the rest of the cash. The task had taken them almost six hours. After adding up the printouts from the counting machine, Wisting made a clean copy on a fresh page of his notepad.

$5,364,400
£2,840,800
€3,120,200

Converted to Norwegian currency, the total value was indeed more than 80 million kroner.

5

Once Mortensen had left, having agreed to return early the next morning, Wisting was ready for refreshment and relaxation. There was still some iced tea left in the jug Line had brought. Wisting added a few more ice cubes and carried it out to the verandah. The daylight had gone. He pulled a chair under the exterior light and sat down with his notebook and the iPad he had received from Line at Christmas.

Through a number of articles on the Internet, he gained a rapid overview of Clausen's political life: he had grown up in a working-class family in Oppegård, Akershus, immediately after the war. As a teenager he began working for a construction company that was erecting apartment blocks in Groruddalen. Through trade union involvement he obtained a job with LO, the Norwegian Confederation of Trade Unions, and became active in the movement, supporting Norwegian membership of the EU. In 1975 he was elected to the local council in Oppegård, and in 1981 he was voted into Parliament after being a deputy representative for two periods of four years.

Following several years on the Parliament's Standing Committee on Health and Care, he became a member of the Committee for Foreign Affairs and the Constitution and later the Defence Committee. At the change of government in 2001 he was appointed Minister of Health. His wife died one year later. In 2003 his son died in a road traffic accident. Clausen withdrew from government at a Cabinet reshuffle but was back on the election campaign trail in 2005 and, that same autumn, he entered government again, this time as the Minister of Foreign Affairs. In his capacity as Norway's Foreign Minister, he was for a period also Chair of the Committee of Ministers of the Council of Europe. In the wake of the general election in 2009, he was chosen as President of the Norwegian Parliament and continued in this role until he officially retired. The most recent articles reported that he was still politically active and poised to contribute to the general election campaign that autumn.

A movement at the extreme perimeter of the garden made him look up and Line, having skirted around the house, appeared in the gloaming.

'How's the little thief doing?' Wisting asked, putting his papers aside.

'She's fast asleep,' Line answered, showing him her mobile phone screen. A camera in the child's bedroom meant she could see and hear her daughter wherever she went, and in such a quiet neighbourhood she did not feel anxious.

Wisting thought of making a comment about sleeping soundly with a clear conscience but let it drop. Instead he went inside and brought her a glass.

'I thought I might write an article about children and stealing,' Line said when he returned.

'Good idea,' Wisting replied as he filled her glass.

Line had trained as a journalist while working in the profession. After having Amalie, she had moved home to Stavern from Oslo, and after two periods of leave she had taken a severance package from the national *Verdens Gang* newspaper. Now she was a freelance journalist who worked on interviews and articles for various magazines.

She also had a weekly column about life as single parent to a young child.

'It would be the closest I've come to crime journalism for a long while,' she said, tongue in cheek.

'Do you miss it?' Wisting asked.

Line refrained from answering. 'What have you and Mortensen been up to, anyway?' she asked instead as she took a drink.

Wisting was twirling his own glass in his hand. 'Counting money,' he replied.

Line looked at him as Wisting left his words hanging in the air.

'We're working on a case where it would be best for the police *not* to be the ones asking the questions,' he told her.

'What kind of case?'

'A case in which I need an in-depth personal portrait of a well-known person in order to bring out fresh, previously unknown aspects of his character.'

'Who are we talking about here?'

Wisting swatted a midge that flew past his ear. 'Perhaps you could help?' he asked.

Line smiled. 'I'm not in the police force,' she answered, knowing that her father usually liked to keep her journalism at arm's length from his work.

'I can get authorization for you,' Wisting told her.

Line laughed but quickly realized he was being serious. 'It's not on, really,' she replied, shaking her head. 'I can't pass myself off as a journalist in order to obtain answers for the police.'

Wisting leaned back in his chair, listening to the grasshoppers sing. 'Of course, you'll be able to publish whatever you dig up, and there's nothing to prevent us from exchanging information, surely. Additional information. The info you get from me can't be published without prior clearance, but it will be a scoop for you all the same. The police and press enter into that kind of agreement all the time. What's more, you won't have an editor to answer to.'

Although he was posing his daughter an ethical journalistic dilemma, in that her interviewees would believe she was working for a newspaper rather than the police, he could see that she was interested.

'What does getting authorization involve?' she asked.

'You'll be given police authority, limited in time and applying only to this specific case, and financial remuneration.'

'I thought this case was confidential?'

Wisting reflected on this. 'It's a case that might turn out to be damaging to the public interest,' he answered. 'If that proves to be the case, you can't write about it. But if not, the police won't be concerned about keeping anything secret, as long as it doesn't undermine an ongoing investigation.'

'So I can write whatever I want once the case has been fully investigated?'

'As long as the information isn't classified as confidential,' Wisting told her.

Line sat staring out to sea, where the Svenner lighthouse beam swept lazily across the water. 'Fine,' she said. 'Who's it about?'

'Bernhard Clausen.'

'The politician? But he's dead! Are there suspicions that . . .'

Shaking his head, Wisting interrupted her. 'He died of a heart attack,' he clarified. 'But he left behind an unlikely fortune. I'm investigating where the money came from.'

He watched as Line tried to gather her thoughts. 'How much are we talking about?' she asked.

'It'll make a good story,' Wisting said with a smile. 'He had just over 80 million kroner stashed in his summer cabin at Hummerbakken.'

Wide-eyed, Line repeated the figure aloud. Wisting went on to explain how it was divided into different currencies and the work he'd undertaken to count it all.

'He'll be buried some time next week,' he added. 'That gives us a window of opportunity when it'll be quite natural to talk to people about his past.'

'And if he won the money on the lottery, then I'll be allowed to write about it?' Line asked. 'But if it comes from something like American war operations, then it's confidential?'

Wisting drained his glass and crunched the last ice cube between his teeth. 'More or less. In either case, it'll be a matter of finding the truth,' he said. 'Let's start with that.'

Line's phone buzzed. Amalie was awake. 'I have to go home.'

Wisting got to his feet, too, and collected the glasses. 'There's a meeting here tomorrow morning at eight,' he said, pointing into his kitchen.

Line gave a smile in answer as she disappeared around the corner of the house. Wisting stacked the glasses in the dishwasher and stood at the kitchen window, following his daughter with his gaze. A black cat sneaked out beneath her garden hedge, rubbing up against a lamppost before prowling on. When it vanished into the darkness, Wisting sat down with a notepad at the kitchen table.

A phone number, a short cable, a key, a few unidentified fingerprints and an approximate time frame – that was all they had. The answer lay somewhere in Bernhard Clausen's past; he just needed to find where.

He sat studying the timeline he had sketched out. This was how he worked at the start of an investigation. He jotted down times, key words, stray thoughts and little reminders. Sometimes he doodled and made ink drawings, scribbled absent-mindedly.

Bernhard Clausen's life had been long and eventful, but it was a non-political aspect that Wisting began homing in on. His son. Lennart Clausen.

Bernhard Clausen had described the accident in an in-depth interview following his return to politics. His son had died in a motorbike accident in Kolsås, Bærum, in the early hours of 30 September 2003. Two friends had been with him at the time. Lennart Clausen had been overtaking but lost control of his bike and drove off the road. He was declared dead at the scene.

After his son's death, Clausen had no close family left. Nevertheless, Wisting had noted two names. One was Guttorm Hellevik, the long-time leader of the Labour Party group on Oslo City Council who had been Clausen's best man at his wedding and probably his closest friend. Another name that had cropped up in a couple of articles was Edel Holt. Bernhard Clausen had described her somewhere as a loyal political comrade. In another article, she was named as the woman behind the great man.

It was after midnight when he rose from his chair. He headed for the bathroom and brushed his teeth while wandering around the house, checking that all the windows were closed and the doors were locked.

6

A distant noise roused Wisting from sleep, and he lay there, struggling to locate its source. It was still dark outside and the clock radio on his bedside table showed 5.13.

Pushing aside the quilt, he planted his feet on the floor and listened intently, but the sound had gone.

He got up and made for the bathroom, since he was wide awake now. On retracing his steps to the bedroom, he heard the noise again. It was coming from somewhere inside the house, down in the basement.

It dawned on him that it must be the new alarm system. He rushed to find the keys to unlock the door to the basement.

He opened the door, flicked on the light and stepped inside. His movements made the control panel light up, demanding the access code. After keying in the four digits, he heard the noise again, but it came from elsewhere in the room. He tried to find his bearings and follow the sound. Halfway across the basement, he realized that it was Bernhard Clausen's mobile phone ringing. It lay on the table with his wallet and gold watch, and Mortensen had connected it to a charger.

He grabbed it to find some way of turning off the noise. The display glowed with the caller ID *Alarm Company*. Wisting hesitated for only a second before answering. 'Yes, hello?'

'Am I speaking to Bernhard Clausen?' the young woman at the other end asked.

'I'm speaking on his behalf,' Wisting replied. 'Is this about an alarm?'

The woman explained that she was phoning from the Guardco central switchboard. 'We've received an error message from Hummerbakken 102,' she told him. 'Are you there now?'

'What kind of error message?' Wisting demanded.

'The wrong alarm code has been keyed in three times,' the woman said. 'A security guard has been dispatched. I need a password to switch off the alarm.'

'No,' Wisting answered. 'I'm not there.'

'That's odd,' the woman commented.

'What is it?' Wisting asked.

'The fire alarm has just gone off,' she told him. 'At the same location.'

Wisting swore under his breath and ordered the alarm-company operator to call the fire brigade, before throwing on some clothes and bolting out to his car.

The fiery yellow glow lit up the night sky from afar and its intensity grew as he approached the scene.

Neither the police nor the fire service had turned up as yet, but a security vehicle was parked, with its warning lights flashing. Wisting manoeuvred around it and drove down to the patch of grass beside the water to avoid obstructing the fire engines when they arrived.

He felt the scorching heat as soon as he stepped out of his car. Orange, yellow and red flames entwined and enveloped the entire cabin.

As a window exploded, a huddled group of neighbours from nearby cabins backed away. The flames surged out, licking their way along the wall and darting out under the roof.

Wisting stood back, like the others. The dry timbers creaked and cracked, and his skin tensed in the searing heat.

Another explosion sent plumes of blue flame up through the roof, and burning planks and huge red cinders were tossed up into the air. The security guard told everyone to draw back.

The first blue lights appeared after a few minutes, two fire engines followed by a police patrol car. The fire fighters set to work with the water they had on board while they rolled out hoses down to the shore.

Wisting introduced himself to the officers in the patrol car. Without divulging anything about the background, he told them that the alarm had been triggered and the cabin had been unoccupied.

When the security guard headed for his vehicle, Wisting pursued him. He showed his police ID and asked if he had seen anything of significance.

'What did the fire look like when you arrived?' he asked. 'Did you notice if any part of the cabin was burning more than another?'

'The flames were certainly more vigorous at the back of the cabin,' the guard told him. 'It looked as if the fire started there.'

'Did you encounter anyone on your way down here?'

The guard shook his head. 'People from the neighbouring cabins had already gathered here, though.'

'What about along the road?'

'There was the odd car, but nothing I paid any attention to.' He opened the car door and sat inside. 'Why do you ask? Do you think the fire was started deliberately?'

'I spoke to the operator at your central switchboard,' Wisting said. 'Someone had keyed in the wrong access code before the fire alarm was set off. That is grounds for further investigation.'

'I have a dash camera,' the guard told him, pointing up at the rear-view mirror. 'My whole shift is recorded. You can't have the file right now, but I can make sure you get a copy some time tomorrow.'

'That would be a great help,' Wisting said. He moved to the front of the vehicle and spotted the small, discreet camera. 'Are you filming now, too?' he asked.

'All the time,' the guard replied, nodding.

Glancing at his watch, Wisting registered that it was 6.01.07. He took out a card with his contact details and handed it to the security guard. A sudden noise made them both turn their eyes to the burning cabin, where the roof had now collapsed. The front wall swayed before it split open and half slid back into the shattered roof. A shower of sparks flew upwards, carried by the hot, smoky air. The fire fighters had their generators working and were drenching the flames with seawater, but by now it was not a case of saving the cabin but simply damping down and controlling the blaze.

Dawn was breaking around them as Wisting strode across to his car, sat inside and took out his phone. He sent a brief text message to Espen Mortensen, telling him what had happened and asking that they meet up at Wisting's house asap. Then he sent a similar message with the same information to the Director General, adding that the valuables had been secured and the fire would be investigated as a case of potential arson.

7

The sun spilled in through the kitchen window as Wisting put a cup of coffee in front of Mortensen and produced a few slices of bread from the freezer.

'Have you eaten?' he asked as he popped them into the toaster.

'Yes, but thanks anyway.'

Wisting brought out some butter and marmalade. Through the kitchen window, he saw his daughter park her car in the street. 'Line's joining us,' he said, explaining how he had let her in on the investigation the previous evening.

Mortensen seemed sceptical but did not pass any comment.

When Line entered, she took out a cup and dropped a capsule into the coffee machine.

'Where's Amalie?' Wisting asked.

'Sofie's taking her today,' Line explained, naming her friend, who also had a young daughter and frequently babysat for her.

The toaster clicked as it spat out the two slices of bread. While he buttered the toast Wisting told them about the fire at the cabin.

'The cabin is just a smoking heap of ashes,' he concluded. 'I've arranged with Hammer to put an officer on guard at the scene until it can be examined.'

Mortensen sipped his coffee. 'The fire makes things

easier for us,' he pointed out. 'We can use the investigation into it as cover for our questions.'

Wisting took a bite of toast. 'Mortensen and I have an appointment with the pathologist at ten o'clock,' he said, looking in Line's direction. 'And then at the Party office at eleven. After that we'll drop into Kripos and pay a visit to Clausen's home. I suggest we do as planned and then we can go and take a look at the scene of the fire this evening.'

'Where should I begin?' Line asked.

Dipping into his notebook, Wisting took out a Post-it note and jotted down a phone number. 'This number was on a scrap of paper in one of the boxes of cash,' he told her.

'Gine Jonasen in Oslo,' Mortensen interjected.

'Find out who she is,' Wisting said, adding her date of birth and address. 'There's nothing on her in the police records,' he added. 'See if she has any connection whatsoever to Bernhard Clausen, or if she knows anything that might be helpful.'

'OK,' Line replied. 'What else?'

'Guttorm Hellevik and Edel Holt,' Wisting said, writing down their names and contact information on a note for her.

'I know who Guttorm Hellevik is,' Line said.

'As well as being a political colleague, he was also best man at Bernhard Clausen's wedding,' Wisting elaborated. 'Edel Holt was some kind of personal assistant to him.'

He made a list of key points concerning information he was keen to extract from her interviews with them. Line had a number of questions regarding what she could and could not say. They discussed the case before Wisting gathered up the coffee cups and stacked them in the dishwasher.

'Then let's meet back here this evening,' he said, rounding off the meeting.

Line used her own car and Mortensen drove the unmarked police car. Neither he nor Wisting had much to say en route. They passed Sandefjord and Tønsberg.

'I've been thinking about the fire and those peepholes,' Mortensen said, glancing in the mirror. 'Without a doubt, something went on at that cabin. Something someone thought important enough to hide every trace of. Something not necessarily connected to the money.'

Wisting had been harbouring the same thoughts, but neither of them could make an educated guess about what might be at the bottom of it all.

One hour later, Mortensen turned into the hospital grounds at Ullevål and followed the signs to the laboratory buildings. They introduced themselves in the office and produced documents from the Director General that gave them authority to collect fingerprints and a DNA sample from the deceased politician. An attendant was called to accompany them, and they were ushered along several corridors to a tiled room that reeked of disinfectant. At one end of the room was a refrigerated facility in rust-free, acid-resistant steel for the storage of corpses. The doctor drew out a moveable trolley, opened one of the fridge doors and checked a label before removing the dead body and transferring it to the trolley.

Mortensen prepared his instruments for taking fingerprints while the doctor pushed the trolley towards a work lamp and folded aside the white sheet.

Wisting stood by the door, reading the post-mortem report, as Mortensen worked on securing prints from Bernhard Clausen's stiff fingers.

His medical history was described in some detail. His first heart attack had struck him two years earlier, caused by a blood clot in one of the coronary arteries. The artery had been unblocked and he was prescribed blood-thinning medication. About a year later he suffered another heart attack and a stent was inserted. The most recent heart attack was massive and damaged extensive parts of the heart muscle, and when a further attack occurred it had caused total heart failure.

Mortensen did not take long to complete his task. The doctor slid the stretcher back into place in the storage facility and followed them out. From Ullevål, they drove directly to the Labour Party offices in Youngstorget.

They located the appropriate entrance and took the lift to the fourth floor of the enormous building. The walls of the reception area were plastered with election posters and photographs of Party leaders. A picture of Clausen in a thick, black frame was displayed on the counter beside a flickering candle. The woman behind the counter stood up and escorted them to a spacious corner office when Wisting told her they had an appointment with Walter Krom.

Krom, smaller in stature than Wisting had imagined from the times he had seen him on television, rose to his feet when they were shown in. 'Georg Himle will join us in half an hour,' he said, gesturing with his hand towards a conference table, where coffee and biscuits were already laid out.

'Thanks for seeing us at such short notice,' Wisting said as he sat down in one of the leather chairs.

The Party Secretary took a seat opposite him and filled the cups. 'Have you made any progress?' he asked.

'We've counted the money,' Wisting replied, explaining how it was divided into different currencies.

'Is there any way of tracing it?'

'We're conducting a number of searches on the serial numbers through various channels to see if it's flagged up anywhere,' Mortensen said.

'Flagged up?' Krom repeated.

'If the notes come from a consignment of cash that's gone missing, for example after a robbery.'

The Party Secretary nodded slowly, as if taking time to absorb all the possibilities.

'We'll need your fingerprints,' Mortensen said. He opened the briefcase he had carried with him and placed the stamp pad and registration card on the table in front of them. 'To eliminate your prints on the cardboard boxes,' he added.

'Of course,' Krom answered.

Standing up, he took off his suit jacket and rolled up his sleeves. Mortensen guided him as he moistened each individual finger with printer's ink and applied each in turn to the fingerprint form.

Wisting got him to relate in detail how he had let himself into the cabin and found the money. As Clausen's next of kin, he had been given both key and code. He explained how he had cut open the tape on three of the boxes before letting himself out again.

'What's your theory?' he asked.

Walter Krom shook his head. 'It's absolutely incredible,' he said. 'I've no explanation for it whatsoever.'

'How long have you known Bernhard Clausen?'

'A long time,' Krom answered, picking up a moist tissue to wipe his fingers. 'For thirty years at least.'

45

'And nothing happened, either politically or personally, in those thirty years that you can link to the money in any way?'

The Party Secretary shook his head and went to drink from his cup.

'Wait a moment,' Mortensen said. 'I need a clean saliva sample from you, too.'

Packing away the fingerprinting equipment, he took out a DNA testing kit. Krom leaned back in his chair and opened wide as Mortensen swabbed the inside of his mouth.

'Do you have any idea who else might know something?' Wisting asked, once he had finished.

'Georg Himle might have some knowledge, based on their time in government. But nothing of that nature, I should think,' Krom replied. 'He'll be here shortly, as I said.'

'Have you been out there often?' Wisting inquired. 'At the cabin, I mean.'

'Well, we normally had a trip out there each summer – at least we did once he was on his own.'

'Did you spend the night there?'

'Not always, but usually.'

'Can you recall when he started locking the back room?'

'That was his son's bedroom,' Krom told him. 'It was at the far end of the hallway, furthest away from the living room. I don't know when he began to lock it but, after Lennart died, visitors never used that room.'

'Tell me about his son,' Wisting requested.

'There's not much I can say about him,' Krom said. 'He was pretty much an immature, unruly boy, but there was no badness in him. It became a real challenge when Bernhard was left on his own with him.'

'What do you mean by "unruly"?'

'It might be more accurate to say that he was a lad who was easily led. And in revolt against everything his father stood for.'

'How was that?'

Walter Krom took another mouthful of coffee, as if he needed time to choose the right words. 'Lennart was twenty-four when Lisa died,' he began. 'You know the story? That she had a rare form of cancer?'

Wisting nodded.

'It was difficult for Lennart to appreciate why she couldn't be given medicine that might extend her life. He blamed his father for that. Everything he did afterwards I believe he did to hurt his father.'

'Such as what?'

'He dropped out of his studies and hung out with the wrong kind of people.'

'What sort of people?'

'People who drive around on motorbikes in the middle of the night without paying any heed to the speed limits,' Krom replied, referring to the night Lennart Clausen had been killed.

'Criminal friends?' Wisting asked.

'Well, narcotics were involved, but I don't know the details. I don't think it ever went far enough for the police to take an interest.'

Walter Krom lifted his cup but put it back down again. A pensive air had come over him. 'There *is* an heir,' he said. 'Do you know about that?'

Wisting raised his eyebrows to signal that this was news to him. 'Another child?' he asked.

'A grandchild,' Krom clarified. 'Lennart Clausen had a

girlfriend when he died. "A female friend" might be a better description. It turned out that she was pregnant, and she gave birth to a daughter seven months later.'

Wisting prepared to take some notes. This would be an assignment for Line.

'I'll find her name and contact information,' Krom offered, glancing in the direction of his desk. 'The little girl must be almost a teenager now.'

'Did they have any contact?'

Walter Krom shook his head. 'None whatsoever,' he answered. 'That was the mother's choice. I think Lennart had told her far too many negative things about his father for her to allow him any contact.'

'Such as what?'

'That he'd let his mother die.'

Krom turned the conversation to other aspects of Bernhard Clausen's character and related a number of anecdotes from his political life, until there was a knock at the door. It opened before anyone had time to answer and Georg Himle entered the room with the same authoritative bearing as he had shown as Prime Minister.

Wisting got to his feet and they shook hands, before all four sat down again around the table. Georg Himle was first to speak. 'I'm concerned about three things in this case,' he said. 'Honesty, integrity and discretion.'

He continued without waiting for the others to comment. 'Bernhard Clausen is a great loss to us, that can't be denied. We're the opposition, and Clausen would have been extremely useful for us in the forthcoming election campaign. He was a down-to-earth, popular politician who represented the true face of social democracy. When I heard about this, I didn't know what to think, but I do want the truth to emerge. At the same time, I'm anxious to avoid rumour and gossip. That would be damaging to everyone.'

'We hope you can shed some light on the cash found in Clausen's cabin,' Wisting said. 'You can rest assured that we intend to avoid rumour and gossip. We're working in the utmost secrecy.'

Georg Himle shook his head. 'I'm afraid I had no knowledge of the money at all.'

Wisting let him know about the time frame to which they were now able to trace the banknotes. 'That suggests they originate from a period when Clausen was a member of your government,' he summarized.

Georg Himle answered with only a brief nod of his head.

'Are there government funds in the form of cash reserves kept for emergency purposes, or anything like that?' Wisting asked.

The former Prime Minister looked thoughtful. 'Nothing that's out of control. Anything of that sort is tightly monitored,' he replied.

'Could other countries have deposited funds of that kind with Clausen?'

Himle leaned forward in his chair. 'I understand you have to ask that question, but the answer is that it's absolutely inconceivable.'

'A few days ago it would have been considered inconceivable that Bernhard Clausen had more than 80 million kroner in cardboard boxes in his summer cabin,' Wisting reminded him.

'But there's no credible explanation for why he might receive funds of that nature,' Himle replied. 'I really have to reject it out of hand.'

Wisting nodded. 'We need an overview of the people in the organization he had closest contact with,' he said. 'All advisers and personal secretaries.'

Georg Himle delegated the task to Krom with a flick of his hand.

'Who is there we can talk to outside the Party?' Wisting queried. 'Someone who can tell us about his personal life?'

Himle and Krom exchanged looks. 'There's Edel Holt, of course,' Krom answered. 'Apart from that, I don't think there is anyone, at least not after Lisa and Lennart died.'

'Yes, you must speak to Edel,' Himle said. He stood up, indicating that the meeting was over, as far as he was concerned.

'Edel worked closely with Clausen,' Krom explained. 'Both here at the office and while in government. No one knew him better than she did.'

8

Edel Holt lived in Hausmanns gate, within walking distance of Youngstorget, where she had worked for Bernhard Clausen.

Line had been unsure how to approach her when she rang to request a meeting. Introducing herself as a freelance journalist, she explained that she wanted to write an article about Bernhard Clausen. Although Edel Holt explained that Clausen's death had been sudden and unexpected, and she was still reeling from the shock, she nevertheless invited Line to her home that same day.

Edel Holt was a short woman with a round face and fine, delicate features. The eyes behind her glasses twinkled with warmth. She showed Line to a table beside the living-room window overlooking the Akerselva river. Cups were set out, as well as a small plate of biscuits.

'I've made some tea,' she said. 'Or would you rather have coffee?'

'Tea's fine, thank you,' Line said.

Edel Holt disappeared into the kitchen and returned with the teapot.

'They say you're the one who knew him best,' Line began.

'I worked with him until the Party lost the election and the government stood down in 2009,' she explained. 'I was already past retirement age by then. It became difficult for me when everything had to be done on computer.'

Line looked at the grey-haired woman facing her, aware that she was ten years older than Clausen. 'Haven't you been in touch since then?'

'I was a professional resource, organizing Clausen's political work. When he left politics, our relationship naturally dwindled away.'

'What did your work consist of?'

'The most important aspect was managing his calendar, arranging meetings and events, filtering incoming communications and sending them on to wherever in the country Clausen happened to be. Most of all, it was a case of finding practical solutions and clearing up everyday problems, both large and small.'

'Such as what?'

'If he suddenly needed a clean shirt or a dark tie, or was on his way to a meeting and got delayed. There could be major consequences. The other participants had to be informed – some of them might have flights to catch that they'd no longer make, and so on.'

'You got to know each other well?'

Edel Holt nodded. 'I was a part of his daily life for twenty-eight years. I was never treated as a casual employee who could be easily replaced. We had respect for each other.'

She smiled as she went on: 'Sometimes I said to him, "I think you should sleep on that," or something even less diplomatic. He always took it well.'

'So you were on familiar terms?'

'I would say so. But of course he didn't discuss confidential government business with me,' Edel Holt said. 'I had no need to know anything about it, but I got to know him well and was well acquainted with his needs. I made sure he had peace and quiet whenever he needed it.'

'So you became a kind of care-giver for him?'

'Care?' The old woman gave this idea some thought. 'Actually, it wasn't so much a matter of care-giving but of organizing things so that he could do as good a job as possible. For instance, he was in New York for a week and travelled to Brussels on his way back, so I blocked out a day in his calendar for him to relax on his return. Everyone does a better job when they're well rested. It's just a question of being professional.'

She put her cup to her lips to indicate there was nothing more to be said.

Line moved the conversation on to talk about Clausen's work with Prime Minister Himle and visits from leaders of foreign governments. They also spoke about Clausen's wife's illness and the accident that killed his son.

'He decided to sell the summer cabin when Lisa became unwell to cover the costs of the experimental treatment,' she said, 'but that would have meant avoiding the queues in the Norwegian health service and buying privilege. It was also highly uncertain whether it would be successful and it could have prolonged her suffering.'

Line took notes. This would be an interesting angle if she were to write something about Bernhard Clausen.

'I felt lucky to have been able to work with him,' the woman on the opposite side of the table rounded things off. 'He was a principled, steady and shrewd man. Always friendly, always present.'

'Always?' Line asked.

Edel Holt took another gulp of tea and sat for a while without swallowing, as if she had too much in her mouth. 'There were three times when I've known him to be different,' she finally said. 'Distracted and confused. The first time was when Lisa became ill and died. There was something melancholy about him then. He withdrew into a kind of internal place of refuge, if you understand what I mean. He began to go on lots of long walks, often late in the evening or even at night. The same thing happened when he lost his son. Family was important to him, and when both his wife and son were gone, it all became too much. He drew back and then resigned as Health Minister, but he returned after the election and was appointed Foreign Minister.'

'And what was the third time?' Line asked.

'That was one time between the death of his wife and his son.'

'What was the reason for that?'

Edel Holt shook her head. 'There was no single incident that sparked it off,' she said. 'At least not that I knew of. I figured that it was the aftermath of losing his wife, but it seemed to happen more or less overnight.'

'Do you remember when that was?'

'It was in 2003, six months or so after Lisa died.'

Curiosity mounting, Line felt she had touched upon something. 'Would it be possible to find out more exactly?' she asked. 'Are there any appointment books or anything from that time?'

'I have kept my calendars,' the old woman told her. 'But I don't know how I'd find the date. It can't be helped, anyway. And Bernhard Clausen's no longer here to answer for himself.'

9

Wisting and Mortensen had three further appointments in Oslo. The first was at Ullevål University Hospital's Forensics Department, where Mortensen deposited the material for DNA analysis. In addition to the saliva sample from Walter Krom, there were swabs with scrapings from the key, the scrap of paper with the phone number on it and the radio plug.

From the forensics department, their journey moved on to the Kripos laboratories at Bryn. Mortensen had already filled in the required forms detailing what he wanted done. First and foremost was fingerprint examination.

'It has top priority,' Wisting said.

The woman in a lab coat who recorded the items lifted her glasses. 'Everyone asks for top priority,' she said, smiling. 'Everything's urgent.'

Wisting returned her smile. 'This does actually have to go to the front of the queue,' he said, pointing to the special reference number.

The woman shrugged. 'Some people have the right contacts,' she said.

'When can we expect the results?' Mortensen asked.

'You should receive a phone call around this time tomorrow.'

They thanked her and moved on.

Their next stop was Kolbotn, on the eastern side of the Oslo fjord. Lisa and Bernhard Clausen had set up home in Holteveien immediately after their son was born. The drive from the city took just over quarter of an hour.

The street comprised small houses with gardens and ancient trees. Mortensen identified the right one, a grey-painted, two-storeyed detached house with white window frames and a pitched roof. The coarse gravel in the drive-way crunched under the tyres as they swung in.

Another empty house, Wisting thought. He had visited a lot of these. That was his job: venturing into houses that lay empty, either because the person who had lived there had suffered a sudden death, or because it belonged to a perpetrator he had taken into custody. In both cases his work entailed finding traces of the lives of the human beings who had lived there.

A train passed somewhere in the vicinity when they got out of the car. Wisting marched up to the door, unlocked it and switched off the alarm.

The air was dry and dusty. The kitchen was straight ahead, the living room to the left, and to the right there was another corridor with doors into the bathroom, bedroom and office, as well as a staircase to the upper floor.

First, they did the rounds of the upper storey. It consisted of two bedrooms, a small sitting room and a compact bathroom. None of these looked as if it had been used for a long time. One of the bedrooms had apparently belonged to the son. It contained a stereo system and there was a collection of CDs on a shelf, but otherwise it seemed as if all the personal touches had been cleared away. The desk drawers and cupboard shelves were empty. The only thing left hanging on the wall was a photograph of him.

On the ground floor they walked into the office. A large desk stood in front of the window with a clunky computer and stacks of newspapers and magazines. The walls were lined with bookshelves overflowing with non-fiction titles, political biographies and books about American history. A filing cabinet was placed in one corner. Wisting pulled out the top drawer and leafed through the files – judicial registration documents, public service testimonials, old examination papers, insurance documents, tax returns, invoices and receipts. The next drawer held a variety of newspaper cuttings and personal correspondence. A separate folder, with sparse contents, was labelled *Lena*. It didn't take Wisting long to realize that this was Clausen's grandchild. There was a newspaper cutting with a photograph from a special occasion at nursery, a similar clipping from a school event and announcements of Lena Salvesen's birth and baptism.

The bottom drawer contained two jam-packed files. The larger of these was crammed with hospital correspondence in connection with Lisa's illness and death. The other held a collection of papers to do with Clausen's son, everything from school report cards to his death certificate.

The school reports showed that the boy had initially performed well in several subjects but his absences had increased and his marks had deteriorated as a result. It emerged from a number of notes and comments that his schoolwork had been affected by lack of concentration. There were also papers concerning an inquiry about ADHD, though this did not seem to have drawn any conclusions.

Mortensen had taken a seat at the desk and was rummaging through the drawers.

'Diaries,' he said, taking out a bundle of small red yearbooks from the bottom drawer.

They were organized chronologically and spanned the

years 1981 to 2005. Wisting picked up one from 1998 and flicked backwards and forwards through it. Each double page was a week, with nine lines for weekdays and four lines for Saturdays and Sundays. Clausen had noted various appointments, some in abbreviated form, others with names recorded. A few had been scored through and others were underlined. No personal comments were attached to the appointments, merely the time and place of different meetings.

Mortensen laid them aside to take away with them.

The next few hours were spent systematically searching the office. Bernhard Clausen did not seem to be a man with anything to hide; there was no safe and none of the drawers or cupboards was locked. Nothing of what they found gave the impression of being compromising in any way.

Mortensen found the computer password scribbled on a note on the underside of the desk pad. He logged on and clicked through the files without finding anything of interest.

As well as the diaries, they took an address book containing a comprehensive list of phone numbers and addresses.

Before they left, Wisting was keen to check the two garages. One was attached to the house and the other was located near the road. The keys for both hung in a key cupboard in the hallway. The garage beside the house was not locked so he flipped up the retractable door and peered inside. At the far end he could see a workbench with a tool shelf above it. A snow shovel and a yard brush were propped up against the wall. Apart from that, there was nothing to be seen.

They closed the door and locked it before checking the other garage. The door hinges screeched as they pulled it up. Unlike the other garage, the interior was a mess of motorbike parts, tools, engines and other pieces of equipment strewn across the floor.

'The son,' Mortensen remarked as he stepped over an oilcan. His shoes left footprints in the dust and dirt on the concrete floor.

'It must have been left like this since he died,' Wisting said. He stayed outside while Mortensen peered into various cupboards and tried a door at the far end.

'I don't think we'll find anything in here,' he said as he came out again. 'It doesn't look as if Clausen senior ever set foot inside the garage.'

Wisting agreed and drew the door down. If they were to find answers, they would have to search elsewhere.

10

Line fired up the engine but remained staring straight ahead without moving. She had spent considerable time with Edel Holt and asked all the questions her father had wanted her to ask, but nothing specific had really emerged. She hoped her father and Mortensen had been more successful at the Labour Party offices.

Her next interview was with Guttorm Hellevik, who had held several different posts in the Labour Party. Line remembered him from newspaper coverage as an overweight man with thick, grey hair.

It was his wife who opened the door and welcomed her in. 'She's here!' she called out. Guttorm Hellvik shouted back an answer and his wife led Line into a workroom.

Hellcvik rose from his desk and came forward to greet her. 'I've started writing a eulogy,' Hellevik said, gesturing to the desk behind him. 'Someone else will probably speak at the church, but I wanted to write down some of my memories of him.'

They sat down in a little seating area. 'What do you remember best?' Line asked.

'His dry sense of humour, his warm-heartedness and our good conversations,' Hellevik replied. 'He was always so enthusiastic and interested.'

'You were one of the people closest to him, weren't you?' Line asked.

'Well, in the past, anyway,' Hellevik said, nodding, as he

went on to relate how they had met as shop stewards in the sixties and joined the labour movement together.

Hellevik's wife brought in coffee and buttered pancakes. Hellevik spoke about how Clausen had met his wife and what she had meant to him.

He told Line anecdotes and stories about Bernhard Clausen as a politician and friend that supported the popular impression of him as a magnanimous, generous, outspoken and wise man, who had meant so much to so many people.

'But then he changed,' he added. 'After all, he lost both his wife and his son within a short period of time. He took it badly. His wife's death affected him more than people realized. From the outside, he seemed strong and steady, but it was terribly hard for him not to be able to help her. And when his son died, it all became too much for him and he was forced to take a break from politics.'

'Were you with him much at that time?'

'I should have been, but he wanted to be on his own. He wanted to go on walks by himself. He didn't want anyone close to him then. He became a different man.'

'How do you mean?'

Guttorm Hellevik mulled this over. 'He was always so enthusiastic and interested in people but, after Lisa died, he grew quiet and distant. Before that, he was usually one of the loudest voices around a table, but he turned silent and submissive. Withdrawn, lost in his own thoughts.'

His description reminded Line of what Edel Holt had told her only a few hours earlier. 'Did anything else happen at that time to affect him?' she probed.

Guttorm Hellevik did not seem to understand her question.

'Something political?' she added.

Hellvik shook his head. 'No, but he probably began to change his political views on many issues.'

'Such as what?'

'The Labour Party stands for freedom, justice and community, but he began to have different thoughts about these terms. He did not feel free. He thought our society was too regulated, intruded too much on people's private lives and put obstacles in the way of people who wanted to achieve things. He felt an increasing need to be independent, rather than part of a community.'

Hellevik continued to describe the political discussions he had had with Bernhard Clausen. 'To Georg Himle and other senior officials, he was starting to become something of a thorn in the flesh,' he said. 'He began to speak out against some of the Party's fundamental ideologies.'

'But he came back as Minister of Foreign Affairs, didn't he?' Line asked.

'It took time for him to change his viewpoint,' Hellevik explained. 'This was later, towards the end of his political career, but I think he'd begun to think in other political directions when he was left to his own devices after the deaths of his wife and son.'

Keen to home in on something that would shed light on the money, Line made an effort to steer the conversation away from politics. 'Did you spend much time at his summer cabin?' she queried.

'Every summer,' Hellevik confirmed.

'Including the summer his wife died?' Line added.

'Yes,' Hellevik said, nodding, and went on to talk about their fishing trips and late-summer evenings and about collaborating on different projects. He said that, near the end of the summer, Clausen's mood had lifted a little, but then his son had been killed so tragically.

After half an hour or so, Line wrapped up the interview and left.

Back in the car, she went through her notes, ready to write a report of each interview for her father. For her, this was an unaccustomed method of working. She usually gathered her notes a little here and there, some from her notepad, some stored on her Mac and others simply kept inside her head. Then she would summarize everything in a final article. Now it would be her father rather than her who tied all the various strands together to tell the whole story.

The notes from her conversation with Guttorm Hellevik drew a slightly different picture of Bernhard Clausen from the one she had formed earlier. Although it had afforded a fascinating glimpse into his political and personal life, she still did not feel she was any closer to what she was really after, some clue about the mysterious piles of cash left behind after his death.

The most interesting assignment she had been given by her father was the scrap of paper with the phone number on it found in one of the boxes of money. She took out his note of the person's name, address and date of birth. Gine Jonasen. It had not been possible to find much information on her. She lived alone, had no children and worked part-time in a bookshop.

Line tapped the address into her GPS and found that it was twenty-six minutes away. She drove off and followed the directions, which led her to a basement apartment in Kolsås. When she arrived she saw a young woman, around her age, sitting at a table in the garden. She glanced up from her book and Line grabbed her notepad.

'Hi!' she said as she slammed the car door behind her. 'Are you Gine Jonasen, by any chance?'

The woman put her book down on the table. 'Yes?'

Line approached and introduced herself. 'I'm working on a story about Bernhard Clausen,' she said, explaining that she was a journalist.

There was nothing other than bafflement to be seen on the other woman's face.

'I'd like to have a little chat with you about him,' Line went on.

'With me?'

'Yes, you knew him, didn't you?'

The woman shook her head. 'I think you must be mistaken,' she said. 'I know who he is, but I didn't know him.'

Line looked down at the note her father had written for her. Gine Jonasen had been born in 1988. 'But maybe you knew his son?' Line asked on the spur of the moment. 'Lennart Clausen?'

The woman laughed. 'I think you must have the wrong Gine Jonasen,' she said.

Line read out the phone number and date of birth from the note.

'That's me,' the other woman confirmed.

'And there's nobody else who uses your phone?'

The woman leaned down and grabbed a bottle of water from underneath the table. 'No,' she said, twisting off the lid.

A sudden thought struck Line. 'How long have you had that phone number?'

'Always.'

'What does that mean?'

'Since I got my first phone when I was sixteen.'

'So, in 2004?' Line calculated.

'That's probably right,' Gine Jonasen said, nodding. 'Nowadays, youngsters get mobile phones when they go to nursery, I guess.'

Line smiled. 'OK,' she said. 'I think this must be a misunderstanding, after all. Sorry for disturbing you.'

She returned to her car and sat inside. She looked up to see that Gine Jonasen had risen from her chair and was beckoning to her. Line rolled down the passenger-side window and leaned across the seat.

'There's one thing,' Gine Jonasen said as she approached. 'It just dawned on me that someone called a few times when I first got the phone. I think he was looking for the person who had the number before me.'

Line nodded. So that was it. Numbers that had been out of use for a while were allocated to new customers. 'Do you know who was calling?'

'No, but he was asking for someone called Daniel.'

'You can remember that?'

'Yes, because my father's name is Daniel. I thought he meant Dad. It caused a bit of confusion.'

'So the person who used the number before you was probably called Daniel?'

'Yes, but that was ages ago.'

Thanking her, Line bit the lid off her pen and jotted down the name on a blank sheet of her notepad. *Daniel.*

11

Wisting opened two tins of stew, poured the contents into a pan and turned the hotplate up full blast.

Four people were seated around the kitchen table. He shoved some of the papers into the middle, put a plate down in his own place and set the table for Mortensen, Line and Amalie.

'I'm not sure he was exactly like this,' Line said, casting aside Bernhard Clausen's obituary. 'The Party describes him as a monolith. But Guttorm Hellevik told me he changed his political outlook on a number of topics. Apparently, they no longer used him as a speaker on 1 May, Labour Day.'

Wisting reflected on how this contradicted what he had been told at the Party office earlier that day.

'No one wants to speak ill of the dead,' Mortensen commented, continuing to type on his laptop.

'Two of the fingerprints on the cardboard boxes have already been identified,' he said, without looking up from the screen.

Amalie picked up a fork and started banging it on the table. Line grabbed it out of her hand.

'Whose?' Wisting asked, moving back to the stove.

'Bernhard Clausen and Walter Krom. They've been identified from the reference samples. Clausen's seem to be on all the boxes, whereas Krom's are only on some of them. But they've also found some unidentified prints which they're running through the records.'

'When will we get the results of that?' Line asked.

'Tomorrow.'

'Do they say anything about the note with the phone number?' Wisting asked as he stirred the stew.

Mortensen shook his head. 'This looks like it's just the preliminary feedback,' he said. 'But if they'd found something, they would have said so.'

'There are four people named Daniel in Clausen's address and phone book,' Line told them. 'But none with a phone number matching the note.'

'He must have been allocated a new phone number,' Wisting reminded her.

'One of them is the number for Daniel Nyrup, the Danish politician,' Line said, laughing. 'Another one belongs to Daniel Rabe, *Aftenposten*'s political journalist.'

The stew began to bubble and Wisting set the pan down on the table. Line tied a bib on Amalie, ladled out a portion for her and used a fork to mash the chunks of meat.

'Do you think the phone company will have a list of the people previously allocated that number?' she asked.

'I've come across this before,' Mortensen said, pushing his laptop away. 'They don't have historical data so far back, but I'll check, to be on the safe side.'

The phone rang just as Wisting was about to help himself.

'Jonas Hildre from *Dagbladet* newspaper,' the caller introduced himself. 'What can you tell me about Bernhard Clausen?'

The question was sudden and unexpected. 'What are you referring to?' Wisting asked, returning the ladle to the pan.

'An investigation is under way,' the journalist said.

'There's been a fire at his summer cabin,' Wisting replied. 'Christine Thiis, the police prosecutor, is dealing with that,' he added. 'You can speak to her about it.'

'I'm just after some background information to start with,' the journalist insisted.

Wisting did not want his name in print but, if he gave the journalist the brush-off, it would place Christine Thiis in an awkward situation. She had no knowledge of his investigation and would not be able to provide any explanation for it.

'OK,' Wisting replied, anxious to end the conversation, 'but I don't want to be quoted or named.'

'That's fine with me,' the journalist replied. 'As I said, I'm just looking for some simple facts. For example, have you discovered the cause of the fire?'

'No,' Wisting answered.

'But arson is suspected?'

'We have to identify the cause first.'

'I have information suggesting there was an intruder in the cabin just before the fire started.'

Wisting regretted having accepted the call. The journalist was well informed. He must have received a tip-off from someone in the alarm company, which made the information difficult to deny.

'That's something we're looking into,' he said. 'The security company has reported that they received a number of different alarms and signals.'

He stood up and moved some distance from the table. 'We're expecting a report from them,' he added, in order to insinuate that the various alarms could have been a matter of technical failures.

'Do you regard Clausen's death as being linked to the fire?'

'What do you mean?' Wisting asked, in an attempt to fluster the journalist.

'Could there be a connection between his death and the fire?'

Strictly speaking, the answer was yes. In Wisting's eyes, the former had triggered the latter. 'And what might that connection be?' he asked.

'I don't know,' the journalist replied. 'But is that something you're looking into?'

Wisting had to weigh his words carefully to avoid saying something that might lead to headlines and attract media attention. 'We're talking here about a death from natural causes following a verified history of illness.'

'Could someone have broken in because it was known he was dead and the cabin was lying empty?'

'I don't want to enter into any kind of speculation.'

The journalist was obviously preparing to draw the conversation to a close. 'When will you know more about the cause of the fire?'

'The cabin is completely demolished,' Wisting told him. 'It's not certain that the investigations will lead to any definite answers.'

'But you will find out if there are traces of a flammable liquid?'

'That's a routine part of the investigations,' Wisting confirmed.

The journalist had not received the answers he wanted to hear but expressed thanks before ringing off.

'Jonas Hildre from *Dagbladet*,' he said, glancing at Line.

'Political journalist,' she told him. 'It was probably just an initial inquiry to sound out the situation. He won't give up, though.'

Wisting was about to store the number when he was interrupted by a text message. He had to put on his glasses to read it, and it took some time before he realized it was the security guard who had been called out to the fire at the cabin in response to the alarm. A link in the message led to a site where he could download the film from his dashboard camera.

'Can you access this?' he asked, holding up the phone to Mortensen.

Mortensen took the mobile and forwarded the message to himself before placing his laptop in the middle of the table so that everyone could see. Soon an image from the cab of the security van appeared. Wisting recognized it immediately. The security vehicle drove down the street past the Wassilioff Hotel in the centre of Stavern and turned to the left at the deep-water quay. The video quality was surprisingly good. A strapline at the foot of the picture showed that the time was 5.14, and faint music played from the car radio.

While Wisting chewed his food, he registered that the stew was almost tasteless. A ringing noise sounded from the screen. Wisting understood that this had to do with an alarm being triggered and listened as the address in question was given.

The RPM were ratcheted up as the vehicle moved out of the town centre. The streetlamps disappeared and the headlights lit up a dark country road with fields on either side. A sign cancelled the speed limit and they could hear from the engine noise that the vehicle's speed was stepped up considerably.

At the end of a straight stretch, the headlights from an oncoming vehicle appeared. They approached quickly and passed by. The front lights blinded the camera, making it impossible to see the number plate.

The journey continued. Yet another oncoming car came into sight. Here, too, it was impossible to make out the registration number, but the taxi sign on the vehicle's roof was clear.

The phone in the security van rang again. Mortensen turned up the volume. It was the alarm company's central switchboard warning that the fire alarm had also been set off at the address he was heading towards.

The guard reported that he would be on the scene in approximately four minutes.

The Hummerbakken turn-off was now close and they could discern the bright glow of the fire in the night sky.

Amalie twisted and turned in her seat, desperate to leave the table. Line lifted her out and set her down on the floor.

'Stop!' Wisting shouted. 'Wind it back.'

'I saw it,' Mortensen said as he pressed a key that made the recording jump back fifteen seconds.

As the guard slowed down to turn off from the main road, a pair of headlights lit up in a small layby at the side of the road. The guard's headlights swept over a grey van starting up.

Mortensen grabbed a pen and noted the exact time.

It was impossible to see the registration number or the person behind the wheel, but the images were good enough for someone with a knowledge of cars to identify the make and model of the vehicle.

The security van continued on to the narrower road and the image began to shake as the road surface deteriorated. Soon the flames appeared.

'It's burning most fiercely at the back,' Mortensen said, letting the recording run on. A few rubberneckers turned up, moving in and out of shot.

'OK,' Wisting said, putting down his spoon. 'Can you find out what kind of vehicle that was, parked up on the road? It seems odd for anyone to be hanging about there at that time of night.'

'I thought it looked like a Berlingo,' Mortensen said, rewinding the video. When the grey van appeared on the screen again, he paused the recording and saved a freeze frame.

'A Citroën Berlingo or a Peugeot Partner,' Mortensen said. 'I can find out for sure.'

Line began to clear the table. Wisting got to his feet, found a toothpick in the kitchen drawer and pressed it pensively between his front teeth.

12

The cabin ruins were still smoking when Wisting and Mortensen parked at the end of the track later that afternoon. Only the chimneystack was left. Bernhard Clausen's car had also sustained extensive damage. Only the garden furniture·down among the trees on the seaward side was unscathed.

A policeman stepped from a patrol car and walked towards them. As news of the fire had gradually spread, a lot of curious onlookers had come to gawp at it but, apart from that, he had nothing to report.

When Wisting and Mortensen ducked beneath the police tape, the acrid smell of smoke wafted towards them. The roof tiles and charred timbers were piled up, and here and there mattress feathers and scraps of metal were scattered about.

'The crime scene investigation will have to wait until tomorrow,' Mortensen said, moving around to the rear of the site of the fire.

Wisting followed him. Nothing was left of the room where the money had been stored. The side of one of the propane canisters deposited inside the cupboard was torn open and it had come to rest in a clump of raspberry bushes a few metres from where the cabin wall had stood. The other canister was nowhere to be seen.

'Where did he moor his boat?' Mortensen asked.

'Are you asking me if Bernhard Clausen had a boat?'

Wisting asked as he looked down towards the jetty, where a man in a green windcheater was loitering.

'I suppose so.'

'I really don't know,' Wisting replied. 'You're thinking of the petrol tank on the bunk bed?'

'And the two petrol cans under the bed, as well as spray cans and propane canisters in the cupboard,' Mortensen said, nodding. 'When the fire first took hold, it would have accelerated like a streak of lightning.'

Wisting glanced down at the jetty again. The man in the green jacket was on his way up towards them, but he stopped at the police cordon. 'That's him,' Wisting said.

'Who?'

'The Director General, Johan Olav Lyngh.'

The police officer on guard duty was making his way from the patrol car. Wisting signalled that he would take care of this.

They greeted each other with a silent handshake. Wisting lifted the police tape to let the Director General duck inside before introducing him to Mortensen.

'Have you made any inroads as yet?' Lyngh asked.

Wisting gave an account of the discoveries they had made in the boxes of cash and the results of their fingerprint investigations so far. 'Would you be aware if the Security Service or the Emergency Squad were in the picture here?' he queried. 'Or the national security authorities?'

'I've conferred with them,' Lyngh replied. 'None of the secret services has actively worked on Clausen. There's no information either to suggest that any officials or politicians of Clausen's stature have behaved in a disloyal manner or to benefit foreign powers.'

A gust of wind set off a wind chime hanging in one of the nearby trees and rattled the chains on a hammock.

'Arson?' Lyngh asked, taking a few steps towards the ruins.

'Yes,' Wisting confirmed, and he went on to explain about the alarm and the vehicle in the security footage.

The Director General stood lost in thought. 'There's one more thing I should have informed you of during our meeting yesterday,' he said, turning to face Wisting. 'It only struck me later that Clausen's name had cropped up once before.'

A nod of Wisting's head suggested that they should sit around the garden table on the paved barbecue area. The Director General pulled out a chair and sat down with his back to the evening sun.

'A great deal of post comes into my office,' he began. 'I'm not thinking just of mail relating to cases, but letters from people who've had bad experiences with the police or with the prosecution service. People who feel they've been unreasonably treated and approach me to complain or to seek support. Then there are cantankerous folk and conspiracy theorists. People who are delusional or have personality disorders and come out with fantastic solutions to criminal cases they've seen covered in the media. Many of these letters come from the secure wards of psychiatric hospitals.'

Wisting nodded. He, too, had received a number of crank letters from people keen to explain away serious crimes as conspiracies by secret alliances between leading figures in society.

'I read all of them,' the Director General continued.

'The ones that are signed receive replies, at least the first time they write to me. They're all filed and we have an efficient system for retrieving all previous inquiries.'

He thrust his hand into the inside pocket of his jacket and produced a brown envelope, folded in two. 'This is a copy,' he said, handing the envelope to Wisting. 'The original's in my car.'

Wisting took it, opened the envelope and withdrew a typewritten sheet of paper. It was a letter dated 11 June 2003, addressed to Director General Johan Olav Lyngh. No sender's name. The letter itself comprised only one line.

Check Health Minister Bernhard Clausen re: the Gjersjø case.

'The Gjersjø case?' Wisting asked.

'A twenty-two-year-old youth disappeared near Gjersjø lake in 2003,' Lyngh clarified. 'Simon Meier. He was reported missing on 31 May, when he hadn't turned up for work for two days in succession. He lived alone and went missing after going on a fishing trip.'

'Gjersjø lake?' Wisting repeated. 'That's in Oppegård, isn't it? Clausen's home district.'

The Director General nodded. 'His fishing gear was located on the eastern side of the lake. The young man himself was never found.' He held back for a moment before continuing: 'There was no substance to it,' he said, indicating the letter in Wisting's hand. 'But just the same, it's an anonymous tip-off. We have procedures for such things. The contents were relayed to the local police station.'

'What happened in the case?'

'It was recorded as a drowning accident, but there's also a possibility that something else occurred. A similar letter arrived six months later.'

He waved his hand to indicate that it was also in his car.

'It's obviously from the same sender and we immediately put it on file,' he went on. 'The content was the same, but a cutting from the local newspaper was also enclosed. The family were not satisfied with the police's efforts. They felt that the search had been called off too early and there were circumstances that meant they could never feel at ease about it. The fishing rod and rucksack were found on the path leading from the fishing spot, together with the day's catch, about twenty metres away from the water's edge.'

'Do you think there's anything in it?' Wisting asked, reading the line of text in the letter one more time.

'Well, these are at least circumstances you ought to know about,' Lyngh answered as he stood up. 'I tried to requisition the case files for you, but they're not in the archives.'

'No?'

'They've been sent out to the Cold Cases Group,' the Director General explained. 'They're evaluating them with a view to reopening the case.'

Wisting had previous experience of working with this new group at Kripos, a team tasked with investigating old, unsolved cases. 'Which investigator has responsibility for it?'

'Adrian Stiller,' the Director General replied.

'I know him,' Wisting said.

'Is he someone you might consider involving in the case?'

Wisting's gaze shifted towards the distant horizon. 'Not really, to be honest,' he said. 'Not if I'm to retain overall control. He's a bit of a maverick and not entirely to be trusted, if my experience is anything to go by. I'll try and find another way to access the files.'

The Director General was on his feet now. Wisting and

Mortensen accompanied him to his car, which was parked in an open space further along the track. Johan Olav Lyngh opened the boot and took out a small package wrapped in grey paper.

'Both the envelopes and the letters are in here,' he said. 'The material hasn't been tested for fingerprints or undergone any other technical examination but I'd really like to know who wrote those letters and why.'

13

The spot where the vehicle was caught by the security van's camera was a patch of gravel at the roadside occupied by mailboxes and rubbish bins for the use of cabin owners.

Wisting parked his car and got out with Mortensen. 'It's about fifty metres from here down to the cabin,' he said. 'Five or six minutes' walk. Faster, if you run.'

'The guard said it took him around four minutes to get here after he received the message about the fire alarm,' Mortensen recalled.

Wisting surveyed the scene, wondering if anything could have been dropped on the gravel. He saw a crumpled beer can, chewing-gum wrappers, cigarette ends and some discarded snuff sachets. Nothing that looked recent.

A car turned in and a woman in her fifties got out, carrying a bag of rubbish. She threw it into the garbage container before checking her mailbox. After dropping a bundle of advertising flyers into the recycling bin, she returned to her car and drove off.

On an impulse, Wisting walked across to the row of mailboxes and located the one marked *B. Clausen*. Lifting the lid, he peered inside. Two copies of the *Dagsavisen* and *Aftenposten* newspapers were stuffed inside, along with some flyers. No personal post.

When he closed the lid his eyes fell on the adjacent mailbox: *Arnfinn Wahlmann* was written in faded letters.

Cabin K622. Clausen's mailbox, meanwhile, was labelled with his correct postal address, *Hummerbakken 102.*

'What's Clausen's cabin number?' Wisting asked, wheeling round to face Mortensen.

'I've no idea,' he replied. 'That's the old numbering method. All the streets have now been given names instead.'

'Do you have your laptop with you?' Wisting asked.

'In my briefcase,' Mortensen answered.

'Can you find the pictures you took in the back room?'

They sat in the car as Mortensen located the photos from the previous day. 'What do you have in mind?' he queried.

'You were the one to mention it,' Wisting told him. 'You wondered whether Clausen had a boat.'

'Oh?'

'Find the pictures of the lower bunk,' Wisting said. 'The ones with the petrol tank.'

Mortensen browsed through the images, selecting a picture that showed the red petrol tank. *K698* was written on it in black permanent marker. 'It's marked with a cabin number,' Mortensen said.

'But is the cabin number Clausen's?'

'It must be possible to find that out,' Mortensen replied, logging into the police computer system, where he would have access to the property register.

Wisting got out of the car again and began to search among the mailboxes. Many had been there for years and were still marked with the old cabin numbers in addition to sticky labels noting which newspapers should be delivered. 'Here!' he yelled. 'It's Gunnar Bjerke's cabin.'

Mortensen was hunched over his laptop. 'That's two cabins further along the track,' he said.

Wisting looked down into the empty mailbox. 'It's possible he's there right now,' he said, returning to the car.

Settling inside again, he made a U-turn and drove back down the road to the cluster of cabins.

Mortensen still had his laptop on his knee. 'It should be that red cabin over there,' he said, pointing as they turned a corner.

Wisting drew up behind a Volvo parked outside the cabin. A man of Wisting's age rose from a chair on the verandah and put down a book.

'Gunnar Bjerke?' Wisting asked as he shut the car door.

'Jan Vidar, actually,' the man replied. 'Gunnar's my father – why do you ask?'

They strode up to him to explain that they were from the police. 'We're investigating last night's fire,' Wisting told him.

The man nodded. 'It woke me up,' he said. 'The police who were here earlier have already interviewed me. Have you discovered how it started?'

'We won't start the technical investigation until tomorrow morning,' Mortensen said.

'But you suspect it was started deliberately?' the man said, nodding in the direction of the patrol car beyond the police cordon.

'There are certainly circumstances we have to look at more closely,' Mortensen agreed.

'Are you missing a petrol tank, by any chance?' Wisting asked.

The man gazed at them in astonishment.

'For a boat,' Mortensen added.

'Well, yes, in a sense,' the man answered, returning to his seat. 'But it was a few years ago. I've replaced it since.'

'What happened when it went missing?'

The man shrugged his shoulders. 'It just vanished,' he said.

'From the boat?'

'No, I had it lying in there.' He pointed at a shed outside with a wooden bar for a door latch. 'Probably some teenagers at one of the cabins further along took it,' he went on. 'We were bothered by that kind of thing for a while. They took the gas canister for the barbecue as well, but we didn't get round to reporting it.'

Wisting gave Mortensen a meaningful look. 'What do you mean, you were bothered by it?' he asked.

'Some teenage boys stayed on at the cabins out here after their parents' holidays were over. There was a lot of partying, all week long, and they drove the boats around like lunatics. They took a petrol tank from the Jansens, too.'

Wisting pivoted round as Jan Vidar Bjerke pointed at a cabin on the opposite side of the track, where the shutters were in place on the windows and the garden furniture was packed away in plastic covers. 'Do you know for sure that it was teenagers?' he asked.

'No, but it was natural to draw that conclusion. After all, they needed fuel for their boats. The same thing happened to several other people.'

'When was this?'

Jan Vidar Bjerke took some time to think. 'The summer of two years ago,' he finally decided. 'Or the year before that. I doubt it has anything to do with the fire.'

Wisting let the subject drop. 'Did you know Bernhard Clausen?' he asked instead.

'We had a nodding acquaintance,' the man replied. 'But I didn't vote for him. Not my Party.'

'When did you see him last?'

'Before the weekend, I think. I gave him a wave from the verandah here when he drove past.'

'Did you notice whether he had any visitors lately?'

'Not really, but well-known politicians do come here from time to time.'

Wisting took hold of the bannister and began to descend the steps from the verandah. 'Thanks for your help,' he said.

'It wasn't much, I'm afraid,' the man replied with a smile.

Wisting returned to the car and reversed out.

'You think it was Clausen who took his petrol tank?' Mortensen said.

'Well, it ended up in his back room,' Wisting said, glancing in the rear-view mirror towards the cabin ruins. 'That room was set up as a fire trap.'

A branch scraped along the side of the car when he was forced to swerve to avoid an oncoming patrol car, probably the relief shift for the police officer on guard duty.

'The holes in the wall,' Wisting added. 'I don't think they were peepholes. I think they were drilled to ensure a flow of oxygen so that a fire would take maximum hold.'

'They would certainly have that effect,' Mortensen confirmed.

Wisting turned in and stopped at the mailboxes. 'That fire was all about clearing up after Bernhard Clausen,' he continued, glancing at Mortensen. 'Everything was made ready to obliterate what was found in the cabin. All it needed was a match.'

'In that case, it lifts the arson investigation on to a completely different level,' Mortensen said.

Wisting agreed. 'Take out your phone,' he said.

Mortensen did as he asked.

'Do you have a stopwatch on it?' Wisting queried.

'Yes, why?'

'I want to find out how long it takes to drive from here to the nearest toll station.'

Mortensen smiled as he opened his phone. It would not be the first time a criminal had been identified through the automatic tollbooths.

They drove the first ten minutes to Stavern in silence, following the main road further towards Larvik.

'Who would be behind it, then?' Mortensen asked. 'The Director General has consulted the secret services. They would have let him know if they were implicated, surely? Then we'd just have been told to pull out and drop the case.'

'Probably,' Wisting replied. 'If any of them were behind it.'

'Do we have other covert services?' Mortensen asked. 'Beyond the Director General's control?'

'Not in Norway,' Wisting answered.

'Oh, bloody hell,' Mortensen swore under his breath.

They were forced to lag behind a car with a horse trailer until Wisting moved out on to the motorway heading for Oslo. After a few minutes, they passed the automatic toll station on the district border between Larvik and Sande-fjord. A signal flashed green and Mortensen stopped the clock. Wisting drove on to the hard shoulder and switched on his warning lights.

'Twenty-four minutes and seventeen seconds,' Mortensen told him.

Wisting glanced in the mirror. Almost 25,000 vehicles passed this tollbooth every twenty-four hours. The drivers were not photographed, but all the car numbers were registered and a precise time given.

'Do you have the exact time the van started up?'

Mortensen took out his laptop and located the freeze frame of the grey van. 'Five twenty-four,' he read out. 'So it should have passed here around 5.48. There's not much traffic at that time of day.'

Wisting took out the notepad he had used on the night of the fire. 'Fast-forward the video to around six o'clock,' he said.

Mortensen did as requested. The cabin was completely ablaze and fire fighters were hosing it with water. 'What is it you're looking for?'

Wisting did not reply but instead stared at the screen until he watched himself enter the frame and stand in front of the security van, staring at the camera on the front windscreen.

'There!' he said when he saw himself raise his hand and look at his wristwatch before jotting something down on his notepad.

Mortensen stopped the film. The clock showed five minutes and eleven seconds past six. Wisting held up his notepad on which he had written *6.01.07.*

'The clock on the dashboard is nearly five minutes fast,' he concluded. 'We're looking for a van passing here around 5.44.'

Mortensen nodded as he closed the laptop lid. 'I should be able to get some answers by lunchtime tomorrow,' he said.

14

Amalie had fallen asleep with her dummy in her mouth. Line rose from the edge of the bed, crossed to the window and leaned her forehead against the glass. It was growing dark and the air from the opening at the bottom of the window was refreshingly cool.

She had not wanted to admit it earlier, but she regretted having left her job as a journalist with *VG*. It had been a choice between heart and head, and common sense had prevailed. She was a single mother and it was difficult to combine that with the hectic daily life of a journalist, but she missed her work. Bernhard Clausen and his hoard of cash had made her realize that.

Further up the street, her father's car swung round in front of his house. She pulled down the roller blind, returned to her daughter's bedside and coaxed the dummy from her mouth.

Amalie had slept in her own room since the start of summer and her cot had been replaced by a child's bed. All the same, during the night she usually found her way in to her mother, and Line had let her sleep there, even though it was a bad habit that might prove difficult to break, just as with the dummy.

Kissing her daughter on the cheek, she tiptoed out and put on some soft music before starting to tidy up the toys in the living room.

All of a sudden her father was standing in the kitchen

doorway. 'I did knock,' he said, sotto voce, pointing at the front door and glancing towards Amalie's room at the same time.

'She's asleep,' Line reassured him.

He had brought his notepad and iPad. 'Can we sit down?' he asked.

Line gestured to the settee. 'Is there some news?'

Without answering, her father sat down and located a picture on his iPad. Line took a seat beside him. 'This is from the back room,' he explained.

The image showed the bunk beds with the cardboard boxes full of money. Wisting used two fingers to enlarge part of the image. A petrol tank.

'This was stolen from one of the neighbouring cabins two years ago,' he said, showing her a picture of the cupboard's interior. The propane-gas canisters were at the bottom and a shelf was filled with various spray cans.

'There were petrol tanks under the bed, too,' her father went on, while he found a photo showing the holes that had been hidden by a poster on the wall.

'The window was nailed shut, but new air vents had been fitted,' Wisting added. 'Everything was arranged so that a fire would develop at breakneck speed.'

'So the fire wasn't just deliberate, it had been well prepared,' Line said slowly. 'Have you come any further in identifying the van spotted on the road?'

'Mortensen will have some answers from the toll company tomorrow,' her father replied, explaining how they had arrived at an approximate time for the van to pass through.

She realized from his demeanour that there was something else, but he was at a loss as to where to begin. 'Do you have any theories on what this whole case is about?' she asked.

'Everything points to the year following his wife's death and the time before his son was killed,' he answered. 'There is one incident from that period which is particularly interesting.'

Line was getting up from the settee to fetch something for them to drink but sat down again. 'What's that?' she asked.

'The robbery at Gardermoen airport in 2003,' Wisting continued. 'It remains unsolved and the money was never found.'

Line had a vague memory of a robbery at the airport. 'I was only nineteen then,' she said by way of excuse, and asked him to go on.

'It was a cash consignment that arrived by plane from Switzerland and was to be transported onwards to DNB bank and the Norwegian Mail headquarters in Oslo. The robbers got in through a gate in the fence, drove out on to the runway and attacked the plane as the money was being unloaded. The cash was in euros, dollars and pounds.'

She studied her father's face. The theft of the money was obviously something he had been thinking about since day one, but for some reason he had been unwilling to share it until now. 'Were there any suspects?' she asked.

'There was a circle of organized robbers at that time, with links to the motorbike fraternity, but no arrests were made.'

'The son,' Line said. 'Lennart Clausen.'

'That's a possibility,' her father said, nodding. 'But the amount doesn't fit. Clausen had more than 80 million kroner altogether; the proceeds from the robbery were no more than 70 million or so. But there's another case that might be of interest, from a timing point of view at least.'

Line tucked her legs up under herself on the settee.

'The Director General turned up while Mortensen and I were out at the site of the fire today,' he went on. 'In the summer of 2003 he received a letter mentioning Bernhard Clausen's name.'

He handed her the iPad with a picture of the letter. '*Check Health Minister Bernhard Clausen re: the Gjersjø case,*' she read out.

'Simon Meier disappeared while on a fishing trip at Gjersjø lake,' her father clarified. 'He was last seen on the afternoon of Thursday 29 May 2003. The robbery took place that same afternoon.'

He moved on to show her a similar letter and a newspaper cutting with a picture of Simon Meier and a summary of the fruitless search for him. Line took over the iPad and read the first few paragraphs. The disappearance had been investigated as suspicious.

'Was Clausen eliminated from the case?' she asked.

'The tip-off was sent on to the local police station,' Wisting told her. 'But I don't know whether they questioned him at all.'

'Is it possible to find out who sent the letters?'

'Mortensen is examining them for DNA and fingerprints, but it's doubtful if anything will come of that.'

'Could there be anything in it?'

'When the Director General received the letter it was regarded as one of the usual conspiracy letters, but now it really has to be looked at in a different light.'

Line read the letter one more time. 'This isn't from a

conspiracy theorist,' she said. 'I had heaps of them at *VG*: page after page, usually with a copy to the King, the Prime Minister and various Members of Parliament. This is quite different in tone.'

She gave him back the iPad. 'We must have the case files sent over,' she said. 'Both the airport robbery and the missing-person case.'

Her father nodded his head. 'There's a problem, though,' he said.

'What's that?'

'The missing-person case isn't in the archives – it's been sent to the Cold Cases Group at Kripos for evaluation.'

'The Cold Cases Group?'

'It's really just a routine re-examination, but it will spark off a lot of questions if we ask to borrow the files,' Wisting explained. 'The case we're working on is too confidential to let that happen.'

'So what do we do?'

'I thought *you* could do it,' her father replied. 'You could write about the old disappearance and contact the Cold Cases Group for access to information. You know the investigator with responsibility for the case.'

'Adrian Stiller?'

Her father confirmed this.

A year ago, Adrian Stiller had led some work in cooperation with *VG* regarding the reopening of an old kidnapping case. Line had made a podcast and a series of articles on the investigation about a young woman named Nadia Krogh who had been kidnapped on her way home from a party. It had taken Line a while to realize that Stiller had a hidden agenda whereby he used her work to provoke a confession from the suspect.

'The roles are reversed now,' her father pointed out. 'You're the one who can hold the cards close to your chest.'

Line relished the idea, as well as the journalistic opportunity. A forgotten disappearance, an unsolved crime mystery, these were the stories she loved to work on, and the connection to Bernhard Clausen meant there would be aspects of the story that had never previously been considered.

'I'll phone Stiller tomorrow,' she said. 'Then you'll have to get hold of the case files for the airport robbery.'

Wisting stood up, pointing questioningly at the room where Amalie was sleeping. Nodding, Line remained seated as her father padded in to his granddaughter, and her gaze rested on an oversized clock on the wall beside the TV. A thought began to take shape.

'She's fast asleep,' he said when he re-emerged.

'Have you adjusted the value of the currencies?' Line asked.

Her father did not understand.

'You said the clock on the security guard's dash camera was fast,' Line explained. 'That you had to adjust the time to arrive at the correct time for the toll station.'

'All the same, we need to give a lot of leeway either side,' Wisting told her. 'And we can't be certain that the van drove that route.'

'Talking of changing the parameters made me think of the stolen money,' Line said. 'Have you calculated the sum using the currency exchange rate from 2003? The Norwegian krone has weakened since that time.'

Her father stared at her as he sat down again before picking up his iPad.

'The dollar was down around six kroner,' he said before

long, glancing up from the iPad. 'The euro was at six as well.'

He produced his notepad and began to count. 'You're right,' he said, looking across at her. 'The currency-exchange adjustments amount to almost 10 million. It could well be the money from the robbery.'

15

The sky had clouded over during the night, and in the early hours of morning it began to rain. Wisting sat at the kitchen table reading Clausen's cabin guest book from 2000 to 2006.

Lengthy spells of those summers had been spent at the cabin and Wisting knew a great deal had happened during those years. Clausen had been appointed Health Minister, his wife and son had died, and he had taken a break from politics before returning two years later as Minister of Foreign Affairs. The guest list was extensive. Many of the people who had visited had been unknown names at that time but had later become central figures in Norwegian politics.

Two thousand and three was the first summer after Lisa Clausen's death. The messages in the guest book were fewer and of a different tone. One weekend at the beginning of June, a whole bunch of Party veterans had gathered to work on a voluntary project. A description was given of how the cabin was painted and the new seating area outside was built. After that, the visits grew in frequency again.

Hearing a car draw up outside, he moved to the window to see Mortensen. The rain's intensity had increased, and the gutters on the roof were gurgling loudly. Line was walking up from her house with an umbrella in her hand and broke into a run for the last few metres. Wisting went downstairs to let them in.

When they sat down at the kitchen table, Mortensen placed his laptop in front of him.

'Line and I came up with something yesterday,' Wisting said, setting down a cup of coffee for his colleague.

'What's that?'

Wisting sat down. 'It kept me awake,' he said, laying his iPad down on the table. 'I searched for an old case and found this.'

He played an archive recording from *Dagsrevyen*, the TV news programme, from 29 May 2003. The footage showed crime scene technicians working on the ground underneath the tail of a Swissair plane. The reporter recounted how the robbery had been effected with military precision and that the perpetrators had escaped with a substantial sum of money in foreign currency. All trace of them ended at a gate in the perimeter fence at the northern end of the runway.

'The amount of cash is in line with the dates on the banknotes and the exchange rate at that time,' Wisting explained. 'The case files will arrive by courier some time today.'

Mortensen leaned back in his chair and spent a few minutes mulling this over. 'The theories in this case spread out in every direction,' he said. 'This could well be a promising lead, but it's totally illogical. What would a Norwegian MP have to do with a currency heist?'

'It could fit with something Edel Holt told me,' Line said. 'During all the years she worked for Clausen, she noted just three occasions when something bothered him so much it impacted his day-to-day life. One was when his wife died and another was when his son was killed. She couldn't remember the specifics of the third, only that it occurred between the first two events. That would be around the same time as this robbery and Simon Meier's disappearance.'

Wisting drew his iPad towards him. 'The news report was broadcast that evening, the same day that Simon Meier was seen for the last time,' he said, explaining how he had thought of using Line to obtain information on the missing-person case.

'I've arranged to meet Adrian Stiller at his office at noon today,' Line said.

'What did he say?' Wisting asked.

'He seemed sceptical, but I think it's more a case of him believing there wasn't much to be done with the investigation. He didn't come across as very optimistic.'

A gust of wind hurled a deluge of rain at the window. Mortensen drank his coffee before carefully putting down his cup. 'They rang from the fingerprint section while I was on my way over,' he said, his gaze fixed on the list of new messages on his phone. 'They've identified two of the fingerprints on the boxes of cash, but it really just makes the case even more confusing.'

Wisting drew his chair closer to the table. 'Who are we talking about?' he asked.

'They're from the same person,' Mortensen replied. 'Someone called Finn Petter Jahrmann.'

The name meant nothing to Wisting.

'He has two convictions for sexual abuse of under-age boys,' Mortensen went on, turning his computer screen towards them. A photo from the records showed a skinny man in his mid-thirties.

'Not exactly the type of guy to commit a robbery,' Line commented.

Sliding the screen towards him, Wisting saw that his first conviction had been in 2005 and the second in 2013.

'He's behind bars in Skien,' Mortensen said.

'Where does he come from?' Line asked.

Mortensen pulled up the personal details from the records. 'Kolbotn,' he answered. 'The same place as Bernhard Clausen.'

'OK,' Wisting said. 'I'll go to the prison to speak to him.' He got to his feet, something he usually did to mark the end of the morning meeting at the police station.

16

Before she got in her car to drive to Oslo, Line had read everything she had found on Simon Meier in the archives. His story was quickly told. He was a quiet lad who mainly kept himself to himself. After high school he had started work in a hardware store and moved into a bedsit. He liked to go fishing. His father claimed in an interview that he had inherited that from him. A family photograph showed the thin, lanky boy holding a large northern pike in his hands.

The Cold Cases Group's remit was to go through old, unsolved cases to see if there was any potential for modern technology to open up new avenues of inquiry.

Adrian Stiller, with rolled-up shirtsleeves, greeted her with a broad smile. 'No tape recorder this time?' he commented.

When she had worked on the podcast about the Krogh kidnapping, she had recorded almost everything she had done. 'Not yet,' she said.

Since then, she had been in touch with Stiller only once, to try to persuade him to be interviewed about his work, but he had adamantly refused.

They took the lift up to the sixth floor, where Stiller escorted her along the corridor and into a small meeting room. A bulging pile of documents, enclosed in a pale-green case folder and held in place with an elastic band, lay in the centre of the table.

'The Gjersjø case,' he said, gesturing with his hand for her to take a seat.

Line pulled out a chair. 'Do you have any particular reason for re-examining this case?' she asked as she sat down.

'It's still unsolved,' Stiller responded with a smile, sitting down beside her. 'That's a good enough reason for us.'

'I was wondering if you'd received any new tip-offs or if any fresh information has come to light to make the case of interest to your team?'

Stiller hesitated slightly before answering that it was a matter of sheer routine. It was just long enough for Line to suspect he was holding something back. 'Any cases where a body isn't found will sooner or later end up being recalled by us,' he added. 'Now it's Simon Meier's turn.'

'What are you doing with it?'

'There are two stages,' Stiller explained. 'We run through the technical details to see if there's any material we can analyse using new, improved technology, then we go through the tactical aspects to see if we can pick up on any mistakes or omissions made by the police at the time.'

Line glanced down at the pile of documents. 'Have you found anything?'

'The most serious mistake was calling it the Gjersjø case.'

'Why is that?'

'Gjersjø lake is almost three square kilometres in size and more than sixty metres at its deepest point. It's full of perch, pike, crayfish and eels, but it's far from certain that the solution lies in there.'

Standing up, he crossed to a worktop and returned to the table with a coffee pot and cups. 'It's always the greatest weakness in unsolved cases,' he went on, 'tying yourself to one specific theory far too early in the investigation.'

Line regretted not having brought her recording equipment with her. Adrian Stiller's thoughts on the old missing-person case would have been well suited to a podcast. Instead, she took out her notepad and jotted them down. 'So you don't believe Simon Meier drowned?' she asked.

'It's not within an investigator's scope to believe anything,' Stiller answered, pouring coffee into the cups. 'But there's actually nothing in the investigation to suggest that.'

'He had gone fishing, though?' Line reminded him.

'Wrong,' Adrian Stiller said. 'He was on his way home *after* going fishing.'

He drew the case files towards him, removed the elastic band and took out a map. The local place name was Eistern, and a track led to an open space beside a disused pump station. From there a footpath ran through the forest to a headland. *Fishing spot* was written on the map. In addition, two photos were glued on, one of a bike locked on to a drainpipe at the old pump station and the other of fishing gear lying on the path. Arrows showed their location on the map.

'It's twenty metres from here to the lake,' Stiller said, pointing at the path to the fishing spot. 'He can't have just fallen in. Something else must have happened.'

The map was pinned to photographs that were glued to sheets of stiff cardboard, just like in an old family album. The first pages were close-ups of the police discoveries on the path. The three fish he had caught were held in a plastic bag. Gashes and holes indicated that birds or other animals had helped themselves to these. It looked as if the bag had originally been inside the rucksack, together with hooks and lures, but had been tugged out with some of the other contents. The fishing rod lay on the grass, almost parallel with the path.

'It seems as if he's put his belongings down carefully,' Line said, 'but the photos give the impression of something different.'

Stiller raised his cup to his mouth as Line pointed at the rucksack and the contents strewn about.

'It looks as if he's just laid them down, but animals have subsequently come along, dragged out the contents and scattered them all over the place.'

'You've got good eyes,' Stiller said over the rim of his cup.

Line leafed further through the files. The gravel patch in front of the disused pump house seemed larger on the map than in the photographs. 'What about any technical evidence?' she asked.

'A few items were gathered in,' Stiller told her. 'Cigarette ends, empty cans and used condoms. They tell you something about what the place was used for.'

'He might have seen something he shouldn't have,' Line said.

'If you're going to write about this, it's important to me that we agree on what I say officially and what is off the record,' Stiller said. 'Unofficially, it's a far likelier hypothesis that Simon Meier witnessed a clandestine affair rather than that he drowned.'

'Have DNA analyses been undertaken?' Line asked, lifting some of the documents from the bundle.

'Some things were analysed at a late stage in the 2003 investigation,' Stiller said. 'We're talking about three condoms, all from the same man. Pubic hair was also found on one of them that gave the profile of a partner. XY-chromosomes.'

Line gave him a look to let him know she did not understand what he meant.

'Both samples had male sex chromosomes,' Stiller explained. 'We're dealing with a homosexual couple.'

Line made a few notes but, as far as she was concerned, this was really of little interest. Simon Meier had probably witnessed something entirely different.

'Do you have DNA from Simon Meier?' she asked.

'The investigators were far-sighted enough to collect some,' Stiller told her. 'Obtained from an electric shaver at his home.'

The Kripos investigator got to his feet. 'What makes the case of interest to you?' he asked.

'Much the same as for you,' Line answered. 'It's unsolved. What's more, I don't believe he fell into the lake and drowned either. That means there's an answer somewhere. Someone must know something.'

'And what do you think happened?'

'Someone took him.'

'Do you have information from anyone apart from the police?' he asked, gazing in the direction of the bundle of files.

'At the moment all I have to go on are media reports from the time mentioning the people who gave statements.'

'So you haven't received a tip-off or found a source to set you on the trail of something?'

Line was uncertain how she should respond. 'My experience is that something always crops up once you start digging,' she replied. 'At the moment I'm just looking to see if it might be possible to make something more out of this case.'

Stiller walked towards the door. 'As I said on the phone, I can't hand over the case files, but you can sit here and go through them at your leisure,' he said, his hand on the doorknob. 'But if you end up writing about this, you must let me know if you turn up anything of significance for the investigation.'

He stood looking at her as if desperate to discover whether something had already cropped up. 'There's coffee in the pot,' he said, before he went out, leaving her on her own.

17

The prison walls were high, thick and imposing, and the rain had given the concrete a darker tinge of grey than usual.

Pressing the button at the gate, Wisting held up his police ID to the CCTV camera, but it took a while for anyone to answer. He explained that he needed to speak to a prisoner in connection with an ongoing case and was told to wait until someone arrived to collect him.

It crossed his mind that investigation was a fluid process. Fresh information bubbled to the surface all the time, and it was a matter of following the case wherever it led.

A prison officer appeared to escort him through the pneumatic doors and on into the main building, where he had to leave his mobile phone before he was allowed to proceed any further.

Finn Petter Jahrmann was waiting at a table in the visitors' room. He had adopted a straggly beard, but apart from that was identical to his photograph. 'What do you want?' he asked.

Wisting sat down and took some time to explain who he was. The eyes of the man on the opposite side of the table darted about, as if he had any number of assaults on his conscience in addition to the ones he was serving time for and was afraid that Wisting had come to tell him that his past had finally caught up with him.

'We don't know each other,' Wisting continued. 'I know why you're here, but that's not the reason for my visit.'

The man shifted in his seat, seemingly anxious to find a more comfortable position. Wisting had learned early in his career that the most important qualities in an investigator was the ability to communicate and to regard each person as an individual. Police work gave him no right to be judgemental. On the contrary – he had to attempt to be open-minded, even though his own opinions on various forms of criminality might be damning.

'I wondered whether you could tell me how you came to know Bernhard Clausen,' he said.

'The politician?'

'Yes.'

'He's dead, isn't he?' Jahrmann asked. 'I saw it on TV.'

'He had a heart attack,' Wisting said.

'But what has that got to do with me?'

'Nothing,' Wisting replied. 'Did you know him?'

'Not really.'

'What does that mean?'

'We're from the same place, but I didn't have anything to do with him. I just saw him at the shop a few times, nothing more than that. Everybody knows who he is.'

'What about his son? You're about the same age.'

'We were in the same year at school,' Jahrmann confirmed. 'He's dead too.'

'Did you know him?'

'Everybody knew Lennart, but we didn't hang out together.'

'Who did he hang out with?'

'Guys who had the same interests as him.'

'A gang?'

'Not exactly a gang, but they were into motorbikes and that sort of thing.'

'If I wanted to speak to the person who knew Lennart Clausen best, who should I talk to, then?' Wisting asked.

Jahrmann answered without hesitation. 'Rita Salvesen. She had a child with him, even though it was born after he was killed.'

Wisting nodded. Her name was already on his notepad. 'Did you have any contact with him or his father around that time?'

Jahrmann shook his head. 'Lennart and his pals spent their time in Oslo,' he explained. 'We didn't see much of them in Kolbotn.'

Wisting spent the next ten minutes persuading Jahrmann to talk about the circle around Lennart Clausen. Some names seemed more important than others. Tommy, Roger and Aksel.

'Was there someone called Daniel?' Wisting asked.

Jahrmann repeated the name but eventually shook his head. Wisting was about to lose all hope of learning anything from this conversation. An old colleague had said that investigation was a matter of finding the right key for a particular lock. He could not recollect who had said it but, as Wisting gained more experience, he tended to disagree. In reality there were several locks and several keys, and no single key was enough to open something that was completely deadlocked.

'Did you know Simon Meier?' he asked, trying a different angle.

'The fisherman?'

Wisting nodded, assuming this was a nickname in popular use.

'This conversation is getting a bit weird,' Jahrmann said. 'You're coming out with lots of questions about people who are dead.'

'Did you know him?'

'Just in the same way that I knew Lennart Clausen – we're from the same place, went to the same school.'

'Did Lennart and Simon know each other?'

'They almost certainly knew each other.'

'What about Bernhard and Simon?'

Jahrmann flung out his arms. 'I've answered all your questions,' he said. 'What's all this really about?'

Wisting pressed the intercom button and announced that they were finished. The simplest thing would be to ask Jahrmann directly how his fingerprints had come to be on the two cardboard boxes.

'It's to do with Bernhard Clausen,' he said as he stood up. 'Have you been out at his summer cabin?'

Finn Petter Jahrmann shook his head and began to laugh. 'What would I be doing there? I'd no idea he even had a cabin.'

Footsteps sounded outside in the corridor. The rattling of keys.

One key, one lock.

Something fell into place.

'You said you'd met Bernhard Clausen at the shop?' Wisting asked.

Jahrmann nodded as the door opened. The prison officer hovered in the doorway. 'Finished?' he asked.

'Almost,' Wisting said, turning to face Jahrmann again. 'Which shop?'

'Co-op Mega.'

'Because you shopped there, or because you worked there?'

'I worked there. Clausen sometimes shopped there.'

Wisting was unsure how to express himself. 'Can you

remember whether there was a particular time you met at the shop when he did something other than shopping?'

'Something other than shopping? What on earth would that be?'

'Sometimes people ask for empty cardboard boxes, for instance,' Wisting suggested.

'It's more than ten years since I worked there,' Jahrmann protested. 'I can't remember . . .' He broke off. 'His wife had died,' he suddenly recollected. 'He came in asking for some cardboard boxes. That's right. He probably wanted them to pack up her belongings.'

'And you were the one who gave them to him?'

'Yes.'

Wisting smiled as he turned to the prison officer again. 'Then we're through,' he said. The prison officer nodded and told Jahrmann to wait while he ushered Wisting out.

The keys rattled again, but it now struck Wisting that the perfect metaphor for an investigation was a jigsaw puzzle. It was just that sometimes you had too many pieces and some of them belonged to a different puzzle.

18

Ulf Lande had been the chief investigator. Line noted the name and also the police lawyer responsible before wading through the introductory papers. It had been Simon Meier's brother who had reported him missing after he had started searching on his own initiative and had found his bicycle and fishing gear at Gjersjø lake.

The report was dated 31 May 2003. Line used her mobile phone to snap a photo of it instead of making notes. This was mainly for her own use, but the layout on the form listing the height, weight, skin colour, hair length and other personal details of the missing man could also be used as a striking illustration for her article.

The search had concentrated on the lake, with divers, surface exploration and inspections all along the water's edge, but patrols had also scoured the forest. Eventually, the character of the case had changed from being a search to a criminal investigation.

Line was used to perusing old crime files. There was a special subfolder for everything relating to Simon Meier as a person: from this it emerged that he had been a loner who lacked friends and, reading between the lines, it suggested that he had been a victim of bullying. His family background was troubled, his parents' marriage volatile and his mother suffered from anxiety. Another folder contained the specifics of the crime scene and everything connected with the technical examinations, and there was yet another folder for all the interviews that were carried out. Everyone who had provided a statement was listed separately with reference to a document number, but Bernhard Clausen's name was not listed.

It seemed as if the interviews had been divided among three police officers and were based on what they called 'voluntary statements'. That is to say, people provided their accounts without interruption. The focus was on anything deemed conspicuous, such as a stranger or a vehicle that did not belong in the area. Near the end of the statements, the investigators interjected with specific questions to help build the bigger picture; one interview built on another. When one witness had noticed a man with a dog, a jogger or an unusual car, subsequent witnesses were asked if they had made the same observation.

Nowhere was Bernhard Clausen alluded to, but Line wondered whether it would have been a different matter if any of the witnesses had been asked if they had seen him.

The most significant item seemed to have been a black car, spotted as it drove down the track to the pump house, but the woman who had reported this could not say what kind of car it was and she was also unsure of the exact day and time. An all-points bulletin had been issued for the car driver but he had never been located.

At the bottom of the bundle she came across a separate folder with the handwritten title *Tip-offs*. Each tip-off was dated and numbered, but apart from that there did not seem to be any system involved.

Line worked methodically through them. Most had come in by phone in the first week and had been jotted down on separate forms. She recognized some of the names from the interviews.

At the very back of the tip-off folder, she also found printouts of class lists from the school where Simon Meier had been a pupil. These were dated ten years prior to his disappearance, and there was no accompanying note to say why the list was included in the investigation material. It could have been used to survey people of the same age who might know something. In addition to Simon's own class, other classes in the same year group and school leavers from the year before and year after were recorded. Line took a photo of them before moving on to the bundle of tip-offs.

Several reports were from people who had seen Simon before he went missing. Others related to cars and hikers that had been noticed. A jogger, and a man with a small dog, were mentioned by a number of people, and some thought they had spotted Meier alive and kicking in different places throughout the country. There were even a few conspiracy theories to do with drinking water, as well as a long, handwritten letter from a clairvoyant woman who insisted that Simon Meier was buried in gravel somewhere. The anonymous letter naming Bernhard Clausen was not included.

Line began to flip through the bundle of case files one more time, just to be absolutely certain she hadn't missed it. She stopped at a report about the letter from the clairvoyant. It had prompted a police search with sniffer dogs in three nearby gravel pits, demonstrating how little the investigators had had to go on. She took a picture of the letter and the report describing the search with the dogs. Clairvoyants were always popular with readers.

Both the jogger and the dog walker were identified and interviewed. The dog owner described where he had walked, but otherwise had nothing to contribute. Nevertheless, Line noted his name. This could be an alternative angle to any eventual article. Maybe the dog would even still be alive, she thought as she pictured in her mind's eye how that could provide a useful illustration of the passage of time.

Adrian Stiller returned after an hour. 'Are you any the wiser?' he inquired.

Line shook her head. 'Is everything here?' she queried.

'Everything we've received, anyway,' Stiller replied. 'Why do you ask? Are you missing something?'

'I'd just thought there might be more tip-offs at least.'

Stiller sat down. 'Sometimes that's a problem with old cases,' he said. 'Tip-offs are left lying here and there and not all of them are gathered up when the case files are packed away. Some tip-offs are checked out but not documented, while others are regarded as of no interest by whoever receives them and never get forwarded.'

'Sounds a bit like a newspaper office,' Line said with a sardonic smile.

'It applies particularly to cases like this, where there's a general perception that Simon accidentally drowned,' Stiller explained. 'But there's a better system in place now than there was in the past.'

'Have you spoken to Ulf Lande?' Line asked. 'The officer in charge of the investigation at that time?'

'Only on a formal level. We haven't discussed the actual case. That won't happen until after we've gone through the files here.'

'So he could have information that's not included in the files?'

'If so, it would probably be along the lines of the various hypotheses they worked from and the judgements they made,' Stiller told her. 'The kind of thing that's never written down in reports but can be read between the lines.'

Line restacked all the papers into a single bundle and drew the elastic band around it. 'What's required in order to solve the case, then?'

'A tip-off,' Stiller replied. 'The right tip-off.'

19

Adrian Stiller crossed to the window and looked down as Line Wisting got into a car and reversed out of the visitors' parking space.

She knew something, he thought. She had been after something, something she had searched through the old documents for but had been unable to find.

Returning to his office, he watched the recording from the camera in the meeting room. She had photographed some of the introductory reports and the documents relating to a letter from the clairvoyant woman, but it looked as if the folder of tip-offs was of most interest to her. She had thumbed through it several times, as if to be sure there was nothing she had overlooked.

He flicked through the tip-offs himself. It was always interesting to delve into old cases and ascertain what changes time had wrought. Just like in old houses where settlement damage and shifts had occurred that, with the passage of time, could cause cracks in what had previously appeared to be a solid construction. Especially when the foundations of an investigation were shaky, as in the Gjersjø case, where there was no certainty whether it had been an accident or a crime.

He picked up the phone and called the chief investigator. 'Any news?' Ulf Lande asked.

'I've only just started looking at the case,' Stiller said. 'But I'm not sure if I've received everything. I don't see a null-and-void folder.'

In major cases there were always administrative documents of no significance to the investigation, and these were usually collected into a separate folder.

'That could well be,' Ulf Lande admitted. 'Is it of interest to you, then?'

'I would at least like to know what's in it.'

'I'll check with the admin office and find out what we have,' Lande said.

Stiller thanked him and added, 'I've had a visit from a journalist who's taking an interest in the case. She'll probably be in touch with you, too.'

'Oh?'

Stiller glanced at the video footage still showing on the screen. 'Line Wisting,' he told him. 'I know her from another case. She's well organized. It could be a good idea to attract some media attention to this. That often leads to new tip-offs.'

Ulf Lande did not sound in complete agreement. Investigators generally reacted in two different ways when old, unsolved cases they had had responsibility for were taken up again. Some were genuinely grateful, whereas others regarded it as a reminder of their failure. Ulf Lande obviously belonged to the latter group. He would not be pleased if anyone else found a solution.

When their conversation ended, Adrian Stiller remained in his chair, watching the recording of Line.

Stiller turned up the sound on the recording and listened to himself say that the key to solving old cases was a crucial tip-off. Maybe Line was aware of such a tip-off?

The screen image went black as he turned this over in his mind. It bothered him that she might know something he did not.

20

When the guard handed back his phone Wisting noticed that he had two missed calls, both from the same number. When he moved beyond the prison walls, his mobile rang again. Wisting delayed answering until he was well ensconced inside his own car.

'Jonas Hildre, *Dagbladet*. We spoke yesterday.'

'Yes,' Wisting confirmed, regretting that he had neglected to store the number.

'Is there any news about Bernhard Clausen?' the journalist asked.

'No.'

'I've talked to someone who told me that the police were inside the cabin and brought out a number of items before the place burned down,' Hildre went on. 'What was that about?'

Wisting turned the ignition. 'It was to do with the deceased's estate,' he replied, though he realized that the journalist would not be fobbed off with that answer.

'In what way?' he asked. 'What was it you carried out?'

'It included some foodstuffs that had been left out,' Wisting responded as he started driving. 'They'd already begun to smell.'

He switched the phone over to the hands-free system. 'As I said, Christine Thiis has responsibility for that case,' he added. 'She's in charge of communication with the press.' Wisting had confidence in Christine Thiis's ability to handle the media and he was keen to get this persistent reporter off his back.

The journalist pressed on regardless: 'Have you had any contact with the Party leaders?'

The wipers slid across the film of grease and grime on the windscreen that was impairing his vision. 'Our contact person there is Walter Krom,' Wisting said.

'What sort of contact are we talking about?'

'A purely practical one. He was listed as next of kin.'

'So you didn't remove anything from the cabin that you subsequently handed over to him or anyone else in the Party?'

'No.'

'You're sure?'

'I was there myself,' Wisting said, aware that his tone had become brusque. 'Was there anything else?'

'Not on this occasion,' the journalist retorted before hanging up.

Wisting saved the number and drove to the police station to find out if the case documents from the airport robbery had arrived.

There was nothing waiting for him. He inquired about them at the counter, and of Karin Berg, the senior assistant in the admin office, but had to content himself that it was still too early.

Christine Thiis, her hair now cut short, was in her office. As he sat down, it crossed his mind that it suited her like that.

'Bernhard Clausen,' she said, picking up a case folder from her in-tray. 'I've read the fire reports, but I get the impression that not everything's included in here.'

'Mortensen is out at the site of the fire now with a couple of other technicians,' Wisting said.

Christine Thiis smiled. 'I was thinking more of what you were actually doing out there in the middle of the night,' she said. 'Nils Hammer told me you'd been put in charge of a covert, high-level project.'

Wisting nodded.

'Does it have anything to do with Bernhard Clausen's death?'

'Not directly,' Wisting answered.

Christine Thiis knew she should not question him any further. 'Just as well that I don't know anything, I suppose,' she said.

'There's one thing you ought to know,' Wisting said. 'The day before the fire, Mortensen and I were at his summer cabin and removed a number of cardboard boxes. Some of the neighbours obviously saw us and passed the information to a *Dagbladet* journalist.'

Christine Thiis leaned back in her chair.

'It concerns us handling some of the deceased's belongings,' Wisting continued. 'It's not part of your arson case and you should not provide answers, should the journalist ask.'

'I understand,' Christine replied, nodding. 'The fire appears to have been deliberate. Is it linked to the project you're working on?'

'There is reason to believe so,' Wisting said. 'We are investigating it in the usual way, in parallel with our project, and will keep you updated.'

Christine Thiis gave him a brief nod. 'I'm relying on you to handle those aspects. Just remember to keep me in the loop, won't you?' she said.

Wisting got to his feet. 'Of course. Thanks,' he said, leaving the door open behind him as he left.

En route to his own office he met Mortensen, who had a cardboard box under his arm. The acrid smell of smoke from the fire had permeated his clothes.

'Are you finished?'

Mortensen shook his head. 'No, the others are going to work for a few more hours, but this is probably the most interesting thing we're going to find.'

He held out the box to Wisting, who saw that it contained a sooty lock case. 'From the front door,' Mortensen told him. 'It's open.'

'Whoever was there had a key, then,' Wisting concluded.

'And the code for the alarm, but it had been changed after the Party Secretary was there on Sunday. Three attempts with the old code triggered the alarm.'

'Have you heard from the toll company yet?'

'I'll check my email now,' Mortensen said, heading to his own office. As Wisting followed he related his conversation with Jahrmann and how he had given Clausen some cardboard boxes while working in the local shop. 'That is a logical explanation, I guess,' Mortensen commented.

Wisting watched the computer screen over his colleague's shoulder and saw that the email from the toll company had arrived half an hour earlier. Mortensen opened the attachment. All transits were listed, together with registration numbers and precise timings, in an Excel file. He had to copy each car number plate into the vehicle records in order to identify the make of vehicle.

Wisting drew out a chair and sat down.

'There, I think we have it,' Mortensen said after the fourth attempt. 'A Peugeot Partner passed through at 5.43. He drove a bit faster than us, but that should fit.'

Wisting focused on the screen image from the vehicle

records. The van was registered to Aksel Skavhaug at an Oslo address. Thirty-seven years old.

Mortensen worked his way through several minutes in each direction, but this was the only transit that matched the vehicle type from the security van's dash camera.

'Check him out in the police records,' Wisting requested.

Mortensen copied and pasted Skavhaug's personal ID number into the computer system that searched through all the various police databases. 'Two convictions,' he read out from the screen. 'Both for narcotics. Nothing recent.'

He clicked on a link and called up a photograph, which was a few years old. Aksel had blond hair, a narrow face and sported a beard.

'See if he has any involvement in other cases,' Wisting said. 'Vandalism or arson.'

Mortensen scrolled though the criminal records to find all the other cases Skavhaug had been implicated in.

'Only a few traffic offences,' Mortensen told him.

'Wait!' Wisting yelled, pointing at the screen to a case from 2003.

Mortensen clicked on the link. The case was coded as a road traffic accident resulting in death. Aksel Skavhaug was listed as a witness.

The fatality was Lennart Clausen.

21

Wisting was stretched out on the floor beside Amalie, who was trying to assemble a jigsaw. It comprised ten pieces with various animals that had to be placed correctly in a farmyard. She seemed more preoccupied by the shape of the pieces rather than the pictures and was determined not to accept any help.

Line sat at the kitchen table with one of the cabin guest books.

'It looks as if they were childhood friends,' she said. 'There's even a photo of him here.'

Wisting's knees clicked as he got up to look, and Line slid the guest book across the table to him. She had reached the summer of 1988. Three photographs from a Polaroid camera were pasted in: one was of four adults around a table. Wisting recognized Bernhard Clausen. A second was of a fair-haired boy with a bare torso holding up a shore crab to the photographer, and the third was of three ten-year-old children sitting on a jetty, each with a crab line dangling in the water.

Lennart, Tone and Aksel was the caption under the photo.

Lennart was the boy who had been holding the crab between his fingers. From the remaining text, they could make out that the Skavhaug family had spent three days at the cabin.

'Tone must be Aksel's sister, then. There's a clear family resemblance,' Line suggested as she continued to browse.

'They lived in the same street in Kolbotn,' Wisting said.

'Grandpa!' Amalie shouted.

Another piece had fallen into place. Wisting sat down with her again and pushed a cow's head closer to its rightful position.

Now that the investigation into the fire at the cabin was completed, it was officially a case of arson. Before he left the police station, he had gathered up all the information they had unearthed and presented it to Christine Thiis. She had acknowledged that there was sufficient evidence to charge Skavhaug with arson. Normally, he would have asked his colleagues in Oslo to conduct the arrest and have him transported to Larvik, but the initial encounter between the police and a possible perpetrator was always crucial. How the first few words came out when Aksel Skavhaug was told of the charge against him could be absolutely vital for the subsequent outcome. They therefore agreed that an Oslo patrol would meet Mortensen and Wisting at Lambertseter and remain in the background during the actual arrest.

'He was there the following summer, too,' Line said.

She joined them on the floor and showed him another entry. Two boys lay close together on a bunk bed, each with a comic and a bowl of crisps. Aksel was glancing up in the photo. Beneath the picture, Lisa Clausen had written something about a rainy day.

'The back room,' Wisting commented. 'The money was piled up on that bed.'

'Could he have known about it?' Line asked. 'Was that why he set fire to it all?'

Wisting looked at the time. He would have to leave soon. 'That doesn't make sense,' he said.

Amalie put the cow's head in place and Wisting clapped his hands. There were only two jigsaw pieces left.

'This is in 1989,' Line said, leafing through the guest book. 'In 2003 they were twenty-five and twenty-six years old. They could have taken part in the robbery at the airport.'

'In that case, why has the money stayed in the cabin for so many years?' Wisting asked. 'Why set fire to it now? What had he to gain by that?'

Line sat down with them on the floor and tried to show Amalie where a pig would fit in, but she was firmly shoved aside. 'Did you examine the rest of the room, or the rest of the cabin, when you were there?' she asked.

'Not thoroughly. We brought out the money. Then the place burned down before we had time for much else.'

'Could there have been anything else in there?'

'What do you have in mind?'

'Whether there was anything in the cabin that Aksel Skavhaug might benefit from having disappear in the fire.'

Wisting mulled this over as he watched Amalie turn one of the last pieces this way and that to make it fit. 'There's nothing to suggest anything of that nature,' he said. 'Not yet, at least.'

A clicking noise came from the jigsaw puzzle as Amalie inserted the pig in the right place.

'Have you heard anything more from that *Dagbladet* journalist?' Line asked.

'He phoned this afternoon,' Wisting replied. 'I got the impression that there was more to it than the fire. He'd spoken to someone who saw us carrying the boxes out of the cabin.'

He could see from Line's expression that she took

exception to the idea of someone else digging into the case. 'What did you say to him?'

'I confirmed that we had turned up in connection with the deceased's estate, nothing else.'

Amalie found the place for the last piece of the puzzle and Wisting clapped his hands again. 'You're going to be a detective!' he said, tickling her.

'I don't know,' Line said with a sigh. 'She tried to take one of Maja's toys today when I picked her up from Sofie's.'

'A two-year-old doesn't know what ownership means, or that she has to ask permission to borrow something,' Wisting reassured her.

'In two weeks' time she'll start at nursery,' Line said. 'Maybe she'll learn something there.'

Wisting helped his grandchild put the jigsaw puzzle back in the box as Line prepared to leave.

'I'm going to have a chat with *VG* about making something out of Simon Meier's disappearance,' she said. 'He deserves that.'

'Is there anything to go on?'

'It's worth a try,' Line said. 'It would make a good story regardless. Besides, it gives me an excuse to conduct an alibi check. The airport robbery took place on the same day that Simon Meier went missing. A report would give me a reason to ask people where they were on that day.'

Wisting nodded in agreement.

Line held Amalie by the hand. 'Can you take her for a few hours tomorrow, while I'm away?' she asked.

'I don't know what's happening tomorrow,' Wisting answered. 'Something might turn up.'

'Just until early afternoon. Sofie's taking Maja for her three-year check up in the morning and I've already made an appointment with the chief investigator in the missing-person case. I want to trace the third biker who was present on the night Lennart died.'

'Tommy Pleym,' Wisting told her, nodding. 'OK, Amalie can stay here with me.'

22

The grey van was parked in the street outside the apartment block. Wisting drove past slowly for a second time and looked directly up at the apartment on the second floor. A woman stood smoking inside the glazed balcony. According to the information in the records, Aksel Skavhaug lived with a partner and two boys aged twelve and fourteen.

He found a parking space and stepped out, aware that rain was in the air. The Oslo police patrol stayed at their post at the nearest intersection. He raised his hand in greeting, and they responded with a brief flash of their headlights.

'Looks like a tradesman's van,' Mortensen said, nodding in the direction of the grey van.

Wisting cast a fleeting glance inside as they walked past. The driver's cabin was dirty and messy, filled with empty bottles and scraps of paper.

The woman on the balcony pinched her cigarette butt and tossed it down to the grass without paying any heed to them.

Wisting and Mortensen crossed the street. The name was listed beside a doorbell at the entrance, but they waited for a few moments to see if anyone might arrive to let them in, before Wisting shrugged and pressed the button.

Some time elapsed before a man answered and Wisting gave his name. 'I'm here to see Aksel Skavhaug,' he added.

The lock release buzzed and Mortensen pulled open the door. High in the stairwell they heard a door open and, when they reached the second floor, Aksel Skavhaug stood in the doorway waiting for them.

Wisting presented his police ID. 'We're from the police,' he said, noticing a worried expression cross the face of the man in front of them.

'I see,' he said.

Wisting pointed into the apartment. 'Could we do this inside?'

They walked into the living room, where his partner was seated on the settee. There was no sign of any children.

'The police,' Skavhaug clarified.

The woman picked up the remote control, switched off the TV and looked around with a touch of panic, as if something had to be hidden.

They remained on their feet while Wisting held out a copy of the charge sheet.

'It concerns the fire at Bernhard Clausen's summer cabin,' he said.

'What do you mean?' Aksel Skavhaug asked.

'We believe it was you who set fire to the cabin,' Wisting replied. 'You'll have to come with us.'

Skavhaug read the papers signed by the police lawyer. 'He asked me to do it,' he said.

Wisting looked at Mortensen. 'What do you mean?'

'Bernhard. He asked me to do it.'

'You know that Bernhard Clausen is dead?' Wisting asked.

'Yes, but this was a long time ago. Three years or so.'

Wisting pointed to a table, suggesting that they should sit down. He put his phone on the coffee table, turned on the recorder function and asked Skavhaug to repeat what he had just said.

'He phoned me,' he continued. 'He asked if I could come out to his cabin in Stavern. He had a job for me, he said. I thought it was something he wanted fixed and wasn't really keen to do it. It would take a lot of time to drive all the way out there, but he insisted he would pay for all that.'

Wisting produced his notepad, but remained seated, listening.

'I knew him from before,' Skavhaug added. 'His son and I were childhood pals. I was there a lot in the summertime when I was little, as well as at their house in Kolbotn.'

'So you went out to meet him?' Wisting asked, in an effort to move the conversation forward.

Skavhaug nodded. 'He wasn't well,' he went on. 'He'd just got out of hospital. Heart attack. That was probably why he'd started thinking about it.'

'About what?'

'That he didn't want any strangers raking around in his belongings after he died. That was why he asked me to do it.'

It began to dawn on Wisting what Aksel Skavhaug meant.

'He wanted me to burn it all down as soon as I heard he was dead,' Skavhaug said, getting to his feet. 'I've got documentation confirming it,' he added, crossing to a sideboard drawer. He rummaged for a while before placing a sheet of paper before Wisting.

The text was typewritten:

I, Bernhard Clausen, wish to confirm that it is my express instruction that, after my death, my cabin at Hummerbakken in Stavern is to be burned to the ground so that all

127

of my posthumous papers are destroyed. For this purpose I have engaged the services of Aksel Skavhaug, who must not be held criminally responsible for the setting of the fire.

Under the signature, a handwritten note was added: *The alarm code is 0105.*

'I was given a key as well,' Skavhaug went on to say. 'It's in my van.'

Wisting looked across at his partner. It looked as if she was familiar with all of this.

'Couldn't he just get rid of the papers himself?' Mortensen asked. 'Burn them in his fireplace or something like that?'

Aksel Skavhaug shook his head energetically, as if he had arrived at the same thought himself.

'He was working on a book,' he explained. 'His memoirs. His whole desk was littered with papers. He needed them for as long as he was working on it but, if he were to die suddenly, he didn't want anyone else looking at them.'

'So you went along with it, just like that?'

'The cabin was insured, so Lena would receive a large insurance settlement all the same.'

'His grandchild,' Wisting noted.

'Lennart's daughter,' the other man agreed. 'She's his sole heir. He told me the insurance money would be more than enough to build a new, modern summer cabin. In addition, she'll get the house in Kolbotn and the money in the bank.'

'But the house wasn't to be burned down?' Mortensen asked.

'No, it was the cabin where he kept all the papers he didn't want anyone to see.'

'What did you get for doing it?' Wisting probed.

'One hundred thousand in advance. He had the cash ready. If I didn't accept the job, he would get somebody else to do it.'

'Norwegian kroner?'

Aksel Skavhaug looked confused by the question, but nodded his head. 'In addition, there was another hundred thousand in a pre-arranged place that I could collect when the job was done.'

Wisting sat back in his chair. 'Tell me what you did, then,' he said.

'What do you mean?'

'When you went down to the cabin on Monday night,' Wisting elaborated. 'In as much detail as possible.'

Aksel Skavhaug stood up, approached his partner and picked up a pack of cigarettes from the table in front of her. 'They announced it on the news on Sunday,' he said, taking out a cigarette. 'That he was dead.'

He lit the cigarette before continuing: 'I drove down to Stavern on Monday night and let myself in, but the code I'd been given wasn't the right one.' He pointed at the sheet of paper with Bernhard Clausen's statement on it.

'Apart from that, everything was as agreed. There was a full can of petrol ready, and the rest of the money was where he had shown me. I just poured out the petrol and tossed on a match. When I was sure it had really caught fire, I ran back to my van.'

'Where was the rest of the money you received for the job?' Mortensen asked.

Skavhaug tapped some ash from his cigarette into a cup. 'In an envelope taped beneath a shelf in the cupboard,' he explained. 'He showed me it when I was there three years ago.'

'In the back room?' Wisting asked.

'Eh?'

'Was the envelope with the rest of the cash hidden in Lennart's old room?' Wisting pressed him. 'Was that where you lit the fire?'

'No, in the room next to that,' Skavhaug corrected him. 'That was the agreement. In the adjacent room.'

Wisting picked up his phone. He believed that Skavhaug had lit the fire on Bernhard Clausen's orders, but not because of his papers. It was the cash Clausen had been keen to get rid of.

'What happens now?' Skavhaug asked.

Wisting gazed at the man in front of him. He seemed naïve enough to believe that Clausen's letter would absolve him. Wisting did not want to be the one to tell him that he had conspired in an insurance fraud and arson was a crime in itself. Even the misuse of police and fire service resources could lead to a sentence of six months' imprisonment. They would charge him, but there was no longer any reason to take him into custody.

'Do you have a lawyer?' Wisting asked.

Aksel Skavhaug nodded.

'Speak to him or her, then,' Wisting suggested as he stopped the recording. He returned his phone to his pocket but remained seated. 'I understand you were with Lennart when he died,' he said. 'In the motorbike accident.'

Skavhaug inhaled loudly. 'It was fucking awful,' he said, pinching the cigarette and blowing out smoke.

'Who else was there?' Wisting asked.

'There was me, Lennart and Tommy. Tommy Pleym.'

'What were you doing out so late at night on the other side of town?'

Aksel Skavhaug looked at him as if he did not understand the question.

'Where were you coming from, and where were you going?' Wisting added.

'Nowhere in particular,' Skavhaug answered. 'We were just out riding.'

'Didn't you have work or college to go to?'

'I did a bit of work for my father, whenever he needed help.'

'What about the others?'

'I don't really remember. Lennart didn't do much after his mother died. He lived at home, but sort of on his own, really, since his father had the parliamentary apartment in Oslo. We spent a lot of time at his house and sometimes Lennart would borrow the apartment in Oslo.'

'Are you still in touch with Tommy?'

'Not really. He won some money on the lottery not long after that, almost 6 million kroner. Started investing in stocks and shares and suchlike and changed completely.'

Mortensen spoke up. 'Who else was in that gang of yours?' he asked.

'We weren't a gang,' Skavhaug protested, but he went on to rattle off a few names.

'Lennart had a girlfriend, didn't he?'

'Rita Salvesen,' Skavhaug confirmed. 'She gave birth to Lena after he died. It was just tragic, all of it.'

Wisting stood up. He wanted to use Line's ploy of steering the conversation round to the time of the airport robbery but without mentioning it directly. 'How old were you at that time?' he asked.

'Twenty-five.'

'Did you know the boy who went missing, the fisherman?'

'You're thinking of Simon?' Skavhaug asked.

Wisting nodded.

'We went to the same school, but we didn't hang out with him. He kept himself to himself.'

'Did you take part in the search for him?'

'There wasn't much to take part in,' Skavhaug replied. 'They used divers and boats but never found him. Why do you ask?'

Wisting put on a slightly apologetic smile. 'Sorry,' he said. 'My daughter's a journalist. She's going to write an article about the case. We talked about it earlier today. She was looking for some people of the same age who could tell her what it was like growing up in Kolbotn at that time.'

'Don't think I can help her, sorry.'

They moved towards the front door, where two boys were kicking off their outdoor shoes.

'We're finished here now,' Wisting said.

23

For the third day in succession, Wisting had gathered the small investigation group for a morning meeting around the kitchen table. Line sat with Amalie on her lap. The case was now taking a clear direction, as they were focusing their attention on the airport robbery. Various theories were tossed around, and Mortensen maintained that both Lennart Clausen and his father must have been involved.

'He was covering for his son,' he said.

'It's an incredible way of going about it,' Line pointed out.

'Do you think Clausen was directly involved?'

Line shook her head. 'But I think it's about something other than the money.'

'It's always about the money,' Mortensen said.

'About something *more* than the money, then,' Line revised her comment.

Mortensen turned to Wisting: 'We have to take a look at how the robbery was investigated,' he said. 'Officially, there were no suspects, but there must be a lot of information on file.'

Wisting's phone vibrated on the table. He held up the display to show Line that it was another call from the *Dagbladet* journalist.

'Take it!' Line encouraged him, putting Amalie down on the floor. 'Tell him that a man has confessed to setting fire to the cabin.'

Wisting switched the phone to loudspeaker.

'It's about Bernhard Clausen,' the journalist began.

'I expected as much,' Wisting said.

'Is there any news?'

'We've charged a man with arson,' Wisting replied. 'He's admitted it all, chapter and verse.'

They heard the clatter of Hildre's fingers on the keyboard at the other end of the line. 'Can you tell me anything about his age and where he comes from?'

'He's in his thirties and comes from the Østland area.'

'What was his motive?'

Wisting glanced at Mortensen, uncertain of how to respond. 'He expressed a personal motive,' he said.

'What does that imply?'

'I can't go into any details,' Wisting replied.

Line made a sign that he should wrap up the conversation as they heard the journalist shuffle some papers.

'You told me yesterday that you took some old scraps of food out of the cabin,' he said. 'But according to our source, a number of large cardboard boxes were carried out, so it can't just have been food.'

'As I said yesterday, it had to do with the deceased's estate. I can't be more specific than that.'

'So you won't say what was in the cardboard boxes?'

Wisting refrained from answering.

'It's rumoured that Bernhard Clausen was spending time at his cabin writing a book in which he criticizes his own Party's politics,' the journalist continued.

Wisting curled his free hand around his coffee cup on the table. 'I don't know anything about that,' he said.

'So you deny it was something of that nature that you carried out?'

'Yes.'

'What about his computer?'

'Nothing like that,' Wisting said.

Line signalled again that he should conclude the conversation.

'Just one more thing,' the journalist said. 'You had a meeting with Georg Himle and Walter Krom at the Party offices on Tuesday. What was that about?'

Line rolled her eyes as she picked up her own phone.

'Practical matters,' Wisting answered. 'Clausen has only one surviving heir,' he added, knowing that the strict rules about reporting on minors would come into play. 'A grandchild, but Clausen's son died before the child was born and the mother had no wish to be in contact with Clausen.'

'I see,' the journalist replied.

'I have another call waiting,' Wisting said as he saw Line's name flash up. 'If there's anything else, you'll have to ring me back later.'

'I'll do that,' Hildre said.

Wisting ended the call.

'He must have a source in politics,' Line said. 'Centrally placed inside the Labour Party. Someone who saw you there. You should have ended the call earlier.'

'Skavhaug also mentioned that Clausen was working on a book,' Mortensen said. 'I thought it was something Clausen had used to persuade him to set fire to the cabin, but maybe there was something in it after all.'

'In that case, I'd really like to read it,' Wisting commented.

His phone rang again. This time it was a number he did not have stored. Wisting hesitated, but after a moment he answered.

The caller introduced himself: 'Audun Thule, Romerike

police.' His voice was gruff but carried authority. 'I see you've asked to have one of my old cases sent over to you.'

This was a conversation Wisting had hoped to avoid. Audun Thule was head of the investigation into the airport robbery. He had addressed his request for the files directly to the admin office, hoping they would send them without involving anyone else.

'Good of you to call,' he said.

'I worked on that investigation for nearly two years,' Thule continued. 'I'm phoning to find out if there's any special reason you want to see the file.'

Wisting understood where he was coming from. He had cases himself that he'd invested a great deal of time and energy in, without reaching any kind of resolution. If someone from another police district suddenly asked to borrow the file, he would not have handed it over without asking why.

'I'm working on a case that involves a large cash consignment of foreign currency. So far, we haven't managed to trace where it comes from, and I want to look into the possibility that it might be the cash from the robbery.'

'How much money are we talking about?' Thule asked.

'A considerable sum,' Wisting replied. 'There were dollars, euros and pounds, all dated before 2004.'

'Where did you find it?'

'That's a bit complicated,' Wisting answered, his eyes roving around the table to Mortensen and Line. It was about time the investigation group expanded.

'Would it be possible for you to come down here and bring the case files with you?' he asked. 'I think what we've unearthed will interest you.'

'I've been waiting for an approach like that for years,' Thule said. 'I can be there in three hours.'

24

Line was no longer known to the security guards at the *VG* front desk and she had to key in her name and the person she wanted to see on a screen.

It had been six months since her last day at *VG*. It had not been commemorated in any way whatsoever. She had gone from being on maternity leave to being a former employee. In the course of her eighteen months of leave, the editorial office had been reorganized, colleagues had changed places, some had left and new faces had arrived. No one had suggested going for a beer or doing anything to mark her departure from the team.

Knut Sandersen was still head of the news desk. Line stood outside the security barrier, waiting for him to come down to collect her.

When she had started at *VG* seven years earlier, she had thought this was the beginning of her future. That she was here to stay. At that time she had only herself to think about, but now her life was different, and she tried yet again to convince herself that she had made the right choice. That she enjoyed being her own boss.

Sandersen greeted her with a hug.

'Thanks for agreeing to meet me,' Line said.

'You're welcome,' Sandersen told her, ushering her through the barriers and into the lift.

She had delivered a number of front-page stories and

been awarded the prestigious *Golden Pen* and *Scoop* prizes for her work.

Sandersen had checked his wristwatch twice by the time the lift reached their floor. Line appreciated that she would not have much time with him.

'I've started to look at an old missing-person case,' she said as she sat opposite him in his glass-walled office.

'What case is that?' the chief news editor asked.

He reclined into the soft padding on his chair, giving her the benefit of his steely gaze.

'One that no one remembers,' Line answered. 'Simon Meier. Disappeared at Gjersjø lake in 2003.'

'Have you got anything new on it?'

'Maybe.'

Sandersen canted his head, looking sceptical.

'The Cold Cases Group is going through the files,' she added.

'That's just routine,' Sandersen said, looking at his watch again. 'They look at all old, unsolved missing-person cases. What's special about this one?'

'It could involve errors made by the police,' Line told him, repeating what Adrian Stiller at Kripos had said, that the investigation should never have been called after the vast lake.

'Police error is nothing unique,' Sandersen broke in. 'As a rule, that's the reason these cases weren't solved in the first place.'

'There were also tip-offs that were never followed up,' Line went on. 'I don't have too much to go on as yet, but I'd like to put my work on a formal footing when I begin interviewing people, so that they know it's for a *VG* story.'

'You're a bit too late, I'm afraid,' Sandersen said,

straightening up. 'We've already commissioned a story about an old disappearance. We've put a lot of resources into it – podcasts, articles, videos, the whole caboodle. You know how it goes.'

'What case is it?'

'Much the same thing. A case that almost nobody paid any attention to when it took place and that everybody has forgotten today. We have a source who says she knows what happened and where the body is. We'll probably start publishing it next week.'

Line understood what that meant. Sandersen would not want to have competing projects running in parallel. She considered showing him the letter with the anonymous tip-off about Bernhard Clausen, but that would be a mistake.

'I'd be happy for you to come back again in six months' time,' Sandersen said. 'Or if you manage to come up with something definitive.'

Line stood up. It would have made things easier if she'd had an editor backing her, but she was not reliant on that. She was not reliant on *VG* at all.

'Thanks for taking the time to see me, anyway,' she said, and saw herself out.

25

Yesterday's rain was gone. The air had grown colder, but it was still pleasant enough to sit outside. Wisting had put Amalie on the settee on the terrace, well tucked in with plenty of cushions and holding the iPad. Her little face was deep in concentration, and now and again noises came from the game she was engrossed in.

Audun Thule had phoned an hour ago to say that he was on his way and asking for a meeting place. Wisting had given his own address and explained that he was not at work but at home on babysitting duties.

He leafed through to a blank page in his notepad and narrowed down the timeline to a few days at the end of May 2003. In the middle of the line he inserted a red dot and wrote *29.05.2003 14.40*. That was the date and time of the airport robbery. Further down on the right of the line he put a pencil mark and wrote *SM – circa 17.00*. That was the last time anyone had seen Simon Meier.

Mortensen sat with an electronic version of the same information. He had been sent Clausen's calendar of political meetings in 2003. It corresponded with the diary they had taken from Clausen's home office but was more comprehensive. On Thursday 29 May, Clausen had participated in a team meeting in the department at 9 a.m. before fulfilling an engagement at the Health Department's premises in Einar Gerhardsens plass at ten o'clock. At noon he had attended a briefing by the Norwegian Society of Paediatricians, and at one he had a short meeting with representatives of the executive board of the Norwegian Dental Association. At two thirty there was another meeting, this time with the Norwegian Biotechnology Advisory Board.

'He cancelled all his meetings the following day,' Mortensen pointed out, showing the screen with a picture of his agenda for Friday 30 May.

Some of the appointments had been entered with new dates, while a meeting with the chief of the Norwegian Institute of Public Health had been marked with a note saying that it had been conducted by telephone.

'Pretty remarkable,' Mortensen said.

Wisting continued to browse through the personal diary. The same appointments were entered. In addition, the annotation *cabin* had been added on Friday, Saturday and Sunday. 'Anything in the guest book?' he asked.

Mortensen looked it up. 'Not until the following weekend,' he replied. 'He had a lot of visitors then.'

Wisting checked to compare this with the diary. *Cabin. Work Party* was entered for the weekend of 7 and 8 June.

'The guest book is used mainly by visitors,' Mortensen added. 'Not as a diary.'

The doorbell chimed inside the house. Wisting got up and looked across at Amalie, who had fallen asleep with the iPad on her lap.

Audun Thule was a big man with a bushy moustache and a broad nose, dressed in jeans, a white T-shirt and sporting his police ID on a lanyard around his neck. He shifted a thick notebook to his left hand and gave Wisting a firm handshake.

'I've never visited a colleague at home before,' he commented.

Smiling, Wisting cast a glance at the car he had arrived in.

'The documents are in the boot,' Thule explained. 'Eight ring binders. We can pick them up later.'

They walked through the house and out to the terrace at the rear. Mortensen got to his feet and greeted the investigator from Romerike while Wisting fetched another coffee cup.

'Tell me about the money,' Thule said when they sat down.

Wisting looked at Amalie, still fast asleep.

'My granddaughter isn't the reason we're meeting here,' he said. 'I'm conducting a special investigation under the direct supervision of the Director General. No one at the station knows anything about it.'

Thule frowned. 'I've never heard of such a thing.'

'It's the first time for me, too,' Wisting admitted. 'I'd like you to join us in the investigation group.'

'I need to know what it's all about first,' Thule told him.

Wisting nodded. 'Everything we discuss today is confidential,' he said. 'You can wait to decide whether you want to take part but in either case you can't speak to anyone about what we're about to tell you.'

'Fine,' Thule answered, without taking time to think it over.

Wisting wondered where he should start. 'Let me show you the money,' he said, standing up. He checked that Amalie was still fast asleep before leaving the terrace.

Thule looked askance at him but pushed his chair out from the table and followed Wisting and Mortensen down to the basement. Wisting let them into the room downstairs and cancelled the alarm.

'You're storing the cash here?' Thule asked.

Mortensen pulled on a pair of latex gloves from a box on the table and picked up one of the cardboard boxes. Wisting held the box of gloves out to Thule. He drew on a pair while Mortensen opened the cardboard box and took out a wad of dollar notes.

'There are nine boxes altogether,' he said, handing the bundle to Thule.

'Five point three million dollars,' Wisting said, '2.8 million pounds and 3.1 million euros.'

'And you have all of that in your basement?' Thule exclaimed, shaking his head. 'Are you mad?'

'We've calculated that the total sum matches the robbery proceeds,' Wisting said. 'About 70 million kroner, according to the currency exchange rate at the time.'

Audun Thule was still shocked. 'That sounds about right,' he muttered. 'I have the exact sums in the case papers.'

He skirted around the table with the box on it and picked up another wad of dollars. 'Has anyone been arrested?' he asked.

'No.'

'Where did you find it?'

Wisting told him about Bernhard Clausen's summer cabin.

'His appointments diary gives Clausen an alibi for the time of the robbery,' Mortensen said.

'In any case, it seems highly unlikely that a serving government minister would have been involved in anything like that.'

'He had a son who died in a motorbike accident four months later,' Wisting added. 'We're investigating the son's circle of friends.'

Thule returned the money and pulled off the gloves. 'If

Clausen was implicated in the robbery in any way, I don't understand why the Director General would protect him with a covert investigation,' he commented.

'If this *is* the cash from the robbery, the whole case will be downgraded,' Wisting said. 'But we can't be sure. Clausen was a government minister, and there's enough money here to have impacted his political decisions and, because of that, to have significance for Norway's national interests.'

'But it doesn't look as if he's spent any of the cash,' Thule pointed out. 'He's just kept it all in storage. That doesn't make sense.'

Agreeing, Wisting related the story of Aksel Skavhaug, who had been paid in Norwegian kroner to set fire to the cabin.

'Have you found any technical evidence on the banknotes?' Thule asked.

Mortensen explained about the fingerprint examinations. 'We're waiting for results of the DNA tests, including a component, possibly part of a walkie-talkie radio, that was in one of the boxes,' he added.

'There was also a key in one box, as well as a scrap of paper with a phone number written on it,' Wisting went on. 'It could be for someone called Daniel. Does that mean anything to you?'

Thule shook his head. 'Not off the top of my head, but it's something to work on, at least. The case files contain almost five hundred names.'

26

The background check on Tommy Pleym showed that he was living with a partner and worked as the sales manager in a finance company a few blocks away from the *VG* building. Line took a seat at one of the café tables outside a bakery and phoned him.

'Can you spare a couple of minutes?' she asked, after introducing herself.

'That depends what it's about,' the man at the other end answered.

'I'm working on an article about the mystery surrounding Simon Meier's disappearance,' Line explained. 'Do you remember that?'

'Yes.'

'I'm looking to speak to someone of the same age as him who grew up in the same place. Just to have a few words about what kind of impression the disappearance made and what you think about it when you cast your mind back today.'

'Then I think you'd be better to speak to someone other than me. Someone who knew him better.'

'I'm sitting here with some old class lists,' Line pressed on. 'Do you think you could help me to pick someone out?'

Tommy Pleym gave this some thought. 'I'm not in touch with any of them these days,' he replied.

'I'm in the *VG* building right now,' Line went on. 'I called you because I see that the company you work for is located in Grensen. I can be there in five minutes and we could take a look at the class lists together.'

'I have a meeting in half an hour,' Tommy Pleym warned her.

Line rose to her feet and started walking. 'I won't need any longer than that,' she assured him.

'OK.'

She hung up and set off along the street. The office block where Tommy Pleym worked was accessed from a back yard and a receptionist let her in via an intercom. She took the three flights of stairs up to where Tommy Pleym was waiting for her at the reception desk. He was dressed in dark suit trousers and a white shirt with the sleeves rolled up.

'So good of you to find the time,' Line said.

'As I said, I don't know if I can be of any help,' Tommy Pleym told her as he led her into the nearest conference room. 'I remember him from school, but he wasn't really someone I hung around with and the accident happened years after we left school.'

Line sat down. 'You think it was an accident, then?'

'Well, that was what was said, at least.'

'Do you remember the day he disappeared?'

'What I recall was a helicopter flying low above the lake at Gjersjø, but that wasn't until a few days afterwards. You see, it took a while for them to realize he was missing before they began the search for him.'

'Did you live in Kolbotn at that time?'

'I had a bedsit,' Tommy Pleym replied. 'I was working in telephone sales.'

'So you were working on the day he vanished?'

'Probably. We usually worked afternoons and evenings, when people were likely to be at home.'

'What did you think when you heard he was missing?'

Tommy Pleym shrugged. 'I can certainly help you with those class lists, but I don't want to take part in any kind of interview about what happened that day.'

'Sorry,' Line said, taking out the printouts of the class lists. The list of Simon Meier's class was on top.

'I remember hardly any of them,' Tommy Pleym said apologetically. 'You see, I was a year older than him, and my friends were older, too.'

Line moved on to the next list, on which Lennart Clausen was second from the top. She had drawn a line through his name and reprinted the list to make it look as if this was how she had received it. 'There's one scored out,' she commented.

'Yes, Lennart,' Tommy Pleym said. 'He's dead.'

'How did he die?'

'A road accident.'

'You were in the same class?'

Tommy Pleym nodded but volunteered nothing more about what had happened. He picked up the class lists and leafed through them. Line thought she could detect some reluctance in his manner.

'I don't know,' he said, shaking his head. 'The only one I can think of is Ingeborg Skui.'

He put his finger on a name near the foot of one of the lists. 'She edited the school newspaper and was on the pupil council,' he went on. 'She was the kind of warm-hearted girl who went out of her way for everyone. If she can't tell you anything, then she might know who could help you.' He handed back the lists.

'Thanks, anyway,' she said, taking her time to sort the bundle of papers.

The conversation had not produced the answers she was after, but she was disinclined to finish up as yet. 'So two boys you were at school with are now dead?' she remarked.

'Lennart was Bernhard Clausen's son,' Tommy added. 'The politician.'

Line nodded, as if this information were new to her. 'Did Lennart and Simon know each other?'

Tommy Pleym glanced at his watch as he got to his feet. 'Well, they didn't live far from each other, at least,' he replied, advancing towards the door.

Line was groping for a way to prolong the conversation. 'Did you and Lennart keep in touch after school?' she asked as she stood up.

'We spent a bit of time together, yes,' he replied.

'What about the day Simon Meier went missing? Were you together then?'

'I don't really remember,' Tommy Pleym said, smiling. 'It was years ago.'

'My mistake,' Line said. 'I'd imagined a story like this would make a lasting impression on local people.'

Tommy Pleym held the door open for her. 'Then you'll have to talk to someone other than me. Sorry,' he said.

Line thanked him for his time. She couldn't help feeling that Tommy Pleym was keen to distance himself from Lennart Clausen and the past. Maybe the motorbike accident was a traumatic memory he preferred not to revisit, but it would have been natural to mention it during their conversation.

When she emerged into the street, she turned around and looked up at the third floor. She thought she could see a figure at one of the windows looking down at her.

27

A train passed outside Ulf Lande's office window. He had been allocated to a new workplace since Simon Meier had gone missing. The local police station had closed down and his new office was on the second floor of the imposing police headquarters in Ski.

'You're writing for *VG*?' he asked.

'I used to be employed there,' Line said. 'Now I work freelance.'

'There was another journalist looking into the Gjersjø case a few years back,' he recalled.

Line took out her notepad and digital recorder. 'When was that, then?' she asked.

'It was while I was at the local police station,' Lande answered. 'Maybe five or six years ago. She'd been in touch with Simon's brother, but I don't think anything came of it.'

'Kjell,' Line said.

Ulf Lande looked as if he had no idea what she meant.

'His brother's name is Kjell,' Line clarified. 'I'm meeting him later.'

'Yes, I remember now, he was our contact person in the family,' Lande said, nodding. 'But I haven't spoken to him in ages.'

Another train passed outside, in the opposite direction this time, and Line waited until the noise had subsided. 'Is it OK for me to record our conversation?' she queried.

Ulf Lande nodded and Line switched on the recorder.

Strictly speaking, it belonged to *VG*. This was equipment she had been given in connection with the podcast series she had done for them previously.

'What do you think happened to Simon?' she asked.

'An accident,' Lande replied. 'I think he's lying in the depths of the lake, buried in the mud at the bottom of Gjersjø.'

'His belongings were found a good distance from the water, though,' Line pointed out.

'That's easily explained,' Lande told her. 'He might have put down his things on the path to run back for something he'd left behind on the shore.'

'What might that have been?' Line probed. 'Nothing was found at the spot where he'd been fishing.'

Ulf Lande shrugged. 'Some fishing gear he might have put in his pocket, or maybe a fishing knife that he slipped back inside its sheath. I think that was why the accident occurred. He went back to look for something and fell in the water.'

'But didn't divers conduct a thorough search?'

'The conditions were hopeless for diving,' Lande explained. 'The bottom of the lake is covered with more than half a metre of clay and mud, and when the divers were moving about, it all swirled up and impaired their visibility.'

'But wouldn't he have floated to the surface eventually?'

'That was what we hoped would happen,' Lande said. 'But he may well have got snagged on something or swallowed up by the soft clay at the bottom. Most likely he lay there until the water turned him into clay as well.'

Line noted that she would have to speak to someone who had been down to the bottom of the lake. 'Who dived there looking for him, then?' she asked.

'The divers from the fire service,' Lande said. 'The local diving club made an attempt, too.'

Line thumbed through her notes. 'So that was your theory?' she summed up. 'A drowning accident?'

'"Hypothesis" is what we call it these days,' Lande said, casting a glance around the modern surroundings in which they were seated.

'Did you try out any other hypotheses?' Line asked.

'We kept all our options open, but nothing stood out, really. It's difficult to imagine a motive for any kind of crime.'

'What if he saw something he shouldn't have?' Line probed.

Ulf Lande smiled. 'You're thinking of the condoms?'

Actually she was not. All the same, she said: 'For example.'

'We found them when we did a fingertip search of the parking space and the area around it. What we were looking for was something that might indicate a crime scene, but we found nothing. No broken branches, no traces of blood. Nothing.'

'Were all the tip-offs you received followed up?'

'Yes,' Lande assured her. 'We even went up to a gravel pit because a clairvoyant woman had "seen" him there.'

'Did you get any tip-offs about specific people?'

'What do you have in mind?'

She had Bernhard Clausen in mind. 'Tip-offs from anyone naming a possible suspect,' she said.

Ulf Lande shook his head. 'As I told you, the most likely explanation is a drowning accident.'

'How many tip-offs did you get altogether?' Line asked, even though she knew the answer.

'Around fifty,' the investigator replied. 'Most of them were from people who thought they'd spotted him in Oslo after he disappeared.'

'Adrian Stiller at Kripos told me that it's easy for some tip-offs to slip through the net,' Line said. 'Especially in cases where you think you already know what's happened. Then information that points in a different direction can seem insignificant.'

She saw from his expression that he disliked her insinuation that the case had not been very well handled.

'Well, of course that's a problem for anyone in charge of an inquiry,' he said. 'Lots of messages end up at the police districts around Oslo and not all of them are forwarded on. But I choose to believe that I'd have been told if anything crucial had turned up.'

'What do you think about the Cold Cases Group re-examining the files?'

'We just have to be grateful for that,' Lande told her. 'We don't have the resources to do anything like that ourselves. But I can't really see what else can be done. I'm not entirely sure what you think you're going to achieve either.'

With a smile, Line reached out for the recorder and switched it off. In fact, she had thought she might find Simon Meier, but she did not say that aloud.

28

'The first message was received on the emergency phone line at 14.40,' Audun Thule explained, without having to refer to his notes. 'The robbers struck on the runway in front of the terminal building, just as the money was being unloaded from the aircraft and on to an armoured security vehicle. We had the first patrol car on the scene at 14.46, but they had difficulty locating the crime scene in the vast airport. It was the airport police who got there first, but by then the robbers had already made themselves scarce.'

Amalie listened to him wide-eyed as she chewed a slice of bread.

'Two robbers were actively involved,' Thule continued. 'Wearing dark overalls and balaclavas, and carrying machine pistols. They drove a black Grand Voyager and made their way on to the runway by cutting a padlock on one of the gates in the wire netting to the north of the airport.'

Wisting nodded. Everything Thule told him was familiar from the media coverage.

'Initially, we concentrated on establishing checkpoints on all the roads in the vicinity,' Thule went on. 'At 15.07 a message was received about a vehicle ablaze on the E16 east of Kløfta. A Grand Voyager, to be more precise. That gave grounds for believing that the thieves had fled eastwards, towards Sweden. The officers were sent in that direction and roadblocks were set up on the border. That turned out to be a diversionary manoeuvre. The right vehicle, the one actually used in the raid, wasn't found until a week later, burning in a disused welding workshop in Sand, a small village ten minutes south of the airport. The workshop was usually deserted, but we found a burnt-out Grand Voyager and a dirt bike in the ruins. The car had been stolen from Hauketo six months earlier and the plates taken from a similar vehicle in Bjerkebanen. The car used in the diversionary tactic had been stolen from the car park behind the old Østbanehallen railway depot in Oslo.'

Thule opened his notebook for the first time. 'We concentrated the investigation on trying to find an inside man,' he said. 'Someone employed at Gardermoen, in the security company or the airline, must have tipped the robbers the wink about routines and arrivals.'

'Did you find anyone?'

'No. The work was extensive and time-consuming and we ended up with a few candidates, but nothing concrete.'

'What information do you have?'

'The raid was well planned, prepared far in advance and implemented with military precision,' Thule said. 'There are only a handful of people among Norway's criminals who would be capable of carrying out such a plan. We used our informants in various camps, and one name emerged from that: Aleksander Kvamme.'

Wisting knew the name. For many years, Kvamme had been the kingpin in organized crime circles around the Østland area, with contacts in the Yugoslavian mafia, which was already so well established in Sweden. He had also been accused of an execution-style killing but was never convicted.

'We ran some sham attacks on him,' Thule went on. 'Including getting him charged in a narcotics case so that we could see what he was up to, but all that came out of it was an alibi. At the time of the robbery, he was sitting in a tattoo parlour having an eagle etched on his upper arm.'

'Watertight?'

'If we're to believe the tattooist and his next customer. We also found a receipt with the time and date. Cases like that usually start to crack once the money starts circulating, but that never happened. Our theory was that the money was either taken straight out of the country or that it was frozen.'

'Frozen?'

'Hidden in a secure place in the expectation that the police would scale down the investigation,' Thule clarified.

'What do you think now you know the cash may have been found in Bernhard Clausen's possession?' Wisting asked.

'I've no idea what to think,' Thule answered. 'I'll have to go through the whole case again with that as the starting point, but I really can't imagine Clausen having any connection to the airport robbery.'

Wisting filled him in on Clausen's son and what he knew about the circles in which he mixed.

'Sounds like a totally different level from someone capable of carrying out a stunt like this, though.'

'There's one further point,' Wisting continued.

Thule sat up straight, his interest piqued.

'On the same day as the raid at the airport a twenty-two-year-old lad from Kolbotn went missing,' Wisting said. 'Simon Meier. An incident the media called the Gjersjø case.'

'Means nothing to me,' Thule said.

Wisting picked up the iPad from the settee, where Amalie had now fallen asleep again and opened the folder of pictures.

'A week or so after the boy disappeared, the Director General received an anonymous tip-off.'

He showed Thule the letter with the short message: *Check Health Minister Bernhard Clausen re: the Gjersjø case.*

'So there's a possible tie-up here,' Wisting said, using his finger to draw lines of connection in the air, 'linking the raid, the disappearance and Bernhard Clausen.'

Amalie woke and reached out for the iPad. Wisting let her have it and once again propped her up among the cushions on the settee. Audun Thule headed out to his car and Mortensen helped him to carry in the cardboard boxes filled with the airport robbery case files. In the meantime, Wisting made a phone call to the Director General.

'Any news?' Lyngh asked.

'We have a suspicion about where the money came from,' Wisting answered. 'The raid at Gardermoen airport in 2003.'

There was silence at the other end.

'The time frame and the amount of cash match up,' Wisting continued.

'That's certainly one hypothesis,' the Director General replied. 'But surely it doesn't make any sense for Clausen to be connected to it?'

'The robbery took place on the same day that Simon Meier went missing,' Wisting added.

'Do you see a connection, then?'

'Not yet, but I need you to pull a few strings for me.'

'OK, how?'

'I'd like you to talk to the Police Chief in Romerike and have Audun Thule released from his duties and allocated to me.'

29

Branches scraped across the roof and sides of the car as Line turned on to the overgrown gravel track. She had had difficulty finding it, but this had to be the same track along which Simon Meier had cycled with his fishing gear in 2003.

She drove slowly. After a hundred metres or so, the old pump house appeared. Cracks in the masonry and walls were covered in moss. Stinging nettles grew tall along the foundations and several of the tiny panes of glass in the single window were smashed. The drainpipe to which Simon Meier had locked his bike was missing.

Driving around the pump house, Line parked and took out her camera. She lingered for a while, soaking up her surroundings. The forest had grown in recent years, reducing the size of the area, and from where she stood she could not catch as much as a glimpse of Gjersjø lake.

She located the footpath leading down to the fishing spot. It still seemed well trodden, with smooth pine roots lying on top of the hard-packed earth. Either animals frequented it or people still came down here to fish. Maybe even both.

Very soon the terrain opened out into a promontory beside the water and a gentle breeze ruffled the surface of the lake.

The edge of the mountain sloping down to the water was ragged, and the waves splashed in, making the mountainside wet and slick. She could see that there was a real chance of losing your footing and hitting your head on the rocks then ending up unconscious in the water. The offshore wind, as now, could also force a body out into deeper water, where it could become submerged.

Traces of fish blood had been found in several places on the promontory, but nothing to support the theory that Simon Meier might have fallen and knocked himself out. No hairs or human blood. However, such traces might have been difficult to find after two days.

A duck, its wings flapping rapidly, took off from the rushes on her left and flew low across the lake. Behind her, she thought she heard a car.

Again retracing her steps for some distance along the path, she raised her camera as the sunlight fell obliquely through the foliage above her head. She directed the lens at the headland where Simon Meier had once stood, focusing on one of the twisted roots on the path and adjusting the depth of field before she took a few sample photographs. The scene would add drama to any articles she might publish.

She took some more photos before walking back to the pump house. A car door slammed and a man with a fishing rod emerged from the other side of the building.

Line exchanged a smile and a nod with the driver, a man of East European appearance, and took a chance. 'Are you going fishing?' she asked. Answering in broken Norwegian, the man told her he was going to catch something for dinner, before vanishing into the trees along the path.

Line skirted around the pump house, where the man had parked in the shade. She had intended to replicate the photo the police had taken of the bicycle in the case folder, but the man's car was in the way.

However, it was the door and pump-house entrance that provided the most evocative shot. The obvious decay suggested that something sinister could easily have happened there. She worked a little on the light until she felt satisfied with the picture and then approached the door. Brown streaks of rust ran down the panels.

Although the door was locked, it showed signs of an attempted break-in and the doorframe was now reinforced with steel casing. The window was too high on the wall for her to see inside, but an old pallet was propped against it, acting as a ladder. She climbed on it and peered through one of the small panes where the glass was missing. The floor inside was a metre below ground level and in the centre of the room stood an enormous generator, with pipes snaking out in all directions. There were a few cabinets on the wall, an ancient control panel and an open door leading into another room. Through that doorway she could just make out the outlines of a hatch in the floor.

She stood for a while before jumping down, finding her phone and calling Ulf Lande's number. 'Sorry to bother you,' she said, 'but I'm taking a look at the old pump station and just had to ask: did you examine the old pump house when you were searching for Simon?'

'Of course,' the chief investigator answered. 'The search party broke in there.'

Line cast a glance at the door. 'What about the hatch in the floor?' she asked.

'I was in there myself and looked down into it,' Lande replied.

Line thanked him and apologized once again for disturbing him. When she rang off, she felt embarrassed. Of course the police would have investigated that possibility.

It was almost 1 p.m. now. She wondered whether she should phone her father to remind him that Amalie would need some food but shook off the idea. Instead she settled behind the wheel and keyed Kjell Meier's address into her GPS.

The car bumped along the narrow track as she followed the directions to Langhus, finishing up at the end of a row of grey-painted terraced houses.

Simon Meier's brother welcomed her and showed her through to the kitchen, where an open ring binder lay on the table, filled with newspaper cuttings and other information from the missing-person case.

'Thanks for agreeing to meet me,' Line said. 'Especially at such short notice.'

'No trouble,' he said.

He was different from how she had imagined. Kjell Meier was short and plump, whereas Simon had been tall and skinny.

'I spoke to Adrian Stiller yesterday,' she said.

'Was he able to tell you anything?' Kjell Meier asked. 'Was there any news?'

'I think it was still too early,' Line answered. 'I paid a visit to Ulf Lande today and he told me there had been another journalist looking at the case a few years ago.'

'Yes, she was certainly persistent and enthusiastic,' Kjell Meier told her. 'Her research went on for a long time and she uncovered some mistakes that the police had made, but nothing was ever published.'

'Why not?'

'The newspaper she worked for went bust. I don't think she got paid either, even though she spent hours on the story. She went through everything and made fresh inquiries. Things that the police should really have done.'

'Do you remember the journalist's name?'

'Henriette something or other,' Kjell Meier said, starting to browse through the ring binders on the table. 'I can find out for you.'

'I thought it might be worth speaking to her,' Line said.

He found what he was looking for in the first few pages. 'Henriette Koppang,' he said, sliding the open page towards Line. 'She was very well informed. Do you know her?' he asked.

Line shook her head as she scribbled down the phone number. She vaguely recognized the name and wondered if she had worked for the online newspaper *Nettavisen*, but she knew nothing more about her.

'I work freelance these days and don't have a connection to any particular publication,' Line went on. 'I can't guarantee I'll get anything into print, but since the Cold Cases Group at Kripos is now examining the case, it should be of interest to a number of media outlets.'

Kjell Meier nodded.

'Can I take a look at this?' Line asked, turning the pages of the ring binder.

'Be my guest.'

The ring binder appeared to contain all the press coverage of the case. There were a couple of minor write-ups in *Dagbladet* and *Aftenposten*: otherwise, it seemed to be the local newspapers that had followed up the disappearance. In addition to the cuttings, there were copies of correspondence between the victim's counsel and a police lawyer, complaining that the investigation had been closed down too early. She also found a number of legal documents that declared Simon Meier as officially dead, three years after his disappearance.

'You had engaged a victim's counsel,' Line commented as she made a note of the name.

'We had to pay him out of our own pocket,' Kjell Meier told her.

Line continued browsing. The ring binder fell open at a photograph of Simon.

'I have to admit I no longer give him much thought,' his brother said. 'Days and weeks can pass between the times I think of him, but I'd really like to know what happened and where he ended up.'

'What do you believe yourself?' Line asked.

'I've considered every possibility, but I don't think he's in the lake. I think someone abducted him.'

'Why would anyone do that?'

'The most worrying explanation is that some perverted sadist took him, kept him prisoner and abused him. It's not particularly rational, but things like that do happen, at least in other countries, and usually to girls. That fear has kept me awake at night. A simpler explanation would be that there was an accident. A car reversed into him or something and the person responsible carted him off and dumped him somewhere.'

Line took notes. Both scenarios were just as likely as the police's drowning theory. 'Have you received any tip-offs from people who might not have approached the police?' she asked.

'There was a clairvoyant woman who got in touch, but we passed that on to the police. She insisted that Simon was buried under stones and gravel. They checked out the stone-crushing plant at Vinterbro, but stones and gravel aren't exactly a specific description.'

'What do you remember from the day he went missing?' Line asked.

'It was a Thursday,' Kjell Meier said, 'and the last person to see him saw him on his bike with a fishing rod. I didn't speak to him that day, but on Saturday his work phoned me and asked about him. So I went to his house, saw that his bike was gone and assumed he had gone fishing. I went to the pump house at Eistern, where he usually went to fish, and found his bike and fishing rod on the path. That's when I realized that something was wrong.'

Line wanted to go back to the Thursday, the day of the robbery. 'Do you remember what you were doing that day?'

Kjell Meier shook his head. 'I just remember the Saturday,' he told her.

Line made notes as he told her about his anxiety and confusion that day. About when the police arrived, the divers that were sent out and the Red Cross that formed a search party.

She stayed for another hour, asking about Simon's friends and his social circle, steering the conversation round to his old school pals to try to engineer an opportunity to talk about Lennart Clausen, but his name did not crop up.

Line prepared to leave. 'Did you know Bernhard Clausen, by any chance?' she asked as she stood up. ' Isn't he from round here?'

Kjell Meier nodded. 'I heard he died at the weekend,' he replied. 'Why do you ask?'

'I wrote an article about him,' Line said, hoping this sounded credible. 'He had a son about Simon's age who was killed in a motorbike accident.'

'Lennart,' Kjell Meier confirmed. 'We grew up in the same street.'

'Were he and Simon friends?'

'When they were younger. Simon spent some time at his house and they played together.'

Kjell Meier got to his feet and accompanied her to the door. Line thanked him for his time before leaving. She couldn't help feeling as if she had missed something, but couldn't put her finger on what it was.

30

Just before twelve o'clock, *Dagbladet* had released the news that a man had been charged with setting fire to Bernhard Clausen's summer cabin. Wisting was pleased to see that his name was not mentioned in the article. Christine Thiis would be the one to field phone messages from the rest of the press.

When it clouded over, the three investigators moved inside from the terrace, into the kitchen. Wisting read through the documents from the airport robbery. It was often easy to spot holes and deficiencies when looking back at old cases, but so far he could not identify any errors in the investigation.

Thule sat down beside him and leafed through the photos from Bernhard Clausen's cabin. 'There's something almost artistic about it,' he said, peering at the picture of the array of boxes on the bunk beds in the back room.

'How do you mean?'

'That the money's just been sitting there, year after year, without him touching any of it,' Thule explained. 'It's a bit like an eccentric collector who buys stolen art and hangs it on his walls without showing it to anyone.'

Mortensen thought aloud: 'If the son was involved in the raid, Clausen may have found the cash after he died and quite simply had no idea what to do with it. It would have created a humiliating scandal if it had come out.'

'But he could have just got rid of it, then,' Thule said.

'Burned the notes in the fireplace or buried them somewhere. Just keeping them here involved taking a risk that they might be discovered some day.'

They heard the front door open and Amalie glanced up from her drawing book.

'Mummy's back,' Wisting told her.

His grandchild leapt up and ran to meet her mother. Mortensen received a phone call and moved into the living room to take it. Line introduced herself to Audun Thule before admiring the drawing her daughter had made.

'Any news?' Wisting asked.

'Not really,' she replied, going on to recount the day. 'I bought a map in the bookshop,' she added, and spread it out on the kitchen table.

She had already marked the fishing spot and the house where Bernhard Clausen lived but, before she had time to update the others, Mortensen returned from the living room. 'DNA results,' he said. 'They've found a profile for sample B-2.'

'The radio plug,' Wisting specified.

'The key and the scrap of paper produced nothing new, but they found a profile on the plug that called up a result in the DNA register.'

'Who?'

'Oscar Tvedt,' Mortensen answered, sitting down at his laptop.

Audun Thule swore. 'The Captain,' he said, grabbing one of his ring binders.

'Who's that?' Wisting asked.

'Ex-Special Forces,' Thule said. 'He was an associate of Aleksander Kvamme right up until the Alna showdown.'

'Never heard of it,' Wisting commented.

'It was an isolated incident handled by the Oslo police, but we received copies of everything that went on with the hard-core bunch of criminals at that time.'

He browsed through the ring binder until he found what he was looking for. 'We didn't make a connection at the time, but this could be a real breakthrough. His DNA on a component from the walkie-talkie used in the robbery means he may well have been one of the raiders.'

'What happened at Alna?' Line asked.

'The emergency services received a phone call about a severely injured man in the car park where the Radisson Hotel now stands. Paramedics found Oscar Tvedt severely beaten up. It was categorized as an internal confrontation and no one was ever brought to book for it.'

'What did Oscar Tvedt have to say about it?' Wisting queried.

'Nothing,' Thule replied. 'He was unconscious for weeks and woke with serious brain damage. He was left paralysed and lost the ability to speak.'

'Where is he now?'

'When this report was written, he was in a rehabilitation facility at Ullevål Hospital.'

'Could he have recovered from his injuries since then?' Mortensen asked.

Audun Thule began to pack up his belongings. 'I'll follow it up,' he said. 'I have to clear up one or two things back at the office, but I'll be back tomorrow.'

Mortensen also prepared to leave. Wisting accompanied them both to the door. It was colder outside now, and the air had taken on a touch of autumn.

31

'*VG* turned down the story,' Line said, going on to tell her father about the meeting with the head of the news desk.

'Maybe just as well,' he told her. 'Fundamentally, this is an investigation, not a news item. You've landed in a pretty delicate double role.'

'I've led Simon's brother to believe that I'm going to publish something. There was another journalist who worked on the same thing a few years ago, but nothing came of it.'

'In any case, you can't print anything as long as the investigation is still under way,' her father said. 'Maybe *VG* will show interest later, when we know a bit more about what has happened.'

Line took out her camera. 'Maybe so,' she answered, letting her father see the pictures from the fishing spot and the pump house. 'If not, I'll approach a few other media outlets with it.'

Simon Meier was part of a far bigger story, she thought. That was the story she really wanted to tell.

'Do you have a babysitter for tomorrow?' Wisting asked. 'Yes, why?'

'I want you to talk to Bernhard Clausen's old friends, the ones close to him in the spring and summer of 2003.'

Line looked at her father. Something about the way he had said this annoyed her. 'Must it be tomorrow?' she asked. 'I was thinking of making contact with the journalist who investigated Simon's disappearance.'

'Clausen has been dead for almost a week now,' her father replied. 'The funeral's on Monday. You need to speak to his friends before it becomes too suspicious.'

Line sighed at the idea of having to return to routine assignments. It felt like going through the motions and she had no faith that it would yield results.

Wisting gave her a reproving look, one she had not seen since she was a teenager. He didn't need to say anything. It was a clear reminder that she was part of an investigation team under his leadership.

'Do you have a list of likely candidates?' she asked.

Her father brought out one of the cabin guest books. 'A whole gang of them did some work at his cabin the weekend after Simon Meier went missing,' he said, handing her the book opened at the right page. 'Mainly old Party colleagues. I want you to start with Trygve Johnsrud.'

'The Finance Minister?'

'They were elected to Parliament at the same time and have been close ever since. Besides, he has a cabin down here, too. If you're lucky, he'll be around for the weekend.'

Line doubted she would be granted an interview. 'I can give it a try,' she said.

'I'll speak to the Party Secretary and get his phone number for you,' he said.

'Great.'

Once she had packed up Amalie's belongings, she went home to her own house.

The black cat that had been slinking around in the garden over the past few days was sitting on their front steps. It looked like Buster, the cat her father used to have after he was widowed but had simply disappeared one day.

'Puss!' Amalie yelled.

Letting go of Line's hand, she ran towards the cat. It jumped down from the step, darted out into the garden and sneaked around the corner of the house, with Amalie tearing after him. Line followed them round to the back of the house, just in time to see the cat vanish under the hedge and into the neighbour's garden.

'Puss!' Amalie shouted again, but it was gone.

Line had to persuade her daughter to come inside. They spent the next few hours together, and at Amalie's bedside Line downloaded an e-book about Pettson and Findus. Amalie was a bit too young to understand all of it, but she found the idea of a cat that walked around in striped trousers great fun. Afterwards she insisted they draw a cat and then they pinned the drawing on the wall above her bed.

Line's father had sent her a message with Trygve Johnsrud's phone number, and she tried to ring him, but received no answer.

She checked that Amalie was fast asleep before making herself a cup of tea and heading down to her office in the basement. It had no windows and the desk was placed against a wall where a cork board hung. She had pinned up cuttings from the Gjersjø case, which now filled the entire left side of the board. On the right-hand side she had started working on a relationship chart centred on Lennart Clausen. Post-it notes were displayed around a photo of him, with names of his associates placed depending on how close their relationship to him had been. Those closest were his childhood friends Aksel Skavhaug and Tommy Pleym, and Lennart's girlfriend.

In the basement office she also had a desktop Mac with a large screen. All her work was synchronized automatically so that she could begin work on the laptop and continue with it in the basement, but the desktop machine was faster and easier to work on.

She logged on and conducted a search for Henriette Koppang. It looked as if there were several women of the same name, but only one was a journalist. All the articles were several years old and it appeared as if she had been connected to *Nettavisen* and various film and TV production companies. Her profiles on social media were private and provided little information. A photo revealed that she was blonde with a round face.

There was something lively and energetic about the voice that answered when Line phoned. She introduced herself and explained that she was working freelance. 'I've started looking at a missing-person case,' she said. 'Simon Meier. I understand you did some work on it a few years ago.'

The voice at the other end changed character and grew serious. 'Is there any news?'

'Not really,' Line answered. 'Kripos are carrying out a routine investigation, but I was keen to give it some prominence. I'm not so sure that it was an accident.'

Henriette Koppang shared her opinion. 'There really are too many unanswered questions,' she said.

'You never published anything?'

'No, to be honest, I've got a guilty conscience about the whole business,' Henriette admitted. 'I was working for *Goliat* at the time and was five months pregnant. Suddenly, they had no money to pay me and I didn't even get my expenses covered. Then they went bankrupt, and I was heavily pregnant and without a job. It was all just a mess, and I had more than enough to think about.'

'Did you discover anything?'

'Nothing other than that the police had very thin grounds for shelving the case.'

A child called out in the background. Henriette turned away from the phone and shouted that she would be back in a minute.

'What do you think happened?' she asked when she returned to the call.

'The way I see it, he was most likely the victim of a crime,' Line replied.

'You think he was murdered?'

'That's the way I see it, really,' Line confirmed, weighing her words. 'He may have witnessed something and was killed to keep another crime hidden.'

'What kind of crime?'

'Not necessarily a crime, exactly,' Line said. 'But maybe he saw someone where they shouldn't have been.'

'You're thinking that the place where he disappeared was a well-known shagging spot?'

Line laughed at the explicit description. 'What about you?'

'I actually think he may still be alive,' she answered.

Line had not really considered that as a possibility. 'What makes you believe that?' she asked.

'Firstly, that he's never been found – a body usually turns up sooner or later – but there are also other things that point to it.'

Line's mind turned to the tip-offs. A couple of them had insisted that Meier had been seen abroad.

'His mother was from Chile, you see,' Henriette went on. 'He was fluent in Spanish. That's a good basis for starting a new life in a different country.'

Someone spoke in the background again. 'Let's have a

coffee together tomorrow,' Henriette suggested. 'Then we can discuss this further.'

'I live in Stavern,' Line said.

'No problem. I can come down to you. As I said, I have a bad conscience about it all, because I feel I let the family down, and it would be great if someone else could make something of it.'

They arranged to meet at a local café before rounding off their conversation.

Line was still doubtful that Simon Meier could have survived but had to admit she had locked on to the theory that he had been disposed of, in the same way that the police had become fixated on the theory that he had drowned in the lake. If Simon Meier was still alive, he had broken every link with his family. Meaning he wanted to flee from something.

32

Just before midnight, Wisting finished his review of the airport robbery files. Some documents he had merely skimmed, but others he had read several times over. He agreed with Audun Thule that the raid had been exceptionally professional in its execution.

The documents showed how much manpower had been devoted to gathering information, without the investigation ever really taking off. More had happened in the course of the past few days than at any previous point. The entire proceeds of the robbery had apparently been found, and they had also secured DNA evidence.

Getting to his feet, he walked into the living room and began to pick up Amalie's toys, which were still scattered across the floor. One of the jigsaw pieces had ended up far beneath the settee.

It was a cow, and he stood with the piece in his hand, casting his mind back to his conversation with Finn Petter Jahrmann in prison. The trip had turned out to be a wild-goose chase, one surplus piece that did not fit into their picture.

The right key for the right lock, he muttered aloud. He still struggled to recall which of his older colleagues had mentioned this.

He returned to the kitchen and studied the map Line had left on the table. She had marked a cross on the old pump house near Simon Meier's usual fishing spot. The distance from the airport to that location was around sixty kilometres, and it was only a short detour from the E6 motorway, leaving room for a certain possibility.

He carried the thought with him into the bathroom while he brushed his teeth. After he had gone to bed, he lay tossing and turning. He knew from experience that it would be hours before he fell asleep, hours of useless mental turmoil that would lead to nothing but fatigue.

Half an hour later he threw aside the quilt and got up. Collecting Line's map and the rest of what he needed, he checked that the alarm in the basement was activated before heading for his car and reversing out of the courtyard.

In the rear-view mirror he noticed that the light was switched off in Line's living room. He put the car in gear and drove slowly out of the street.

He turned on to the motorway and had to make a stop to fill up with fuel. It was almost 2 a.m. when he took out the map and searched for the turn-off that led down to the old pump house.

His headlights shone on mugwort and other weeds growing at the edges of the track. The opening was easier to find than he had anticipated, but the track looked as if it was no longer in use. As he turned on to it, he heard shrubs and grass brush along the undercarriage and sides of the car.

The darkness was total on all sides. Wisting leaned forward in his seat, hunched over the steering wheel in an effort to make out any obstacles that might lie ahead.

After a hundred metres the narrow track opened out into a wider space that had been gravelled at one time, but now tufts of yellow grass protruded from the crushed stones on the surface. In some places the grass was squashed flat and he could see tyre tracks.

He stopped, but left his engine running. The headlights lit up the entrance to the disused pump station, where insects darted in and out of the beams of light. Somewhere between the dark trees a large bird flew up, maybe a wood pigeon or an owl.

Wisting got out of his car and made for the door, watching as his own shadow danced on the grey brick walls. In his pocket he had the evidence bag that Mortensen had marked B-3. Drawing on a pair of latex gloves, he broke the seal and plucked out the key they had found in the final box of money. He guided it towards the cylinder lock on the old door and pushed it in.

The key was reluctant, and stuck almost halfway in. He wrenched it out, inserted it again and turned it several times, but it still proved obstinate.

Returning to the car, he opened the bonnet, withdrew the oil dipstick and dribbled a couple of drops on to the key before heading back to the door. This time, the key slipped in more easily, and he could turn it round. Raw, chilly air wafted towards him as the door slid open.

Investigation is a matter of finding the right key for a particular lock.

It occurred to him that it had been Ove Dokken, head of the criminal investigation department when Wisting had started there in 1984, who had said this.

He stood for a moment before heading back to the car for his torch.

A flight of five steps led down to the floor of the pump house. As plaster crunched under his feet, the noise echoed off the walls.

In the middle of the room stood a large pump. Pipes rose from the floor on one side and disappeared out through the wall on the other. A door leading into a second room was wide open and the room beyond lay empty, but there was a hatch in the floor. The hinges screeched when he lifted it. He shone the torch towards the opening and let it sweep around the empty space, which measured about two metres in height and one in depth. The walls were mottled with black damp. He was about to close the hatch when he spotted something lying in one corner. A padlock with a key inserted. He considered jumping down and taking it with him but decided to leave it and instead lowered the hatch carefully back in place.

Standing up straight, he was fired up with adrenaline, certain now about what he had found. This was the place where the airport cash had been 'frozen.' Now he just needed to find out what had happened next.

33

Overnight, a grey sea mist had swept across the landscape. Wisting had encountered the first wisps as he approached Larvik at around 4 a.m. Now it was so thick that he could not even see Line's house from his kitchen window where he stood, staring out into the distance.

A pair of headlights sliced through the fog and drove up in front of Wisting's house while he stood beside the coffee machine. Espen Mortensen, turning up promptly, as usual, for their morning meeting. Wisting put out another cup and went downstairs to let him in.

'Sleep badly?' Mortensen asked as he studied Wisting's face.

'I slept well enough, but not for long,' Wisting answered.

'What were you up to?'

Wisting retrieved the evidence bag containing the key from the kitchen table. 'I took this and went for a drive late last night. I didn't get back until early this morning,' he said, going on to explain where he had been.

Mortensen sat down. 'The money from the robbery was stored there, then?' he asked.

'Most likely,' Wisting replied.

'Have you spoken to Audun Thule?'

'Not yet. He'll be here soon.'

Mortensen produced a bundle of papers from his folder. 'Good,' he said. 'I've come across something else of interest.'

They heard a noise at the door downstairs as Line let herself in.

'Have you talked to Trygve Johnsrud?' Wisting asked her when she entered.

'Good morning to you, too,' Line replied.

Mortensen glanced up from his papers. 'The Finance Minister?' he queried.

'He visited Clausen at the cabin immediately after Simon Meier disappeared,' Wisting explained. 'I want to know whether he has anything to tell us about that time.'

He turned to face Line again. 'Have you spoken to him?'

'You'd have known about it if I had.'

'But have you made an appointment with him?'

'I tried to call him yesterday,' Line said. 'He didn't answer.'

'Try again,' Wisting insisted.

Line gave him a long-suffering smile. 'I'll follow it up.'

'We have to speak to Lennart Clausen's girlfriend as well,' he said, finding her name on the pad: 'Rita Salvesen. She's the nearest we'll come to a relative of Bernhard Clausen.'

He fixed his eye on his daughter to indicate that this would be something for her to tackle. 'It's only natural for a journalist trying to find fresh, obscure aspects of a politician's character to ask what he was like as a grandfather.'

'I thought they had no contact, though,' Line said.

'She must have become pregnant by Lennart Clausen not long after the airport robbery,' Wisting told her. 'So they may have had some contact in the past.'

'She lives in Spain now,' Mortensen broke in. 'Has done for the past three years.' He leafed through his own notes and handed her a piece of paper with the address and phone number.

'You said you'd found something interesting?' Wisting reminded him.

Mortensen nodded. 'I've started to chart Lennart Clausen's circle of acquaintances with a view to matching them with the airport raid,' he said. 'We got some names from Aksel Skavhaug,' he pointed out. 'One of them is really interesting. He worked for Menzies Aviation at Gardermoen in 2003.'

Wisting began to search through Thule's case documents to find the ring binder that dealt with the attempts to identify the informant the raiders must have had on the inside at the airport. 'What was his job there?'

'I don't know what he did exactly, but they operate most of the ground services at the air terminal.'

'Name?'

'Kim Werner Pollen.'

Wisting ran his finger down a list of names. 'He was interviewed,' he said, locating the interview record in another folder.

'He wasn't at work when the robbery took place . . .' he said, skimming further: 'A part-time employee for eight months. Worked on loading and unloading aircraft as well as other technical services for various airlines.'

'We could be on to something here,' Mortensen ventured.

'What does he do nowadays?' Line asked.

'He lives in Asker, runs a petrol station,' Mortensen said. 'Married, two children.'

Line flipped up the lid of her laptop. 'When was he born?' she asked.

'Nineteen eighty-one. Why do you ask?'

'He's the same age as Simon Meier,' she said, homing in

on the old class lists. 'They were in the same class at school. I can have a chat with him.'

The doorbell rang and Wisting went downstairs to let Audun Thule in. They all sat around the kitchen table and updated him on their latest findings.

'I can't get all this to add up,' Thule said. 'We've found Oscar Tvedt's DNA on the banknotes. We know he was connected to a professional criminal ring, but this doesn't link up with the gang of boys from Kolbotn.'

'There's some point of contact, though,' Wisting continued. 'How did the raiders get hold of the key to the pump house, I wonder?'

'The police broke in when they were searching for Simon Meier,' Line said. 'The building must belong to the local authority or the water board or something like that. Maybe Ulf Lande knows something more.'

'Can you follow it up?'

Line nodded and made a note.

Wisting turned to Audun Thule: 'Have you any news about Oscar Tvedt?'

'He'd been living at home with his mother in Nordstrand until she died this summer,' Thule explained. 'She was given a carer's allowance for looking after him. Now he's living in a nursing home near Østensjø lake.'

'Can he talk?'

'No.' Thule was searching for something in his notes. 'He has multiple brain injuries that have affected his cognitive functions. He's able to express what he wants and doesn't want, grunts and gestures, but no more than that.'

'Were there any suspects for the showdown at Alna?'

'Not really – it was regarded as an internal confrontation.'

'What do you mean by "internal"?'

Audun Thule took out a folder and removed the elastic band. 'We've already discussed Aleksander Kvamme,' he said, setting down a photo of a muscular man with a shaved head and a scowling expression.

'This is Jan Gudim,' he went on, laying down a picture of a man with curly hair. 'Leif Havang, Rudi Larsen, Jonas Stensby,' he continued, adding various headshots. 'They're the most central characters, the core group.'

The photographs of these hardened criminals from police records suggested that these men operated at a completely different level from Lennart Clausen and his circle.

'Who were the ones thought to be involved in the gang of robbers?' Mortensen asked.

'Not Leif Havang. He was too unstable, and still is. They wouldn't have taken the risk of bringing him along. All the others are serious candidates. Jan Gudim has taken part in motor sports and is likely to have been the driver. Jonas Stensby usually played supporting roles and could be the one who set fire to the bogus robbery vehicle.'

'Were their alibis checked at the time?'

'We didn't get as far as that, but we monitored their movements afterwards. None of them went abroad in the following six months, and none of them showed evidence of high expenditure. That was the sort of thing we looked for at the time. In hindsight, that wasn't enough.'

Line picked up the picture of Jonas Stensby. In contrast to the others, he seemed short and puny. 'Was there any-one called Daniel in that gang?' she asked.

Audun Thule shook his head. 'You're thinking of the phone number in the box of cash?' he asked. 'Your father's already asked me that.'

'Do you have any telecomms data from that time?' she continued.

Thule stood up to fetch a ring binder from one of his cardboard boxes. 'Printouts of calls from the base stations around Gardermoen for one hour before and after the raid,' he told her. 'I have them on computer disk as well, but I didn't bring them, I'm afraid. I'll get someone who still has a disk drive to locate them and send them over to us.'

Wisting got to his feet. He could now make out a possible chain of events. 'The cash from the robbery was stored in the old pump station,' he said, as he crossed to the kitchen worktop. 'Around the same time, Simon Meier disappears from the same place. What we know is that the robbers never reaped the benefits of the money they stole. Could it be that Oscar Tvedt was blamed for that? That it was his role to store the cash but the police search meant that the place he'd chosen wasn't so secure after all?'

'Someone who took part in the search may have found the money,' Mortensen suggested.

Wisting looked at his daughter. 'Are there any lists of names or an overview of the people who took part in the search?' he asked.

'I didn't see anything of that kind among the case documents,' Line answered. 'The chief investigator said someone had broken into the pump house, but didn't disclose their identity.'

'Do we know if Clausen's son or any of his pals took part in the search?' Thule asked.

'According to Aksel Skavhaug, they didn't,' Wisting replied.

'All the same, this is pretty hard to swallow,' Line said.

183

'The search was conducted from the area outside the pump house. If anyone found the money or took it from there, it must have been noticed. It's more straightforward to believe that the money disappeared along with Simon Meier.'

Wisting had to agree with her. 'The only snag is that the money didn't actually disappear,' he said. 'For some reason or other, it ended up with Bernhard Clausen.'

34

Adrian Stiller opened the thick envelope that arrived from Follo police station and drew the contents out on to his desk.

One folder was labelled with Simon Meier's name, case number and a note of how case expenses were to be registered. Papers dealing with the same subject were fastened together with a paperclip. The first bundle included an official complaint. The parents' committee at Østli school had written to say that the door to the old pump house had been left open after the police search and it could have endangered the children playing in the vicinity. The attached answer from the police directed the complainant to the water and sewerage board.

The next documents were copies of the final report from the Red Cross, an attachment listing those involved in the search, the expenses they claimed and the main rescue coordination centre.

There was further correspondence between the victim's counsel and Simon Meier's family, as well as a copy of the court record declaring him dead.

Towards the very back of the bundle, two sheets of photocopied paper were stapled together. The first one was written by the Director General of Public Prosecution: *Forward to the local police office in Oppegård.* Enclosed was a letter with a single line of text: *Check Health Minister Bernhard Clausen re: the Gjersjø case.*

A faded Post-it note was attached bearing one name: *Arnt Eikanger*. Stiller recognized the name as one of the investigating officers. He had probably been asked to follow up the tip-off.

'Bernhard Clausen,' he said aloud, speaking to himself.

Something clicked into place. Stiller did not believe in coincidences – investigators never did. Experience told him that one event was usually triggered by another.

He liked the feeling produced when he uncovered hidden connections. Just to be certain, he did a quick online search and found the reports of Bernhard Clausen's death and the fire at his cabin in Stavern.

So Line Wisting did have an agenda. She knew more than he did.

35

There were several empty tables outside the Golden Peace café, but Line went inside and left her belongings at one nearest the back before returning to the counter to buy herself a latte. When she sat down, her phone buzzed. It was Henriette Koppang, letting her know she'd be a quarter of an hour late.

Line drank some of the milky foam at the top of the cup and then looked for the phone number for Trygve Johnsrud, the man who had served in government with Bernhard Clausen. She had seen a different side to her father over the last few days and gained an insight into what he was like as a boss. Her father's micro-managerial style irritated her. Especially as he did not tell the other members of the investigation group how to prioritize or figure out their tasks.

When Trygve Johnsrud answered, Line introduced herself and asked when he might have an hour to spare to talk about Bernhard Clausen.

'Not until after the funeral,' the former Finance Minister said. 'I'm in France at the moment, but I'm coming home on Sunday.'

'Sometime next week, then?' Line suggested.

'What are you intending to write?' Johnsrud asked.

'It will be angled towards the election,' Line said. 'About why the old Labour Party ideals that both you and Clausen stood for are so important today.'

'What sort of thing do you have in mind?' Johnsrud asked. It sounded as if he was testing her.

'That social democratic policies, such as a strong welfare state, are vital to ensure Norway's future,' Line heard herself reply.

'What about Wednesday?' Johnsrud suggested.

'Wednesday would be fine,' Line answered. 'We could meet at your cabin in Kjerringvik? It's not too far from my house.'

'I can be there. You can come at ten o'clock.'

Line thanked him and took a sip of coffee while she noted the date and time in her diary. Her father would probably be annoyed that it was five days away, but at least she had an appointment with Johnsrud. Anyway, she had little faith that a conversation with an old Party colleague would lead to anything.

There was still some time left before Henriette Koppang was due to show up. Line rang Ulf Lande's number and the chief investigator answered almost at once.

'Sorry for pestering you,' Line said. 'I realize I should really collect all my questions together instead of disturbing you every time something turns up.'

'It's perfectly fine,' Ulf Lande assured her.

'It's about the old pump house,' she explained. 'You said the police broke the door open. Do you know who it was who did that?'

'It would be someone from one of the patrols.'

'But you don't know who exactly?'

'I can't give you a name. I wasn't there myself, not at that point. Why do you ask?'

'I'm just looking at various angles, purely from a

story-telling point of view. There's nothing about it in the case documents.'

'I see,' Lande said. 'That's to do with the administrative side of things,' Lande clarified.

'What does that mean?'

'That some information doesn't impinge on the actual investigation.'

'But surely there is a record of who did what?' Line asked.

'To a certain degree,' Lande answered.

'Is that something I can take a look at?'

'It shouldn't be a problem, it's probably in the null-and-void folder, but I've just sent it all over to Kripos.'

'So Adrian Stiller now has the administrative case documents?'

Ulf Lande confirmed this.

'Do you know who owns the pump house?' Line continued. 'Who is the key holder?'

'I would imagine it's the water and sewage board,' Lande replied. 'It's stated somewhere on the papers Stiller has. You see, we had to break down the door and so received a bill for the damage.'

'Wouldn't it be normal for the person who broke in to be named?'

'If the police have incurred expense as a result, that would have to be accounted for, and then they would most certainly be mentioned in some report,' Lande confirmed. 'But not among the actual case documents. The null-and-void folder contains most of the bits and pieces of admin paperwork.'

Line thanked him for his help and contemplated phoning Adrian Stiller, just as the café door opened and Henriette

Koppang looked around. Line recognized her from her photograph on the Internet and waved across.

'Would you like anything?' Line asked as Henriette sat down.

'The same as you're having,' Henriette replied with a smile.

Line bought another latte and brought over two glasses of water.

'I understand you used to work at *VG*?' Henriette asked.

'For almost five years before I got pregnant,' Line told her. 'I took a severance package six months ago. Now I'm freelance, working mainly for weekly magazines and periodicals.'

'You've achieved a lot in those five years. Loads of major stories.'

'Mostly because I've been lucky,' Line said. 'Been in the right place at the right time, along with the right people.'

'I had fairly grand ambitions when I started out in the industry,' Henriette admitted. 'But I wasn't the only one. There are a lot of smart people around, and increasingly fewer jobs.'

'Are you still working as a journalist?'

'I keep a toe in the water, but I don't have a permanent post. Right now I'm engaged as a researcher for *Insider*, where I'm able to use some of my old contacts.'

'I watch that,' Line said, smiling. *Insider* was a true-crime documentary series.

'Everything changed when I got pregnant and had Josefine,' Henriette added. 'I didn't have a permanent job, you see, and couldn't work as much as I had before. It doesn't take long to nosedive down through the ranks, no matter how good you are.'

'Are you on your own with her?' Line asked.

Henriette Koppang pulled a face. 'Not really,' she said, brushing it off. 'Let's just say it's complicated. What about you?'

'It's complicated,' Line said, smiling. 'But I live alone.'

Henriette Koppang drank her latte. 'Do you work from home, or do you have an office somewhere?' she asked.

'I have an office in the basement at home,' Line replied.

'And what have you discovered about Simon Meier?'

'Not much,' Line admitted. 'But enough to doubt the police's conclusion.'

Henriette Koppang agreed. 'I spoke to a biologist about the conditions on the bottom of Gjersjø lake,' she said. 'He was adamant that a human body would not vanish into the mud unless it had been weighted down with something heavy. I still have his name somewhere. I can certainly give it to you.'

'Ulf Lande thought the body might have got snagged on something down in the mud,' Line commented.

'The divers used sonar,' Henriette objected. 'They would have seen something on the pictures if anyone was down there.'

Line had only flicked through the documents detailing the sonar searches.

'That was the sort of thing we did at *Goliat*,' Henriette explained. 'We picked cases apart and presented the mistakes we found in the investigation to the police. It was quite a job. Sometimes we found fresh answers ourselves or helped advance alternative theories.'

'You thought he could be abroad somewhere?' Line queried.

'In Spain,' Henriette said, nodding. 'There were two different tip-offs that suggested he'd been seen in Marbella.'

'That would suggest he had planned it,' Line said. 'And that there was something he was keen to run from.'

'All the same, he left behind a hellish life,' Henriette said. 'He was a victim of bullying, had a badly paid job in a shop. No friends or girlfriend, no future.'

She took another mouthful of coffee. 'I also spoke to some of his schoolfriends,' she went on. 'His family bonds weren't very strong either. His father was violent and his mother had mental health problems.'

'So you think he ran away?'

'The police never checked passenger lists on planes or boats,' Henriette Koppang argued. 'Also, the Øresund bridge had opened by then. You can drive straight to Marbella in thirty-six hours. Even though we live in a world full of computers, electronics and surveillance, it's still possible to disappear and start a new life if you really want to.'

'But it's quite challenging,' Line pointed out. 'He would have needed money, for a start.'

'You're right,' Henriette said, with a nod. 'Many people who live unfulfilled lives buy lottery tickets and hope for better times. Maybe something happened that brought a large sum of money into his hands? Maybe that was why he disappeared so suddenly?'

Line shifted in her seat. Henriette Koppang was presenting a very interesting theory, but there was one problem: Simon Meier had not possessed the money.

'How would that have worked?' she asked.

'Maybe he found a stash of money or narcotics?' Henriette suggested, not paying much attention to the fact that her theory sounded fantastical. 'I travelled down there to search for him, you know,' she added.

'You went to Spain?'

192

'My boyfriend has an apartment in Malaga and we have a few friends down there,' Henriette clarified. 'You have to remember that two separate tip-offs pointed to Marbella. Two independent tip-offs. Considering there are more than ten thousand towns in Europe, those tip-offs are interesting, but they were never followed up by the police.'

'Did you find out anything down there?'

'I spoke to the individuals who said they'd seen him. They were pretty certain, but nothing came of it. He could have moved on, of course, changed his appearance or something.'

Line had little faith in the Spain theory but she was keen to take one premise in a different direction.

'Let's say he'd found some drugs money or saw something he shouldn't have,' she began. 'Someone else could have spotted him and wanted to get rid of him?'

Henriette Koppang sat deep in thought. 'Another crime,' she echoed. 'What are you thinking about?'

Line had no wish to mention the airport robbery, at least not yet. 'Blackmail, for one thing,' she suggested, picturing in her mind's eye what might have taken place inside the old pump house.

'Do you have a suspect in mind?' Henriette asked.

In the scenario she imagined, Lennart Clausen would be involved, but it was too early to bring up his name. 'I'm working on it,' she said instead.

Henriette had a gleam in her eye. 'You have a lead,' she said. 'Something new has come up to make you think that!'

Line felt her blood pumping, unable to hide that Henriette Koppang had hit the nail on the head. 'I don't know yet,' she said. 'It may not be significant at all.'

'What have you got?' Henriette asked. 'Is this something I could work on with you?'

Line withdrew a little in her chair. She had taken a liking to this woman. 'Maybe,' she answered. 'You're still working for *Insider*?'

'Do you think this could be a suitable story for them?'

Line had not given this any thought, but of course it was a possibility and would displease Sandersen at *VG*. 'You said you had contacts that could be useful,' she said.

'Yes, from the time I worked at *Goliat*,' Henriette replied, nodding. 'We had a series of interviews with known criminals which drew a more nuanced picture of them than the police had done. Those contacts are probably the most valuable data I gained from that newspaper.'

Line considered whether she should play another card. It was no secret that the airport raid had taken place on the same day that Simon Meier went missing – it was just a connection that had not been picked up before. Talking about it wouldn't put her father's case at risk.

'Did you write anything about the airport raid in 2003?' she asked.

Henriette Koppang opened her mouth but sat gawping before bursting into fits of laughter. 'My God,' she said, lowering her voice. 'Do you think there might be a connection there?'

'The only thing I know is that the robbery took place on the same day that Simon Meier disappeared.'

'That's absolutely crazy!'

'Do you have any informants that might know something?' Line asked.

'Well, I do know who to ask.'

'You'll have to be extremely discreet,' Line warned her. 'You mustn't let anyone know anything.'

She suddenly regretted sharing the information without her father's permission, but at the same time this might lead them closer to the truth.

'I know how this game works,' Henriette assured her. 'Do you have a name? A tip-off about who committed the robbery?'

Line shook her head. This was information she was unwilling to share at present. 'All I know is that no one was caught and that the money from the robbery was never found.'

'This story could be really huge.'

Line agreed. 'Just keep it to yourself for now, though.'

36

The kitchen was no longer suitable as a centre of operations for the investigation. There were too many papers. Mortensen had helped Wisting to shift everything down into the basement, where the money was still stored.

They had placed the table in the centre of the room, along with the chairs from the garden, so that they could hold meetings around it. One wall had been cleared and was used instead as a noticeboard. All the ring binders from the airport robbery investigation were on display. In one corner, Audun Thule had made a workstation for himself and linked up his laptop to the police networks. Mortensen sat with his back to him, engrossed in one of the forensic analysis reports.

Wisting's mobile phone rang, and he saw it was a number he had saved from an earlier case: *Adrian Stiller.*

He considered not answering. Stiller was busy examining Simon Meier's missing-person case, but it was the same story with him as with any police colleague in the Security Service branch: always looking to receive information, never to share.

'Aren't you going to take the call?' Mortensen asked.

'Yes, of course,' Wisting answered, swiping the screen with his finger.

Stiller came straight to the point: 'What's the connection between Bernhard Clausen and Simon Meier?' he asked.

Wisting moved the phone to his other ear and chose to

be equally direct: 'I'm trying to find that out,' he said. 'Do you have anything for me?'

'That depends,' Stiller replied. 'The Cold Cases Group has been sent the old missing-person files for a fresh assessment, but you probably already know that. Could Bernhard Clausen have anything to do with it?'

'What makes you think that?'

'He's named in a tip-off,' Stiller explained.

'I have the same tip-off,' Wisting admitted. 'Originally sent to the Director General.'

Adrian Stiller confirmed that they were talking about the same piece of information. 'Could there be anything in it?' he asked.

'We're investigating other circumstances relating to Clausen,' Wisting replied. 'This was something that cropped up, and we had to take a look at it.'

'Cropped up?' Stiller repeated. 'How can an old tip-off in a missing-person case simply crop up? What exactly is it you're investigating?'

Wisting had no answer to that.

'Bernhard Clausen is dead,' Stiller said. 'Does it have to do with that?'

'I can't discuss that over the phone,' was Wisting's response, as his eyes flitted around the room. Mortensen had turned towards him and was listening in to the conversation.

'I can come down to see you,' Stiller offered.

Wisting saw no option other than to include Adrian Stiller in the covert investigation group. Although he had reservations about the man's approach and methods, he could nevertheless bring creative skills that would benefit the investigation. 'I think that might be a good idea,' Wisting said. 'When can you get here?'

'I've one thing I need to check on first. What about tomorrow? Are you going to work on this over the weekend?'

'Tomorrow's fine,' Wisting confirmed. 'You can come to my house.'

'I'll be there at ten o'clock,' Stiller rounded off. 'I expect Line's there too?' His last remark contained a trace of sarcasm.

'She is,' Wisting told him before he rang off.

Mortensen got to his feet.

'Adrian Stiller,' Wisting said. 'Cold Cases.'

'You're letting him join us?'

'The tip-off about Bernhard Clausen has turned up in the old Simon Meier case documents,' Wisting explained.

'We were going to have to involve him anyway,' Mortensen told him. 'I've received the results from the examination of the tip-off letter.'

Thule turned around.

'Several fingerprints, but none identified,' Mortensen went on. 'We can collect the prints of employees in the Director General's office for exclusion purposes, but all the same, we won't find the sender in police records.'

'It sounds as if there's a *but* coming,' Thule commented.

'The envelope,' Mortensen answered. 'It was sliced open with a letter opener, but it had been sealed by moistening the glue on the back flap.'

'Spit,' Thule said. 'DNA?'

'We have a DNA profile,' Mortensen said. 'And we have a match.'

Wisting felt a frisson of anticipation as he cast a glance at the computer screen behind Mortensen. He had doubted that the envelope would yield any results, but now the case could be about to open up.

'Who is it?' he asked.

'I don't have a name, but there's an interesting result in the trace register.' The trace register contained DNA profiles of unknown identities from unsolved cases. 'The letter writer is the same person as the condom-user in the Gjersjø case,' Mortensen explained.

Audun Thule required further elaboration.

'In the area beside the old pump house where Simon Meier disappeared, used condoms and male pubic hairs were found,' Wisting told him.

'That makes sense,' Thule replied.

'He was there,' Wisting said, referring to the anonymous letter writer. 'He saw something.'

37

It was Friday afternoon and the traffic was nudging its way out of the capital city. Adrian Stiller sat with his hands on the steering wheel, thinking of Line Wisting. He could not quite work out her role in this. Whether her father had sent her to gain access to the Gjersjø case files, or whether she actually did intend to write a story about a cold case. Either way, it must have been her father who had tipped her off about Simon Meier.

He looked down at the sheet of paper on the passenger seat beside him, the note that had dragged Bernhard Clausen into the case. He had understood why the yellow note attached to it had Arnt Eikanger's name on it. Eikanger had worked as an officer in the local police station in Oppegård when Simon Meier went missing, but he was also politically active. He had been a local councillor and chair of the executive committee, as well as Deputy Leader of the Labour Party in the period from 2003 to 2007. The officer in charge of the investigation must have thought it practical to ask him to make contact with Bernhard Clausen.

Arnt Eikanger lived in Myrvoll, just beside Gjersjø lake, only a couple of kilometres from the fishing spot frequented by Simon Meier. The drive through the afternoon traffic took double the usual time.

When the local police station was closed down, Eikanger had quit the police and concentrated entirely on politics. In the run-up to that autumn's general election, he was in fourth place on the Labour Party's list vote for members of parliament for the region in Norway's proportional representation system. Stiller had not given Eikanger notice of his visit. The whole trip could prove to be a wasted journey, but he liked to speak to people without giving them an opportunity to prepare.

He located the house and turned into a paved courtyard. As he stepped out of the car, it crossed his mind that police officers ought to be careful about expressing political viewpoints. A neutral political standpoint in the force would surely instil greater public confidence and trust.

Arnt Eikanger was at home. A grey-haired man with glasses, he stood in the doorway while Stiller introduced himself.

'I don't mean to disturb you,' he said. 'It's just that I was in the neighbourhood and thought I'd swing by and see if you were at home. We've taken up the Gjersjø case again and I'm following up some leads.'

'I see,' the former policeman answered. 'Then you really must come in.'

They sat down together at the kitchen table. 'Is there anything new?' Eikanger asked. 'Has he been found, or something?'

Stiller shook his head. 'There's nothing new,' he said. 'But there are a few unanswered questions from that time.'

'It was Ulf Lande who led the investigation,' Eikanger pointed out. 'I had more responsibility for the operative details, such as organizing the search party. Ulf still works in the police force, at the police station in Ski.'

Stiller drew out the letter that named Clausen.

'I've spoken to him,' he said. 'But he couldn't answer everything. He didn't know how this was handled.'

He pushed the letter across the kitchen table. Eikanger adjusted his glasses and read the brief text several times over before tearing off the note with his own name and then attaching it again.

'I checked it out,' he replied.

'In what way?'

'I spoke to Bernhard Clausen.'

'You knew him?'

Arnt Eikanger nodded. 'We knew each other for years.'

'Through the Labour Party?'

There was a trace of reproach in his voice as Stiller posed this question.

'Loads of police officers are politically active,' Eikanger replied. 'We see all the dysfunctional aspects of society and experience in the force is a good thing to bring into the political arena. The aim has always been the same, as far as I'm concerned: taking part in the creation of a safer and better society. I left the police a few years ago and actually believe I can help to make a greater difference when I become a Member of Parliament.'

The reply seemed rehearsed but Stiller refrained from passing comment.

Instead, he replied: 'There's no record of your conversation with Clausen.'

'There was nothing to record,' Eikanger explained.

'What do you mean?' Stiller asked, trying not to sound churlish. 'If you spoke to him, surely you wrote a report about what he said?'

Arnt Eikanger pushed the paper back across the table. 'He didn't have anything to contribute to the investigation,' he said. 'He knew nothing about it.'

Stiller left the document lying between them. 'Is that

what you call checking him out?' he queried. 'You spoke to the person highlighted in a named tip-off, and when he says he doesn't know anything about it, you're satisfied with that?'

'Listen!' Eikanger said, obviously annoyed. 'I knew Bernhard Clausen. I'm going to his funeral on Monday. There's nothing to suggest that he had anything to do with Meier. There was no reason an anonymous tip-off should drag him into the investigation and place him under suspicion. He had enough problems on his plate at that time.'

'What kind of problems?'

'He'd been widowed and was finding his son very challenging.'

'Did you ask him where he was on the evening Simon Meier went missing?'

'He'd had a long day of meetings before returning to his parliamentary apartment in Oslo,' Eikanger said. 'He was there all week and just went home to Kolbotn at weekends, if he wasn't at the cabin in Stavern.'

'Did you check that this was correct?'

'I saw no reason to question it. There was nothing to suggest that any crime had been committed.'

'So you didn't even commit any of it to paper?'

'I reported back to Ulf Lande.'

'Verbally?'

'I told him what I had done. I've no idea whether he entered that information anywhere. If it hadn't been for the letter being sent directly to the Director General, we probably wouldn't have done anything about it at all. We were investigating a drowning accident.'

'Why do you think someone would bring him to the Director General's attention?'

Arnt Eikanger shrugged. 'A political opponent trying to tarnish his name?' he said.

Adrian Stiller retrieved the letter from the table. 'So, you reckon it was politically motivated,' he commented.

'Clausen thought it had just been a misunderstanding.'

'What kind of misunderstanding?'

'He occasionally went for walks in the forest around Gjersjø lake when he needed time to think. That happened more often after Lisa's death. He liked to be on his own. To be left in peace. Sometimes he parked his car at the pump station. He thought someone might have seen him there and mixed up the days.'

'Mixed up the days? In what way? What day *had* he been there?'

'Another day.'

'But he was in Oslo all week, wasn't he? When had he been at Gjersjø with his car?'

'I don't know.'

'Wait a minute,' Stiller said. 'By his own admission, Bernhard Clausen links himself to the crime scene, but you don't write a report on it or follow it up in any way whatsoever?'

A deep frown appeared on Arnt Eikanger's forehead. 'There is no crime scene,' he said, unruffled. 'The case was filed away as a drowning accident. Are you really intending to spend time on this?' he continued, rising from the table. 'Bernhard Clausen is dead. If you were thinking of blackening his name, it will be without my involvement.'

Stiller also stood up. 'Good luck in the election!' was his parting shot as he headed for the door.

38

At 7 p.m. the house was empty. Wisting activated the alarm, locked the basement door and climbed upstairs to the kitchen. Unearthing some sausages in the fridge, he put three in a pan with water and turned the heat up high.

When his phone rang in his pocket, he fished it out, saw that it was Line and crossed to the window to gaze across at her house before answering.

'Have you seen *Dagbladet*?' she asked.

He looked around for his iPad. 'No,' he replied.

'They're reporting on the book that Clausen was working on,' Line told him.

Once he located the iPad on the coffee table in the living room, he sat down and found the story.

POSTHUMOUS MANUSCRIPT VANISHED WITHOUT TRACE was the headline.

He read the report with Line still on the line.

Former Finance Minister Trygve Johnsrud confirmed that, prior to his death, Bernhard Clausen had been working on a book about his time in the Labour Party. It had been a topic of conversation when Johnsrud had visited him at his cabin three weeks ago. He was unwilling to divulge anything about the contents, but from what the newspaper had learned, the book would be regarded as controversial. A number of issues were raised on which Bernhard Clausen had voiced opinions contrary to Party policy and put forward a more liberal political viewpoint in which he became a spokesman for a greater degree of economic and personal freedom.

'The police are accused of running errands for the Party leadership and helping them to get their hands on the manuscript,' Line continued.

Wisting found the paragraphs she was referring to. Christine Thiis, the police prosecutor, confirmed that they had removed several boxes of Clausen's personal effects from the cabin shortly after the politician's death but refused to confirm or deny that a manuscript featured among those or that the material they took included his computer. This meant that the manuscript had possibly been lost in the fire, the online newspaper concluded.

'Krom,' Wisting said. 'The Party Secretary. He said he was in the cabin on Sunday to check that the windows were closed and the doors were locked. That was how he came across the cash. Of course, he must have been after the manuscript.'

'So he'd have nicked it?'

'He'd at least have wanted to get hold of it before anyone else did,' Wisting told her.

'What are you going to do about it?'

Wisting was about to answer when a noise from the kitchen caught his attention.

'The sausages!'

He dashed out to the stove and found the water had boiled over and was sizzling on the hotplate. He pulled the pan aside and made his apologies to Line.

'You can come and eat with us,' Line offered. 'I've got a lasagne in the oven.'

The sausages in the pan had burst open.

'That would be lovely.'

'Can you come down after Amalie's gone to bed, then?' she asked. 'I might have some information for you about the gang behind the airport raid.'

'I'll do that,' Wisting promised.

He left the spoiled sausages in the pan and phoned Christine Thiis.

'Have you read the *Dagbladet* report about Bernhard Clausen?' he asked.

'Not yet,' Christine Thiis answered. 'But I expect, as usual, to be cast in a bad light on behalf of the police force and get blamed for running errands for the Labour Party top brass.'

'Sorry,' Wisting said. 'I had no idea about any book manuscript. We didn't take anything like that out of the cabin. What I'm working on has to do with something entirely different.'

'I'm longing to ask you what that is, but I'll just have to resist.'

'You'll be one of the first to know,' Wisting promised.

When he hung up, he tracked down Walter Krom's number.

'This manuscript,' Wisting said when Krom answered. 'I want you to send it to me.'

Krom was wise enough not to deny that he had it. 'I've read through it,' he said. 'There's nothing in it that might explain where the money came from.'

'We're interested in every aspect of Clausen's life,' Wisting replied. 'If he wrote anything resembling memoirs, then I'd like to read them and decide for myself.'

'We regard the manuscript as an internal Party matter,' Krom said.

'But I don't,' Wisting snapped. 'If you send it over by courier, then it'll reach me some time tomorrow.'

Krom had nothing more to say on the matter. 'Have you found out anything else?' he asked instead.

'We know where the money came from,' Wisting replied. 'When the time is right, you can read about it in the newspapers,' he added, closing down their conversation.

He headed to the kitchen drawer, where he found a fork, and fished the three sausages out and on to a plate before wolfing them down with a generous dollop of mustard.

Line had served a portion of lasagne and placed it in the microwave by the time her father arrived.

'Is she asleep?' he asked, glancing towards Amalie's bedroom.

'She went out like a light,' Line said, smiling. 'Have you spoken to anyone about Bernhard Clausen's manuscript?'

Wisting drew out a chair and slung his jacket over the back. 'I'll get it tomorrow,' he replied as he sat down.

The microwave beeped a signal. Line took out the plate, added some salad and set it in front of him.

'I had an interesting meeting today,' she said, and went on to tell him about Henriette Koppang. 'She tried to write a story about Simon Meier a few years back. Nothing came of it, but she thinks he ran off to Spain.'

Wisting began to eat. 'What did she base that on?'

Line put on the kettle for tea. 'There were two different sightings in Marbella,' she said. 'But her theory hinged on the idea that he'd found a stash of drugs or money, and had taken either the hush money or the cash and run.'

'She does have a point there.'

Line was reluctant to tell him the rest of the story. Her father would not be happy that she had introduced Henriette Koppang to the link with the airport robbery.

'I thought so, too,' she said. 'I pointed out that the raid at Gardermoen had taken place on the same day that Simon Meier went missing.'

Her father put down his fork.

'It *is* information in the public domain, after all,' she added.

'Do you know her from before?' Wisting asked.

'No.'

'Have you checked any references?'

'She works as a researcher for *Insider*,' Line told him.

'The TV programme?'

'That's the whole point. She has contacts in criminal circles. She knows people who might have some information.'

'But you can't trust her!' her father groaned.

Line raised her voice. '*You* have to trust me!' she said. 'This might lead us further, as opposed to going around in circles talking to old Party colleagues. She's a professional and knows how to handle informants.'

Her father did not say anything.

'She won't publicize any connection to the Gjersjø investigation,' Line went on. 'She's putting out some feelers about the robbery under the pretext that *Insider* is keen to make a programme about it.'

Wisting seemed slightly pacified. 'You didn't mention Bernhard Clausen?'

Line glanced up at him in dismay, shaking her head. 'You must have some faith in me and give me some room for manoeuvre,' she told him. 'You don't micro-manage what the others are doing.'

'The others are experienced investigators,' her father pointed out.

'You were the one who wanted me in this group,' Line

said. 'You have to let me use my own experience, let me do things my way.'

'I just don't want you to make a wrong move,' Wisting said. 'Sorry.'

The kettle was boiling. Line poured water into a cup and left it while she filled the infuser. 'Would you like a cup?' she asked.

Wisting shook his head.

'By the way, do we know whether the money found in the cabin is all the cash from the robbery?' she asked.

Her father resumed eating. 'Audun Thule went through that today. There is a few thousand kroner difference. But that can be blamed on miscounting or the raiders taking a handful before they stashed the money away.'

Line took a seat and they sat in silence.

'Adrian Stiller phoned today,' Wisting said after a while.

'What did he want?'

'He came across the tip-off that named Bernhard Clausen in the Gjersjø case,' her father explained. 'It was passed on by the local police.'

'What did you say to him?'

'To begin with, his inquiry was only a shot in the dark, but, once he'd scored a hit, I couldn't give him the brush-off. He's coming here tomorrow.'

'So he's going to join the investigation group?'

'We need full access to the case documents from that time,' her father said, nodding.

Line heaved a sigh. She should have envisaged this situation arising, but she did not like it one bit.

'He's going to see through me and realize what I was up to.'

'I think he already has his suspicions, but you haven't

done anything wrong. Besides, I think he'll respect you for it.'

Line had to agree. To Adrian Stiller, his investigations were games of strategy in which he set the players up against one another, held the cards close to his chest and did not always play fair.

A faint, high-frequency noise sounded in the distance. Line carried her teacup to the window and looked out but was unable to place the sound.

'We had a DNA result today,' Wisting said.

Line turned to face him.

'The sender of the anonymous tip-off about Clausen is the same person as the condom-user at Gjersjø,' her father went on to say.

'And you don't mention that until now?' Line complained. 'That gives the tip-off credibility. The letter writer has been at the pump house!'

They heard the buzz of a text message and Line checked her phone.

'It was yours,' she said to her father.

Wisting fumbled for his phone in his jacket pocket on the back of the chair. Another message arrived.

'The alarm!' he yelled, rushing for the door.

It took a couple of seconds for Line to realize what he was talking about. She raced after her father and caught up with him halfway up the hill. The noise of the alarm siren grew louder.

'Wait here!' Wisting ordered.

Ignoring him, she stayed hot on his heels all the way to the front door.

Her father had the key ready. He let himself in, located another key and opened the door to the basement.

Line switched on the light. Everything looked normal. Her father reset the alarm before inspecting the room. The boxes of money sat untouched.

'False alarm,' he decided.

'Something set it off,' Line said, looking around to find an explanation.

Wisting stood clutching his phone.

'There's a camera in the detector,' he said. 'I've received some footage.'

Line hovered by his side, gazing at the images on his phone that followed the alarm alert. There were two detectors, one on either side of the room, and the one that had triggered the alarm covered Audun Thule's workstation and the windowless wall.

'Maybe it was a mouse or something,' her father suggested.

Line walked across to the wall being used as a noticeboard. Audun Thule had pinned up photos of the suspects in the airport robbery.

'It was this guy here,' she said, picking up the photo of Jan Gudim that had detached from the wall and fluttered to the floor. The movement had set off the alarm.

'Then at least we know it works,' her father concluded.

His phone rang. 'Mortensen,' he told her. 'The alarm goes to him as well.'

He took the call and reassured Mortensen.

Line rehung Jan Gudim's photo beside the others. He had sharp, deep-set eyes, a strong chin and his nose looked as if it had been broken.

She took out her mobile and photographed the entire row of images.

'Is there nowhere else you can store the money?' she asked.

Wisting had sat down by now. 'We'll find a solution to that over the weekend,' he said. 'This investigation is no longer about the money.'

Line checked the babysitter app on her phone and saw that Amalie was fast asleep. 'What do you mean?' she queried.

'It's now about what happened to Simon Meier.'

'Maybe he got the blame for something he hadn't done,' Line suggested. 'Maybe they thought he had run off with the cash?'

She stood staring at the photographs on the wall as she mulled over this new theory. Although she could not make all the pieces fit, she nevertheless agreed with her father. If they discovered what had happened to Simon Meier, it might unlock everything else.

39

Everyone was assembled in the basement in Wisting's house when Adrian Stiller arrived the following morning. The Cold Cases investigator stood at the door and looked around.

'Are you working from here?' he asked incredulously, his gaze lingering on Line before he turned to face Wisting.

'We're dealing with a highly confidential case,' Wisting said with a nod. 'I've put together a special investigation team. Line's included.'

Line, who sat with Amalie on her knee, acknowledged him with a little wave.

Stiller and Mortensen had met before. Audun Thule introduced himself as a detective from Romerike police district.

'Romerike?' Stiller repeated, but he was given no further explanation.

Wisting drew out a chair and Stiller sat down, placing his notebook on the makeshift conference table.

'What do you really have on Bernhard Clausen?' he asked.

'We're working on an assignment from the Director General,' Wisting said as he sat down opposite him. 'You can't report anything you learn here to Kripos.'

'Understood,' Stiller agreed.

Wisting gave a sign to Mortensen, who, moving to the wall and picking up one of the boxes of dollar notes, produced a knife and began to open the seal.

'When Clausen died, he left behind about 80 million kroner in foreign currency,' Wisting said.

Stiller stood up to inspect the contents of the box Mortensen had opened.

'He kept it at his cabin,' Mortensen said, going on to explain how the money had been found.

Stiller glanced across at the boxes along the wall. 'You've got the money stored in here?' he asked. 'Does the Director General know about that?'

Wisting nodded his head. 'We initially thought this money had been put aside to bribe foreign powers,' he went on. 'However, the investigation has taken us in a different direction,' he added, with a nod towards Audun Thule.

'On Thursday 29 May 2003, a consignment of cash from Switzerland was stolen from Gardermoen airport,' he said. 'The proceeds were around 80 million kroner.'

'Twenty-ninth of May,' Stiller repeated. 'The same day that Simon Meier disappeared.'

'Among the cash at Clausen's cabin we also found a key to the old pump station at Gjersjø lake,' Wisting continued. 'We believe the proceeds from the robbery were stored in there and that they have some connection to his disappearance.'

Stiller resumed his seat. 'You found the key to the pump house with the cash from the robbery?' he asked.

Wisting explained how he had driven to Kolbotn the night before last to try the key in the lock.

Stiller glanced across at Line. 'That means we may have a crime scene,' he said.

Wisting also looked at his daughter.

'The search party broke open the pump-house door to

see if Simon was there,' she said. 'But the crime scene technicians never went inside. Nothing suspicious was found so they concluded that Simon had drowned.'

Stiller nodded.

'They examined the area outside the pump house and the path leading to the fishing spot but found no evidence of violence. Whatever happened to Simon Meier most likely happened in the pump house.'

Wisting now turned to Mortensen. 'Might it still be possible to find something there?' he asked.

'The files say that the pump house has remained empty and locked since that time,' Line interjected.

'If nothing else, we might find traces of blood,' Mortensen said.

Stiller began to drum his pen on his notebook. 'Do you have the equipment you need?' he asked.

'I have everything in the van,' Mortensen replied. 'We can go there after the meeting.'

Adrian Stiller jotted something down and gripped his pen between his teeth. 'Nevertheless, the question remains as to how the money ended up with Bernhard Clausen,' he said.

'That's what the Director General wants us to solve,' Wisting said. 'But to find the answer, we most likely have to solve the robbery and the Gjersjø case.'

'What do you have to go on regarding the robbery?' Stiller probed.

'Strictly speaking, nothing on the robbery itself,' Thule said, before going on to give Stiller a quick summary of the old investigation.

'We believe the raiders were equipped with walkie-talkies,' Wisting added. 'A jack attached to an earplug cable was also found among the cash. The DNA profile from that matches Oscar Tvedt, a known member of a formidable criminal gang in Oslo.'

Stiller raised his eyebrows. Thule took the photo of Tvedt down from the wall and handed it to him.

'He was beaten up a fortnight after the raid,' he said, going on to explain his medical condition. 'He can't help us with any of this.'

'In addition, there was a note hidden in the banknotes with a phone number on it that we haven't been able to identify,' Mortensen said.

Wisting went on to explain about the fire at Bernhard Clausen's cabin and the son who had died in a motorbike accident. It felt useful to talk through the case in order to bring a new member of the investigation team up to speed. He rounded off by mentioning that the DNA from the envelope containing the anonymous tip-off belonged to the same man who had disposed of a used condom beside the pump house.

Stiller had sat with his arms on either side of his notebook on the table, listening intently, without writing anything. 'Do you have a strategy for the next steps in the investigation?' he asked.

'The most important thing will be to consider the two cases as connected,' Wisting replied.

Stiller nodded. 'The tip-off was never followed up properly,' he said. 'An officer, who was also an active local politician, spoke to Clausen. Arnt Eikanger. He's now the fourth candidate on the Labour Party list in Akershus and almost assured of a place in Parliament. I spoke to him yesterday. He personally vouched for Clausen.'

Mortensen got to his feet and found one of the visitors'

books from the cabin. 'That name's familiar,' he said, starting to leaf through the book. 'He's been a frequent visitor to Clausen's cabin. The latest visit was only a fortnight ago. They're close friends.'

'Is there any chance of discovering the identity of the letter writer?' Thule asked. 'He would be a key witness. What he actually saw could be conclusive.'

'A homosexual guy from the local neighbourhood,' Mortensen commented. 'The tip-off was probably anonymous, because he would have had difficulty explaining what he was doing there in the first place.'

Amalie had been sitting drawing pictures. Now she grew restless, and Line put her down. Wisting could see that his daughter was racking her brains.

'He could just have sent the letter anonymously to the local police station, though,' she said. 'Instead he sent it to the Director General.'

Wisting waited for her to continue.

'It could be that he didn't trust the local police because a close Party colleague of Bernhard Clausen worked there. Sending the tip-off to the Director General was a guarantee that it would be chased up.'

'Good point,' Stiller said. 'We probably already have his name somewhere in the paperwork.'

Wisting realized what his reasoning implied: 'He might have been interviewed by Arnt Eikanger but didn't feel he could mention Bernhard Clausen.'

'Or even worse,' Stiller said, 'he told him but it wasn't recorded and he realized it wouldn't be followed up.'

'Let's start there,' Wisting said. 'Make a list of all the witnesses who were interviewed by Arnt Eikanger or were in contact with him by some other means.'

He turned towards Stiller. 'You've brought the case documents with you?'

'I have them here,' Stiller said, producing a memory stick from his shirt pocket. 'Everything's been scanned using OCR. All the text is searchable.'

'I can take a look at that,' Line said, stretching out her hand. Stiller hesitated for a moment before tossing the memory stick across to her. 'Are the null-and-void documents there too?' she asked.

'Everything,' he assured her, before turning to Mortensen. 'Shall we go?'

40

When the courier from the Party office arrived just before noon, Wisting signed for the parcel and opened it. It contained Bernhard Clausen's laptop and a bundle of papers.

Setting the computer down in Mortensen's place so that he could examine it on his return, he took the manuscript across to an armchair.

It was quiet in the house. Line had taken Amalie and gone home to work on the Gjersjø case, while Audun Thule was continuing his task of gathering updated intelligence on the current robbery suspects.

The manuscript, obviously unfinished, consisted of around 250 pages of well-spaced lines.

Although it lacked a title, it was introduced by a quotation from the French philosopher Jean-Paul Sartre about humankind being condemned to be free.

I claim that freedom for myself, he went on to write on the next page, quoting the Norwegian writer Jens Bjørneboe: *That is where the secret of the essence of freedom lies. You claim it for yourself. No one grants us freedom – we have to claim it for ourselves.*

The text contained nothing about Bernhard Clausen's private life. He wrote about contemporary political issues, and how he was disillusioned with current Labour Party ideals. As Wisting continued reading, it became clear that Clausen had held neo-liberal views and had nurtured a growing mistrust of social democracy.

The reasons for Clausen's political shift to the right were not given, but much of what he wrote was surprising and would cause quite a storm if it were ever published.

Wisting got to his feet, stretched his legs a little and spoke about the book's content to Thule. 'For instance, he writes that we need more wealthy people and that he would get rid of wealth tax,' he said. 'He believes increased private capital will create more jobs and employment.'

'Maybe that's how you start to think when you've got 80 million kroner lying in your cabin,' Thule replied.

With a smile, Wisting returned to the manuscript. At first he had to agree with Walter Krom. There was nothing here that impinged on the investigation but, all the same, there was something in Thule's comment. Something had made Bernhard Clausen change his fundamental political beliefs, and it looked as if that had happened after he had got his hands on the money.

41

Stiller drove up beside Mortensen's CSI van and stepped out. He had never visited the location where Simon Meier had gone missing and had only seen the old pump house in photographs.

As he slammed the car door behind him, the wind rustled through the foliage above him and a flock of birds twittered in the treetops.

Having donned the obligatory white overalls, Mortensen tossed him a pair of shoe covers. Stiller pulled these on and followed the crime scene technician up to the door. The key was in an envelope. Mortensen took it out and remarked how thoughtless it had been of Wisting to use engine oil, since it would have erased any possible DNA traces.

It slid easily into the lock, but the hinges protested loudly when he yanked the door open. Stiller waited while Mortensen set up a spotlight on a tripod and connected it to a battery in his van.

He could see footprints in the dust and dirt on the floor, presumably Wisting's. The prints led across to an open door at the far end of the room and then on to a steel hatch in the concrete floor.

Mortensen remained standing beside the spotlight, as if keen to take in every detail of the space.

'What are you looking for?' Stiller asked.

Mortensen did not respond immediately but moved

further into the room. 'This could be difficult,' he said, without explaining what he meant.

He went back to his van, took out a tarpaulin and a roll of tape. 'We'll have to cover the window,' he said, holding up one corner of the tarpaulin.

Stiller grabbed it and blanketed the window for Mortensen to tape up, ensuring that no sliver of daylight could slip through.

Working with old, unsolved cases meant that Stiller rarely had the chance to watch a crime scene investigation. As a rule, he only read technical reports and looked through folders of photographs or old videotapes. However, he knew technicians could find blood even if it had dried, been scrubbed or painted over. The process itself was simple – they used a sensitive chemical solution that glows in the dark when it comes into contact with blood. If blood were found here, a DNA analysis would reveal whether or not it came from Simon Meier.

Mortensen returned to his van and brought back a spray bottle. 'We'll give it a go,' he said.

They headed inside again. Mortensen put on a pair of protective goggles, crouched down and shook the bottle. A fine jet sprayed out from the nozzle and settled on the floor and the nearest pipes. 'OK, then,' he said, straightening up. 'Turn off the light.'

Stiller pulled out the plug on the spotlight, plunging the room into darkness. A few speckles on the moistened area glimmered with a fluorescent blue light.

Stiller was impressed by the sheer simplicity and effectiveness of the process.

'I was afraid of that,' Mortensen said.

'Is something wrong?' Stiller asked, turning on the light again.

'Luminol reacts to the iron in red blood cells,' Mortensen explained. 'That means it also reacts to rust.'

Stiller looked around. 'What do we do, then?'

'I'll have to collect samples and have each and every one of them analysed,' Mortensen said. 'It's going to take time, both the collection and the analysis.'

'I see,' Stiller replied. 'Can you handle it on your own? I have something else I need to attend to.'

In response to Mortensen's nod, Stiller waved his hand in thanks and left. The branches in the dense forest on both verges of the gravel track scraped the sides of his car as he drove out. Once back on the main road, he took a left turn.

He had been ready to return the Gjersjø case with no recommendation to reopen it when Line Wisting had contacted him. He had been through the case files without finding anything to work on. Reinvestigation of cold cases was often triggered by technical evidence, but the Gjersjø case had yielded nothing, until now.

He checked the time and picked up speed.

The other potential trigger was someone who knew something beginning to talk. He had always said that resolving an old case was a matter of the right person coming forward. But what if the right person had already spoken to someone unwilling to listen?

The trip from Gjersjø lake to Ski took fifteen minutes. Parking beneath a *Strictly No Parking* sign, he peered through the side window at the entrance to the Storsenter shopping mall. A number of political parties had set up stalls and were handing out election leaflets to passers-by.

He spotted Arnt Eikanger, dressed in a red T-shirt, speaking to an elderly woman.

Stiller waited until he was free before emerging from his car to approach him. On spotting him, Eikanger looked uncomfortable. He handed a red rose to a man of similar age before trying to engage him in conversation, but the man walked on.

Stiller accepted a rose from a Party colleague before accosting Eikanger.

'You again,' Eikanger said, with a nod.

'I have another question for you,' Stiller told him.

'Here?' Eikanger asked. 'I'm a bit busy.'

'One question,' Stiller insisted. 'It won't take long.'

Without waiting for a response, he said: 'You interviewed nineteen men in connection with the Gjersjø inquiry. Did any of them mention Bernhard Clausen's name?'

'Haven't you read the documents?' Eikanger asked.

'I know what they say,' Stiller said. 'What I asked was whether any of them said anything about Bernhard Clausen.'

Arnt Eikanger opened his mouth to speak.

'Think carefully,' Stiller told him, before he had a chance to say anything. 'I'm considering asking all nineteen of them the same question.'

Eikanger closed his mouth again and smiled to a woman passing by. 'It was years ago,' he said. 'I can't remember now.'

It was a liar's easiest answer.

'You and Bernhard Clausen were close acquaintances,' Stiller said. 'You were friends. Wouldn't you remember if his name had cropped up in an interview?'

'You said you had one question,' Eikanger said. 'It's been answered.'

'Vegard Skottemyr,' Stiller said. 'I'm speaking to him first of all.'

Eikanger turned his back on him and continued handing out election pamphlets. Stiller headed back to his car. He had drawn up a list of the nineteen men Eikanger had interviewed. Although there was no guarantee that the anonymous letter writer would be among them, Eikanger's reaction had reinforced his belief in what had happened.

The names had originally been listed in alphabetical order and Stiller had looked up each individual in the population register. Married men with children were moved to the bottom of the list. Unmarried men with no family responsibilities were pushed to the top. Although this sorting method had its weaknesses, he knew the man they were searching for most likely hid his sexual orientation, which meant he might be found further down the list.

The selection process brought the name Vegard Skottemyr to the top of the list. He suited the potential profile perfectly. Aged forty-four, he was unmarried and worked as a customer adviser in DNB bank, he had no children and his address history suggested that he had never had a live-in partner either. He had three older sisters and his father was a pastor in the Free Church.

Stiller started the car and pulled out into the traffic. Vegard Skottemyr lived half an hour away.

42

Line sat at her computer in her basement office. She should have gone out to the local playground with Amalie, but for the moment her daughter looked happy enough to sit on the floor with the iPad.

The file she had received from Adrian Stiller was extensive and the machine worked sluggishly, but it would be far easier to negotiate her way around the electronic edition of the Gjersjø case files than a thick bundle of papers.

She typed *Clausen* into the search field and was taken aback when it produced two hits. The first was for Lennart Clausen in the old class lists from the school where both he and Simon Meier had been pupils. The next result was the letter to the Director General that was now included in the inquiry.

There were eighty-seven hits for Eikanger. Most of these were in connection with the interviews he carried out. In total, he had interviewed nineteen men and eleven women, and this included the man who had been walking his dog.

With the anonymous letter writer in mind, the male interviewees were of primary interest to her. She would have a thorough read of what they had said, but the search function had sparked an idea. She keyed in the phone number from the note found with the money. No result. Then she searched for the name Daniel. That yielded five results, including one for the Red Cross leader. Neither he nor any of the other Daniels seemed to fit the bill.

Before she began to read the interviews, she was keen to look at the null-and-void documents that had been omitted from the case files the first time she had looked at them.

Stiller had collected these into a special subfolder. She recognized many of the documents from her visit to Simon Meier's brother: letters to and from the victim's counsel and a copy of the death declaration. Arnt Eikanger's name appeared in a statement concerning the damaged pump-house door. He was the one who had broken it open during the search activities. The damage was not to the lock itself but to the door and the doorframe. The destruction was repaired and the appropriate council department informed. Three months later, the parents' committee sent the letter to the police, pointing out that the door to the pump house was still lying open. Arnt Eikanger reported that a representative from the water and sewage board had visited the pump house with a key and locked it up before the police left the scene. In a fairly arrogant tone, the complaint had therefore been dismissed.

Amalie came over and stood at the edge of the desk. 'Shall we go out to play?' Line suggested.

Amalie nodded.

'Mummy is just going to finish reading this,' Line told her, moving on to the next page.

It was a copy of a letter from Oppegård local authority to Østli school, thanking them for drawing attention to the state of the old pump station that had been left unsecured and stating that they had now closed the building.

Amalie began to play with a stapler on the desk. Line took it out of her hands and patted her daughter on the head.

'OK, then,' she said, skimming through the rest of the document. 'Let's get dressed and go out.'

She was about to stand up, but something on the screen pinned her to the chair. A tiny detail about to flit past, a name. The letter from the local authority was written by the person in charge of the water and sewage board, Roger Gudim.

Gudim was not a common name. She thought of the photo of Jan Gudim and the other potential raiders on the wall of the basement in her father's house. In some way or other, they had obtained the key to the disused pump station.

Gudim. There could be a family connection.

Amalie tugged at her sleeve. 'Mummy.'

'Yes, sweetie,' she replied, turning away from the image on the screen. 'Now we'll go out.'

She helped Amalie with her shoes and found their cycle helmets.

The black cat was stretched out on the ground in front of the car when they ventured outside, but leapt up and ran out into the street, with Amalie racing after it.

'No!' Line yelled.

She bounded after her daughter and caught her just before she reached the road.

'Cars could come!'' Line chided.

'Puss!' Amalie said, pointing down the street.

'Now we're going to the play park,' Line said, donning her cycle helmet.

No children of Amalie's age lived in their street, but they usually cycled to the park in Vardeveien, where there were sometimes children they knew.

Amalie sat in the seat behind Line on the bike and sang as Line pedalled, her little body rocking from side to side.

Her father had access to the population register, Line thought as they swayed along the road. A quick search would reveal whether the manager of the water and sewage board in Oppegård was related to one of the suspected robbers. In that case, it would draw an even clearer picture of how this all connected.

There was no one at the playground, but Amalie made a beeline for the slide, clambered up and slithered down. Next time, Line had to go with her. After two turns, Amalie wanted to move on to the swings, and Line pushed her hard as her daughter squealed in delight.

Her phone rang and she saw that the caller was Henriette Koppang. Line answered and headed towards one of the picnic benches to sit down.

'Are you out working?' Henriette asked.

'I'm at the park with Amalie,' Line replied. 'Have you found out anything?'

'I've had a few interesting conversations,' Henriette said. 'Will you be at home tomorrow?'

'Yes.'

'Could we meet at the same café as before, so that I can tell you more?'

Line glanced across at the swings. 'I'd have to bring Amalie along,' she said.

'Then I'll bring Josefine. That'll be nice.'

'What have you discovered?' Line asked.

'The rumour is that the robbers were robbed,' Henriette explained. 'The money was stolen from them.'

'Does anyone know who the robbers were?' Line queried, tempted to share the names she already had.

'Let's chat tomorrow,' Henriette suggested. 'I'm meeting an informant this evening.'

Amalie shouted that she wanted another push.

'OK,' Line said. 'Twelve noon?'

'Twelve noon is fine.'

She put her phone back, crossed to the swing and gave Amalie another big push.

A dad appeared with two small boys, who started to play in the sandpit, and Amalie wanted to get off the swing to play with them. Line sat down on the bench again and saw her daughter watch the two boys before tentatively borrowing a spade.

Line had seen the father before. Three or four years younger than her, he lived somewhere in the neighbourhood. He sat down on the opposite side of the picnic table.

'Out for a breath of air,' he said with a smile.

Line returned his smile.

'How old is she?' the man asked, nodding towards the sandpit.

'She's just turned two,' Line answered. 'What about yours?'

'They're three and four.'

Amalie toddled over. 'Thirsty,' she said.

'I didn't bring anything with us to drink,' Line said, getting to her feet. 'But now we're going to visit Grandpa. You can get some juice from him.'

Amalie did not seem entirely happy with that suggestion but made no protest when Line put the helmet on her head.

The vehicles belonging to Mortensen and Thule had left when Line turned into her father's driveway. Taking off her helmet, she went round to the terrace at the back. It looked deserted now that the garden table and chairs had been carried down to the basement. Only a sofa was left.

The terrace door was closed and she asked Amalie to

knock on the glass. Her father appeared and let them in. 'Have you had a visitor?' he asked.

'A visitor?'

'A man came out of your house not long ago,' her father said. 'I saw him from the kitchen window.'

'We haven't been at home,' Line told him. 'We've been for a ride on the bike. Amalie's thirsty.'

'I have some juice,' her father said, with a smile.

Amalie accompanied him into the kitchen and Line followed behind. She stood at the window and looked towards her own house: she had no idea who the visitor might have been.

'Well, it looked as if he came from your house,' Wisting said, producing three tumblers. 'He walked on down the road.'

He mixed some squash and water, gave Line a tumbler and let Amalie drink some before she carried her tumbler carefully out on to the terrace.

Line sat down in the doorway while her father took a seat on the sofa outside. He held Amalie's tumbler for her while she scrambled up to join him.

'I think I know where the robbers got hold of the pump-house key,' Line told him. 'The boss at the water and sewage board is called Roger Gudim.'

'Jan Gudim,' her father commented.

'Can you find out if they're related?'

Her father fetched his iPad. It took him a while to log into the correct system but, once he was in, the answer popped up quickly.

'Father and son,' he confirmed, getting to his feet. 'Thule has produced a folder on him.'

He disappeared and re-emerged with a plastic folder

with *Jan Gudim* written on it in black marker pen. He drew out the top sheet and skimmed through it. 'A number of convictions,' he said. 'Looks as if he's in jail now.'

'For what?'

'Narcotics and breach of the gun laws. He's served two years of an eight-year sentence. Aleksander Kvamme was charged with the same crimes, but no prosecution was brought.'

He handed the papers to Line. There was little detail in the printouts, but the case related to the import of a total of twenty kilos of amphetamines. Two other men had received shorter prison sentences in the same case.

Wisting lifted Amalie on to his lap. She had started to whimper and wanted some food.

'We're moving towards something,' he said. 'Making good progress.'

Line took out her daughter's dummy. 'Henriette Koppang phoned,' she said. 'She's going to meet an informant tonight. The story going round is that the proceeds of the robbery were stolen. She's coming over here tomorrow.'

'Keep that to yourself,' her father said abruptly, with a nod in the direction of Jan Gudim's folder.

Line stood up, returned the folder to her father and took charge of Amalie.

'Of course,' she said.

Amalie nuzzled into the crook of Line's neck, and Line stroked her daughter's hair. 'We'd better head home,' she said.

Wisting gave them each a hug before she carried Amalie around the house again and wheeled her bike along the street. Halfway there, she put her daughter down to walk the rest of the way.

Amalie toddled up the steps as Line put her bike aside. 'Wait,' she said, rummaging for her keys, but Amalie had already gone inside.

Line stared at the open door. 'Wait!' she shouted sternly.

Amalie stood in the hallway.

'Wait here,' Line said, walking ahead of her into the house.

She might have forgotten to lock the door – that had happened before – but what her father had said about a man leaving her house rang alarm bells.

She moved through the kitchen and into the living room, with Amalie waddling after her.

'Wait here,' she said again.

She checked the bedrooms and the basement to be sure there was nobody inside the house. Then she went out to the hallway and locked the front door before hoisting Amalie on to her hip again and doing another circuit to see if anything looked different. She could not find anything untoward. Her laptop was still on the kitchen table, exactly as she had left it. Her bag was slung over the back of a chair, her purse safely inside it. All the same, she could not shake off the feeling that someone had been in the house.

The bedroom windows were open slightly to air the rooms. They were old and of the type that could be opened from the outside if you put a stick or something similar into the opening and pushed up the child lock on the frame.

She entered her own bedroom. The window overlooked the garden at the back. On the window ledge there was a framed photograph of her mother and a glass unicorn. They did not appear to have been moved, and there were no prints or marks to suggest that anyone had climbed in that way, but it was certainly possible to do so before leaving through the front door.

Amalie squirmed and wanted to get down. Planting her on the floor, Line crossed to the window, pulled it shut and chased away her thoughts.

43

Vegard Skottemyr had moved from Kolbotn in 2004 and had been listed at three other addresses since then. The last of these was a modern terraced apartment in a cul-de-sac in Lørenskog. Adrian Stiller drove slowly past and parked at the end of the street. Before he stepped out, he skimmed through the statement Skottemyr had provided in 2003. Several people had noticed a man out jogging in the blue and white colours of the local sports club. Once this had been mentioned in the local newspaper, Vegard Skottemyr had made contact with the local police station. On the afternoon of Thursday 29 May 2003, he had taken a detour from his usual run to take a leak and ran a few metres down the track leading to the disused pump station. He had not noticed anyone or anything, but it was quite possible that he had been observed from cars passing on the main road.

Placing the papers in a separate folder, Stiller brought them with him and walked up to the apartment. There was only one name on the mailbox and one name on the doorbell.

A buzz sounded inside when he pressed the button and a man in a tracksuit appeared at the door, his top soaked through with sweat.

Stiller showed him his police ID. 'I work on old, unsolved cases,' he explained. 'I'd like to talk to you about Simon Meier, who went missing from Gjersjø in 2003.'

'Right now?'

'If possible,' Stiller said. 'It won't take long.'

The man at the door took a step back and ushered Stiller in. 'Is there any news?' Skottemyr asked.

'It's really more of a routine run-through,' Stiller clarified. 'We're talking to everyone interviewed at that time, mainly to confirm their statements.'

Vegard Skottemyr showed Stiller to a seat at the kitchen table and filled a bottle of water before sitting down himself.

'Do you live alone?' Stiller asked as he took out the old interview form.

The other man nodded.

'Do you remember what you said at that time?' Stiller went on.

'More or less,' Skottemyr said. 'I was in the habit of jogging past the track down to the pump house. I ran a short distance down the track to have a piss.'

With a nod, Stiller pushed the interview form across the table to him. 'Would you read it through, please?' he asked.

Skottemyr drew the paper towards him and read quickly through the statement. It was no more than a page and a half of typewritten text. In addition to the detour from his jogging trip, Skottemyr had described the clothes he had been wearing, when he had left home, the route he had taken and when he had got back. At that time, he had been living in a basement apartment beneath his parents' house. They would be able to confirm the exact time when he returned home.

'Did you already know the officer who interviewed you?' Stiller asked. 'Arnt Eikanger?'

'I knew who he was,' Skottemyr answered. 'Everyone knew the folk who worked in the local police station to some degree. He's a politician these days.'

'Yes, of course,' Stiller replied, smiling. 'Did you vote for him?'

Skottemyr returned the smile. 'Wrong party.'

'Did you tell him anything that isn't written down here?' Stiller asked.

Vegard Skottemyr took a swig from the water bottle before shaking his head. 'I don't think so.'

'Have you remembered anything else since?'

'There wasn't much to tell,' Skottemyr replied, handing back the statement.

Stiller grew frustrated. He was convinced that the man facing him was the anonymous letter writer and had thought it would be an easy matter to persuade him to talk about it. He would have to be more direct in his questioning.

'Do you know who Bernhard Clausen is?' he asked.

'Of course.'

'Did you see him that day?'

Skottemyr cast a glance at the interview form. 'Everything I saw and didn't see is here,' he answered.

Stiller considered querying his sexual orientation but decided against it. 'What we also do in these run-throughs of old cases is to ask all those involved to give a DNA sample,' he said instead.

'I wasn't exactly involved,' Skottemyr commented.

With a smile, Stiller produced a testing kit. 'You were in the area the day Simon Meier disappeared,' he said. 'That means we'd like a sample from you. New technology makes DNA more relevant than it was at that time. Is that OK with you?'

'I don't really see the point,' Skottemyr replied.

'It's simply a matter of eliminating you,' Stiller told him as he took out the swab. 'It's over and done with very speedily. You just need to put this in your mouth.'

Vegard Skottemyr took the swab and followed the instructions Stiller gave him. The sample was then bagged and sealed, and Stiller got to his feet. 'Is there anything you'd like to add before I go?' he asked.

Skottemyr rose slowly from his chair. Stiller had the impression that there was something, but Skottemyr ended by shaking his head.

44

Just before 6 a.m., Amalie came padding into Line's bedroom and crept up into her bed. Line could not get back to sleep. Her laptop lay beside her from the previous evening. She pulled it towards her, flipped open the lid and lay reading the last interviews of the men Arnt Eikanger had questioned. The statements were fairly alike in style and content. The men recounted their observations and their own movements. The one who had been closest to the crime scene was a jogger called Vegard Skottemyr, who had ventured fifteen to twenty metres down the pump-station track to urinate. That had been just before 7 p.m. At the end of his statement, it emerged that he lived in the basement apartment of his parents' house and that they could confirm the time of his return. This gave the impression that he was single.

From the introductory personal information, she worked out that he was born in 1971 and had been thirty-two when Simon Meier went missing.

At eight o'clock, Amalie began to stir. They got up and ate breakfast together. For the next couple of hours Line struggled to get some work done as Amalie kept clinging to her and getting in the way. Line tried to persuade her to play in her room or find something else to amuse herself, but her daughter just threw herself on the floor and lay kicking in a tantrum.

As her meeting with Henriette Koppang approached,

Line grew increasingly restless. Line would prefer to have interviewed the informant herself. This was what she was good at and, anyway, she liked to have control.

As the time ticked closer to eleven o'clock, she let Amalie help her to pack a bag. They mixed squash and filled bottles, brought a packet of biscuits and two bananas. Before they left, Line checked that the windows were closed tight and made sure the door was firmly locked behind her. Then she put Amalie into the child seat on the bike and wheeled it up past her father's house to the top of the street. From there, it was downhill almost all the way to Stavern.

Having left early, she cycled down to the harbour. There, they sat on a bench and shared the biscuits with the swans. Just as they were about to pack up and leave for their meeting with Henriette at the café, she received a text message from her to say that she would be fifteen minutes late. She replied *OK* and spent the time wheeling her bike through the town-centre streets.

Amalie had a smoothie while Line chose a latte at the counter. They sat down at the same table where she and Henriette had sat the last time.

Henriette did not arrive until twenty minutes later and this time she had a little dark-haired girl with her. 'Sorry for being late.'

Line half rose from her seat and gave her a quick hug. 'It's fine,' she reassured her.

'You must both say hello to Josefine.'

Josefine said hello nicely but Amalie turned away and crept up on to Line's lap to hide her face there.

Henriette returned to the counter and bought something to drink.

'Did you meet him?' Line asked, once she had sat down again.

'Yes, but I didn't get as much out of him as I'd hoped.'

Line nodded. She had worked in close proximity to criminal circles herself. It could prove to be a test of patience.

'It was as I said,' Henriette went on in a hushed voice. 'After the robbery, the money was hidden in what was thought to be a safe place but, when they went to collect it, it was gone.'

'Does your source know where the hiding place was?'

'Only that it was somewhere just outside Oslo.'

'Does he know who took part in the raid?'

'I got the impression that he does, but he didn't mention any names. Just gave me the brush-off when I asked about that.'

Amalie began to whimper, wriggling around on Line's knee and reaching for the dummy she knew Line had in her pocket.

'Was anyone suspected of the theft?' Line asked, letting her daughter have the dummy.

Henriette nodded and took a gulp of coffee. 'I didn't get any names, but it didn't seem as if Simon Meier was involved. There was talk of someone who had been killed in a motorbike accident a few months after the robbery. The rumour is that he hid the money and the cash is still there now.'

Line pushed Amalie's arms away. Of course, it could be as simple as that. Lennart Clausen took the money and hid it in his family's summer cabin. When he died, his father continued to hide it.

'What about Simon Meier?' she asked. 'How does he come into the picture?'

'No idea. I couldn't start asking about that – he would have cottoned on that we know more than I was saying.'

Line agreed. 'But if Simon Meier has something to do with the case, then the airport robbers must have considered that possibility, too,' she said. 'If the cash was hidden near the spot where he disappeared, it must have really stressed them out. I mean, all of a sudden, there's an official search in operation right by their hiding place. That must have sparked some speculation later about what happened to the cash.'

'True,' Henriette answered, but she had nothing more to add.

Line was disappointed about how little had emerged from the meeting with the informer. 'Didn't he tell you anything more?' she asked.

Henriette shook her head. 'Not on this occasion.'

'But do you think he knows anything more?'

'Well, he will at least make some inquiries for us, ask around, but that can take time. These are dangerous people, so he has to tread carefully.'

Amalie had settled and wriggled down from Line's lap with the dummy in her mouth. Line suggested that she could show Josefine the playroom further inside the café. She was unwilling at first but let herself be persuaded.

'The terrible twos,' Henriette said with a smile when they were left on their own. 'Josefine was like that as well.'

'Do you know anyone else you could talk to?' Line asked. 'Someone who might know something more? We need some names.'

Henriette received a text message and took out her phone and read it. 'What would really make a sensational story would be if we could find out what became of the money,' she said as she keyed in a response. 'Do you have your laptop with you?'

'Yes, why?'

'There can't have been too many deaths in motorbike accidents in 2003,' Henriette continued. 'I tried to do a bit of a search on the Internet last night, but I didn't get very far with it.'

Picking up her bag, Line took out her laptop. She knew the answer already, but it would be too complicated to start explaining that now. She had to keep Henriette in the dark about everything to do with Lennart Clausen and his father. 'What search terms should I use?' she asked after logging in.

Henriette put down her phone. 'Fatal accident, motorbike, 2003,' she suggested.

They found a total of eleven accidents in the official statistics. Three of them had occurred prior to the airport robbery. Line cut and pasted key phrases from the other eight fatal accidents and collated a list. Then she arranged them in order of what seemed most likely. Accidents in the north of Norway were moved down the list and accidents in the Oslo area were given priority. In the end, Lennart Clausen's accident in Bærum on the night of 30 September 2003 landed in third place.

'A twenty-five-year-old,' Henriette commented. 'I think maybe he should be moved up.'

The accidents in the top two places dealt respectively with an eighteen-year-old on a light motorbike and a married couple in their fifties who had both died.

Line highlighted the text relating to Lennart Clausen, cut it out and moved it to the top of the list.

'We have to try to find out more about the people who died,' she said speculatively.

'Send the list to me,' Henriette told her. 'I know some-one in the police that I can ask.'

'I have someone I can ask, too,' Line said, but refrained from telling her that her father was a police officer. It seemed almost odd that Henriette had not discovered that when she had googled who she was and which of her stor-ies *VG* had published. The crime stories she had covered in the past had often mentioned Chief Inspector Wisting.

'I can check it out,' Henriette insisted.

'OK,' Line agreed.

Something happened over in the play corner. Amalie had obviously not got her way and was starting to complain loudly. 'She's getting tired,' Line explained, rising to her feet.

She went to fetch Amalie and lifted her on to her knee. 'When are you going to meet your informant again?' she asked.

'He'll phone if he has anything more to tell me.'

'We need more info on the robbery,' Line told her. 'Some names.'

Henriette agreed, and they remained sitting there, dis-cussing the possible connections to Simon Meier.

'The only thing I can think of is that Simon and the motorbike guy were together on taking the money,' Hen-riette said. 'Maybe they shared it. Simon went to Spain with his share, while the motorbike guy died. I used to think Simon had run off with the money on his own, but since I heard the rumour about the motorbike guy, I think it's more likely he had help.'

Line had spent the past few days trying to find a con-nection between Simon Meier and Lennart Clausen. The only thing that linked them so far was that they had grown up in the same street.

'You still believe he might be in Spain, then?' she remarked, as she returned her laptop to her bag.

'I think if we do find him, we'll find the answer to everything,' Henriette replied. 'Or if we find the money from the robbery,' she added with a smile.

Line returned her smile but felt constrained by not being able to tell her everything she knew. It would be difficult to work with Henriette once she realized that Line had withheld crucial information.

Henriette sat studying her facial expression. 'Penny for your thoughts,' she said. 'Do you have a theory about what happened to the money? Or is there something you haven't told me?'

Line busied herself with Amalie. 'I'm thinking of my news editor at *VG*,' she said, in an attempt to laugh off the question. 'He didn't want this story. At least, not before.'

Henriette chuckled along with her. 'He'll be sure to kick himself when he reads it,' she said.

45

Mortensen turned his laptop screen to face the others. 'I think this is blood,' he said, showing them an image of the steel edge on the pump machinery where one part of the metal was darker than the surrounding area. 'It reacts to luminol,' he added. 'I've prepared a sample for analysis.'

He went on to select another picture that showed a larger portion of the room. The place where Mortensen thought he had detected blood was marked with an arrow. In addition, there was an arrow on the floor, below the first one.

'I have a similar sample from there, too,' Mortensen told them, pointing. 'If it proves to be blood, then that will at least tell us something about what might have happened in there.'

Wisting tried to interpret what he could see. 'His head may have struck the steel edge before he fell to the floor.'

Mortensen nodded. 'It could have been an accident or the result of an argument,' he suggested. 'Pushing and shoving.'

'With fatal consequences,' Stiller commented.

'That's entirely possible,' Mortensen replied. 'But on the other hand, it might not be blood at all or have anything to do with our case.'

'Did you find anything else?' Wisting asked.

Mortensen produced a picture of a padlock with a key that he had found lying on the floor under the hatch. 'It's possible we may have some fingerprints on this,' he answered. 'I'm letting the Kripos lab take a look at it.'

Wisting was relieved he hadn't picked it up. 'Line has found something of interest regarding the pump house,' he said, explaining that Jan Gudim's father had held the original key. 'He was the manager of the water and sewage board.'

'They probably used it to hide drugs for years,' Audun Thule said.

Stiller agreed. 'But the chances of bringing charges are slim,' he decided.

'Was Gudim's alibi for the day of the robbery ever checked?' Wisting asked.

'Only as far as tracing his phone use. It was located at his home.'

'Where was his home at that time?' Mortensen probed. 'Where did he live?'

'In Kolbotn.'

'Do you think he'll talk if we bring him in for interview?'

'Doubt it. He's never confessed to anything or cooperated with the police in any way.'

Wisting glanced up at the board with the pictures of the possible robbers. 'We think Gudim drove the vehicle used in the raid?' he asked.

'Without a doubt,' Thule replied. 'His hobby is rally driving.'

'So, Jan Gudim and Aleksander Kvamme?'

'All the intelligence we have suggests that Kvamme was the main man,' Thule answered. 'Everything also suggests that Oscar Tvedt took part and got the blame when the money disappeared.'

Stiller stood up, walked across to the noticeboard and

took down the photo of Jan Gudim. 'We won't make a dent in this with traditional investigation methods,' he said. 'We'll have to approach them in a different way, with a different strategy. A tactical move.'

Wisting leaned back in his chair, realizing that Stiller had come up with a plan.

'Instead of confronting Gudim with shaky evidence, we'll have to use it to draw out something new,' Stiller went on. 'We have to coax out information about who else was in on the action.'

'How do we do that?' Thule asked.

'We'll use what we already know and have,' Stiller answered. He returned Gudim's picture to the board before taking out one of the boxes of cash and lifting it up on to the table. 'We use the money,' he said.

The three others in the room waited for him to continue. Stiller turned to face Audun Thule. 'You said Oscar Tvedt's mother died this summer?' he asked.

Thule nodded.

'Then we'll pay Gudim a visit in prison and show him the picture of one of the boxes of cash and say that it was found at her home after her death. That we've found the key to the pump house inside it and DNA belonging to Oscar Tvedt.'

Wisting liked the idea. It would hopefully provoke a reaction and, because Jan Gudim was in prison, they had complete control over everyone he was in contact with. All phone calls in and out of the prison were monitored, and all visits could be observed.

Stiller was a few steps ahead: 'We'll give him the impression that Oscar Tvedt has begun to communicate,' he went on. 'We'll tell him what nursing home he's in and that he's willing to talk to us. That should entice the other robbers to visit him to make sure he keeps his mouth shut.'

Audun Thule leaned forward across the table. 'You're going to occupy the wing where he's a patient?'

'I'll equip it with cameras and recording equipment and then pose as a patient or a nurse when he has a visitor,' Stiller said, smiling.

'That will have to be cleared at a high level,' Mortensen interjected.

'I can arrange that,' Wisting promised.

They discussed the details until Line arrived with Amalie and Wisting updated her with Stiller's plan.

'Henriette has a source in the circles around the robbers,' she said, repeating the theory that whoever stole the cash was later killed in a motorbike accident.

'Lennart Clausen,' Wisting said.

'That sounds likely,' Stiller agreed.

'Do you know the identity of her source?' Thule asked.

'No, but she conducted a series of in-depth interviews with professional criminals when she worked at *Goliat*,' Line explained. 'It's probably one of them. I have to go into Oslo tomorrow to speak to Kim Werner Pollen, Simon Meier's schoolfriend, who worked at Gardermoen. Then I thought I'd pop into the National Library and read those interviews. I know someone who works there who can look them out for me. Maybe there will be some interesting names there.'

Amalie, unsettled, tugged impatiently at her mother's arm. 'We'll have to go home,' Line said with a sigh as she lifted up her daughter.

Wisting accompanied her out.

'How much did the burglar alarm cost?' she asked, hoisting Amalie into the child seat at the back of her bike.

'I haven't had the bill yet,' Wisting told her.

'I think I want an alarm,' Line said. 'It's an old house, easy to pick the window locks.'

'I can phone Olve and get a quote,' Wisting suggested.

'Could you?'

He nodded and stood watching as she wheeled her bike home.

46

The air in the house was hot and stuffy. Line locked the front door behind her, but opened the verandah door in the living room as well as the window in Amalie's bedroom. Then she headed into the kitchen to butter a couple of slices of bread for her daughter.

'Mummy?'

Line turned around. Amalie approached, carrying the black cat from the garden. As she held it with both arms outstretched the animal made no protest.

'Be careful!' Line warned her, afraid that the cat might scratch and bite.

Her daughter laid her cheek on its unkempt fur. The cat calmly accepted this for a little longer, but then began to thrash about. It twisted out of her grasp, landed on all fours and darted away.

Amalie began to scream, mainly from surprise. Its claws had left two scratches on the back of one hand. Line gave Amalie her dummy and brought her into the bathroom, where she washed the wounds and applied a plaster.

After eating, Amalie was ready for a nap. She still slept for an hour or so in the middle of the day and snuggled her head into the pillow as soon as she lay down. Line drew down the roller blind to darken the room.

'Puss,' Amalie whimpered from the bed. Line leaned over her and ran her hand across her hair. Amalie was pointing at the wall. 'Puss,' she repeated from behind the dummy.

Line realized what she meant. The drawing they had made together a few days earlier was gone. All that was left was a tiny pinprick in the wall where the drawing pin had been.

'Yes, where is the pussycat?' Line asked, casting around for the drawing in case it had slid down between the bed and the wall.

It was nowhere to be found. Amalie could not give her any explanation and soon lost interest. She turned her head to one side and found a soft corner of the quilt to rub against her face.

Line carried the laundry into the utility room. In one of Amalie's pockets, she found a red crayon that her daughter must have taken from the play corner in the café.

With a sigh, she loaded the clothes into the washing machine, switched it on and headed downstairs to the office in the basement. Before she sat down, she stood staring at the noticeboard, which she had divided into two. On the left-hand side, she had hung pictures and clippings about the Gjersjø case. The right-hand side contained information about Lennart Clausen and his circle. Until now, she had failed to find any clear lines of connection between the two sides of the board.

She still had not spoken to Rita Salvesen, the mother of Lennart's child. Line had been unsure how to approach her. She lived in Spain and would have to be contacted by phone. It seemed contrived to call her under the pretext of the Simon Meier case. After a while, she worked out a plan.

The phone rang for a long time before anyone answered and then a bright, cheerful voice confirmed that she was Rita Salvesen.

Line identified herself. 'I work as a journalist, but I'm not calling to interview you or anything,' she said. 'I was just wondering if you knew that Bernhard Clausen was dead?'

A moment's silence ensued at the other end of the line. 'I've seen it in the news,' Rita Salvesen confirmed. 'But no one told me about it.'

'You're the only heir,' Line went on. 'That is to say, your daughter is.'

There was another silence.

'Why are you phoning, actually?'

'I've been working on an article about him,' Line explained. 'About his life. That was how I found out about you and Lennart. They say he's left everything to the Labour Party and that he has no heirs, that you've relinquished all claim.'

'That's not right,' Rita Salvesen said, her voice sounding obviously perturbed. 'I just saw no reason to have any contact with him after Lennart died. He and his father hardly ever spoke to each other, anyway.'

'That was what I reckoned,' Line said. 'That was why I phoned. I wanted to assure myself that everything was being handled fairly and above board.'

'What do I do now?' Rita asked.

'You can just get in touch with the district court in his home area and they'll help you with it. But the easiest way is probably to make contact with a lawyer.'

'Can you recommend anyone?'

Line had actually written an article about the distribution of deceaseds' estates and gave her the name of the lawyer who had helped her with it.

'Why weren't Lennart and his father on speaking terms?' she asked.

'His father was self-centred and mostly taken up with

politics,' Rita replied. 'He was always preoccupied with helping others instead of his own family.'

It sounded as if she was repeating something that Lennart had told her.

'In what way?'

'Well, for instance with Lennart's mother. She got cancer and died. There was medicine that could have helped her, but his father thought it would show a lack of solidarity if she were to get it.'

'Lack of solidarity?'

'He was mainly thinking about himself, about how it would look if he, as Health Minister, changed the rules just so that his wife could live longer.'

'Have you ever spoken to him?'

'Not when Lennart was alive. We hadn't been together long when he died, you see. But his father came to see us when Lena was one.'

It sounded as if Rita was reluctant to say anything further.

'Why did he come?' Line asked, mostly to keep the conversation going.

'I wondered about that, too,' Rita answered. 'He gave me a card with his direct number on it and said that if we needed help with anything just to get in touch. I called him a few years ago because we were going to move to Spain, and asked if I could borrow some money. He told me that wasn't what he had meant.'

'What did he mean, then?'

'That he could help if we were ever seriously ill or something.'

'Did you inherit anything from Lennart?' Line asked, in an effort to close in on what she was really after.

'No. He died before Lena was born.'

'Did he have money?'

Rita Salvesen gave a brief burst of laughter. 'He didn't even have a permanent job,' she said. 'But I suppose he got some money from his father.'

'But he had bought himself a motorbike?'

'I think he'd taken out a loan for that.'

'So you didn't get the impression that he had much money?'

'No.'

Line changed the subject before Rita Salvesen could start quizzing her about why she was asking.

'On a different note,' she said. 'You're from Kolbotn, aren't you?'

'Yes.'

'I'm going to write about an old missing-person case,' Line told her. 'Simon Meier. Do you remember him?'

'He was the one that drowned?'

'He disappeared near Gjersjø lake, yes,' Line replied. 'I've spoken to a number of people who grew up with him to find out how the other young people felt about someone of their own age disappearing like that.'

'Are you asking me about it?'

'I've spoken to Tommy Pleym, among others.'

'Tommy.' Rita laughed when she spoke his name. 'Surely he wasn't too bothered about it?'

'He didn't remember much,' Line replied.

'I don't either, to be honest.'

'Do you remember the day he disappeared?'

'Yes, they were searching with helicopters and all sorts, but I don't recall anything more than that.'

'That was when he was reported missing,' Line said. 'He went AWOL two days earlier.'

'I just remember the helicopter. But Lennart knew him.'

Line sat bolt upright and grabbed a pen. 'Oh, how?'

'They had played together when they were little, went to school together and all that. Simon lived just a few houses further along the street, but he was a bit strange. I don't think he and Lennart had any contact after they left school.'

That chimed with what Simon Meier's brother had told her.

'How did Lennart react when he went missing?' Line probed.

'I don't know if he reacted in any particular way, but he did mention that he knew him.'

'Was that long afterwards?'

'I think it was while it was in the newspapers and they were all talking about it.'

'How did he behave?'

'What do you mean?'

Line mulled this over for a few seconds but decided that the simplest thing would be to ask a direct question: 'Did he say or do anything that suggested he knew what had happened to Simon Meier?'

Rita did not react to the question. 'No, but he drowned, didn't he? That's what they all said.'

Line realized she would get no further with this and prepared to end the conversation. 'Someone thought they'd seen him in Spain,' she said, attempting to sound flippant.

'Well, I've never seen him,' Rita answered.

Line had no more questions. She rounded things off and leaned back in her chair. She may not have probed particularly deeply into the relationship between Simon Meier and Lennart Clausen, but it was enough to link the two sides of her noticeboard together.

47

Jan Gudim was incarcerated in Halden prison. They set off at 9 a.m. to arrive there by noon. Wisting was driving, with Thule beside him, while Stiller sat in the back seat. First they reached Horten, where they took the ferry across the Oslo fjord and then the motorway down to the jail, which was located near the Swedish border.

The prison was situated at the top of a hillside, surrounded by forest. The heather beyond the smooth, circular walls was scorched brown. Several of the pine trees on the fringes of the forest were bare and black, as if in the grip of some destructive disease.

It was one of the most modern prisons in the country. Education, vocational training and excellent opportunities for cultural and social diversion were the tools used for rehabilitation. But the impression created in the media was not entirely correct. Several years of cutbacks and budget trimming meant that prisoners spent increasingly lengthy periods of time behind closed doors.

They parked in an empty space at the far edge of the large car park and walked up to the entrance. Wisting rang the bell, gave their names and explained that they had an appointment with the prison governor.

Inside, two guards were waiting for them on the other side of an X-ray machine with a metal detector. Wisting took a plastic tray from a stack, emptied his pockets and pushed it across to the guard manning the X-ray machine.

The other waved him through the detector. Although the machine did not react, he had to undergo a body search all the same.

Thule and Stiller submitted to the same process before all three were escorted to the administration block, where they had to hand in their mobile phones.

'I need mine,' Stiller said. 'I have a case ongoing.'

The prison guard on the other side of the glass wall protested about this breach of normal procedure, but his arguments did not prevail.

The prison governor met them in a room equipped for monitoring the inmates. His name was engraved on a black badge fastened above his left breast pocket. *E. Kallmann.* They informed him about the case, without going into too much detail, and showed him the documents that gave them permission to listen in on Jan Gudim's phone conversations.

'Where does he call from?' Wisting asked.

'From the guardroom in his section.'

'From which phone? Can you show us?'

'Gudim is in section C, so we'll have to go out and walk.'

Wisting gave him a nod.

Kallmann led them out of the building, through a small grove of trees, towards another building further inside the area.

The prison was divided into separate building complexes. Kallmann explained that the idea behind this was to recreate everyday life, with prisoners moving from their residence to their employment and a separate activities space. It was intended to give them a perspective of time and place.

'Can he see us?' Thule asked, glowering at the two-storey building.

The prison governor shook his head. 'His living quarters are at the rear,' he said.

They let themselves in through a series of doors and walked along grey corridors with linoleum floors that squeaked under their shoes. They could hear some of the prisoners from another section hammering on metal and concrete. A shout reached them, muffled by locked doors and zigzag corridors.

The prison governor stopped in front of a cubicle and pointed at a cordless phone on a charger. 'They can either ring from here, or take the phone with them into their cell.'

'And when you're monitoring the calls?' Stiller asked. 'How does that work?'

'From an extension in the guardroom,' Kallmann explained. 'The conversation is set up from there.'

He nodded towards the adjacent room. Its glass walls looked out into the common areas. A prison guard was seated in front of a computer with the phone on the table beside him.

The three detectives exchanged looks. 'That won't work,' Thule said.

'Is there somewhere else we can sit and listen in?' Wisting asked.

The prison governor shook his head. 'Gudim doesn't have phone time until tomorrow evening,' he told them.

'Can he phone someone if something important crops up?'

Kallmann smiled. 'You're in a prison now,' he said. 'He can call his lawyer or the public authorities, and those are conversations we're not allowed to monitor.'

'I need the number of that phone,' Stiller said, pointing into the cubicle.

The prison governor nodded. He let himself into the guardroom, spoke to the guard sitting there and emerged clutching a note of the phone number.

Stiller took out his mobile phone. Kallmann raised his eyebrows but handed over the note and the number without a word and Stiller keyed it in. Shortly afterwards, the phone in the cubicle began to ring.

'OK,' Stiller said. 'We just need a guarantee that this is the phone he's going to use and that some other guard doesn't let him borrow his office.'

'I'll let my staff know,' Kallmann assured them.

He ushered them out of the building. On their way back to the administration building, Stiller called his colleagues at Kripos to action formal phone surveillance. 'Up and running in half an hour,' he said after ringing off.

Stiller and Thule were the ones who would conduct the interview. Wisting would watch via a monitor in the adjacent control room and observe through a one-way mirror. They received instructions about how they could contact the guard on duty when they were finished and spent a little time activating the video equipment before asking for Gudim to be brought in.

Wisting waited in the side room. He could hear everything they said, but they could not hear him.

Stiller flicked through to a blank page in his notebook. Thule had his notes collected in a folder. They had devised a detailed plan but were also prepared to improvise.

Almost ten minutes passed before the door opened. A guard nodded at the two officers and moved a metre or so into the room to check that everything was as it should be. Then he stepped aside and let Gudim enter.

He was tall and broad-shouldered with taut facial muscles.

Stiller and Thule stood up and gave their names without offering handshakes.

Gudim stepped forward to the empty chair but waited until the guard had left the room before he sat down.

'I haven't anything to say to you,' he said, leaning his arms on the table in front of him.

This opening remark was anticipated. Wisting had heard it many times before.

'You don't need to,' Stiller assured him. 'We can do the talking, but it's important that you listen.'

The man opposite didn't say a word.

'I work with a group at Kripos dealing with old, unsolved cases,' Stiller went on. 'Audun Thule is an inspector with Romerike police district,' he added with a gesture to one side. 'In 2003 he was responsible for the investigation of a robbery at Gardermoen airport.'

It was difficult to see on the monitor, but it seemed that a muscle twitched on Gudim's face.

'The case has been taken up again because part of the stolen money has been found,' Thule explained.

He drew a picture from his folder and pushed it across the table. The previous evening, they had gained access to Mrs Tvedt's apartment, which had lain empty since her death. Placing one of the boxes of cash at the bottom of a wardrobe, they had taken photographs of it.

'There's a total of 650,000 British pounds,' Stiller said.

'Along with the money, we found this,' Thule continued, putting down the picture of the torn-off cable with the jack plug attached. 'That's from the lead for earplugs on a walkie-talkie radio,' he clarified. 'Oscar Tvedt's DNA profile was found on it.'

He laid down the report from the DNA database.

'You know him,' Stiller said. 'You were arrested together in 2002.'

They had discussed the possibility of the conversation going two ways from this point onwards. Either Gudim would put a stop to it there and then, in order to speak to his lawyer, or he would come up with some kind of explanation.

Gudim cleared his throat.

'Oscar was a radio officer in the Telemark battalion,' he said. 'He worked on that sort of thing. Bought damaged equipment, tinkered with it, repaired it and sold it on. It could well be that he's had his fingers on it, but that doesn't mean he robbed the plane.'

'This photo was taken in Else Tvedt's home,' Thule said, pointing at the money. 'Oscar's mother. She died not long ago.'

These were rehearsed sentences. Wisting liked them. Their backs were covered if they had to play the recording of this interview at some future time.

On screen, Gudim turned away from the two investigators, as if he regretted having said anything at all.

'Together with the cash, we also found something interesting,' Stiller went on.

He put down a picture of the key. They had agreed not to say anything more. As far as Jan Gudim was concerned, the photo would reinforce the seriousness of the situation.

'Have you spoken to Oscar Tvedt lately?' Thule asked instead.

This question would create the impression that Oscar Tvedt was sufficiently recovered to be capable of holding a conversation.

'He stays at the Abildsø Nursing Home now, near Østensjø lake,' Stiller added. 'He's still in a wheelchair, but he's doing well.'

'We're meeting his lawyer again on Wednesday,' Thule said, as he began to pack up the papers. This was not a lie either. Frida Strand acted as Oscar Tvedt's guardian and Thule had made an appointment with her.

Stiller got to his feet and approached the intercom on the wall. 'Are you still refusing to speak to us?' he asked.

Gudim did not answer.

Stiller pressed the call button and declared that they were finished. Then he returned to the table and put down his business card.

'You know how it works,' he said. 'The first person who talks to us gets a deal.'

The door opened and a prison guard stepped inside. Stiller and Thule hovered for a moment before following the guard out and leaving Jan Gudim in the room.

Wisting turned towards the door as Stiller and Thule came in and walked up to the mirror.

'He's got something to think about now,' Thule said.

Gudim sat with his head tilted back, staring at the ceiling. Then he leaned forward, ran one hand over the table and swept up Stiller's business card. He glanced at it, turning it this way and that, before stuffing it into his pocket.

They waited in the control room until Gudim was collected and led back to his section, then they were escorted to the exit.

Wisting checked his phone when he had it returned to

him. Two missed calls, but nothing urgent. A guard led them through the various doors. As he opened the final door, his walkie-talkie radio crackled.

He answered the call.

'Are you still with the police officers?'

'Yes.'

'Just a brief message from the prison governor: he asked a moment ago to call his lawyer. They'll know who that refers to.'

The guard looked at Wisting.

Wisting nodded. They were well underway now.

48

Line parked her car in a marked space at the petrol station and ran through what she knew about Kim Werner Pollen. He had been in Simon Meier's class at primary and high school. After school he had been employed in a number of different jobs, including one as a baggage handler at Gardermoen airport. Now he ran his own filling station.

A couple of the petrol pumps were closed down, physically cordoned off, and a man was dismantling them. It looked as if a rubbish bin had caught fire.

Line waited until fewer customers were around before she switched on her recorder, dropped it into her bag and stepped out of her car. She had not found a phone number for Kim Werner Pollen, but she had called a number registered to the petrol station. One of the employees had answered and told her that Pollen would be in the office today.

A long-haired girl behind the counter was turning over hotdog sausages.

'I'd like to speak to Kim Werner Pollen,' Line said.

'In there,' the girl replied, using the tongs to point at an open door at the end of the counter. 'The last door on the left.'

Line followed her directions and found a chubby man in a T-shirt behind a desk.

'Hi,' she said, knocking on the doorframe. 'Kim Werner Pollen?'

The man looked up. A recent graze was evident on one cheek. 'That's me,' he said.

Line told him who she was. 'I'm trying to find out what happened to an old classmate of yours,' she explained. 'Simon Meier.'

'Then you'll need to take a course,' the man suggested.

Line did not understand what he meant.

'A diving course. Simon Meier's lying on the bottom of Gjersjø lake. You'll find him there.'

Line took a few steps into the room, moving towards an empty chair. 'I'm writing about the missing-person case,' she pressed on.

'You shouldn't bother,' Kim Werner Pollen interrupted her. 'All you'll achieve is to tear open old wounds and create false hope. Maybe it'll sell a few newspapers, maybe you'll be able to show off a bit and get some praise from your boss, but it won't help his family and friends any.'

His contemptuous comments sounded rehearsed. The arguments sounded learned by heart, as if he had been waiting for her and had prepared to give her the brush-off.

'Were you friends?' she asked.

'We were in the same class, at any rate.'

Line refused to budge. 'I've read all the old case documents,' she said. 'I got the impression that he didn't really have many friends.'

Kim Werner Pollen cocked his head. 'Is that what you're going to write?'

'I'm trying to search out a few different angles, and I'm really looking for someone who can tell me what they remember about the day he disappeared.'

The man behind the desk crossed his arms on his chest.

'Do you remember that day?' Line asked.

Kim Werner Pollen smiled condescendingly and shook his head. None of the others Line had spoken to had remembered the actual day Simon Meier had gone missing either.

'It was the same day as the robbery at Gardermoen airport,' Line went on. 'Didn't you work up there at that time?'

This was a question she had planned. It would seem casual and allow her to watch his reaction when she mentioned the robbery. His mouth opened and his jaw dropped; he blinked rapidly a number of times as the colour slowly drained from his face.

'I wasn't at work that day,' he said, and got to his feet. 'Actually, I'm a bit busy right now, so . . .'

'Yes, sorry,' Line said, half turning towards the door. 'It looked as if there had been a fire in one of the bins outside.'

'Just a minor inconvenience,' Pollen said, skirting around the desk. 'Someone must have thrown in a cigarette end or something.'

'Have you checked the CCTV cameras?'

'What?'

'The CCTV cameras,' Line repeated. 'To see what happened.'

'Out of order,' Pollen said, touching the wound on his cheek and ushering her out.

'It could have been a lot worse,' she said.

Pollen followed her out towards the retail area. 'Yes, it could,' he answered. Part of the scab on his cheek had loosened and she saw a trickle of blood. 'Fortunately, it was OK this time.'

Line wondered whether she should buy something before she left and try to drop Lennart Clausen's name into the conversation, but Pollen's tone of voice had changed from sour and sarcastic to somewhat hostile. Mumbling her thanks, she left and glanced up at the nearest CCTV camera before clambering into her car and switching off the recorder.

The airport robbery was something Kim Werner Pollen was obviously reluctant to discuss. In 2003 he had worked on baggage handling and could have had access to the internal information the robbers required.

After turning on the ignition, she made her way towards Oslo. As she drove, she played back the entire conversation from the petrol station. She listened to it twice, and the feeling that had come over her in the office was reinforced. Kim Werner Pollen seemed to have prepared what he was going to say, as if someone had warned him that she might turn up. Maybe even heavy-handedly, she imagined, thinking of the cut on his cheek and the fire in the bins.

She wondered whether she should call her father but decided that she had perhaps read too much into it. She had been travelling around asking questions for several days now but could not envisage who might have put pressure on Pollen. Maybe he had just been having a bad day. He had injured himself and had had to cope with an arson attempt. That was more than enough to make him grumpy. And anyway, her father had other things on his mind at the moment.

49

Immediately after they had crossed the River Glomma, Wisting turned off from the E6 motorway and drove into a petrol station. He filled the tank while Stiller phoned his colleagues at Kripos to play back the conversation between Jan Gudim and his lawyer. He connected his phone to the hands-free set-up in the car so that all three of them could hear it:

'Harnes here.'

'It's Gudim.'

'It's been a while.'

'You must come down here to see me.'

'Has something happened?'

'I need to talk to you.'

'I can come down on Thursday.'

'You have to get in a car this minute and come right now. At once.'

Silence ensued.

'That'd be difficult,' was the lawyer's eventual response.

They could hear Gudim's breathing.

The lawyer cleared his throat. 'What is this about?'

'I had a visit from two detectives today. One of them was from the Cold Cases Group at Kripos.'

'I see,' the lawyer said, and suddenly his voice grew cautious.

'The other one was in charge of the investigation into the airport robbery at Gardermoen in 2003.'

Another silence.

'Did they have any documents with them?'

'Photos and DNA reports, but no charges, if that's what you're thinking of. But it seemed as if it's just a matter of time.'

The lawyer took a deep breath. 'Sounds as if I'd better come, then. I'll be in my car within half an hour.'

'Great.'

Then the connection was cut.

'Just as expected,' Wisting remarked. 'He hasn't said anything compromising on the phone, not even to his lawyer.'

'I know Harnes,' Stiller said. 'Gudim is going to use him to relay messages from the prison.'

'He'll warn the others in the gang,' Thule said, nodding. 'Get them to make sure Oscar Tvedt keeps his mouth shut.'

Wisting opened the car door. 'I need a hotdog before we drive any further,' he said.

50

There were no free parking spaces in the streets around the National Library, and Line ended up parking her car as far down as the Vika neighbourhood. While she walked back, she rang Sofie to find out how Amalie was doing.

'We've only just eaten,' Sofie told her.

It dawned on Line that she felt hungry, too. 'Sorry for dumping so much on you,' she said. 'But this has involved more work than I thought.'

'Isn't that good, though?' Sofie asked. 'You'll be submitting an invoice for every hour, won't you?'

'Yes, I guess so,' Line assured her. 'And luckily, she'll start at nursery next week.'

'You'll need to get used to that,' Sofie advised. 'You won't be able to travel into Oslo whenever you like. You'll have to be around to pick her up from nursery every day.'

'I know,' Line replied as she climbed the steps outside the hundred-year-old library building. 'Hopefully, I'll be able to finish up this week.'

The entrance doors of the huge edifice opened in front of her. She thanked Sofie once again for helping her out before she set foot inside.

She had been here several times while she worked in *VG*. Most of the material was held in storage and had to be ordered in advance. She knew that if she phoned before 9 a.m., whatever she was looking for would be available by noon. The bundle of magazines was already laid out in the reading room for her, all in chronological order. *Goliat* had published twenty-seven editions before it folded in 2012.

She flicked through the bundle and fairly quickly found Henriette's name in a report about the crime division of Oslo police. In the next edition, she located a story about security guards and then a report about Norwegian criminals in Spain. In the following issue, the magazine introduced a series of in-depth interviews with known criminals. The first of these was with the leader of Norway's Hells Angels. In the next number, a prominent alcohol smuggler told his story. This was followed by a gang leader serving a sentence for murder.

She leafed further through and found an interview in which a man stood with his back to the photographer. He was referred to as 'one of the most powerful figures in the Norwegian underworld'. He had been acquitted of killing a Pakistani gang leader and the Director General had recently indicted him in a major narcotics case. The report drew a picture of how he had been caught in a network of criminals but had himself never committed any serious crime. It sounded as if this man could be Henriette's source.

The homicide case was described in detail and illustrated with archive photographs. Line felt her unease gradually increase as she continued reading. She took her laptop from her bag and opened the folder Audun Thule had collated on the airport robbery suspects. The date of the homicide given in the interview coincided with the murder of which Aleksander Kvamme had been acquitted. This could not be a fluke: Henriette must have interviewed Kvamme. She also noted that the narcotics case was the same one for which Jan Gudim had been convicted.

Her unease was replaced by a feeling of panic that lodged deep inside her chest.

The man suspected of being the ringleader of the airport robbery could well be the informer Henriette had been speaking to. She could quite simply be implicated in recruiting Aleksander Kvamme as a source. A tremor ran through Line's body as she realized what this meant, that Henriette could be in danger.

She was relieved that she had withheld information about the Clausen link and the discovery of the cash from her colleague.

Line used her phone to take photos of the pages before hurrying out of the building. She headed for her car and called Henriette, but her phone rang out, unanswered.

Slinging her bag over her shoulder, she began to write a text message asking Henriette to phone her. Just at that moment she felt a powerful push on her back, propelling her forward and making her drop her mobile. At the same time she was whirled around and someone yanked at her bag. Screaming at the top of her voice, she grabbed hold of her bag and held it close to her body. A man in dark clothing, his face hidden by a motorbike helmet, raised his hand and punched her head. She staggered but did not let go of her bag. The man struck again, this time a harder blow, and she was sent flying, finally landing sprawled on the ground. He tugged at the bag strap and kicked her in the stomach. Line released her grip and covered her head with her arms. Her attacker snatched the bag and ran. When Line looked up, he was on his way into a side street, where he pulled out her laptop, threw away her bag and leapt on to a waiting motorbike. Line struggled to her feet. The number plate was bent, making it impossible to read the registration. With a roar, it was gone.

Line looked around, but no one seemed to have realized what had happened. Or if they had, no one had paid any attention.

She picked up her phone. The screen was smashed, but it looked as if it was still functioning. Crossing the street, she retrieved her bag and gathered her scattered belongings. Only once she was settled behind the steering wheel of her car did the reaction come. She shook uncontrollably, sobbed and gasped for breath. Finally, she managed to collect her thoughts. It could have been a random attack, but they had only been after her laptop. Her purse and the rest of the contents of her bag had been of no interest to them.

Her Mac contained all the information she had accumulated on Simon Meier, Lennart Clausen and his father, as well as photos, notes and all the reports she had written for her father. Thankfully, everything was stored on iCloud, so she could access all of it from her computer at home. But the more she thought about it, the more convinced she became that the attacker wanted to know what she knew. The same person who had threatened Kim Werner Pollen to keep his mouth shut at the petrol station. Fortunately, her laptop was password protected. It would not be easy to gain access to it.

She checked her phone again. Instead of calling the police, she dialled her father's number.

51

It was 5.30 p.m. when Wisting parked outside Abildsø Nursing Home in Oslo. Somewhere along the E6 they would have passed Harnes, Gudim's lawyer, on his way to Halden prison.

The nursing home where Oscar Tvedt was a patient was barely distinguishable from the other residential blocks, but it was more rustic, with extensive recreation areas adapted for wheelchair users.

They met the manager in her office. In addition to a charge nurse, a lawyer from the local authority was also present. She sat stiffly with a grim expression on her face.

Stiller led the conversation. 'Thanks for seeing us at such short notice,' he began. 'As I explained on the phone, we believe one of your patients is under threat.'

'Who are we talking about?' the manager asked.

'We've received information about threats made in connection with a major, ongoing case,' Stiller continued. 'It's very important that no one finds out anything about our presence here.'

The three women nodded.

'The patient we're talking about is Oscar Tvedt,' Stiller went on.

A short cry of surprise came from the charge nurse. 'But he's practically in a vegetative state,' she protested. 'And has been for more than ten years.'

'We're aware of that . . .' Stiller replied. 'But that doesn't change the level of threat. I can't go into much detail, but we must take precautionary measures.'

'In what way?'

'We'll place two undercover detectives here until the situation is resolved.'

The lawyer leaned forward. 'Wouldn't it be more appropriate to remove the patient and install him in a more secure location?' she asked, adjusting her glasses.

'We don't think that would be in Oscar Tvedt's best interests. This is where he lives, and this is where he receives the daily medical care he needs.'

'What about the employees and other patients?' the manager asked. 'The rest of the patients here are elderly and suffer from dementia. Changes in routine can be disturbing for them.'

'That's been taken into account,' Stiller assured her. 'We expect the situation will be cleared up in no more than a couple of days.'

Wisting felt his phone vibrate inside his pocket. He fished it out and glanced at it. He saw it was Line, but she would have to wait.

'How will you arrange this surveillance, from a practical point of view?' the charge nurse asked. 'There are visitors here every day.'

'Our people will look like ordinary visitors,' Stiller explained. 'We also intend to equip Tvedt's room with video cameras to record anything suspicious.'

'You're going to film our staff inside his room, while they're working?' the charge nurse queried.

Stiller fixed his eyes on her. 'Is that a problem?'

He received no answer.

'There will be a rota,' he continued. 'I'll come back tomorrow morning to be here in person.'

The lawyer held up her hand in warning. 'Wait a minute,' she said. 'It seems as if you're using the patient as a kind of bait. Do we have any guarantee that no one will be injured?'

Wisting glanced at her. She was sharp, he thought, and should really use her legal expertise somewhere other than the local-government sector.

'I can't guarantee anything if we don't take appropriate measures,' Stiller objected. 'As I said, we're talking about a very short period of time until the situation is cleared up.'

Line phoned again. Wisting excused himself and stepped out into the corridor to answer.

'It's me,' Line said.

Wisting could discern a note of desperation in her voice.

'Has something happened?' he asked.

'Someone has stolen my laptop,' Line told him.

'Where did this happen?'

'In the street, after I'd been to the National Library. A man in a motorbike helmet and gloves came along, grabbed my bag, took my laptop and then jumped on a motorbike.'

'Are you hurt?'

'A few scratches,' Line said, pausing for a moment before adding: 'I don't think it was random. I think it has to do with the investigation.'

'Have you phoned the police?'

'Should I?'

'This was a robbery, Line. You have to report it.'

'OK.'

'Where are you now?'

'In my car, in a street down from the National Library.'

'I'm in Oslo, too,' Wisting told her. 'I'll come to you.'

They ended their conversation and Wisting returned to the others. 'We have to go,' he said.

Thule and Stiller got to their feet. 'We're finished here anyway,' Stiller said, with a nod. He checked the time and turned to the manager: 'Our people will be here in an hour.'

None of the three women had any further comment to make.

'What's up?' Thule asked when the door closed behind them.

'Line's been attacked,' Wisting said. 'Someone stole her laptop. She's down at the National Library.'

He rushed out ahead of them and jumped into the car. Stiller directed him through a short cut while Wisting told them what he knew. A police patrol vehicle was parked behind Line's car when they arrived and a police officer with a notepad and recorder was taking her statement. A woman in uniform scanned the ground.

Wisting hung the lanyard with his police ID around his neck before he stepped out. Thule and Stiller followed suit.

The officer taking the statement looked as if he had finished. Thrusting the recorder into his pocket, he turned to face them. His gaze rested on their police IDs.

'I think we have everything under control here,' he said in a quizzical tone.

'I hope so,' Stiller said. He lifted his police ID from his chest. 'Adrian Stiller, Kripos,' he said. 'She's one of us,' he added, with a nod in Line's direction.

'A colleague?' the policeman asked, turning towards her.

Line shook her head. Wisting approached her, held her by the shoulders and pulled her towards him.

'She's working with us as a special adviser,' Stiller clarified. 'She was on duty when she was attacked.'

The policewoman who had examined the ground where the attack had taken place now joined them.

'I suggest you call out the crime division,' Stiller suggested. 'They'll be able to gather all the CCTV footage in the vicinity. One of the cameras might have caught the motorbike.'

'Is this linked to the case you're working on?' the police officer asked.

'We can't exclude that possibility,' Stiller replied.

'Bag-snatching isn't uncommon,' the policewoman commented.

'On this particular occasion, it's an unusual occurrence,' Stiller said.

He fumbled in his inside pocket. 'Here's my card,' he said, handing it to the policeman. 'I'd like you to let me know if you track down the motorbike.'

The policeman took it. 'We're finished here,' he said.

Stiller turned to Line. 'We'll take your car,' he said, meaning himself and Thule. 'You can go with your father.'

Line gratefully handed over her keys. Wisting appreciated Stiller's quick thinking but refrained from saying anything.

'This might have nothing to do with the case,' Thule said. 'But we have to take it into consideration. It means we have a different situation now. The stakes have been raised.'

Stiller agreed. 'But all the same, we're the ones who make the rules,' he added.

52

The chairs scraped across the floor when they drew them up to the table in the basement at Wisting's house. Line sat at one end. A headache was brewing and she felt how swollen the left side of her face was where the punches had landed.

Espen Mortensen had also arrived and he was keen to know how anyone could have traced her. 'How did they find you?' he asked.

'I think someone may have followed me from the petrol station,' Line answered, explaining her encounter with Kim Werner Pollen. 'I think he may have been the inside man at the airport.'

'But how could they know you were working on the case?'

Line had spent her time in the car on the way home from Oslo reflecting on the various possibilities. 'Someone I've spoken to must have been directly involved in the airport robbery, or else Henriette must have mentioned me to her informer.'

She had forwarded the pictures she took of the interview with Aleksander Kvamme to her father and now used his iPad to show them to the others.

'But surely that also puts her in danger,' Thule pointed out. 'Have you spoken to her today?'

Line shook her head. 'I was trying to get hold of her when I was attacked.'

'Try again,' Stiller instructed.

Line took out her phone. It rang, but there was still no answer.

'Wouldn't she have phoned you back when she missed your call?' Stiller asked. 'It's been more than two hours since you tried.'

Line wrote a brief message asking Henriette to call her. 'She might be busy with something,' she said, but realized that she felt troubled. 'How much can I say when I speak to her?'

'We have to warn her,' her father said. 'You can tell her a police source has told you that Aleksander Kvamme is a suspect in the robbery investigation.'

'That's not a problem,' Thule agreed. 'Who else have you spoken to about the robbery?'

'No one,' Line answered. 'I've just been talking about Simon Meier.'

Mortensen sat back in his chair and tried to summarize: 'So if the attack has something to do with the case, we don't really know whether "the case" is the airport robbery or the missing-person investigation?'

'They're both connected,' Thule pointed out.

'Who have you spoken to about the missing-person case?' Stiller asked.

Line had drawn up a list, but it was not a lengthy one. In addition to Henriette, there was Simon's brother, Kjell Meier, and the officer in charge of the original investigation, Ulf Lande.

'The only outsiders were Tommy Pleym and Kim Werner Pollen,' she said.

'I'll take a closer look at them,' Thule told her.

Just then, Stiller received a phone call, got to his feet and headed outside.

'You've spoken to people about Bernhard Clausen as well?' Mortensen asked.

'Only people in the Party,' Line replied. 'Edel Holt and Guttorm Hellevik. I also have an appointment with Trygve Johnsrud on Wednesday.'

Audun Thule stood up. 'I have to get back to my hotel,' he said. 'But all things considered, this could benefit the investigation. These people have been lying low for years, believing that both the robbery and the missing-person case have been forgotten. Once we started rooting around, we scared them out. That's good. People like that are always easier to catch when they're on the move.'

Having finished his phone conversation, Stiller returned. 'It was from Halden prison,' he explained. 'Harnes, the lawyer, arrived at a quarter to four. He's just left.'

Thule looked at his watch. 'Almost three hours,' he commented. 'They must have had a lot to talk about.'

Stiller's phone rang again. He took the call without leaving the room this time, answering, 'Yes,' and 'OK,' before he finished. 'The undercover detectives are in place,' he told them, referring to the nursing home at Abildsø. 'The cameras have been installed. They're wireless. We can watch from here, if we like.'

'I have to pick up Amalie,' Line said, pushing her chair away from the table. Her father offered to do that for her. 'It'll be fine,' she insisted.

Stiller returned her car keys. On the way out she visited her father's bathroom and looked at herself in the mirror. The skin was blue, almost black, beside her left eye.

*

Sofie and the girls were out in the garden when she arrived. Amalie ran towards her and threw her arms around her mother's neck. Line swung her up.

'What's happened?' Sofie asked.

'I tripped,' she said. 'Dropped my phone and broke the screen as well.'

Amalie pushed away from her and looked up at her face.

'It's all right,' Line told her, kissing her daughter on the cheek.

'Have you seen a doctor?' Sofie asked. 'You could have concussion.'

'It honestly looks worse than it is,' Line replied, smiling. 'I think I'll just go home and rest.'

Sofie followed her to the car. 'Shall I take her tomorrow, too?' she asked.

'You don't need to,' Line answered, putting Amalie into the child seat. 'I'm not planning on going anywhere tomorrow.'

When they parked at home, the black cat was sitting in front of the steps, licking its fur. Amalie rushed towards it, but the cat, alarmed, leapt up and disappeared.

As Line let herself in, it crossed her mind that she must remind her father to talk to the alarm company for her. The idea that a stranger had sneaked inside her house appeared more likely following the attack.

For their supper she made a smoothie with yogurt and fruit. Afterwards, she gave Amalie a bath and read to her for a while before she fell asleep.

When she sat down in front of her computer in the basement office, it dawned on her that her travel insurance might well cover the theft of her laptop. She logged into the insurance company's website but found that she needed both confirmation from the police and the exact specifications of the stolen machine.

There was also a function on the stolen Mac that meant she could trace its whereabouts at any time, but that depended on the laptop being connected to the Internet. She checked all the same, but nothing came up.

She sat reading the online newspapers. Bernhard Clausen's funeral received extensive coverage, with photographs of the well-known politicians and former ministers who had attended. Jonas Hildre had been present, representing *Dagbladet*. The report was followed by links to other stories, including an article about the arson attack at his cabin and the book he had been working on.

There was also an interview with Arnt Eikanger. He spoke of Bernhard Clausen as his political mentor and talked about their friendship. The interview included pictures of Eikanger in a checked shirt, chopping wood. Other Party colleagues were also present and told of how Eikanger had filled Clausen's shoes. It concluded with speculation as to whether he would be the country's next Justice Minister if the Labour Party won the general election in four weeks' time.

53

Amalie's crying woke Line. The clock on the bedside table gave the time as just past 5 a.m. She cast aside the quilt and went in to see her.

Her daughter was sitting on the bed. 'The man,' she said, stretching out her arms.

Line lifted her up. 'It was just a bad dream, sweetheart,' she consoled her daughter, and handed her the dummy.

Amalie buried her head in the crook of Line's neck as her mother carried her into her own bed. Line could feel her heart hammering inside her small ribcage.

Switching on the light above the bedside table, she snuggled up to her daughter. Amalie lay babbling behind her dummy. Line stroked her hair until she grew quiet and was breathing more evenly.

Line lay wide awake. The motor on the fridge kicked into action and hummed steadily. A car started up somewhere and drove off. Her head ached. She got up again, took a painkiller and returned to bed. Only once the first rays of daylight began to filter through the sides of the roller blind did she finally drop off.

When she woke again, it was nearly half past eight and her headache had dissipated. Already awake, Amalie had gone to her room to fetch some dolls and was playing happily.

'We have to hurry,' Line said. There was a meeting at her father's house at 9 a.m.

She let Amalie play with her dolls at the table while they ate. Then she headed to the bathroom before getting her daughter ready.

'Shall we go see Grandpa?' she asked.

'Grandpa!' Amalie yelled with delight.

A note fell on to the steps when she opened the front door. It must have been caught in the gap between the door and the frame.

Line felt a stab of anxiety. She picked up the paper and unfolded it. It was Amalie's cat drawing, the one that had been pinned to the wall in her bedroom. Beneath the sketch, something was written in clumsy handwriting: *Curiosity killed the cat.*

Amalie tugged at her. 'Mummy.'

Line looked all around as the door started to close behind her. 'Wait,' she said.

She wanted to go back inside and find a plastic bag so that the drawing could be forensically examined, but as she turned, she caught sight of it. The black cat was hanging by the tail from a rope looped over the door handle. Its lips were drawn back and the teeth exposed in a deathly grimace. Something was running from its open mouth and dripping on to the steps.

Her stomach tensed with a mixture of disgust and fear. She whirled around again.

'Mummy,' Amalie whimpered. There was nothing to suggest she had seen the dead cat.

'Let's go,' Line said, hurriedly pushing her daughter in front of her, towards the street, without either closing or locking the door behind her. She was filled with panic but knew better than to do anything that might contaminate the scene.

54

Wisting stood in the doorway. 'What's happened?' he asked.

Line looked over her shoulder. 'There's a dead cat hanging on my front door,' she mouthed, gasping for breath.

Wisting stepped aside and let his daughter and grandchild move inside. 'What did you say?' he asked as he closed the door behind them.

Line handed him the sheet of paper: *Curiosity killed the cat.*

'The cat,' Line explained in a whisper. 'The one Amalie's been playing with. Someone has killed it.'

Espen Mortensen and Audun Thule appeared from the basement and Wisting showed them the drawing.

'Yesterday's attack wasn't random, then,' Thule said. 'They wanted to know what you'd found out, and now they're scared you might dig up more.'

'I just left the house,' Line told them. 'The door's still open and the cat's hanging there.'

'Mortensen will take care of it,' Wisting said. Mortensen nodded and made for the door.

'Have you spoken to the security company?' Line asked. 'I need that alarm. The drawing was on the wall in Amalie's bedroom. Someone's been inside my house. In Amalie's room.'

Mortensen's CSI van started up outside. Wisting carefully laid aside the sketch. 'I'll phone them,' he reassured her. 'But until then I think you and Amalie should move in here with me.'

Line made no protest.

Wisting picked up his granddaughter. 'We'll go upstairs,' he said, locking the basement door.

'When did that drawing disappear?' Thule asked, once they were seated at the kitchen table.

'It must have been on Saturday,' Line answered, 'while Amalie and I were at the play park. When I got home, the door wasn't locked.'

She turned to face her father. 'You said you'd seen a man come out of my driveway.'

Wisting nodded. He had noticed him behind Line's parked car. When he emerged, he had turned right and walked down the street. The man had been dressed in dark clothing: that was all he could say about him.

'In that case, it was before you'd spoken to Kim Werner Pollen?' Thule asked.

'Yes.'

'I've checked on Tommy Pleym as well,' Thule continued. 'It can't have been him. He's been in hospital since Sunday.'

'Why's that?'

'I don't know yet,' Thule replied. 'I got it from a message on the operations log. It's coded as a violent crime, with him as the victim, but I haven't spoken to the investigator yet.'

'I must get hold of Henriette,' Line said. 'She may be even more at risk than I am.' She grabbed her phone. 'She's still not answering,' she said, removing the phone from her ear. 'Can you check police records and see if anything has happened to her?'

They sat in a huddle at the kitchen table. Wisting took out his iPad and logged on to the search tool.

'Henriette Koppang,' Line reminded him.

Wisting keyed in the name, confining the search to the last seven days. No result.

'Is there anyone else you can call?' he asked. 'Someone who knows her?'

Line shook her head.

'I can find her parents,' Wisting suggested, opening the population register.

There were three listings of her name.

'Her daughter's called Josefine,' Line told him. 'She's five.'

Wisting found the right Henriette Koppang. Her mother was dead, and her father was listed as living abroad.

'See who Josefine's father is, then,' Line asked. 'I think they live together.'

Wisting keyed in the further search but, at that moment, Line's phone rang. 'It's her,' she said. She answered and turned on the phone's loudspeaker.

'Hi,' Henriette said. 'I know you've been trying to call me. Sorry. There's been a lot going on here at home.'

'Has something happened?' Line asked.

'We've bought a new car, you see,' Henriette explained. 'Neither me nor my bank account were ready for that.'

Wisting lifted Amalie on to his knee and let her take charge of the iPad.

'Apart from that, I've spoken to the guy I know in the police,' Henriette went on.

'Oh?' Line replied.

'I think I've found out who may have taken the money. The guy who died in the motorbike accident was called

Lennart Clausen. He was the son of the politician, Bernhard Clausen.'

Wisting moved closer. Line glanced across at him, uncertain of how to respond. 'The one who just died?' she asked.

'Yes,' Henriette answered at the other end.

Wisting wrote *Aleksander Kvamme* on a sheet of paper and pushed it towards her.

'I've also spoken to someone in the police,' Line said. 'Somebody who works in intelligence. He told me that a man called Aleksander Kvamme was probably the ringleader in the airport robbery.'

Henriette Koppang repeated the name.

'Do you know him?'

'I know who he is,' Henriette replied. 'I interviewed him for *Goliat* once, but I don't think he's a front-runner. I got the impression that he likes to boast about things. The police fall for it, of course, but most of the charges against him have been dropped. They once thought he'd killed a Pakistani guy, but he was later acquitted.'

'Have you spoken to him recently, in connection with Simon Meier?'

'No, but if your policeman thinks there's something in it, maybe I should.'

'I don't think you should do that,' Line warned her. 'At least not until we have more information. I think we should concentrate on Lennart Clausen.'

'Agreed,' Henriette said. 'We must find out more about him. If he took the money, he must have hidden it in a secure location. We have to find someone who might know where that would be.'

'I can try to track down some of his friends,' Line said.

'Then you can continue to make inquiries in criminal circles.'

'OK,' Henriette said. 'How are things otherwise?'

Wisting saw that his daughter looked hesitant.

'Fine,' she answered. 'Just fine.'

'Great – we'll speak later, then!'

The conversation drew to a close and Line rang off.

'I think we should prioritize a chat with Tommy Pleym,' Wisting said. 'Find out who beat him up.'

'I looked into Kim Werner Pollen,' Thule said. 'The fire wasn't reported to either the police or the security company.'

'Suspicious,' Wisting commented.

'I found one more thing,' Thule went on. 'In 2002, according to the vehicle licensing authority, he bought a motorbike from Jan Gudim. Those two know each other. He has to be the inside guy – he worked at the airport at the time.'

55

The sun slanted through the venetian blinds in the private ward and one of the shadows settled on Oscar Tvedt's face and eyes.

Stiller crossed to the windows and adjusted the slats. Oscar Tvedt blinked and his twisted mouth made a gurgling sound. According to the charge nurse, that was as much as he could articulate. He was both physically and mentally disabled. Despite physiotherapy and other forms of exercise, he was slipping more and more into a vegetative state. He could open his eyes and breathe unassisted, but had no voice and very seldom responded to what was happening around him. He was reminiscent of a doll. His eyes were open, but his face was emaciated and his eyes were empty.

Stiller cast around for something to say, struggling to explain his presence. 'I'm a police investigator,' he said in a loud voice, as if speaking to an elderly person.

The face of the man in the bed was unresponsive, but it was possible he could hear and understand what Stiller was saying.

'We've found the cash from the Gardermoen airport robbery,' he continued. 'All of it. Worth more than 80 million kroner today.'

Another gurgling sound came and Stiller moved closer to the bed. Oscar Tvedt lay with his arms by his sides. The palms of his hands seemed dry and his nails were long.

'It was a perfect robbery, until the cash went missing.' Stiller leaned over the man in the bed. 'I think you got the blame for that,' he said. 'Your gang agreed that you had run off with the cash. They needed a scapegoat, someone to blame so that they could take their anger out on him. That person was you.'

There was no reaction to be detected on Oscar Tvedt's face. He appeared unperturbed, as if he lay there resting.

'They say you don't possess the power of logical thought,' Stiller went on. 'That the brain injury they inflicted on you means your ability to learn, remember and understand is limited. But I'd like to believe there's one thing you've spent your time here thinking about. The money. What happened to the money?'

He crossed to the other side of the room and pulled a chair slightly towards the bed. When he sat down, Oscar Tvedt had closed his eyes.

'Fine,' Stiller said. 'I don't know what happened to it either. That doesn't really interest me, but whatever happened, it cost Simon Meier his life. That's why I'm here. That's why I'm going to find out what took place.'

His earplug crackled. The detective seated at the entrance of the nursing home whispered: 'Two men in blue overalls just went in. Muscular-looking brutes. Apparently from Flex Ventilation. One of them is carrying a large bag. I'm going in after them.'

'Copy,' he answered, pushing the chair back into place before he left the room.

Further along the corridor there was a table with a Thermos of coffee and some cups laid out. Stiller sat down, took out his phone and found the live-stream of Oscar Tvedt's room.

The men in overalls appeared at the foot of the corridor, where they knocked on the nearest door and went inside without waiting for a response. Presumably, no one was there, as the men returned a couple of minutes later. One was holding an iPad in his hands while the other was carrying the bag. Stiller did not recognize either of them.

They knocked on the door on the other side of the corridor and stepped inside. Stayed for two minutes again and then re-emerged. The same procedure was repeated as they trawled along the corridor. They nodded briefly to Stiller, disguised as a care worker, as they passed.

The next room was Oscar Tvedt's. When they knocked and went inside, Stiller got to his feet. 'Come now,' he spoke into the microphone.

The detective made an appearance at the end of the corridor. Stiller headed for the door, adjusted the gun concealed inside his jacket, and watched the footage on his phone.

'There's someone lying in here,' the man with the bag said.

'He's sleeping,' the other man replied. 'Just let's get this over with.'

The first man drew a measuring instrument shaped like a funnel from his bag. He lifted it to the ceiling and opened the air-vent valve.

'Eight seven two,' he said, reading off a number on the instrument display.

The other man seemed to make a note of this. Several values were read off.

Stiller raised his left wrist to his mouth. 'I think they're measuring the room temperature,' he said into the microphone.

The detective further down the corridor held up his thumb before returning to his post at the nursing-home entrance.

The men exited and moved into the next room while Stiller filled a cup with coffee. His phone buzzed as he took the first mouthful. He swallowed and answered quietly.

'This is Einar Harnes, I'm a lawyer,' the caller introduced himself. 'Jan Gudim is my client. I understand that you and one of your colleagues interviewed him in Halden prison yesterday.'

'We had a chat with him,' Stiller corrected.

'He'd like to pick up from that meeting,' the lawyer explained.

'What's it about?'

'He wants to make a statement about the airport robbery,' the lawyer answered. 'Can we make an appointment? Preferably today. He's ready to talk.'

56

Wisting put the phone down on the table and turned to Thule. 'Jan Gudim wants to give a statement,' he said.

Audun Thule put his arms behind his head and leaned back in his chair. 'That's a surprising turn of events.'

'What does it mean?' Line asked.

'It means that Stiller's plan won't work,' Wisting told her. 'His lawyer contacted us instead of some of the other robbers.'

He turned to face Thule. 'You two were a bit too convincing, perhaps.'

'I'll take a confession any time,' Thule said with a smile.

'Do you think he's going to confess?' Line asked.

Thule shrugged. 'It remains to be seen, but I can't see any other reason for him to speak to us again.'

'Stiller has made an appointment for five o'clock,' Wisting said. 'This case could be done and dusted by tonight.'

'Then we'll have to get moving,' Thule said. 'An Oslo detective is going to Ullevål Hospital at two o'clock to interview Tommy Pleym. We have permission to accompany him. Then we can pick up Stiller before heading for Halden.'

Wisting glanced at his daughter. 'You'll be left on your own,' he said. 'Is that OK?'

'It's fine, as long as you keep me posted.'

Wisting looked around the basement. 'Will you sit in here or upstairs?'

'Upstairs,' Line replied. 'You can lock up this area, but I'll need my computer. It's at home.'

'I'll come down with you to get it.'

They brought Amalie with them too. Mortensen had placed the dead cat in a box and was busy washing down the door when they arrived.

'I've had an answer from Kripos,' he said, straightening up. 'There was blood in the pump house, right enough.'

'DNA?' Wisting asked.

'That's the next step.'

Line and Amalie went inside to pack some toiletries, clothes and other items they would need if they were going to be away for a few days. Mortensen moved to the CSI van and brought something from the passenger seat.

'I found this on Line's car,' he said, holding up an evidence bag containing a black plastic box about the size of a matchbox. 'It's a GPS tracker with a magnet bracket,' he explained. 'It was attached under the wheel arch.'

'A tracker unit,' Wisting said thoughtfully.

'Someone has been following her movements,' Mortensen confirmed. 'That's professional equipment.'

Line emerged with her belongings. When they explained what Mortensen had found, she took the bag and peered more closely at the little block.

'What should we do about it?' Mortensen said. 'If I deactivate it, the person who put it there will know that we've found it.'

'We'll leave it here,' Line said, tossing it into the hallway before locking the door behind her.

Wisting carried her largest bag up to his house. 'Are you sure you don't mind being left on your own?' he asked.

'It's fine,' Line assured him.

'I can get a patrol car to drive past every hour.'

'I'm sure that's not really necessary, Dad. We'll be fine.'

She and Amalie both received hugs before Wisting and Thule got into the car.

The traffic on the motorway into Oslo was flowing smoothly. When they passed Tønsberg, Wisting's phone rang.

'Christine Thiis,' he read from the display on the dashboard.

'I've missed you,' she said.

'You're on loudspeaker,' Wisting told her cheerfully. 'I'm with a colleague from Romerike, Audun Thule.'

'Hello,' Audun said.

Christine Thiis laughed. 'We all miss you, then,' she said. 'Do you know how much longer your investigation might take?'

'No, but I think we're closing in now.'

'Good. I'm calling about the fire at Bernhard Clausen's cabin. I know it has some connection to what you're working on.'

Wisting did not reply but waited for her to continue.

'I thought it might be of interest for you to know that Aksel Skavhaug has disappeared,' Christine Thiis went on.

'What do you mean by "disappeared"?'

'Well, he confessed that he had set fire to the cabin. I have the report from your questioning, and he was supposed to come in for a formal interview today. He didn't turn up.'

'Have you tried to phone him?'

'He's not answering,' Christine Thiis explained.

'He has a live-in partner and two small children,' Wisting said.

'We've spoken to her. She says he went to a job yesterday.

299

He had said he might be late, but he didn't come home at all last night.'

'What kind of job?'

'He was to lay a new roof on a cabin in Østfold. We're working on trying to find out who it was for.'

'OK,' Wisting said, explaining that they were on their way to Oslo but would be driving through Østfold en route to Halden later that afternoon. 'Call me if there are any developments.'

Wisting rounded off the conversation and looked across at Thule. 'Line robbed, Tommy Pleym beaten up and Aksel Skavhaug missing,' he said. 'There's a lot of movement going on now. I don't like it one little bit.'

They drove on in silence. The fields and forest that flanked the car were replaced by tall buildings as they approached Oslo. Wisting turned off on to the ring road that led to the hospital at Ullevål.

A plain-clothes Oslo detective met them outside the ward where Tommy Pleym lay. Wisting understood him to be a chief inspector who worked in the violent-crime division and that his name was Wibe.

'He's been given a real going-over,' he told them. 'Two cranial fractures and a punctured lung are the most serious of his injuries.'

'What do you know about it?' Wisting asked.

'It was a taxi driver who found him,' Wibe said. 'He came crawling out of an old industrial building that's being renovated down in the city centre. We've located the crime scene. It's covered in fucking blood.'

'Any witnesses? Evidence?'

The chief inspector shook his head before opening the door into the ward and showing them inside.

'The officers on patrol spoke to him while they waited for the ambulance, but they got very little out of him except that it was two guys in balaclavas.'

'Masked?' Thule queried. 'So we're not talking about a random attack?'

Wibe stopped outside a numbered door. 'Well, you wouldn't be here if that was the case,' he commented. 'I don't know what kind of crime you're investigating, but to me it looks like some kind of confrontation. Your friends have probably been messing with the wrong people. I doubt we'll get anything whatsoever out of him.'

'We'll see,' Wisting replied.

Wibe pushed open the door.

Tommy Pleym, his head bandaged and his left arm in plaster, was in a single room. His nose had also received treatment of some kind. He peered up at them through crusted eyes.

The Oslo detective made the introductions. 'Can you tell us what happened?' he asked.

'They took me with them,' the man in the bed whispered.

'Who did?' Wibe asked.

The answer came in fits and starts, blunted by painkillers. 'Don't know . . . strangers . . .'

He raised his plastered arm but let it drop again. 'Balaclavas . . .' he went on. 'They took me with them in a car.'

Tommy Pleym swallowed and moved his head slightly to one side to look around. Audun Thule picked up a glass and put the straw into his mouth.

'It had to do with Lennart,' Pleym added.

Wisting took a step closer. 'Lennart Clausen?' he asked.

The chief inspector glanced across at Wisting as Tommy Pleym nodded.

'Lennart has been dead for years,' Pleym went on.

'We know that,' Wisting said, nodding. 'Motorbike accident. You and Aksel Skavhaug were with him.'

Tommy Pleym's battered, discoloured face looked puzzled, as if he could not understand how Wisting knew that.

'What did they say about Lennart?' Thule probed.

'That he'd stolen money from them . . . that I had been in on it.' Tommy Pleym pulled a face. 'I don't know about any money . . . they drove me into a backyard. Dragged me into a building. Wanted to make me talk. I didn't know anything.'

Wisting could guess what had happened. Line's journalist friend had started to ask questions in the criminal fraternity. A rumour swirled that the cash had been stolen by someone who died in a motorbike accident and that the money was still where he had left it. Tommy Pleym had been one of Lennart Clausen's closest friends. It was only natural to home in on him.

'Lottery . . .' he said.

'You won the lottery?' Wisting recalled.

Tommy Pleym nodded. 'My money . . . they thought I . . . that it was theirs . . .'

Wisting nodded.

'A journalist,' Tommy Pleym barked out. 'A journalist visited me before the weekend . . . She asked about Lennart, too, and about Simon Meier.'

Line, Wisting thought.

'Haven't spoken about Lennart for years . . . Now twice in one . . .'

'Who is Simon Meier?' Wibe asked, but the conversation was interrupted by a nurse.

'Sorry,' she said. 'Will this take much longer? We have to prepare the patient for an MRI scan.'

Wibe glanced at Wisting, who shook his head. 'We can do the rest another time,' Wibe said.

The three policemen were left standing as Tommy Pleym was wheeled out.

'Hope you got more out of that than I did,' Wibe commented.

'More or less,' Wisting answered.

'Would you like to share what this is all about?'

'A misunderstanding,' Wisting replied. 'We're going to try to clear things up. You can suspend your investigation for now.'

57

Stiller was standing outside waiting when Wisting swung up in front of the nursing home.

'Waste of time,' he said, casting a glance at the building behind him as he sat down inside the car.

'Do we still have him under surveillance, though?' Thule asked.

Stiller nodded. 'We're still none the wiser,' he said. 'We don't know what Jan Gudim wants to say, or who he's been in contact with.'

Agreeing, Wisting gave an account of their meeting with Tommy Pleym at the hospital.

His phone rang as he turned out on to the E6. It was Christine Thiis again.

'Have you found him?' Wisting asked.

'No, but we've traced his phone. It's somewhere in a group of cabins in Son. That fits with what his partner told us.'

They passed an exit sign for Vinterbro. 'That suits us fine,' Wisting said. 'We're only twenty minutes away from there at the moment.'

'I can send a patrol car,' Christine Thiis offered.

Wisting checked his watch. They had plenty of time before their appointment at Halden prison. 'We'll see to it,' he said. 'Send me the exact position,' he added, before ending the call.

'What was that about?' Stiller asked.

'Aksel Skavhaug,' Wisting explained. 'The arsonist. He didn't turn up for interview today. No one can get hold of him.'

He received a text with the precise location of Skavhaug's phone. 'Would you key it in?' he asked, handing the phone to Thule.

Thule tapped the coordinates into the GPS and they followed the directions that led them down towards the Oslo fjord.

'Three hundred metres,' Thule commented as Wisting turned into a narrow track of hard-packed gravel.

They rounded a bend and emerged on to the brow of a hill overlooking the Oslo fjord, where four cabins were situated. A grey van with materials balanced on the roof was parked outside one of them. Wisting recognized it immediately.

'That's his vehicle,' he said, pointing.

Driving forward, he parked beside it and three car doors slammed. Only a week ago, this area would have been buzzing with people enjoying the summer holidays. Now, it was quiet. All that could be heard was the screech of gulls from the sea.

They walked around to the front of the cabin. The sun was reflecting off the huge panorama windows, making it difficult to see inside.

'Skavhaug!' Wisting shouted. No answer.

Adrian Stiller pushed open the verandah doors as Wisting and Thule followed.

They found Aksel Skavhaug in the kitchen, slumped over a massive oak table with his hands stretched out on either side.

'What the fuck?' Thule exclaimed.

Skavhaug lifted his head when he realized there were people in the room. Threads of dribble hung from his nose and mouth.

'Help me,' he begged.

It took no time at all for Wisting to grasp the situation. Aksel Skavhaug was literally nailed to the table. A rough square nail had been hammered through each hand into the wood. Blood from the wounds had coagulated and blackened. His phone and a disposable syringe lay between his hands.

'We need a doctor,' Stiller said, taking out his phone.

Wisting found a glass in the kitchen cupboard, filled it with water and helped Skavhaug to drink while Stiller moved out into the living room to call for reinforcements.

'What happened?' Wisting asked.

'They nailed me down,' Skavhaug began, looking at his nail gun on the floor. 'Wanted to make me talk. Threatened to give me an injection. I didn't know anything, you see,' he continued, sounding desperate. 'I couldn't tell them anything. Nothing they wanted to know.'

Wisting found a couple of dish towels. He dried Skavhaug's nose and mouth with one before rinsing the other in cold water to wipe his face.

'Who was it?' he asked.

'I've no idea. It was two men in balaclavas. They came here yesterday, just after I arrived. They must have followed me here.'

'The same guys,' Thule murmured.

Stiller entered again. 'The emergency services are on their way,' he said.

Skavhaug groaned and laid his forehead on the table top again. Wisting laid the cold cloth on his neck.

'What did they want?' he asked.

'They didn't say.'

Aksel Skavhaug tried to sit up but grimaced in pain and leaned forward again.

'They said I knew why they were here,' he went on. 'That I'd helped Lennart Clausen with something before he died. Something that Lennart had stolen from them, and they wanted it back. They thought I knew where it was. Where Lennart had hidden it. But I don't know anything about it.'

He glanced at the syringe on the table in front of him. Wisting followed his gaze. 'Did they use it?' he asked.

'Air,' Skavhaug answered. 'They threatened to inject air into me.'

Thule had brought a pillow from one of the bedrooms and placed it on the table for Skavhaug to rest his head on.

'How did you find me?' he asked, glancing up at Wisting.

'You should have come for an interview today,' he replied. 'We traced your phone.'

'Anette has been calling,' Skavhaug said, peering at the phone in front of him on the table. 'Probably a thousand times.'

'Do you want me to phone her now?' he asked.

Aksel Skavhaug shook his head. 'I'd rather wait till later,' he said.

They heard sirens in the distance. Within minutes, the cabin was filled with paramedics and police officers from the local station. They discussed various methods of releasing Skavhaug. In the end, they injected his hands with anaesthetic and a policeman lay underneath the table and tapped the nails back a few centimetres to create a gap between the head of each nail and Skavhaug's hands. The heads were then clipped off with pliers so that they could lift his hands free.

'We're dealing with ruthless criminals,' Thule commented when the ambulance drove Skavhaug away.

Wisting glanced at his watch. They would be late for their appointment at the prison but, then again, Jan Gudim wasn't going anywhere.

58

The letters on the screen vanished, one by one, until the entire paragraph was gone. Line usually had no difficulty writing, but this time she was struggling. She deleted, reworked, read through, added and scored out again. In the course of the past few hours she had managed to write just six hundred words. She was probably being premature. They did not have all the details she needed, but she was keen to produce a rough draft, ready to fill in the final, conclusive information.

Normally, she would have taken her material to *VG*. Sandersen had encouraged her to return when she had something for them, but after their last meeting she felt more inclined to be published elsewhere.

She began to construct the article around the three parallel stories that all began on the afternoon of Thursday, 29 May 2003. It started with Simon Meier packing his fishing gear and heading out to Gjersjø lake. At around the same time, two robbers were sitting in a car watching as Swissair flight LX 4710 landed at Gardermoen airport, before they pulled down their balaclavas. In the Ministry of Health, Bernhard Clausen left a meeting with the Bio-technology Advisory Board. She had also included another name: Lennart Clausen. She knew little about his whereabouts at the time but placed him in his garage at home, tinkering with a motorbike.

At some point, their paths crossed. When and how were

details she would have to fill in later, but what was about to happen that day would be pivotal in all their lives.

Amalie was sitting in front of the TV, watching a children's channel. Line had to make the most of her time while her daughter was occupied.

She pieced together a few paragraphs about the anonymous tip-off sent to the Director General. She had been optimistic to think that she might find the sender among the men who had been called in for interview, but they had not made any further progress with that.

Amalie slid down from the settee, toddled over and tried to catch her attention. They should really go out for some fresh air, but they couldn't leave the house.

'Mummy has some work to do,' she tried to explain.

Amalie turned around, padded into the kitchen and came back with her Grandpa's iPad. 'Play,' she said, handing it to Line. She needed the code.

'OK,' Line said, smiling, as she keyed in the four digits: 2412. The iPad had been a Christmas present to her father, but he mainly used it for work.

The onscreen image was still showing the population register from when they had tried to find Henriette's parents and live-in partner a few hours earlier. She had phoned while they were conducting the search, and they had abandoned it, but now, with the search left open, a name had appeared on the screen: Daniel Lindberg. At first she paid no attention to it, but then her skin started to tingle.

Daniel.

The phone number on the note inside the box of money.

Daniel. One of the robbers, in all probability.

Amalie tugged at the iPad. Line read the name again to

be absolutely certain and took a screen shot before opening her daughter's favourite game.

She sat back in her chair and let one thought lead to another. Then something slowly dawned on her. Anxiety gathered in the pit of her stomach.

If Henriette Koppang had a child and lived with one of the robbers, that explained a lot. She had visited the chief investigator in the Gjersjø case and gained access to the police documents not as a journalist but to discover what had happened to the cash.

Line felt compelled to get to her feet. Henriette must have told the robbers that Line was working on the robbery case. They had followed her and broken into her home to find out what she knew. Henriette did not have a source. The information she had come up with had been information the robbers had stumbled upon when they broke into her house. They must have seen Lennart Clausen's name placed in the centre of the noticeboard, with lines of connection to all the people around him.

Henriette had asked to use her laptop in the café. She had been sitting beside her when she keyed in her password. The robbers knew everything. Everything apart from the money being found in Bernhard Clausen's cabin.

She took out her phone. She had to call her father.

59

Wisting's phone vibrated in the plastic tray after he had handed it over to the prison guard. 'I'll take the call later,' Wisting said, waving his hand.

They were already late. Jan Gudim and his lawyer had been waiting for half an hour.

A guard accompanied them to the interview room. Wisting stood at the other side of the one-way mirror. Gudim and Harnes, his lawyer, were seated on one side of the table, each with a paper cup. The lawyer in shirt and suit, with his jacket draped over the back of the chair, Jan Gudim in T-shirt and trainers. They stood up when Thule and Stiller entered the room.

Wisting started the video recording. A red bulb was lit up on the interview-room wall. He stood listening as Stiller apologized for being late before moving on to the formalities: time and place of interview and names of those present, the case to which it referred, as well as Gudim's right to silence.

The lawyer leaned forward to the microphone. 'My client wishes to admit culpability for involuntary participation and subsequent assistance in connection with the airport robbery, as well as a number of lesser offences,' he said. 'He is willing to confess his own role in these matters.'

Wisting sat down, satisfied with the words he had heard. This was a significant first step.

'Tell us,' Adrian Stiller said, with a nod.

Jan Gudim shifted slightly in his seat, as if unsure where to begin, or even if he should say anything at all. For a moment, Wisting feared that he had changed his mind and that they would not get their hands on a statement after all.

'I agreed to do a job,' he finally said. 'I was to drive a car and then set it alight. I thought it was just an insurance fraud.'

There was no more. Stiller began to prompt him. 'What kind of car? What did you do with it?'

'A Grand Voyager, at the Kløftakrysset intersection. On the way to Kongsvinger. I had to check that a plane was on time, and then I was to drive and set fire to the car. It had to happen thirty minutes after the plane had landed.'

Again, Stiller had to force more details out of him. 'How was that to happen?'

'I got the car a few weeks in advance,' Gudim explained. 'I kept it parked up in a garage. There was room for a little crosser bike in the back of it, a Yamaha YZ125. On the day of the raid I drove the car out, took the bike to the airport and waited in the arrivals hall until I saw that the plane had landed. Then I rode back and set fire to the car.'

The lawyer leaned forward to the microphone again. 'I would like to stress that Gudim did not know at this point in time why he was doing this. He had no knowledge of the robbery plans. He just undertook a job.'

'Who gave you this job?' Stiller asked.

Gudim glanced across at Harnes.

'My client is only willing to give a statement about his own role in this,' he broke in.

Stiller filled a glass of water. 'What plane are we talking about?' he asked.

'A flight from Switzerland. It was to land at around half past two.'

'And was your job over once you'd done that?' Thule asked. 'When the car went up in flames?'

'I had to pick something up as well,' Gudim went on. 'At an old workshop south of the airport. And drive three men to the city centre.'

'On a crosser motorbike?'

'They had a vehicle there. A big van. I left the crosser bike behind. That was the first time I realized what it was all about. They had a lot of black bin bags stuffed with cash.'

Wisting jotted down some notes. So far, the statement matched what was in the public domain. The diversionary manoeuvre with the car that was set on fire and the workshop where the real robbery vehicle and the crosser bike were parked.

'What did you do with them?' Stiller queried.

'Drove them to Oslo.'

'With the bags of money, I mean,' Stiller set him straight.

'I had nothing to do with that. I got out when we reached the city centre and handed the van over to them.'

Adrian Stiller shuffled a sheaf of papers. 'But we know now that the cash was stored in the cellar at the old pump house at Gjersjø lake. You were the one who had access to that place. Your father was the manager of the water board. You got them a key.'

Jan Gudim shook his head. 'We used the pump house to store narcotics.'

'Tell us about the key.'

'I arranged that years ago,' Gudim said. 'Dad got me a summer job at the water board. That was the year the new

314

water treatment plant at Stangåsen was completed. The old pump house was just being closed down. I thought it would be a good idea to have a key for it, so I had a copy made.'

They ran through the statement once more. This time, it was Thule who led him through what had happened. He managed to winkle a few more details out of him, about the car he had stolen, the fire and the crosser bike, but the main points of the statement remained the same.

'Do you know anything about the boy who disappeared?' Stiller asked.

The lawyer grew wary. 'What boy?' he asked.

'Simon Meier,' Stiller clarified. 'He went missing the same day as the airport robbery. All trace of him ends at the pump house at Gjersjø.'

'Now we're moving on to territory my client has no knowledge of,' the lawyer pointed out.

'I don't know anything about that,' Gudim answered. 'I really don't.'

'But you must surely have given it some thought?' Stiller insisted. 'When the police set up a command post at the pump house? And you knew that the bags of cash were hidden in there?'

Jan Gudim squirmed in his chair.

'When did you discover that the money was gone?' Thule demanded.

'I didn't have much to do with that,' he replied. 'I don't know any more than that the keys weren't where they should have been and the money was gone.'

'We know you're lying. The keys?'

'One was to the pump house and the other for a padlock on the hatch on the floor. It was down there that we stored stuff.'

'Where were the keys supposed to be?'

'Under a stone.'

'Were you present when they went to fetch the cash?'

Gudim nodded. 'The money must have disappeared before the search took place. The search didn't start until a couple of days after the robbery, a couple of days after the guy went missing,' he said. 'The police were inside the pump house and they didn't find it. I mean, there were at least seven or eight bin bags. They must have found them if they were there.'

'You must have wondered what had become of the money?'

The lawyer interjected: 'We'll give speculation a wide berth, if you don't mind.'

Thule rearranged his papers again. 'We've also charged Oscar Tvedt in this case,' he said. 'Do you have any comment on that?'

The question was directed at Gudim, but it was his lawyer who answered.

'As we said at the beginning, my client wishes to give an account of his own role in this case. He has now done so. I request it be recorded that at this point in time, neither he nor I have had sight of the case documents and this statement is given on a free and independent basis. I expect there to be a follow-up interview, when I will anticipate receipt of copies of all papers pertaining to the case, including statements made by the others implicated in this crime.'

Stiller nodded. His bluff that Oscar Tvedt was in a position to give a statement would be exposed, but by then it would be too late.

Thule summarized the facts before the interview was formally ended. Wisting stopped the recording but could still hear what was said on the other side of the mirror window.

'I believe my client has some additional information,' the lawyer said.

He nodded in the direction of the dimmed recording light to give a clear understanding that this information should not be recorded. In other words, that Jan Gudim was about to squeal.

Wisting leaned forward, closer to the monitor.

'Of course, it goes without saying that we'd expect the prosecuting authorities to look favourably on the admissions he has made as far as sentencing is concerned. That the circumstances involving any potential criminal consequence are given credence.'

'Such as what?'

'That he didn't have prior knowledge of the robbery, that he believed it had to do with an insurance scam.'

'We can't guarantee what the public prosecutor will believe,' Thule interjected.

'You'll get the names of everyone involved,' the defence lawyer added.

'We already have the names,' Thule replied. 'What your client comes out with is worthless if he's not willing to give the same information in a court of law.'

'You'll get the answer book,' the lawyer said with a strained smile. 'It's always easier to solve a puzzle when you know all the answers.'

Wisting crossed to the mirror window and knocked on the glass. All four men on the other side swivelled towards him.

'We'll be back,' Stiller said, beckoning to a prison guard, who let them out.

'I need my phone,' Wisting said when the guard brought his colleagues in to join him.

'No phones are allowed in this section,' the guard told him.

'I need to phone the Director General,' Wisting said.

The guard gave him a long, hard look before nodding his head.

'What's on your mind?' Thule asked.

'I think we can come to an arrangement here,' Wisting answered. 'The airport robbery is no longer the most important aspect. The most important thing is to find out what happened to Simon Meier.'

His two colleagues agreed. Wisting's phone was brought into the room. He had two missed calls, both from Line.

'Calls from Line,' he told the others, holding the phone display up to them.

His anxiety increased with each ring that sounded. When she finally answered, her voice sounded breathless.

'Is everything OK?' Wisting asked.

'Yes, I'm just busy with Amalie.'

'You called?'

'I've found Daniel,' his daughter replied. 'The one whose phone number was on the note discovered in the box of cash.'

'Wait,' Wisting told her. 'I'm switching you to loud-speaker.'

He placed the phone on the table.

'Daniel Lindberg,' Line said.

The three men exchanged looks.

'Doesn't mean anything to me,' Thule said.

'He's Henriette Koppang's partner. They have a daughter together.'

Wisting fell silent. 'Exactly how much have you told her?' he asked.

'I haven't said anything to damage the investigation,' Line explained. 'The problem is that she was sitting beside me when I logged into my laptop. She may have seen my password. Everything on that computer could be open to them.'

'That's not a catastrophe,' Stiller broke in. 'They don't know that we have made the connection. We can use that to our advantage.'

'Don't answer your phone if she rings,' Wisting said. 'We'll be back in a few hours and we'll talk then.'

Line seemed reassured. They said their goodbyes and Wisting found the Director General's number.

'I'm at Halden prison,' he said. 'We've just finished an interview with Jan Gudim, who is serving a lengthy sentence for a narcotics crime. He's told us about the part he played in the airport robbery.'

'What does that involve?'

'He was responsible for the diversionary tactic, the car fire, but says at that time he had no idea it was part of a planned robbery. Afterwards, he met the robbers in a pre-arranged place and drove them to the city centre.'

'And the money?' the Director General asked.

'He had a key to the pump house, but not for this purpose. He was not present when the money was stashed in there.'

'You mentioned the part he played – does that mean he hasn't implicated anyone else in his statement?'

Walking over to the one-way mirror, Wisting gazed at Gudim and his lawyer sitting in silence in the adjacent room.

'No, but he's willing to give an additional statement off

319

the record,' he explained. 'I think it may well be the lever we need to open up the whole investigation.'

'What does he want in return?'

'A reduced sentence and an indictment in line with what he has confessed – complicity and accessory after the fact.'

'We can't guarantee that,' the Director General pointed out.

'It has to be one of the conditions of the agreement,' Wisting replied.

'If that's what you need and what you recommend, then let's go for it,' the Director General said. 'Who's his defence counsel?'

'Einar Harnes.'

'Good. Let me speak to him.'

Wisting handed his phone to Stiller, who took it with him into the interview room. Wisting had never before experienced the Director General himself going along with such an arrangement. Presumably, neither had Harnes.

'For you,' Stiller said, handing Harnes the phone.

Harnes glanced sceptically at the phone before taking it.

'This is Einar Harnes,' Wisting heard him say.

His facial expression changed dramatically when the Director General introduced himself. Harnes looked across in amazement at the one-way mirror, as if the person he was speaking to was located in there. His answers came in staccato words of one syllable and were accompanied by brief nods of the head. After only thirty seconds, he handed the phone back. Stiller took it and drew out a chair.

'Let's talk,' he said.

60

Everyone's eyes were now fixed on Gudim. Wisting watched it all from the side room. It looked as if the man being interviewed was still unsure whether he should go through with it. The loudspeakers on either side of the monitor crackled whenever he wriggled in his seat. Then he took a deep breath in through his nose and slowly let it spill out through his mouth.

'Daniel Lindberg and Aleksander Kvamme,' he said. 'It was Daniel's scheme. He was the one who planned it all.'

He paused before continuing. 'I'm not grassing on them here,' he went on. 'I owe them nothing. Quite the opposite, in fact. I've already taken on a lot for them. I've served two years for something they should have gone down for. Aleksander was acquitted. Daniel wasn't even charged.'

He was referring to the narcotics charge for which he still had several more years to serve in prison. His voice was filled with bitterness.

'Go on,' Stiller told him.

Jan Gudim swallowed hard. 'They used a black Grand Voyager,' he explained. 'Daniel first stole the keys from a used-car salesman in Hauketo and then he came back a few days later and took the car. He kept it parked in a garage in Jessheim for a few months before the robbery. The plates were stolen from another Voyager in Bjerkebanen.'

Wisting saw how Audun Thule took notes, even though they already had this information.

'On the day of the robbery they used an old workshop that Daniel had kept under observation. The owner had been dead for a number of years. His wife was in an old folks' home. I met Daniel and Aleksander there after setting fire to the car in Kløfta. They were busy breaking open the cases from the currency consignment. Aleksander was using a blowtorch on them. They didn't have colour ampoules or anything like that, just locks and seals. They transferred the cash into bin bags and took them in the vehicle to Oslo. They then tossed the empty cases into the robbery vehicle. The clothes they'd worn were put into an oil drum half full of petrol. A week later, Daniel came back and set fire to the whole workshop.'

Thule nodded in acknowledgement. Gudim's story matched the details in the report given by the technicians who had examined the site of the fire.

'Daniel and Aleksander got changed and I drove them into Oslo. Aleksander had an arrangement with a guy at Iron Ink Tattoos downtown. He was to come in through the back way, put a sticking plaster on a tattoo he'd had done a couple of days earlier, get a receipt and make himself known to some of the people sitting waiting. Arrange an alibi, in other words. Daniel was to be picked up by a ticket inspection on the subway. He knew a guard and got information about where the inspections were taking place. He made sure to lose his temper and instigate a shouting match, so that he would be noticed. Even though it was more than an hour since the robbery, he reckoned it would work. I drove back and stored the money at Gjersjø. I don't know any more than that.'

'So you *were* the one who put the money in the pump house?' Stiller asked. 'That's not what you told us earlier.'

'Accessory after the fact,' Harnes pointed out. 'It's within the bounds of everything already admitted.'

'What kind of vehicle did you use when you drove from the welding workshop?' Stiller asked. 'Since you left the car used in the robbery behind, along with the bike and all the other gear?'

'That was a legal car,' Gudim replied. 'A Ford Mondeo estate that Aleksander was supposed to fix for his uncle.'

'Colour?'

'Red. Daniel thought it was perfect. Escape cars are usually dark or grey to make sure they don't stand out. That was what the police were looking for. An ancient red old fogey's car wouldn't be noticed.'

Stiller nodded and jotted something down.

'What about Oscar Tvedt?' Thule asked. 'We've picked up his DNA.'

'That's what I told you here the first time,' Gudim answered. 'He'd been a communications officer in the army and knew about things like that. We got the radio set from him. He was originally supposed to take part, but he pulled out the day before. He gave the excuse that he was ill, and blamed food poisoning or something. It was too late to postpone Daniel's plan. It was now or never, so we went ahead without him.'

'But he became the scapegoat when the money disappeared?' Stiller asked.

Gudim nodded. 'Once things had calmed down after that business with Simon Meier, Daniel and I went to the pump house to check on the money. We thought it would be there. Nothing had come out in the media about it being found.'

The sound of footsteps in the corridor reached inside.

Gudim waited until they had passed by before continuing: 'We realized when the key was not where it should be. Daniel broke open the door, but the money was gone, of course.'

Wisting nodded. That corresponded with the documents from the Gjersjø case. The pump-house door had been broken open twice, first by Arnt Eikanger in connection with the official search, and later by the robbers. Some of the parents had complained to the local authority because they felt it might be dangerous for the children who played there.

'Could anyone have seen you?' Stiller asked. 'Could there have been anyone who saw where you had hidden the key?'

'It's possible,' Gudim said. 'The guy who went missing had been there, at least. I saw his bike. It was attached to the pump-house drainpipe. We did wonder whether he might have run off with the cash, or whether one of the policemen had taken it, but in fact it was Oscar.'

Wisting ran his hand through his hair. The last time they had spoken to Gudim they had given him the impression that some of the robbery proceeds had been found at Oscar Tvedt's mother's house. It dawned on him that this would complicate the statement he was giving now.

'Daniel was already convinced of that at the time,' Gudim went on. 'He and Aleksander were the ones who beat him up. I wasn't involved in that. Afterwards, they were no longer so sure. He denied everything.'

Gudim sat bolt upright in his chair as if something important had just struck him. 'Daniel's girlfriend made some inquiries,' he continued. 'She wrote for *Goliat* and pretended she was preparing an article about the guy who went missing. She was allowed to see all the investigation documents, but she was none the wiser after that. She thought the man who disappeared had maybe gone to Spain with all the money.'

Stiller left that hanging. 'Where did the information about the cash consignment come from?' he asked instead.

Jan Gudim leaned back in his chair. He seemed unprepared for that question. 'Daniel talked to a guy who worked up there,' he answered.

'Who?' Thule demanded.

'It was Daniel's plan,' Gudim replied. 'He didn't share details about that sort of thing with anyone else.'

'Kim Werner Pollen,' Stiller said.

Wisting could see through the mirror window that the name provoked a reaction.

'You were the one who knew him,' Stiller added. 'It's going to bounce back on you if you don't tell us everything now.'

Gudim was clearly worried sick. His lawyer did not look comfortable either. 'That was long before the robbery, nearly a year before, and in a totally different connection,' Gudim finally admitted. 'Daniel asked if I knew anyone who worked at Gardermoen airport. I told him I knew of Kim Werner. I thought it was to do with importing drugs. That he was after someone who worked in the baggage-handling section and could get stuff out without going through Customs. I didn't think any more of it afterwards, to be honest.'

The lawyer cleared his throat. 'This doesn't change the basis of our agreement,' he said. 'The fact is that Gudim had no knowledge of the specific plans for the robbery until after the robbery had been committed.'

Thule nodded. He was willing to accept this version of events. 'Where did the guns come from?' he asked instead.

'I've no idea,' Gudim replied. 'Probably from Oscar. After all, he'd been in the Special Forces. They called him the Captain. He was the guy who handled weapons, the one you went to if you needed that kind of thing.'

Stiller had taken notes during the entire conversation. Now he folded his notebook shut. 'I work in the section dealing with old and unsolved cases,' he said.

Gudim nodded.

'The investigation I've reopened now is the Gjersjø case,' Stiller went on.

'I thought it was the robbery you were working on,' Gudim said.

'That was Thule's case,' Stiller answered with a nod to one side. 'I'm trying to find out what happened to Simon Meier.'

He waited for a beat before continuing: 'You have an agreement with the Director General. It would be far more valuable to us, and beneficial to you, if you know something about that case.'

Gudim shook his head. 'Nothing more than what I said about Daniel's girlfriend looking for him in Spain,' he replied. 'Apart from that, there was some talk of him being buried in a gravel pit.'

'Where did you get that from?'

'From Daniel, or maybe it was something his girlfriend had picked up from the police reports. There was a clairvoyant woman who had seen him in gravel. But they also had another theory. It seems highly likely now.'

'What's that?'

'That Oscar had taken care of him, you know? That he

had seen Oscar with the money and Oscar was then forced to get rid of him. It seems obvious now that you've found the money. Anyway, I don't think he drowned, since he's never been found. It's a bit too much of a coincidence for it to have happened at the same time that the money was stolen. Maybe Oscar buried him somewhere in the gravel, just like that clairvoyant woman said.'

Wisting used the control stick on the video camera in the interview room to zoom in on Gudim so that his face filled the monitor screen. He agreed. Simon Meier could have seen something he shouldn't have and been killed in order to keep quiet. But it was not Oscar Tvedt who had taken him or the money. The money had ended up with Bernhard Clausen.

61

The printer in the corner of the basement was working steadily. Line studied a sheet of paper on its way out on which the picture of Daniel Lindberg was slowly taking shape. He was dark-haired and good-looking, with a sun-tanned face and white teeth. Line recognized some of the features from his daughter. The chin, the transparent freckles on the nose and the dark, close-set eyes.

Audun Thule took the printout and hung the picture on the wall beside Aleksander Kvamme.

'We have very little intelligence on him,' Thule said. 'The photo in our records was taken when he was called in for disorderly conduct at an outdoor café three years ago. He works at a fitness centre he runs with his brother. That's probably where he and Aleksander Kvamme crossed paths.'

Stiller turned to face Line. 'They're trying to find out what happened to the money and thought you knew some-thing,' he said. 'From what they've discovered on your laptop and the noticeboard beside your office desk, they believe that Lennart Clausen took the cash.'

'That's a rational theory,' Thule agreed. 'Lennart is from the neighbouring area. The fact that he died not long after gives them reason to believe that the cash is still intact.'

'It could be that's exactly what has happened,' Mortensen broke in.

'They're following your tracks, Line,' Stiller went on. 'According to your summary, Tommy Pleym and Aksel Skavhaug were Lennart Clausen's closest associates at that time. If anyone knew where he had hidden the money, it would have to be one of them.'

'They're going to go on searching,' Thule suggested.

'Then we'll give them some help,' Stiller said.

'How will we do that?' Line asked.

'Our advantage is that they have no idea that we know about Henriette's double role. Next time you talk to her, say that you think you know where Lennart Clausen may have hidden the money. We'll lead them there and catch them red-handed.'

'The same tactic we tried to use with Oscar Tvedt,' Thule commented.

'We'll move the undercover operators and the cameras,' Stiller said, nodding.

'But where?' Line asked. 'Where is it likely that Lennart Clausen would have hidden the money, and how could I possibly have found out about it?'

'The garage,' Wisting said.

'What garage?'

'At his father's house,' Wisting clarified. 'The garage is full of motorbike parts and tools. It's been left like that ever since Lennart died.'

'That's perfect,' Mortensen said.

'I ought to have a more detailed background story, though,' Line said.

'Talk to his girlfriend,' her father suggested. 'The woman in Spain. Get her to tell you about the garage, and then you can use that.'

'Go ahead,' Stiller said, indicating the phone on the

table. 'Then you can arrange a meeting with Henriette tomorrow.'

Line drew the phone towards her. 'I already have an appointment with Trygve Johnsrud tomorrow,' she said.

'Cancel that,' Mortensen suggested.

'He used to be Finance Minister,' Line reminded him. 'It wasn't easy getting an appointment. I can't just call it off now.'

'When is it?' her father asked.

'Ten a.m., at his cabin in Kjerringvik.'

'Then you can manage both,' Wisting told her.

With a nod of the head, Line took the phone out of the room. Standing at the kitchen window, she gazed down at her own house while she made the call. She should have switched on some lights, she thought. Twilight came increasingly early and darkness was already closing in now.

The ring tone was faint and quivering, but the voice sounded close when Rita Salvesen answered.

'How are things?' Line asked. 'Have you spoken to that lawyer about the estate settlement?'

'Yes, he's going to take care of everything. It seems there's no will or anything like that. Lena will inherit everything, so thank you for phoning me about it. Maybe we can meet up when I come to Norway?'

'That would be lovely,' Line replied. 'What were you planning on doing with the house?'

'Selling it.'

'You wouldn't consider moving back to Norway?'

'Not yet, at least.'

'I drove past it, in fact, when I was in Kolbotn,' Line went on. This was not true, but she was keen to turn the conversation to the house and garage. 'It's in a beautiful situation, great for a family with young children,' she added.

'I know.'

'Were you there much when you and Lennart were together?'

'We mostly spent time at my place.'

'Lennart spent most of his time in the garage, as far as I understand?' Line said.

Rita laughed. 'You'd better believe it,' she answered. 'He worked on those motorbikes day and night. It was practically forbidden for anyone else to set foot in there.'

That was perfect, Line thought. She could use what Rita had said in her conversation with Henriette. 'Why not?' she asked.

'I don't know. But I paint, and I really don't like anyone to see my paintings while I'm working on them. I won't show a picture until I've finished it. I think it was something similar with Lennart, too. He assembled motorbikes, cleaned and painted them. He certainly didn't want anyone to look at them until he was completely finished. It's probably like that for you as a journalist as well. You don't want anyone to read your first drafts.'

'That's true,' Line said.

'It grew worse during the summer before he died,' Rita went on. 'I think maybe he was working on a motorbike for me. At least, he was desperate for me to pass my test so that we could go out biking together.'

'Did you do that?'

'I never got that far.'

Line had all the information she needed, but went on chatting all the same. 'Send me a message, then, whenever you're in Norway,' Line finally said, to round off the conversation.

'It won't be long,' Rita promised. 'I'll probably have some papers to sign soon.'

'Great!'

They hung up. Line stood deep in thought, considering how to tackle her conversation with Henriette.

Her father entered the room behind her. Line turned her back to the window and leaned towards the kitchen table. 'It's not certain she'll answer,' she said.

'Try,' her father told her. 'Maybe she'll call back again.'

Line switched on the loudspeaker function. There was music in the background when Henriette picked up.

'Any news?' she asked.

'You could say so,' Line replied. 'Something's happened to make me consider dropping the whole story.'

The music was turned down. 'What's that?'

'I was attacked,' Line told her. 'My laptop was stolen. I think it may have something to do with the investigation.'

'What happened?'

Line explained about the assault but did not mention anything about having been to the National Library to read Henriette's old articles.

'Why do you think it had something to do with the airport robbery?' Henriette asked.

'Other things have happened, too,' Line continued. 'It's complicated, but I think someone knows I've starting digging into this.'

Her father nodded to indicate that it was a smart move to give the impression that the threats had made an impact on her.

'Who could that be?'

'I don't want to talk about it on the phone.'

'So you're withdrawing from it all entirely?' Henriette asked.

Line struggled to work out if she was pleased or not.

'I'm not really sure,' she said. 'But I do have a theory about where the money may be hidden.'

'Where?'

'An obvious hiding place.'

'You can't give up now,' Henriette told her. 'Could we meet up, maybe tomorrow?'

'I have another appointment in the morning,' Line said, 'and I only have a babysitter until two o'clock.'

'I can come down to you,' Henriette said. 'We could meet at the same place as last time.'

'I'm not sure,' Line said. 'This whole business is starting to get dangerous.'

'You've started, so you should finish,' Henriette insisted. 'At the very least, you owe me the information about where you think the money is located, after all the time I've spent approaching my sources. If you're not going to follow this up, then I will. It'll make a sensational story if the cash is found.'

'OK, then,' Line said. 'Let's meet at one o'clock.'

62

The temperature had plummeted overnight. The sky was covered in a layer of grey cloud and a light breeze made the trees sway. Line was in her own house, pulling on a sweater and collecting a jacket for Amalie. Before she drove off, she brought the tracking device that Mortensen had found into the car, so that whoever was following her would see she was on the move.

After dropping off Amalie, she drove into town and further out to the eastern side of the Larvik fjord. A narrow, twisting track took her the final few kilometres to the old harbour near the open sea where the former Finance Minister and Bernhard Clausen's Party colleague had his country house. She followed the signs to a white captain's house in a sheltered area under the steep, craggy hillside by the shore. Nevertheless, with a shudder, she drew her shoulders together as a keen blast of sea air assailed her.

'We'll sit inside,' Trygve Johnsrud suggested when he appeared at the front door.

Line followed him into a living room with panorama windows overlooking the sea. Johnsrud cleared away newspapers and magazines from the dining table to make space for them both.

'Well, then, Bernhard Clausen,' he began. 'He leaves behind quite a void.'

'A few different things have emerged about him since we arranged our meeting,' Line said.

'You're thinking of his book?'

Line nodded. 'Do you know what he was writing in it?' she asked.

Johnsrud smiled. 'I haven't read any of it,' he answered.

'I spoke to Guttorm Hellevik last week,' Line continued. 'I got the impression that Clausen had become a freethinker who no longer felt attached to social democratic ideals.'

The former Finance Minister agreed. 'A good politician is usually regarded as one who stands firm, but I believe the ability to change your point of view as a result of social debate or personal experience is an excellent political attribute.'

'What signs did you see that he had changed his opinions?'

'We mostly discussed financial politics,' Johnsrud explained. 'Bernhard disagreed with the tax proposals put forward by the Labour Party. He wanted a lower tax threshold, leading to higher personal consumption. He thought that we politicians should have greater confidence in allowing people the right to choose what they wanted to spend their own money on. He felt that hard work and private initiative should be more generously rewarded. Maybe that was a natural consequence of having worked hard all his life.'

He got to his feet and fetched two cups and a coffee pot.

'When did he change his political viewpoint?' Line queried.

Johnsrud filled the cups.

'I'm not so sure that "changed his political viewpoint" is the right way to put it. That sounds so dramatic, but he had strong opinions about individual freedom and personal responsibility. They weren't really evident until his last period in government,' he answered. 'But those close to him noticed a change after his spell of sick leave when he was Health Minister.'

Line seized the opportunity to direct the conversation on to the time in Bernhard Clausen's life that interested her most.

'After his son died?' she asked.

Trygve Johnsrud gave this some thought. 'It was probably really after his wife died,' he said. 'I think that triggered a lot of soul-searching.'

'In what way?'

The Labour Party veteran picked up his coffee cup and drank deeply before putting it down again. 'Health care is one of our most important welfare benefits, but to retain a good service we can't help everyone with everything. The medicines Lisa needed cost millions and would probably have given her a year or two more, at most. The decision-making committee had already turned down that treatment, both on the basis of price, and also because there was no proof of its efficacy. I remember some talk of an operation in Israel, but her doctors didn't support it. In many ways, Bernhard Clausen became a political hostage. He made up his mind to sell the cabin in Stavern and buy private health care but it meant he would have had to resign as Health Minister.'

Trygve Johnsrud pursed his lips, as if he had said more than he should have.

'In the end it was Lisa who begged him not to do it. The point is that he did not feel free to choose what was best for him and his family. I think, eventually, that spurred his thoughts towards a more liberal view.'

'I understand that Lennart blamed his father for his mother's death,' Line said.

'Indeed he did, but not as much as Bernhard Clausen blamed himself. It wasn't something that divided them.'

Line disagreed as Trygve Johnsrud stood up. 'The relationship between father and son can be difficult,' he said, crossing to the other side of the room. 'I'll show you a photo.'

He opened a sideboard drawer and took out an envelope full of photographs. 'I came across this when I was leafing through some old photos yesterday,' he said, placing a picture of Lennart and his father in front of her. They stood with their arms around each other's shoulders. Bernhard Clausen held a hammer in his free hand and both smiled broadly at the photographer.

'Isn't that a good photo?' Johnsrud asked.

Line lifted it up. There was something about their smiles – they did not seem genuine.

'Is that at the cabin in Stavern?'

'That was the summer after Lisa died,' Johnsrud told her, putting down the other photographs. 'There was a get-together at the cabin so that we could help him to build a new patio. Lennart came down on his motorbike with some documents Bernhard had left behind.'

Line had read about that work party in the cabin visitors' book. It was the weekend after Simon Meier's disappearance. She recognized a few of the politicians in the picture.

'Who is that?' she asked, pointing at a man with a paintbrush.

Trygve Johnsrud leaned across the table. 'That's probably our next Minister of Justice,' he said, smiling.

'Arnt Eikanger?' Line asked. 'But surely he was working as a police officer in those days?'

'He knows where the shoe pinches,' Johnsrud replied. 'He's a major political talent. Bernhard acted as a kind of mentor to him.'

Line lingered on that photograph before looking at the others. She recognized Guttorm Hellevik from Oslo City Council in one of them. He stood tossing sand into an old-fashioned cement mixer along with a man in a red Labour Party cap.

'Could I borrow this one, please?' she asked, holding up the picture of Lennart and his father.

'Take them all,' Johnsrud suggested. 'It would be a good idea to use the one of Eikanger,' he added, perhaps thinking that the work-party pictures would have a positive impact on the forthcoming election campaign.

'We worked together throughout the day,' he went on, 'and in the evening we carved out our political plans.'

Line collected the photos, leaving the one of Lennart and his father on top.

'That's probably the last photo of the two of them together,' Johnsrud said with a smile. 'Family was important to him, and Bernhard loved that boy. The cancer that claimed Lisa was hereditary. He was afraid his son would be affected, too, but only a few months after that photo was taken, he was killed in a motorbike accident.'

Line nodded. 'Did you all stay at the cabin that weekend?' she asked, placing the photos in her bag.

'Yes.'

'Don't you think it's a bit odd that the cabin has burned down?'

'It's more difficult to envisage Bernhard being gone, to be honest.'

After almost two hours, Line had enough material to write an article about how the old social democratic ideals were crucial to the renewal of the welfare state but not much more about what had happened in the summer of 2003.

63

The hinges on the garage doors screeched when Wisting pulled them up. The piercing noise sounded like the agonized cry of someone in pain.

Two windows were placed high on the wall and a heavy work lamp hung from the ceiling in the middle of the untidy space. Beneath it stood a motorbike stripped of its tyres and petrol tank, propped up on a frame. The engine lay in pieces on the concrete floor with tools and dirty, twisted rags. A pair of overalls was draped over the back of a camping chair beside an open tool chest. Around it were dotted other half-finished projects, cases of engine parts, boxes of screws and half-filled oilcans.

They strode in, with Stiller pointing out where he wanted to mount the hidden cameras.

The technician from his section at Kripos set to work at once. The tiny cameras would relay the live-stream to Bernhard Clausen's office, where the police would monitor what was going on.

'We won't get them sentenced for robbery even if we can prove they broke into a garage,' Thule commented.

'We'll use this to break their weakest link,' Stiller said. 'Henriette Koppang. She's the one who'll lead them here. She's the one who has to start talking.'

Wisting flicked through an instruction book left open on a workbench. It contained advanced illustrations of various motorbike parts. He felt optimistic at the thought

340

of a breakthrough. The possibility of a prison sentence and the consequences for her daughter would be enough to make Henriette Koppang spill the beans. Simon Meier's disappearance would be a different matter. The people who might know something were both dead: Bernhard Clausen and his son.

'What's this in here?' Stiller asked, tugging at the handle of an interior storage room on the far wall of the garage.

Thule pointed down at the floor. 'It's secured with an extra padlock,' he said.

A metal bar and lock had been fitted across the threshold.

'We could use that room,' Stiller said. 'If anyone wanted to hide something here, they'd use that storeroom.'

He cast around and found a large pair of wire cutters. 'I want a camera in there, too,' he said, struggling to cut off the padlock.

'I saw a bigger pair somewhere,' Thule said, turning around.

He found a large pair of bolt shears on a shelf and used them to cut through the padlock. The lock on the door itself was a standard interior-door lock. Stiller returned to the house to find a key in the key cupboard there.

'Maybe the money really was in there,' Wisting suggested when Stiller returned.

'Well, he has certainly secured this door well,' Stiller said.

Inserting a key, he turned it and pulled the door open. A clammy, cloying smell wafted towards them and combined with the miasma of oil and engines out in the garage. Stiller located the light switch.

The room inside was about two square metres in size with a desk against one wall, a grubby office chair on wheels and a few shelves on the wall. A padlocked wooden chest was pushed against the other wall and above it was displayed an *Easy Rider* film poster depicting Peter Fonda and Dennis Hopper on their motorbikes. In the right-hand corner of the poster a bunch of dried-up air fresheners was nailed up.

Stiller was first to step inside, with Wisting close on his heels. A beer bottle had toppled on the desktop and the spilled beer had dried up, leaving brown stains on the surface and the pile of papers.

One of the drawers was half open. Wisting pulled it all the way out and found a bundle of motorbike magazines with a spray can of air freshener and several hanging air fresheners, still in their cellophane wrappers.

Stiller delivered a kick to the large wooden chest. 'It's locked,' he said.

Thule arrived with the bolt shears, but Stiller's phone rang before he had the chance to do anything. 'It's Gitte, from the DNA register,' he said on first glance at the display.

He answered and switched the phone to loudspeaker. Thule stood waiting with the shears in his hand.

'We've come up with a result on the quick analysis of biological material from Vegard Skottemyr,' the woman from the DNA register explained, and went on to provide a reference number.

Wisting strained to hear more clearly. Vegard Skottemyr was the man they thought had written the anonymous letter to the Director General.

'You've requested a specific comparison with the trace sample marked B-8 in case 15692 for 2003 from what was previously Follo police district,' the woman continued in a formal tone.

'The condom from the area beside the pump house,' Stiller explained to the others.

'There's no match between the samples,' the woman said solemnly.

Wisting sighed. The possibility of finding an eyewitness at Gjersjø seemed to be slipping away from them.

'We've run an additional search in the trace register,' the woman at the other end of the line continued. 'That matched sample B-14 in the same case.'

'What's B-14?' Thule asked.

The woman from the DNA register seemed confused by another voice breaking in. 'It's described here as pubic hair,' she replied.

Stiller gave a broad smile. 'It takes two to tango,' he said. 'We've got him. Vegard Skottemyr was at the pump house, and left a few pubic hairs behind.'

The woman explained how the analysis and test results would be sent to them.

'Do you have any results from the new investigations inside the pump house?' Wisting asked. 'They were submitted by Espen Mortensen in the same case for comparison with the missing person's DNA profile.'

'We've just received that,' the woman told him. 'I'll phone Mortensen next.'

'What do the test results say?'

'It's a match,' the woman replied, and now she had dispensed with her formal tone. 'Trace samples F-1 and F-2 belong to Simon Meier.'

'The steel edge and the floor,' Wisting clarified, mostly for his own benefit.

The woman on the line did not catch what he had said. Stiller turned off the loudspeaker function and put the phone to his ear. 'Thanks for calling,' he said.

'So Simon Meier died in the pump house,' Audun Thule summarized when the phone call had ended.

'And we may have a witness,' Stiller said. 'I'll drive down to Kolbotn and have another chat with Vegard Skottemyr. You can both finish up here.'

He negotiated his way past his colleagues and out of the cramped space. Thule lifted the bolt shears and a metallic click was heard as the hoop on the padlock was snapped through. Wisting lifted the lid.

The locked chest was almost empty. It contained a few pieces of chrome work, a registration plate and a vehicle registration document. Thule lifted up a bag containing the dried shoots from a marijuana plant and a hash pipe.

'Not particularly exciting,' he commented as he let the bag drop.

Wisting closed the lid.

64

Henriette was standing at the counter with her bank card in her hand when Line came in. 'What would you like?' she asked.

Line stopped by her side. 'Caffè latte,' she said.

Henriette passed on the order and the barista set to work. 'How are you doing?' she asked, placing a hand on Line's shoulder.

'I'm not really sure,' Line answered. 'So much has happened.'

'You must tell me all about it,' Henriette replied.

The coffee glasses were placed on the counter. 'I'll pay,' Henriette said, inserting her card into the machine.

Line took the coffee and stood watching as Henriette keyed in her pin number. The card was declined. She tried again, the same four digits, but the transaction did not go through.

'There must be something wrong,' Henriette said with a sigh.

'I'll pay,' Line offered, and put a hundred-kroner note on the counter.

'Thanks,' Henriette said as she returned her card to her purse, picked up her coffee glass and led the way to the table.

'What's happened?' Henriette asked, lowering her voice.

'I haven't told anyone and I've no intention of doing so either,' Line said. 'You have to promise me that you won't tell anyone about it.'

'Of course.'

'I'm only telling you because I'm not sure you're safe either.'

Henriette merely nodded her head without saying anything.

'It started after we spoke for the first time,' Line continued. 'I got the feeling that someone had been in my house.'

'That's awful.'

Putting the straw to her mouth, Line drank while making eye contact with Henriette. She wanted to tell her that she knew it was her partner or his associate. That he had been down in her basement and stood in front of her pin board, looking at the line of connection she had drawn between Simon Meier and Lennart Clausen.

'Was anything stolen?' Henriette asked.

Line shook her head. 'Just a child's drawing,' she replied.

'A drawing?'

'We've had a cat prowling around our house over the past few weeks,' Line explained. 'Amalie wanted to draw it and I gave her a hand. We pinned it up beside her bed.' She felt her eyes brimming and had to steel herself as she went on to tell the story of the dead cat and the warning note.

'My God,' Henriette groaned. 'It couldn't have been some perverted teenager in the neighbourhood or something like that?'

Line shook her head.

'Did you call the police?' Henriette asked.

'No. I threw the cat in the bin before Amalie caught sight of it, but I phoned a security company to have a burglar alarm installed.'

She had been cradling her coffee glass on her lap, and now she placed it on the table. 'I've made up my mind,' she said. 'I'm dropping the whole business. It's just not worth it.'

'Are you sure?'

Line nodded.

'I respect that,' Henriette said. 'But you mentioned that you thought you might know where the money from the robbery was?'

'Maybe.'

'Where, then?'

'I spoke to his ex-girlfriend,' Line explained.

'Lennart Clausen's ex-girlfriend?' Henriette asked.

Line nodded. She was reluctant to disclose her name, even though the information about Rita and her daughter had been stored on her stolen laptop. 'She told me about Lennart.'

'Yes?'

'He had a garage at his father's house where he used to tinker with motorbikes. He spent hours in there and refused to let anyone else come in.'

Keeping her eyes on Line, Henriette continued to drink her coffee.

'The garage is still there,' Line went on. 'It's remained untouched since Lennart died, full of motorbike parts. His father didn't have the heart to clear it out. If that was where he hid the money, it may well still be there.'

She could see that Henriette had swallowed the bait. 'How can we check it out?' she asked.

Line shook her head. 'Not "we",' she said. 'I'm not taking part in anything else. His girlfriend will be coming to Norway soon and will take over the house. She's thinking of selling it. If the money is there, we'll maybe hear about it when she clears out the house.'

Henriette seemed nonplussed. She began to say something about them losing control of the story and the money, but broke off abruptly. 'It would have been a much better story if we'd found the money ourselves instead of it being discovered later, if you know what I mean.'

'Yes, but the whole business just makes me feel sick,' Line said. 'I can't take any more chances. If I had the support of an editor, it might be different, but it is just me, on my own, and I have to think of my daughter as well.'

'I understand,' Henriette said. 'And I totally accept your decision.'

The rest of their conversation turned to everyday topics. Line struggled to show interest and hide the tumult of emotions seething inside, and she was relieved when, after only half an hour, Henriette got to her feet.

'I have to get back,' Henriette said. 'I hope we can stay in touch.'

Line stood up and gave Henriette a quick hug. She remained on her feet, watching as she walked out the door. As soon as she had rounded the corner, she would probably take out her phone to call Daniel.

She turned around to pack up her own belongings and discovered Henriette's phone left on the chair where she had been sitting, tucked down a gap.

Her first impulse was to chase after her, as she would in normal circumstances, but she stood rooted to the spot. You had to use a fingerprint or pin code to access it. Line glanced over at the counter and the card machine. *0208*. When Henriette had been struggling with her bank card, she had seen that the four digits might well be the date of birth of her daughter or her boyfriend.

She grabbed the phone and let her thumb slide across the screen. *0208*. It could be as easy as that. The phone opened.

Line glanced at the door. It would not take long for Henriette to discover that her phone was missing.

She went into the messages. Daniel was number three on the list of contacts. She clicked on the messages and scrolled through until she found a small video file that Henriette had sent to him on Sunday afternoon. At first she did not understand what she was looking at, as the camera wobbled back and forth before focusing on a keyboard. Line was gripped by dread. It was her Mac. Henriette had filmed her, the last time they met, typing in her password.

She swore aloud and turned her eyes to the door again before scrolling on. The previous day, Daniel had sent a photo. She opened it. It was the noticeboard in the office in her basement.

Find out as much as possible about these names was the accompanying message.

Line did not need to enlarge the image to see what names he meant. It was the names pinned around the picture of Lennart Clausen. Tommy Pleym and Aksel Skavhaug. Both had been victims of the robbers' own investigation.

The bell above the door tinkled as Henriette reappeared. Line closed the phone and held it up in the air. 'You forgot this,' she said, slapping on a smile. 'It was on the chair.'

Henriette thanked her and returned her smile. 'I feel completely lost without it,' she said.

Line accompanied her to the door, where they said their goodbyes again and Henriette disappeared around the street corner. Shortly afterwards, she drove past in a blue Audi with her phone at her ear. Line took out her own phone to call her father. The game was on.

65

Adrian Stiller followed a young couple into the bank. They grabbed a ticket and sat down to wait their turn. Stiller, meanwhile, strode straight up to an information desk, produced his police ID and asked to speak to Vegard Skottemyr.

The man at the desk peered at his screen. 'He's in a meeting, I'm afraid,' he answered with a customer-friendly smile.

'I can't wait,' Stiller told him.

The man looked at him as if this was a response he had not encountered before. 'I'll go and see if he'll be finished any time soon,' he said, sliding down from his stool.

Stiller followed him to where Vegard Skottemyr was seated in an office with glass walls and a middle-aged woman was preparing to leave.

'You have a visitor,' the man from the information desk told him.

Skottemyr looked out and Stiller met his gaze. A resigned expression came over his face. Stiller allowed the customer to leave before stepping inside and closing the door behind him.

'We meet again,' he said, as he took a seat.

Skottemyr merely nodded his head.

'You weren't completely honest with me,' Stiller continued.

A disconcerted look came over Skottemyr's face. 'I don't know any more than I told you.'

'I don't think it was true that you had go for a piss,' Stiller said. 'That wasn't why you jogged along the track to the pump house. I think you went to meet someone.'

'And who would that be?'

'A lover.'

Skottemyr's face changed colour. Stiller carried on, explaining how the technicians who had examined the area around the pump house had found traces of sexual activity between two men.

'One of them was you,' Stiller said. 'I want to know who the other one was.'

Skottemyr shook his head, 'It doesn't matter,' he replied. 'He's no longer alive.'

'I want to know who it was all the same,' Stiller told him.

Skottemyr gave this some thought. 'He was married, you see,' he answered. 'I don't want to tarnish his reputation.'

'We're now investigating Simon's disappearance as a homicide,' Stiller said. 'You must tell me the name. Either here or at the police station.'

Vegard Skottemyr grabbed a pen and twirled it between his fingers. 'We met at the swimming baths,' he began. 'We went to the sauna together, but we couldn't really talk properly, or be together there, so we found somewhere else.'

'The pump house.'

'That was one of the places. He was married and I lived with my parents. They wouldn't . . . they don't know about me.'

Skottemyr let the pen slip from between his fingers.

'We met once a week,' he went on, leaving the pen where it lay. 'He got a dog to give him an excuse to go out, to take it for a walk. I went jogging.'

Stiller thought through the list of names he had

produced, with Skottemyr at the top. It included a man with a dog who had been placed at the bottom of the list. Stiller could not recall his name, but it would be easy to find.

'Was there someone else there on the day Simon Meier disappeared?' Stiller asked.

'A car was parked there, so I just turned away and went on running.'

'What kind of car?'

'An estate.'

'Colour?'

'Red.'

Stiller felt a buzz of adrenaline. This was the car Jan Gudim had used to transport the proceeds of the robbery.

'Why didn't you say anything about it?'

'You were looking for a black car,' Skottemyr replied.

That was true. A witness had seen a black car drive down to the pump house. She could not say what day that had been but, all the same, the investigators had made a public appeal for information.

'Reidar arrived after me and saw it,' Skottemyr added.

The man with the puppy, Stiller thought. The name fell into place. 'Reidar Dahl?'

Skottemyr nodded.

'What did he see?'

'The black car.'

'What else did he say?'

'Nothing else,' Skottemyr said. 'It was parked outside the pump house. He turned and left when he spotted it.'

'And that was all he said?' Stiller asked. 'He didn't mention the type of car or whether there was anyone inside it?'

Skottemyr shook his head. 'I got the impression that there was something else, but he never shared it with me.

There was so much focus on the pump house for a while afterwards that we didn't go anywhere near it. After what happened, we never met again, not in that way, and if we bumped into each other, we never mentioned the pump house.'

'Might he have spoken to anyone else about what he saw that day?' Stiller probed.

'He certainly spoke to the police,' Skottemyr replied.

'So he did,' Stiller said, getting to his feet. 'Well, thanks for seeing me.'

Skottemyr glanced up at him, obviously taken aback by his sudden departure.

'I'll find my own way out,' Stiller said as he left.

In the car he found the folder marked *Witnesses* in the Gjersjø case. He leafed through it and located Reidar Dahl's interview. Arnt Eikanger was the officer who had taken his statement.

The statement itself was taken over the phone. Stiller had read it before, but skimmed through it again. Reidar Dahl confirmed that he had been the person spotted with the puppy. It was a seven-month Tibetan terrier called Jeppe and had a grey-and-black coat. He explained where he had gone and gave the name of his wife, who had been at home. At the foot of the page there was a line stating that the witness had no further information to give. But that was presumably untrue.

66

Three cameras had been mounted in Lennart Clausen's garage and another two covered the area outside. In addition, they had an undercover detective posted at each end of the street. A group of officers from the local police district, armed and ready to make arrests, was stationed in a side street one minute away.

Wisting sat in front of the TV screens installed in Bernhard Clausen's office. Four hours had elapsed since Line had spoken to Henriette Koppang, enough time for the robbers to swing into action.

'They're probably waiting until it gets dark,' Thule commented.

Wisting checked the computer.

'Where is she?' Thule asked.

'The same place,' he answered, turning the screen to face him.

A red dot on the map marked the location of Henriette Koppang's blue Audi. Mortensen had attached a tracker while Line met Henriette at the café in Stavern. After the meeting she had driven along the main road towards Larvik. There, the car had turned into a car park.

Wisting felt uneasy. He did not like this. There was no reason for Henriette Koppang to stay behind in town. This car park was nowhere near the shopping centre, and they had expected her to drive straight home to speak to Daniel.

'Could there be anything wrong with the system?' he asked. 'Could it have stalled?'

'There's nothing to suggest that,' Thule told him. 'But you can always get a patrol car to drive past and see if it's really there.'

The phone rang. It was Stiller, and it sounded as if he was in a car. 'Any news?' he asked.

'You'd know if there was,' Wisting assured him, switching the phone to loudspeaker so that Thule could also hear the conversation.

'Has there been any movement?'

Wisting glanced at the screen again. 'No,' he replied.

'Maybe she's at the spa,' Thule said, nodding in the direction of the onscreen map. 'The hotel spa is nearby.'

Wisting shifted the phone to his other hand. 'Are you heading here?' he asked.

'Not yet,' Stiller answered. 'I think I've found the anonymous letter writer.'

'Who is it?'

Wisting shut his eyes and tried to remember the names in the bundle of case documents. Stiller explained what he had discovered when he paid a visit to Vegard Skottemyr.

'He's married,' Wisting recalled when Stiller told them about the man with the dog.

'And he's dead now,' Stiller replied. 'But I'm trying to get hold of his wife. His widow.'

'Do you think she might know something?' Thule asked.

'It's worth a try,' Stiller said.

As Stiller drove into a tunnel, they lost the connection and Wisting rang off.

Wisting stood up, crossed to the window and looked

out behind the curtains. Then he went back and sat down in front of the screens again. None of them showed anything for quite a while. Thule checked the wi-fi to ensure they still had contact with the detectives in the street.

'We should have had surveillance on Lindberg and Kvamme as well,' he commented.

Wisting agreed, but there hadn't been time to track them down.

'White delivery van, two men inside,' reported one of the undercover officers in the street.

Seconds later, the van appeared onscreen. It drove past and the detective checked it out at the other end.

'When does it get really dark?' Wisting asked. 'Nine o'clock? Half past?'

'Around then,' Thule confirmed.

'Then we've another three hours left.'

The waiting made him restless. He got up and paced the room before sitting down again. He pivoted round in his office chair, pulled out a desk drawer and pushed it back in again. He pulled out another drawer and found some papers and a glossy brochure from a private hospital in Israel. It advertised new therapeutic methods and experimental treatments for cancer patients.

He replaced the papers, took out his phone and began to read various online articles. From time to time the radio crackled when the undercover operators reported cars on the way in or out of the street.

'Grey Passat, one man driving,' he heard.

Something in the detective's tone made Wisting look up. 'That's the third time it's passed by,' the detective went on. 'Might be doing a recce.'

The car appeared onscreen and drove slowly past.

Thule grabbed the two-way radio. 'Reg number?' he asked.

It took some time for the reply to come: 'Hired car. We're trying to identify the user.'

'Not good,' Wisting commented. 'If our guys have seen him three times, then he's seen them, too. Our cover could be blown.'

Thule rummaged in a bag and took out two baguettes. 'Or it could just be somebody who lives in the neighbour-hood,' he said, tossing over one of them.

Wisting took it and sat chewing as he stared at the immobile red dot on the map. The longer he stared at it, the more he felt that something was amiss.

67

Stiller stood outside a brown-painted house in a street called Bjørnemyrveien, waiting for Ruth Dahl. He estimated it was around fifteen minutes' walk from there to the pump house at Gjersjø lake.

Ruth Dahl was not at home when Stiller had called, but when he explained that he needed to speak to her about her husband and the Gjersjø case, she immediately offered to meet him at her house. It seemed as if this was a conversation she had anticipated, which made Stiller feel optimistic.

When a white estate car turned into the driveway, Stiller stepped out and nodded in greeting to the woman who emerged. Skirting around to the boot, she opened it to release a short-haired, grey terrier that had to be lifted out and set down on the ground.

'This is Jeppe,' she explained. 'He's getting old now.' Stiller hunkered down and let the dog sniff his hand before he patted its fur.

They entered the kitchen, with the dog following slowly at their heels. Ruth Dahl filled a saucer of water for it.

'I thought someone might come,' she said, inviting him to take a seat.

Stiller pulled out a chair and leaned his arms on the table in front of him once he had taken the weight off his feet.

'At that time it was all hushed up, you see,' Ruth Dahl went on as she sat down. 'But he's dead now.'

'You're thinking of Bernhard Clausen,' Stiller said.

The dog lay down under the table.

'Reidar saw him there at the pump house,' Ruth Dahl explained. 'The evening Simon Meier disappeared.'

'He told you that?'

'He told the local police as well, but they didn't do anything about it.'

'Arnt Eikanger.'

Ruth Dahl nodded her head. 'Eikanger insisted that the boy had drowned, but they never found his body.'

'What did your husband tell you?' Stiller asked.

'He was out with Jeppe,' Ruth Dahl began. 'They sometimes went down to Gjersjø lake. He had bumped into Simon Meier there a couple of times.'

Stiller nodded.

'That evening the door to the pump house was wide open. Reidar stopped at the edge of the track and saw a car drive out from behind. Bernhard Clausen got out of it, opened the boot and dragged a bin bag from the pump house and threw it into the car.'

'A bin bag?' Stiller repeated.

'I don't know what was in it,' Ruth Dahl added. 'Reidar didn't know either. He just turned and left, but it must have had something to do with the boy's disappearance.'

Stiller sat back in his chair, taking some time to digest this information. According to what Ruth Dahl was telling him, it was Bernhard Clausen who had taken the cash from the robbery. Eighty million was a great deal of money, of course, a tempting amount of money, but he had not imagined for a second that the then Health Minister would risk his career for that. Especially not to hoard it all away in his cabin.

'Was he certain it was Bernhard Clausen, and not just his car?' he asked.

'I only know what Reidar told me,' she answered. 'But he was on sick leave at that time. That was when his heart began to fail. He began to lose track of the days, and Eikanger thought he'd mistaken the day. But he'd spotted Simon Meier's bike there, too, beside the pump-house wall. It must have been the same day.'

A loud snore came from the dog under the table.

'And he told all this to Eikanger when he was interviewed?' Stiller queried.

Ruth Dahl clasped her hands on the table in front of her. 'Doesn't it say all this in the reports?' she asked.

'Not in as much detail as you've given me,' Stiller responded.

'Reidar suspected as much,' Ruth Dahl said with a sigh. 'He wasn't sure that Eikanger would do anything about it. After all, he was in politics, too. And Reidar wasn't the sort of man to kick up a fuss about things, but I asked him to write to someone further up the pecking order about it.'

'And did he do that?'

'Oh yes, he sent a letter to the Director General.'

68

The food had made Wisting sleepy. He was about to drop off in the chair when his phone rang. It was the journalist from *Dagbladet*. He turned the phone to silent and held it in his hand as it rang out.

The red dot on the map remained at a standstill in the car park outside the hotel in Larvik. Wisting made a mental calculation. Almost seven hours had elapsed now since Line had met up with Henriette Koppang.

'That's a very long spa treatment,' Thule remarked. 'Maybe she's checked in and is staying the night?'

Wisting could not figure it out. The sense that something was wrong had crept up on him in the course of the past few hours. Now it had grown so strong that he felt he had to take some kind of action. He wondered whether he should call Line to find out if Henriette had mentioned anything about her plans for the rest of the day. Instead, he rang the direct number for the Chief of Police in his own police district.

'I'm on an undercover assignment outside Oslo,' he explained after introducing himself. 'We need help to check out a vehicle that seems to be stationary in a car park in Larvik. Have you a patrol car free that you could send out to take a look?'

'I can have it done within half an hour,' he replied. 'What kind of vehicle is it and where exactly is it parked?'

'A blue Audi,' Wisting said, and went on to give the address and registration number.

'I'll get back to you.'

Outside, it was growing dark. Two boys on bikes stopped in the street. They were wearing football kits and each carried a sports bag – probably on their way home from training. They looked around before one jumped off his bike and left the other to hold it steady for him. Venturing into the garden, the first boy peered up at the house before dashing across to an apple tree. He snatched two apples and rushed back to fling himself on his bike.

The phone rang again. It was Jonas Hildre from *Dagbladet* again. He might as well answer. 'It's about Bernhard Clausen,' the journalist said. 'There's been an incident I thought I should let you know about.'

'What kind of incident?'

'Well, I was down in Stavern last week and took photos of the site of the fire. I spoke to some of the neighbours at the cabins there. One of them told me about all the cardboard boxes you had carried out.'

Wisting nodded. He had been well aware of where the information had come from.

'The man I spoke to phoned me back again a few hours ago. He told me someone else had been there asking about the boxes. He thought you ought to know about it, but he didn't want to call you himself.'

Wisting straightened up. 'What do you mean?'

'It was someone who had read about the cardboard boxes in the newspaper and wanted to know more. Eventually he became almost a bit threatening.'

'In what way?'

'He was a big guy, on anabolic steroids, the man he

visited told me. The guy came into his cabin and demanded to know more.'

'What did he tell him?'

'He told him about you.'

'About me?'

'He told him who you were. That you and the other man who carried out the boxes had been back after the fire and talked about the bottles of propane gas that had been stolen. The guy who turned up was very interested in that.'

'In what?'

'In your name and the fact that you are in the police.'

Wisting's gaze was drawn to the blank surveillance screens. Nothing was going to happen now. The robbers knew the police had found the money. They had given up.

'I see,' he said. 'When was this?'

'This morning. A woman was there, too, but she stayed in the car.'

'What kind of car was it?'

'A blue Audi.'

Wisting nodded to himself. 'Thanks for phoning,' he said.

The journalist had not finished. 'Can you tell me anything more about what is really going on?' he asked. 'What was actually inside those cardboard boxes?'

'I've already told you,' Wisting replied. 'It had to do with the deceased's estate.'

Audun Thule nudged him in the side and pointed at the onscreen map. The red dot was on the move.

'Yes, but that could mean anything at all,' the journalist continued.

'Thanks for phoning,' Wisting repeated as he hung up.

The red dot on the screen was on its way back to Stavern. It should have moved up on to the E18 motorway in the direction of Oslo, but instead it followed the main road and drove through Stavern town centre.

Wisting got to his feet. The dot was moving more slowly now, into a residential area very familiar to him. It stopped outside his house.

69

Line worked best when it was dark outside. It was as if daylight gave her a guilty conscience about sitting in front of a computer screen. It was easier for her to concentrate when Amalie was in bed fast asleep.

She was seated in what had once been her mother's office on the first floor, where she had used to sit correcting school assignments and drawing up teaching plans.

Line's work was starting to take shape now.

During the last half hour she had written about Lisa Clausen's cancer. It had been a rare type that originated within the hormone-producing cells of the endocrine system. This kind of cancer was considered one of the most aggressive. There was no known cause for the development of these malignant tumours and this type was therefore characterized as hereditary.

Line flicked through her notes and located what had been said about Clausen's plans to sell his cabin and finance the treatment abroad. It was difficult to find out the cost of the treatment and the value of his cabin in 2003. But after some calculations she found he would not have come close.

She leaned back in her chair. On the other hand, 80 million kroner in foreign currency would have made quite a difference. The problem was that Lisa Clausen had been dead for more than six months when the currency consignment at Gardermoen airport had been stolen.

A noise made her turn towards the door. It was difficult to work out whether it had come from inside or outside the house.

She stood up and moved into the room where Amalie was sleeping on her back with her face upturned. Her regular breathing was deep and peaceful. She looked more like her father. Line sometimes thought about him, and how different their life would have been with him. He worked in the FBI, and she had met him when he was on an assignment in Norway. His work meant it was out of the question for him to move here, but there had been nothing to prevent her from joining him in the States.

Line smoothed the quilt and stroked her daughter's cheek. A thought began to form in her mind.

She hurried back to the workroom and took out the photographs Trygve Johnsrud had given her from the work party at the cabin. The picture of Lennart and Bernhard Clausen was still at the top of the pile. They had the same chin but, apart from that, it was difficult to see any similarities.

In one of the folders on her computer she had a photo of Lisa Clausen stored. When she opened it on the screen, it was obvious where Lennart had inherited his blond hair, blue eyes and round face.

Maybe he had also inherited his mother's illness? If nothing else, then perhaps this was something Bernhard Clausen had feared.

The text she had written claimed that Lennart Clausen had, by chance, come across the cash, and when he was killed his father had found the money and kept it hidden. But maybe Bernhard Clausen took the cash to ensure financial security, should his son be diagnosed with cancer.

Growing eager, she leafed back through her notes from the meeting with Clausen's personal secretary. She'd only jotted down key words and half-sentences, but they helped her remember what Edel Holt had said. Bernhard Clausen had changed after his wife died. His outlook had become gloomy, and he was lost in his own thoughts and had gone for long walks.

She became more convinced the more she thought about it. It was no different from Amalie taking a packet of sweets from the shelf right beside her pushchair in the shop. The opportunity had offered itself. Many others would have done exactly the same thing, but Bernhard Clausen had had a motive. For him, the money could have meant the difference between life and death.

Another thought occurred to her. Something Rita Salvesen had said also made sense. Bernhard Clausen had visited her when his grandchild was one year old. He had handed her a business card with his phone number and said that she should get in touch if there was anything she needed help with. When she had asked to borrow money to move to Spain, he had brushed her off and said he would help if either of them became seriously ill.

If Lisa Clausen's type of cancer was hereditary, her grandchild was also at risk. That could be the explanation for why Clausen kept the money after his son died. Family was important to him. Trygve Johnsrud was the last person to say that when he showed her the photograph of father and son.

What had happened at the pump house began to crystallize. A melancholy Bernhard Clausen goes on a long walk to Gjersjø lake. Although he catches sight of Gudim lugging plastic bags into the pump house, he remains unseen.

Gudim locks up behind him and drives off. Curiosity makes Clausen take the key from its hiding place. He lets himself in and finds the money.

She was anxious to call her father, but another thought struck her. If it had really been Bernhard Clausen who had taken the cash, then maybe he was the one who had killed Simon Meier. Just as the anonymous letter suggested.

Everything suddenly seemed so logical. The explanation had been there in front of her all the time, though fragmented and disconnected.

She began to put her thoughts into words. Writing them down, she formed specific sentences and summarized facts that pointed towards Bernhard Clausen as Simon Meier's killer. It also dawned on her that her notes probably held the answer to where the body was located. Finding Simon Meier would provide the definitive proof that her thoughts had travelled along the right lines.

She stopped at a half-finished sentence and began to search through the papers and notes strewn across the desk. A noise from the floor below made her pause. Someone was inside the house.

70

It sounded like footsteps.

Line sat up straight, in silence, listening intently until she was certain. The fifth step on the staircase creaked. It had always creaked. Someone was on their way up to where she sat.

Her hand cast around for the phone. Grabbing it, she pushed herself up as quietly as she could from her chair.

Whoever was on their way up would find her easily. The stairs led to a small space with a short hallway in either direction giving on to four rooms: one bathroom, her old bedroom, where Amalie lay sleeping, her brother's old room and the room where she now stood.

She opened the keypad lock on her phone, at the same time scanning the room for somewhere to hide or something she could use to defend herself.

Nothing.

Her thumb slid over the cracked phone screen. She dialled three digits: 112, the emergency number.

She could hear it ring, but it was too late to raise the alarm. The doorway was filled with a man in black jogging trousers, a T-shirt, gloves, and a balaclava pulled down over his face.

Line took a step back, nudging the office chair so that she was left standing with her back to the desk. She heard her emergency call being answered and let the phone drop to the seat in the hope that the operator would understand what was going on and trace the call.

The man strode all the way into the room.

'What do you want?' Line asked. Her voice sounded weaker than she had intended.

The man did not reply but instead crossed to the chair, picked up the phone and broke the connection before dropping it on the floor and crushing it under his heel. Then he lashed out at her with a sudden movement. 'Lying cunt!' he snarled. 'Where's your father?'

The blow knocked her off balance and the intense pain made her dizzy. 'Not here,' she stammered, moving her hand to her face.

Her lip must have split open. Blood was trickling down her chin.

'What about your daughter?' he demanded. 'Where's she?'

Line could not bring herself to answer. Another smack was delivered to her face, but she managed to repress a cry of pain.

'Didn't you realize we knew?' the man went on.

This must be Daniel Lindberg facing her, but she had no idea what he meant.

'I know who your father is,' he practically spat out. 'Bloody pig.'

He took hold of her, one hand gripping her neck and squeezing tight. 'What a fucking nerve,' he continued. 'Using his own daughter.'

He ran his free hand over the desk, sweeping notes and photos on to the floor.

Line struggled to breathe, but she still managed to keep a clear head. They had discovered who her father was and had somehow seen through the investigation. They must have known there was no money in Bernhard Clausen's garage, but there was no way they could know that it was here.

'Your two-faced games have made this personal,' the man in the balaclava went on. 'Your father's going to get a personal message.'

He shoved her down on to the office chair. 'This is what you can write to him,' he said, releasing his stranglehold. Slapping a sheet of paper in front of her, he indicated that she should pick up a pen. She did as she was told.

'Don't give a fuck,' he said.

'What do you mean?' Line stuttered.

'That's the message for your father: he should stop giving a fuck. Drop the case. Nothing good will come of it if he keeps going.'

He hovered over her, his breath hot and sickly sweet.

Line began to write. The blood on her hand smeared red streaks on the page.

She suddenly understood why he had come. The robbers knew it was only a question of time before the past caught up with them. They were willing to go to any lengths to kill the investigation. The language they used was violence and threats.

'Then you can draw a cat, since you're so good at that,' he added.

Line's hand began to shake uncontrollably. She drew a cat's ears and a tail, and then stopped with the tip of the pen pressed on the paper, unsure whether the man in the balaclava had heard what she had.

'Mummy!' Amalie yelled again from the bedroom.

71

'Alpha, this is Bravo 3-0.'

Audun Thule grabbed the police radio and answered the call.

'Regarding the silver-grey Volkswagen Passat 1.6 TDI, we have three sightings of it. The driver is a male, but the vehicle is on hire from Hertz by Henriette Koppang of Inside Media.'

'Copy,' Thule replied, sitting up straight in his chair.

Wisting sat with his eyes fixed on the onscreen map. The red dot had made a short stop in the street outside his own house before moving on to stop beside Line's house. Daniel Lindberg was probably in the car with Henriette Koppang. That meant it was most likely that the driver of the Volkswagen had been Aleksander Kvamme. He must have spotted the undercover detectives and realized that this was a trap.

'I think our cover's blown,' he said, without taking his eyes from the map.

Thule disagreed. 'They've been here to do a recce,' he said. 'Now it's grown dark. They'll be back some time tonight.'

Wisting grabbed the phone and called Line. There was silence as he tried to connect, and then came a series of staccato signals. He swore and tried again but could not get through. Instead, he phoned headquarters.

'Sorry,' said the Chief of Police when he answered. 'I

was a bit tied up with a serious road traffic accident, but I was just about to call you. The patrol car has been past. There's no Audi at the address you gave.'

'I know,' Wisting replied. 'They've moved.'

Swallowing, he carried on. 'A situation has arisen,' he said. 'They may have got wind of our operation. As I said, I'm outside Oslo, but our suspect seems to be at my home address. My daughter and granddaughter are there, alone.'

'Are they under threat?' the Police Chief asked.

'I'm not sure,' Wisting replied. 'But I can't get through to them on the phone.'

'Do you want me to send a car?' the Police Chief queried. 'I don't have one available right now, but I will free one up.'

Wisting felt his pulse begin to pound in his ears. Their operation might still be viable. The robbers might still believe the cash was in the son's garage. The red dot outside his house and Line's might not mean anything more than a recce before they drove back to Oslo. Sending a patrol car would ruin everything.

'No,' he answered. 'That won't be necessary. Thanks anyway.'

He hung up and called Espen Mortensen. 'Jump in your car,' he said. 'Drive to my house. Call me when you're almost there.'

Mortensen asked no questions.

'I think it's urgent,' Wisting added.

72

Amalie called out again. 'Mummy!'

Line did not answer and merely watched as the lips behind the opening in the balaclava parted and formed into a grin. 'The money's in the basement,' she whispered.

The man jerked his head as if someone had slapped him. 'What did you say?' he asked.

'The money from the robbery,' Line explained. 'It's in the basement.'

'Here?'

'Yes.'

The man in the balaclava began to laugh. 'Why on earth?' he asked.

'The investigation group . . .' Line ventured. 'They have their base here.'

The laughter subsided as the man suddenly hauled Line up from the chair.

'Show me!' he ordered as he catapulted her towards the door.

Line landed on the floor but managed to scramble to her feet, continually hoping that Amalie had not left her bedroom.

'Mummy!' she heard her daughter shout again.

'Wait!' she yelled back. 'I'm coming soon, sweetheart.'

The man gave her a rough shove in the back, propelling her forward. Line almost lost her balance again but succeeded in making her way to the staircase.

'In there,' she said, pointing at the door to the basement.

The man took hold of the door handle. 'It's locked,' he said. 'Where is the key?'

'My dad has it,' Line replied.

The man took a step back and studied the door with its simple lock. The keys for the other doors in the house would almost certainly fit.

Dragging Line by the arm across to the bathroom, he checked the inside of the door. No key. The next door was a cupboard containing winter jackets and ski trousers. No key.

The man yanked her back to the locked door and tentatively put his shoulder to it.

The alarm would be activated if he forced it open. That would terrify Amalie but might also chase off the intruder and alert her father.

He lifted one foot and readied himself to deliver a hefty kick.

'The alarm,' Line said.

The man planted his foot on the floor again. 'What did you say?'

'There's an alarm in there,' Line told him.

'Do you know the code?'

Line shook her head. 'No,' she lied.

'But the money's in there?'

Line nodded. 'Nine cardboard boxes.'

The man swore, looked around and dragged her across to the hall cupboard, where he flung her to the floor and switched on the light. He cast around, tearing clothes from their hangers, and found a belt before ordering her to put her hands behind her back. The leather chafed her skin as he drew it tight.

Two sleeping bags were stowed on the top shelf. Grabbing one of them, he pulled it over her until her head was at the foot of the bag. Her throat felt constricted. She began to cough and had to fight to hold her panic in check. The man dragged her across the floor and she felt him wrap another belt around her ankles and pull it tight.

'No!' she shouted, bringing on another fit of coughing. 'Please!'

She felt a kick in the stomach and heard him shut the cupboard door behind him. His footsteps disappeared into the distance and she heard the front door close. Then there was only silence.

The air around her grew denser with every breath she took.

She twisted on to her side and began to work on her hands behind her back. There was some give in the leather belt. She wriggled around the other way and felt something cold and sharp against her face. The zip. She applied her lips to it and tried to suck in fresh air through the metal hooks as she twisted and turned her hands to work them loose.

Warm, clammy air wafted over her face, along with the perspiration dripping off her.

The belt loosened as she drew her right arm up towards her and pushed in the other direction with the left. She felt the skin on the back of her hand peel off as she slid her hand through.

Drawing up her knees, she flexed her back against the fabric of the sleeping bag and moved her hands up above her head. If she remembered right, the ring for the zip was at the foot of the sleeping bag.

She followed the zip to the very end and realized that

she was mistaken, but with her hands free it was easier to work on the belt wound around her feet.

She sat up and felt her way to the belt through the fabric and found the buckle. Grasping the end of the belt, she tugged hard and felt it loosen.

She wriggled out and gulped greedy mouthfuls of the fresh air that streamed towards her.

Once she was free, she threw aside the sleeping bag and lay on her back to collect her thoughts.

She heard a noise at the front door, followed by footsteps and voices, but she could not catch what was said.

Line stood up, moved to the cupboard door and put her eye to the keyhole. Depending on which way she tilted her head, she could see the porch, parts of the hallway and the door to the basement.

The man had rolled up his balaclava and she now recognized him from the photos. It was Daniel Lindberg. Close behind him she caught sight of Henriette Koppang.

'Where is she?' she asked.

Daniel Lindberg pointed at the cupboard. 'In there,' he said. 'She won't escape.'

Standing in front of the basement door, he raised his foot and kicked hard. There was an explosion of splinters as the door imploded, the lower hinge burst open and the door was left hanging at a crooked angle.

The alarm began to flash.

Daniel Lindberg stormed in, with Henriette Koppang at his heels. From where Line stood, she could see only fragments of the room before they both emerged again, each carrying a cardboard box.

They dashed out before returning again and grabbing two more boxes. The alarm began to howl as they moved back and forth three more times to pick up all nine boxes. Line waited for a while longer before she ventured out.

'Mummy!' Amalie stood at the top of the stairs, covering her ears with her hands.

Line raced up to her, swept her up into her arms and held her close. 'It's all over now,' she reassured her.

73

The red dot was back in front of Wisting's house. He got to his feet, his mouth dry and his hands clammy. Pressing his tongue to the roof of his mouth, he swallowed hard and called Mortensen. 'Where are you?' he demanded.

'Five minutes away. Maybe less. What's going on?'

Wisting briefed him on the situation and how worried he was for Line and Amalie's safety. He heard a text message deliver as he spoke.

'Wait!' Mortensen broke off. 'The alarm's gone off.'

Wisting took his phone from his ear to gaze at the same message.

'Both sensors have been set off,' he heard Mortensen say.

Two new messages came in from the alarm company. Wisting opened the footage and saw there were two people in the basement. The sparse light made the picture fuzzy, but he could see a man and a woman, each carrying a cardboard box.

'Christ,' he swore aloud.

'Movement!' Thule said, pointing at the onscreen map.

The red dot moved out of the residential area, on to Brunlaveien, and continued north.

Wisting put the phone to his ear again. 'What route are you taking?' he asked.

'The inland road.'

'Then you're going to meet them.'

'Shall I try to stop them?'

Wisting grabbed the chair back with his free hand. 'No, go straight to my house,' he answered. 'Find Line.' He rang off, breathing in and out with jagged breaths.

Another message arrived from the alarm company. He opened it and saw a picture of Line with Amalie in her arms, switching off the alarm.

The sight made his pulse beat a little more slowly. He saw how Line held Amalie's head to her chest and used her free hand to cover her other ear. They seemed unharmed.

Closing the image, he wondered whether he should phone her, but instead he called the number for the switchboard in Oslo.

He gave his name and rank. 'I'm in charge of a special operation assigned by the Director General,' he continued, knowing that this would put a stop to any questions. 'A critical situation has arisen. We have a man and a woman on their way from Vestfold to Oslo by car. They have just broken into an external evidence store and stolen a considerable sum of money. I need back-up to stop them and place them under arrest.'

'One moment,' the operator replied. 'You can speak directly to the senior officer.'

He was transferred and repeated what he had said. 'We have an electronic tracker on the car,' he said, glancing at the map. 'It shows them on the E18 between Larvik and Sandefjord, driving within the speed limit, on their way north. They'll be in your jurisdiction in ninety minutes.'

'Where are you?'

'On the other side of Oslo. Kolbotn.'

'Are you mobile?'

'Absolutely.'

'Then I suggest you meet up with our incident commander at the Shell garage in Høvik and you can make plans for a roadblock from there.'

Wisting made a note of the commander's direct number. Audun Thule headed for the door and summoned the cars outside. 'We're calling it a day,' he said.

In the time it took Wisting and Thule to travel from Kolbotn to Høvik, the red dot had passed Drammen. 'They'll be here in twenty minutes,' Thule reckoned.

They parked up at the petrol station, where the incident commander had gathered a force and issued them instructions.

Wisting had spoken to Line en route. Mortensen was with her. She had not said very much about what had happened but explained her theories surrounding Bernhard Clausen.

Wisting scanned the traffic as it whizzed past on the motorway. It was impossible to imagine what the couple planned to do next. They had to be aware that the net was closing in on them.

Having finished his briefing, the incident commander approached them. 'We've tackled this kind of thing before,' he said, probably to give reassurance.

'What's the plan?'

'We'll put two unmarked cars behind them and stop a bus in the public transport lane further ahead in order to block the road. Then we'll send the unmarked cars forward in the two other lanes. They'll slow down and draw to a halt when they're level with the bus, and then we'll move in from behind.'

It was a good, simple plan, but there was also a great deal that could go wrong.

Almost ten minutes ticked past before the unmarked cars reported that they were located west of their position. 'Two cars in place behind, steady speed,' they reported.

The red dot passed Slependen and approached Sandvika.

A patrol confirmed that the bus had been stopped east of their position and the motorway had been narrowed to two lanes.

A heavy-goods vehicle thundered past, whirling up dust from the road.

'OK, get ready!' the incident commander shouted.

The team moved into their vehicles, which were hidden behind the petrol station. Wisting sat behind the wheel of the surveillance car. Thule sat down beside him in the passenger seat with his laptop on his knee. 'One minute away,' he announced.

Wisting prepared to slip out into the flow of traffic, his eyes fixed on the road as he waited for the blue Audi to appear.

Thule spotted it first. 'Here it comes!'

It was in the right-hand lane. As it speeded past, Wisting could see the cardboard boxes piled up on the back seat.

Accelerating, he moved out a hundred metres behind it. The boxes obviously obstructed the couple's rear view.

The two unmarked police cars increased speed, overtook the Audi and stayed in the fast lane, parallel to and just ahead of them.

The traffic began to slow down. The blue Audi moved out to the left-hand lane and signalled to overtake. Wisting saw the patrol cars appear in his rear-view mirror.

His speed was down to sixty. Behind them, the police cars were gaining on them. They occupied the full width of all the traffic lanes to prevent any civilian vehicles from moving forward and ending up in the midst of all the action.

Further ahead, they could see the bus used as part of the roadblock.

The Audi drew back in again as a taxi passed in the public transport lane to the right. The Audi moved across to do the same, but the policeman in the car in front grasped the situation and moved over to block it.

The Audi flashed its lights and blasted its horn. The speedometer in Wisting's car crept down to forty. The distance to the stopping place in front of the bus was fast diminishing and, by this time, the couple in the Audi must realize something was going on.

Then everything happened in the blink of an eye. The entire carriageway was blocked when the two unmarked police cars stopped alongside the bus. Two men leapt out of each vehicle and stormed towards the Audi, with guns aimed at the front windscreen. Shouted commands rang out.

Wisting saw the reverse lights come on. The Audi swerved towards him but really had no space to make an escape. Behind them, blue lights flashed. To the left, concrete blocks prevented the car from moving into the oncoming carriageway and high noise barriers rendered it impossible to use the ground on the other side.

Wisting stamped his foot on the brake pedal and braced himself for the collision, but the car in front of him lurched and shot forward, causing one of the armed police officers to jump aside. As the driver tried to force the car forward between the two unmarked cars, the sound of scraping metal rent the air and blue-black smoke belched from the tyres.

Several police officers came running. One of them tried to wrench open the driver's door of the Audi, but it was locked. He pulled out a steel baton and struck one of the rear windows. Glass shards flew out but, before he managed to put his hand in to open the door from inside, the reverse lights came on again. The Audi drove back, picked up speed and tried to plough its way forward. Wisting made room for a police patrol car that moved up and drove into the back of the Audi, leaving it no chance to reverse and speed up again. But it received the extra thrust required for it to force its way through. It shot forward out on to the deserted motorway ahead of the roadblock, with the police car following in hot pursuit. Wisting negotiated his way through the same gap.

The police car immediately behind drove into the side of the Audi and flipped it around 180 degrees. One of the rear doors sprang open and two of the cardboard boxes were tossed out. Dollar notes fluttered out across the carriageway.

Wisting drove forward and drew to a halt bonnet to bonnet with the Audi. The woman in the passenger seat yelled and shrieked and held her head in her hands. The man behind the steering wheel met Wisting's gaze.

'We've got him,' Thule said, once another car had blocked the Audi in similar fashion on the other side.

Police officers in overalls charged forward to tear open the doors and drag the couple out from the car. Lying flat on the asphalt, they were quickly handcuffed.

74

A dollar note had caught between two concrete bollards in the centre section of the E18. Wisting shifted his phone to his other hand to draw out the slip of paper. The Director General was on the line.

'We have a patrol car at Aleksander Kvamme's house,' he said. 'The hire car he uses is parked outside. I expect he'll soon be under arrest as well.'

The damaged Audi was hoisted on to a recovery truck. A fireman swept up broken glass from the asphalt.

The Director General was keen to hear more about how the money had ended up in the back room at Bernhard Clausen's cabin.

'I think it was down to a variety of circumstances,' Wisting summarized. 'Clausen was affected by his wife's death and the fear that the same fate would befall his son. When he came across the money, he regarded it as a lifesaver, an insurance.'

The Director General cleared his throat. 'I presume there's a good deal of truth in the old proverb,' he said.

'Which one?' Wisting asked.

'That opportunity makes a thief.'

One lane was now opened and the traffic began to flow past.

'We also think Clausen was responsible for Simon Meier's disappearance,' Wisting said.

'You mean Clausen killed him?' the Director General queried.

'It's happened before,' Wisting commented. 'People have committed murder to hide another crime.'

'Do you have any proof?'

'We're preparing a search,' Wisting answered. 'We're going to try to find Meier tomorrow. If we're successful, it will give us more information.'

'No matter what, we need transparency on this now,' the Director General continued. 'How do we break the news?'

'I have a plan for that,' Wisting answered. 'But first of all, I think we should solve the Gjersjø case.'

75

The steel drill bored down between two of the stone slabs. As one broke and loosened from the ground beneath, a colony of tiny black ants scurried off in all directions.

Wisting drew back to join the others. A puff of air fluttered the crime scene tape surrounding the ruins and an acrid smell of charred timber wafted towards them.

'How long do you think it will take?' he asked, turning to face Mortensen.

'Not long,' he replied above the noise of the drill. 'The concrete layer isn't thick, only fifteen to twenty centimetres.'

Wisting nodded. Clouds of dust enveloped the drill operator. The first layers of concrete foundation were already broken up. Ten days ago, he himself had stood where the man with the pneumatic drill was working.

Line had brought the photographs taken on the day of the work party. A number of central Party members had gathered at the cabin to undertake a number of tasks, including the building of an outside seating area. In the pictures, the ground had already been dressed with gravel, the shuttering was already prepared and reinforcement irons laid out, and several of them showed the leader of Oslo City Council working the cement mixer while Bernhard Clausen and Arnt Eikanger levelled the wet cement.

The concrete had been poured that weekend. Later, flagstones were laid and an outdoor fireplace and sizeable barbecue were installed. Line's theory was logical. Bernhard

Clausen had hidden Simon Meier in the same place as the money.

'I don't think Eikanger ever knew anything of it,' she said. 'I doubt he even harboured any suspicions. I think he just thought too well of Clausen to take the tip-off seriously.'

Thule agreed. 'We'll never be able to convict him of anything.'

Mortensen was engrossed in a phone call. 'The fingerprint register,' he explained on his return. 'They've found Bernhard Clausen's fingerprints on the padlock for the hatch on the pump-house floor. He's certainly been in there.'

After half an hour the compressor fell silent and the drill operator stopped work. Mortensen gave directions to the driver of the small excavator standing by.

The other four members of the investigation group moved in closer as the excavator scooped concrete and flagstones into its bucket and shifted them aside. Line produced her camera and took several photographs.

When the excavator had reached down to the gravel, Mortensen jumped up into the driver's cabin to give instructions. The gravel was moved into a separate pile, with Mortensen monitoring every single bucketful.

Less than forty centimetres of gravel covered the first human remains. Two grey bones and dark shreds of fabric.

Mortensen waved the excavator away and continued the excavation with a spade. Adrian Stiller helped. Line snapped a number of photos while Wisting stood observing the activity. Not until they found a skull did he step forward.

Lifting it carefully from the gravel, Mortensen turned it around and held it up so that the others could see. On the right side at the back of the skull there was a fracture four centimetres long. None of them needed to pass any further comment. The shape of the rough wound was a close match to the steel edge on the machinery in the pump house at Gjersjø lake.

Mortensen carefully placed the grey skull in a cardboard box and went on with his collection of bone fragments.

After another half-hour, Mortensen and Stiller climbed out of the ditch. Mortensen closed and sealed the flaps on the cardboard boxes before directing the excavator driver to fill in the hole again.

'We have a visitor,' Stiller said, nodding in the direction of a car driving across the grass at the end of the track. A tall man in dark trousers, shirt and tie stepped out.

'Who is it?' Thule asked.

'Jonas Hildre from *Dagbladet*,' Line told him. 'What's he doing here?' Her voice contained a touch of irritation.

'I asked him to come and speak to you,' Wisting said. 'He's going to take care of Arnt Eikanger.'

'What do you mean?' Line asked.

'The difference between investigation and journalism,' Wisting replied. 'In journalism, the evidence doesn't have to be weighed by a judge in a court of law. It's sufficient to put it in the public domain, and that can be enough to stop a political career in its tracks.'

The *Dagbladet* journalist made a round of introductions, finally shaking Wisting's hand. 'Can you let me in on it now?' he asked.

'On what?'

'What was really inside those cardboard boxes?'

Wisting smiled. 'I think you'll have to talk to Line,' he replied.

76

Sandersen from *VG* rang after Line had been credited in two stories splashed on *Dagbladet*'s online pages. The first was about the police action on the E18. Four men and one woman had been charged in connection with the Gardermoen airport robbery in 2003. The second revealed that the body of Simon Meier, who had disappeared during a fishing trip in 2003, had finally been found.

Line was anxious to take the call, just to hear what the news editor had to say, but couldn't spare the time. She was busy polishing her main article, in which she linked the two cases together.

Just as she sent the story to the news desk, a news flash arrived on her phone to say that parliamentary candidate Arnt Eikanger had resigned from the Labour Party. He would no longer run in the forthcoming general election as he had decided to retire from politics altogether. Within the next few days everyone would learn what really lay behind his sudden decision.

77

Wisting glanced down at his grandchild as she played on the floor before laying aside yet another page from the manuscript and beginning on the next one. Towards the end, he found what he was after, something he had already read but had not paid sufficient attention to.

The final chapter in Bernhard Clausen's memoir was called *Free Will*.

> But human beings do not hold sway over all events. They do not exert control in such a way that they are able to exercise freedom in every situation. As far as involuntary actions are concerned, we do not always possess the necessary insight into the consequences of these actions, and in some cases the suffering they will inevitably cause for the individuals concerned as well as others.

The text emphasized that, in the split second of decision, it was impossible to discern the magnitude of the choice being made.

Bernhard Clausen's views on free will ranged over several pages. It was not always easy to follow the thread, but it was obviously something on which he had spent a great deal of energy. The text could be read as a comment on the Gjersjø case, as a defence of his own actions. Clausen had landed in the kind of situation where a person shows their true self, just as some people on board a sinking ship help others into the lifeboat whereas others ensure they secure a place for themselves.

As he put down the bundle of papers, he caught some mention of the Labour Party on the radio. Their support had increased by 0.2 percentage points in the most recent opinion poll. The story had not damaged them at all. Voters obviously understood that a political party was more than one man alone.

'Woof woof,' Amalie barked from down on the floor, waving a jigsaw piece shaped like a dog.

Wisting heaved himself out of his chair, dropped down to his knees and crawled across to her. 'Moo,' he said, inserting the cow in the right place.

Amalie laughed and clapped her hands.

They had put together this same jigsaw puzzle many times before, but Amalie seemed equally delighted every time the pieces fell into place.

Wisting smiled. He knew that feeling well.